Abraham Hayward

Autobiography, Letters and Literary Remains of Mrs. Piozzi (Thrale)

Abraham Hayward

Autobiography, Letters and Literary Remains of Mrs. Piozzi (Thrale)

ISBN/EAN: 9783337030902

Printed in Europe, USA, Canada, Australia, Japan

Cover: Foto ©Raphael Reischuk / pixelio.de

More available books at **www.hansebooks.com**

AUTOBIOGRAPHY

LETTERS AND LITERARY REMAINS

OF

MRS. PIOZZI (THRALE)

EDITED WITH NOTES

AND

AN INTRODUCTORY ACCOUNT OF HER LIFE AND WRITINGS

BY

A. HAYWARD, ESQ. Q.C.

Welcome, Associate Forms, where'er we turn ;
Full, Streatham's Hebe, the Johnsonian urn — St. Stephen's

In Two Volumes

VOL. II.

LONDON
LONGMAN, GREEN, LONGMAN, AND ROBERTS
1861

CONTENTS

OF

THE SECOND VOLUME.

ERRATA IN VOL. II.

p. 57, as heading to the verses on the top of the page read "On a Watch."

p. 72, this letter and the one beginning at p. 81 should be transposed.

p. 155, for "1814" read "1816."

p. 174, note, for "swearing-list" read "Swearing Act."

MISCELLANIES

OR

ORIGINAL COMPOSITIONS IN PROSE AND VERSE.

MISCELLANIES

OR

ORIGINAL COMPOSITIONS IN PROSE AND VERSE.*

THE THREE WARNINGS.

A TALE.

THE tree of deepest root is found
Least willing still to quit the ground;
'Twas therefore said by ancient sages,
That love of life increased with years.
So much, that in our latter stages,
When pains grow sharp and sickness rages,
The greatest love of life appears.
This great affection to believe,
Which all confess but few perceive,
If old affections can't prevail,
Be pleased to hear a modern tale.
When sports went round, and all were gay,
On neighbour Dobson's wedding day,

* Under this head I have printed only those which were found
detached. The majority of her fugitive pieces and occasional
verses are contained in the Letters.

Death called aside the jocund groom,
With him into another room :
And looking grave, you must, says he,
Quit your sweet bride, and come with me.
With you, and quit my Susan's side?
With you! the hapless husband cried :
Young as I am; 'tis monstrous hard;
Besides, in truth, I'm not prepared :
My thoughts on other matters go,
This is my wedding night, you know.
What more he urg'd I have not heard,
His reasons could not well be stronger,
So Death the poor delinquent spared,
And left to live a little longer.
Yet calling up a serious look,
His hour glass tumbled while he spoke,
Neighbour, he said, farewell. No more
Shall Death disturb your mirthful hour,
And further to avoid all blame
Of cruelty upon my name,
To give you time for preparation,
And fit you for your future station,
Three several warnings you shall have
Before you 're summon'd to the grave :
Willing, for once, I'll quit my prey,
And grant a kind reprieve;
In hopes you 'll have no more to say
But when I call again this way,
Well pleas'd the world will leave.

To these conditions both consented,
And parted perfectly contented.
What next the hero of our tale befell,
How long he lived, how wise, how well,
How roundly he pursued his course,
And smok'd his pipe, and strok'd his horse,
The willing muse shall tell :
He chaffer'd then, he bought, he sold,
Nor once perceived his growing old,
Nor thought of Death as near ;
His friends not false, his wife no shrew,
Many his gains, his children few,
He pass'd his hours in peace ;
But while he view'd his wealth increase,
While thus along life's dusty road,
The beaten track content he trod,
Old time whose haste no mortal spares
Uncall'd, unheeded, unawares,

Brought him on his eightieth year.
And now one night in musing mood,
As all alone he sate,
Th' unwelcome messenger of fate
Once more before him stood.
Half stilled with anger and surprise,
So soon returned ! old Dobson cries.
So soon, d' ye call it ! Death replies :
Surely, my friend, you 're but in jest ;
Since I was here before
'Tis six-and-thirty years at least,
And you are now fourscore.

So much the worse, the clown rejoin'd,
To spare the aged would be kind;
However, see your search be legal
And your authority — Is 't regal?
Else you are come on a fool's errand,
With but a secretary's warrant.
Besides, you promised me three warnings,
Which I have looked for nights and mornings;
But for that loss of time and ease
I can recover damages.
I know, cries Death, that at the best,
I seldom am a welcome guest;
But don't be captious, friend, at least;
I little thought you'd still be able
To stump about your farm and stable;
Your years have run to a great length,
I wish you joy tho' of your strength.
Hold, says the farmer, not so fast,
I have been lame these four years past.
And no great wonder, Death replies;
However, you still keep your eyes,
And sure to see one's loves and friends,
For legs and arms would make amends.
Perhaps, says Dobson, so it might,
But, latterly, I've lost my sight.
This is a shocking story, faith,
Yet there's some comfort still, says Death;
Each strives your sadness to amuse,
I warrant you have all the news.

There's none, cries he, and if there were,
I'm grown so deaf, I could not hear.
Nay then, the spectre stern rejoin'd,
These are unjustifiable yearnings;
If you are lame, and deaf, and blind,
You've had your three sufficient warnings.
So come along, no more we'll part:
He said, and touch'd him with his dart;
And now old Dobson, turning pale,
Yields to his fate — so ends my tale.

DUTY AND PLEASURE.

DUTY and Pleasure — long at strife,
Cross'd in the common walks of life;
Pray, don't disturb me, get you gone,
Cries Duty in a serious tone:
Then with a smile — keep off, my dear,
Nor force me thus to be severe.
Lord, Sir, she cries, you're grown so grave
You make yourself a perfect slave;
I can't think why we disagree,
You may turn Methodist for me.
But if you'll neither laugh nor play,
At least don't stop me on my way;
Yet sure one moment you might steal
To see our lovely Miss O'Neill;

One hour to relaxation give,
Oh! lend one hour from life — to live.
And here's a bird and there's a flower,
Dear Duty, walk a little slower.
My youthful task is not half done,
Cries Duty, with an inward groan;
False colours on each object spread,
I scarce see whence or where I'm led;
Your bragg'd enjoyments mount the wind,
And leave their venom'd stings behind.
Where are you flown? Voices around
Cry — Pleasure long has left this ground:
Old age advances — haste away;
Nor lose the light of parting day.
See sickness follows, sorrow threats;
Waste no more time in vain regrets.
One moment more to Duty given,
Might reach perhaps the gates of heaven,
Where only — each with each delighted,
Duty and Pleasure live united.

THE STREATHAM PORTRAITS.

MADAME D'ARBLAY'S description of the Streatham
Portraits will be the best preface to the following verses
on them: " Mrs. Thrale and her eldest daughter were
in one piece, over the fire-place (of the library), at full
length. The rest of the pictures were all three-
quarters. Mr. Thrale was over the door leading to his
study. The general collection then began by Lord
Sandys and Lord Westcote (Lyttelton), two early noble
friends of Mr. Thrale. Then followed Dr. Johnson, Mr.
Burke, Dr. Goldsmith, Mr. Murphy, Mr. Garrick, Mr.
Baretti, Sir Robert Chambers, and Sir Joshua Reynolds
himself—all painted in the highest style of this great
master, who much delighted in this his Streatham
gallery. There was place left but for one more frame
when the acquaintance with Dr. Burney began at
Streatham,"

The whole of them were sold by auction in the spring
of 1816. According to Mrs. Piozzi's marked catalogue,
they fetched respectively the following prices, which
appear to vary according to the celebrity of the subjects, and to make small account of the pictures considered as works of art :—" Lord Sandys, 36*l.* 15*s.*
(Lady Downshire); Lord Lyttelton, 43*l.* 1*s.* (Mr.
Lyttelton, his son); Mrs. Piozzi and her daughter,
81*l.* 18*s.* (S. Boddington, Esq., a rich merchant); Goldsmith (duplicate of the original), 133*l.* 7*s.* (Duke of
Bedford); Sir J. Reynolds, 128*l.* 2*s.* (R. Sharp, Esq.,

M.P.); Sir R. Chambers, 84*l.* (Lady Chambers, his
widow); David Garrick, 183*l.* 15*s.* (Dr. Charles Burney);
Baretti, 31*l.* 10*s.* (Stewart, Esq., I know not who); Dr.
Burney, 84*l.* (Dr. C. Burney, his son); Edmund Burke,
252*l.* (R. Sharp, Esq., M.P.); Dr. Johnson, 378*l.*
(Watson Taylor, Esq.), by whom for Mr. Murphy was
offered 102*l.* 18*s.*, but I bought it in." In 1780
Reynolds raised the price of his portraits (three-quarter
size) from thirty-five to fifty guineas, which, Mrs.
Piozzi complains, made the Streatham portraits in many
instances cost more than they fetched, as she had to pay
for them after Mr. Thrale's death at the increased
price. Her own prefatory remarks are:

" With the dismal years 1772 and 1773 ended much
of my misery, no doubt. The recollection of the sweet
and saint-like manner in which my incomparable mother
meekly laid down her temporal existence, sweetened
the loss of her who I shall see no more in this world,
and whose situation in the next will probably be too
high for my most fervent aspirations. The loss of our
dear boy fell so heavy on my husband, that it became my
duty to endure it courageously, and shake away as much
of the weight as it was possible. Among other efforts to
amuse myself and my eldest daughter, — now my daily
companion, and a *charming* one, but never partial to a
mother who sought in vain to obtain her friendship, —
was a fancy I took of writing little paltry verse characters of the gentlemen who sate for their portraits in
the library, and of whose sittings I was cruelly impatient.
No wonder! when such calamity was hanging over our
heads as is mentioned in the last volume. Let that

reflection make you hesitate in censuring the satirical
vein which perhaps does run through them all :

I.

LORD SANDYS appears first, at the head of the tribe,
But flat insipidity who can describe ?
When such parents and wife as might check even
    Pindar,
Form family compacts his progress to hinder :
Their oppression for forty long years he endur'd,
The nobleman sunk, and the scholar obscur'd ;
Till rank, reason, virtue, endeav'ring in vain
To fling off their burden, and break off their chain,
Can at last but regret, not resist, his hard fate,
Like Enceladus, crush'd by the mountainous weight.

II.

Next him on the right hand, see Lyttelton hang ;
Polite in behaviour, prolix in harangue.
With power well matur'd, with science well bred,
He had studied, had travell'd, had reason'd, had read.
Yet the mind, as the body, was wanting in strength,
For in Lyttelton everything run into length ;
Of his long wheaten straw *that* the farmer complains,
Where the chaff is still found to outnumber the
    grains.

III.

In these features* so placid, so cool, so serene,
What trace of the wit or the Welshwoman 's seen ?

---

* She complained in prose as well as in verse of the want of
likeness in her own portrait. Northcote, in his Life of Reynolds,

What trace of the tender, the rough, the refin'd,
The soul in which such contrarieties join'd!
Where, tho' merriment loves over method to rule,
Religion resides, and the virtues keep school:
Till when tir'd we condemn her dogmatical air,
Like a rocket she rises, and leaves us to stare.
To such contradictions d'ye wish for a clue?
Keep vanity still, that vile passion, in view,
For 'tis thus the slow miner his fortune to make,
Of arsenic thin scatter'd pursues the pale track,
Secure where that poison pollutes the rich ground,
That it points to the place where some silver is found.

IV.

Of a virgin so tender*, the face or the fame
Alike would be injur'd by praise or by blame;

observed of Sir Joshua's pictures in general that "they possess a
degree of merit superior to mere portraits; they assume the rank
of history. His portraits of men are distinguished by a certain
air of dignity, and those of women and children by a grace, a
beauty, and simplicity which have seldom been equalled and never
surpassed. In his attempts to give character where it did not
exist, he has sometimes lost likeness, but the deficiencies of the
portrait were often compensated by the beauty of the picture."
Mrs. Piozzi remarks on this passage: "True, in *my* portrait above
all, there is really no resemblance, and the *character* is less like
my father's daughter than Pharaoh's." Speaking of Sir Joshua's
picture of· Lady Sarah Bunbury "sacrificing to the Graces," Mrs.
Piozzi says: "Lady Sarah never did sacrifice to the Graces. Her
beauty was in her face, which had few equals; but she was a
cricket player, and ate beefsteaks upon the Steyne at Brighthelmstone."

   * Her eldest daughter, then a child.

To the world's fiery trial too early consign'd,
She soon shall experience it, cruel or kind.
His concern thus the artful enameller hides,
And his well-finish'd work to the furnace confides;
But jocund resumes it secure from decay,
If the colours stand firm on the dangerous day.

V.

A manner so studied, so vacant a face,
These features the mind of our Murphy disgrace,
A mind unaffected, soft, artless, and true,
A mind which, though ductile, has dignity too.
Where virtues ill-sorted are huddled in heaps,
Humanity triumphs, and piety sleeps;
A mind in which mirth may with merit reside,
And Learning turns Frolic, with Humour, his guide.
Whilst wit, follies, faults, its fertility prove,
Till the faults you grow fond of, the follies you love,
And corrupted at length by the sweet conversation,
You swear there's no honesty left in the nation.
An African landscape thus breaks on the sight,
Where confusion and wildness increase the delight;
Till in wanton luxuriance indulging our eye,
We faint in the forcible fragrance, and die.

VI.

From our Goldsmith's anomalous character, who
Can withhold his contempt, and his reverence too?
From a poet so polished, so paltry a fellow!
From critic, historian, or vile Punchinello!

From a heart in which meanness had made her abode,
From a foot that each path of vulgarity trod;
From a head to invent, and a hand to adorn,
Unskilled in the schools, a philosopher born.
By disguise undefended, by jealousy smit,
This *lusus naturæ*, nondescript in wit,
May best be compared to those Anamorphòses,
Which for lectures to ladies th' optician proposes;
All deformity seeming, in some points of view,
In others quite accurate, regular, true:
Till the student no more sees the figure that shock'd
    her,
But all in his likeness—our odd little doctor.

VII.

Of Reynolds all good should be said, and no harm;
Tho' the heart is too frigid, the pencil too warm;
Yet each fault from his converse we still must dis-
    claim,
As his temper 'tis peaceful, and pure as his fame.
Nothing in it o'erflows, nothing ever is wanting,
It nor chills like his kindness, nor glows like his
    painting.
When Johnson by strength overpowers our mind,
When Montagu dazzles, and Burke strikes us blind;
To Reynolds well pleas'd for relief we must run,
Rejoice in his shadow, and shrink from the sun.

VIII.

In this luminous portrait requiring no shade,
See Chambers' soft character sweetly display'd:

Oh! quickly return with that genuine smile,
Nor longer let India's temptations beguile,
But fly from a climate where moist relaxation
Invades with her torpor th' effeminate nation,
Where metals and marbles will melt and decay,
Fear, man, for thy virtue, — and hasten away.

IX.

Here Garrick's lov'd features our mem'ry may trace,
Here praise is exhausted, and blame has no place.
Many portraits like this would defeat my whole
    scheme,
For what new can be said on so hackney'd a theme?
'Tis thus on old Ocean whole days one may look,
Every change well recorded in some well-known
    book ;
Till with vain expectation fatiguing our eyes,
Nor the storm nor the calm one new image supplies.

X.

See Thrale from intruders defending his *door*,
While he wishes his house would with people run o'er ;
Unlike his companions, the make of his mind,
In great things expanded, in small things confin'd.
Yet his purse at their call and his meat to their taste,
The wits he delighted in lov'd him at last ;
And finding no prominent follies to fleer at,
Respected his wealth and applauded his merit :
Much like that empirical chemist was he
Who thought Anima Mundi the grand panacea.

Yet when every kind element help'd his collection,
Fell sick while the med'cine was yet in projection.

XI.

Baretti hangs next, by his frowns you may know him,
He has lately been reading some new published
    poem;
He finds the poor author a blockhead, a beast,
A fool without sentiment, judgment, or taste.
Ever thus let our critic his insolence fling,
Like the hornet in Homer, impatient to sting.
Let him rally his friends for their frailties before 'em,
And scorn the dull praise of that dull thing, decorum:
While tenderness, temper, and truth he despises,
And only the triumph of victory prizes.
Yet let us be candid, and where shall we find
So active, so able, so ardent a mind?
To your children more soft, more polite with your
    servant,
More firm in distress, or in friendship more fervent.
Thus Ætna enraged her artillery pours,
And tumbles down palaces, princes, and towers;
While the fortunate peasantry fix'd at its foot,
Can make it a hot-house to ripen their fruit.

XII.

See next, happy contrast! in Burney combine
Every power to please, every talent to shine.
In professional science a second to none,
In social if second, thro' shyness alone.

So sits the sweet violet close to the ground,
Whilst holy-oaks and sunflow'rs flant it around.
His character form'd free, confiding, and kind,
Grown cautious by habit, by station confin'd:
Tho' born to improve and enlighten our days,
In a supple facility fixes his praise;
And contented to sooth, unambitious to strike,
Has a faint praise from all men, from all men alike.
While thus the rich wines of Frontiniac impart
Their sweets to our palate, their warmth to our heart,
All in praise of a liquor so luscious agree,
From the monarch of France to the wild Cherokee.

XIII.

See Burke's bright intelligence beams from his face,
To his language gives splendour, his action gives grace;
Let us list to the learning that tongue can display,
Let it steal all reflection, all reason away;
Lest home to his house we the patriot pursue,
Where scenes of another sort rise to our view;
Where Av'rice usurps sage Economy's look,*
And Humour cracks jokes out of Ribaldry's book:
Till no longer in silence confession can lurk,
That from chaos and cobwebs could spring even Burke.
Thus, 'mong dirty companions conceal'd in the ground,
And unnotic'd by all, the proud metal was found,
Which, exalted by place, and by polish refin'd,
Could comfort, corrupt, and confound all mankind.

* Till he got his pension, Burke was always poor; and the
wonder is how he managed to make both ends meet at all.

XIV.

Gigantic in knowledge, in virtue, in strength,
With Johnson our company closes at length :
So the Greeks from the cavern of Polypheme past,
When, wisest and greatest, Ulysses came last,
To his comrades contemptuous, we see him look down
On their wit and their worth with a general frown :
While from Science' proud tree the rich fruit *he*
    receives,
Who could shake the whole trunk while they turn'd
    a few leaves.
Th' inflammable temper, the positive tongue,
Too conscious of right for endurance of wrong,
We suffer from Johnson, contented to find
That some notice we gain from so noble a mind ;
And pardon our hurts, since so many have found
The balm of instruction pour'd into the wound.
'Tis thus for its virtues the chymists extol
Pure rectified spirit, sublime alcohol.
From noxious putrescence preservative pure,
A cordial in health, and in sickness a cure :
But oppos'd to the sun, taking fire at his rays,
Burns bright to the bottom, and ends in a blaze.

ASHERI.

אשרי.

ARABIAN tales, all Oriental tales indeed, are full of imagination, void of common sense. The lady who recounts can scarcely fail to amuse. She is herself so handsome and so charming, the story must please, be it what it will; but they must be listeners like Sir James Fellowes who can feel interest in an old man's narration, and hear attentively the Rabbinical story concerning *A search after Asheri.*

Four young men, then, stood round their father's death-bed. "I cannot speak what I wish you to hear," whispered the dying parent; "but there is a Genius residing in the neighbouring wood, who pretends to direct mortals to *Asheri.* Meanwhile, accept my house and lands; they are not large, but will afford an elegant sufficiency. — Farewell."

Three of the brothers set out instantly for the wood. The fourth staid at home; and, having performed the last filial duties to a father he revered, began to cultivate his farm, and court his neighbour's daughter to share it with him. She was virtuous, kind, and amiable. We will leave them, and follow the adventurers, who soon arrived at the obscure habitation of the reputed sage, bosomed in trees, and his hut darkened with ivy. Scarce could the ambiguous mandates be heard; still less could the speaker (Imagination) be discerned through the gloom. "What is this *Asheri* we are to look out for?" said one brother. "Oh! when once seen, no eye can be mistaken," replied a voice from within the grot. "Three beautiful forms uniting under one radiant head, compose the sighed-for object." "*I* am a passionate admirer of *beauty*," interrupted the youth. "Shall I not find the lovely creature at Grand Cairo?" "Seek your desire there," was the reply; "the soil will be congenial to your nature." He set off without studying for an answer.

When the next brother made application: "I wonder," said he, "how this renowned *Asheri* should ever be found without obtaining court-favour, and permission to proceed in the search." "At Ispahan, Sir, you may procure both. Here are letters for the young .Sophy of Persia, scarce thirteen years old, and her mother the Sultana Valadi." A respectful bow constituted this youth's adieu, and he put himself immediately on progress.

The third, who till now had been employed in laughing at and mimicking his companions, remained a moment with the Genius of the wood; and "Well, Sir," said he, "which way shall *I* take towards finding this fabulous being, this faultless wonder, this non-existent chimera, *Asheri*?" "Oh, you are a wit: make your *début* at Delhi; 'tis the only mart for talents." Aboul, willing to try his fortune, soon set out: and after fifteen years—for so long my tale lasts — he was observed by two mendicants of ragged and wretched appearance; who, fainting with hunger and exhausted by disease, addressed him as he sate upon a stone by the wayside leading to Kouristan, 400 miles from Delhi. "I have no money, my honest friends," said he; "but you shall share my dinner of brown bread and goat's milk. You have scarcely strength, I see, to reach the cottage: I will run home and fetch two wooden bowls full." He did so, and they were refreshed, and recognised each other. It was now who should tell his hapless history; but Aboul was ablest and gave the following account: —

"You left me," said he, "with that rascally conjuror, Imagination by name, whose delight it is to dress up a phantom for poor afflicted mortals to follow, and he calls it *Asheri*. My destiny led me to seek in Delhi the bright reward of superior talents; but it was never my attention to claim applause till I had deserved it; so my lamp went not out at night till I had composed a book of tales for publication, — short ones, but well-varied, — for novels were the mode at Delhi. In a week's time the book was in every hand that could hold one. The reviews criticised, but the ladies bought it, and the criticisms did me more good than harm. An ill-spent note called me to the toilette of a great lady; invitations then crowded round me, suppers without end, and dinners undesired. At first this was not unpleasant, and I began to think Asheri not far distant. I wrote elaborate poems in praise of my protectress, entered into none of her intrigues; but against all the people she hated there were store of lampoons and

choice of epigrams ready, composed by the fashionable
author, your hapless brother Aboul. Favoured by one
society, therefore, persecuted by another; adored by
one set of ignorant females, tormented by another set;
stared at by a neutral class as if I had been a monster;
everything I said repeated, and *wrong* repeated; everything I did related, and *wrong* related; I gained information that my patroness was on the eve of losing
her friend the vizier's confidence, which a younger beauty
(a woman she despised) was stealing away. My business
was to satirize the vizier, who could not read; but soon
understanding from others that it was done with acri-
mony of which Aboul only was capable, my Fatima
was threatened; and to save *herself,* promised to give me
up; but, in the clothes I exchanged instantly for those
of a grateful slave, my escape was perfected, and you
will not suspect me of seeking this invisible *Asheri* in
the mean character of a village pedagogue, — for such
you find me, after fifteen years' separation, — though,
really, explaining to babies the rudiments of literature
is at least a far less offensive employment than that of
trying to instruct self-sufficient fools who take up their
teachers out of vanity and discard them out of pride.
I have been long enough a wit and an author. Now
tell me *your* adventures."

"*Mine,*" said the passionate admirer of beauty, "are
soon told. I dashed at Cairo into the full tide of what
the world calls *pleasure,* till dissipation was no more a
name. Five of the fifteen years were spent in ruining myself and others. The ten remaining proved too few for

my repentance, too many for my endurance. My frame exhausted, my very mind enfeebled, life is to me only a lengthening calamity. What was *your* course, Mesrou?"

"My *course* was wretched," replied Mesrou; "but my aim was well taken, and the goal I aimed at *grand*. Resolving to subdue all meaner passions, and dedicate myself to ambitious pursuits, I entered Ispahan with hope swelling in my heart, and presented my credentials to Sultana Valadi. She was old and ugly, amorous and vindictive. No matter; she guided the helm of State for her young son, whose honour she conceived would still be best secured by keeping his subjects continually at war. I was a coadjutor completely to her taste in public and private, having small care for the nation, and few scruples of delicacy. We spared no expenses for the support of the army, but our generals were sometimes beaten and disgraced us; sometimes victorious, and then they came home to insult us. My sultana's temper, crooked as her person, grew wholly insupportable; every misfortune was set down to my account as minister, and money became hard to find. Taxes offended the people, and the soldiers refused to enforce them. The lady was affrighted at the spirit she had raised; and, when I observed her one evening as if mixing some powders in the Cherbette we were to drink after supper, I was affrighted too: and, grasping her so roughly that resistance was vain, I held the prepared potion to her own lips. Fortunately for my innocence, the Valadi, in her ungovernable fury at such treatment, broke a blood-vessel, and I left her to expire unpitied on the sofa, while the bustle gave me time to drop my turban; and, snatching the lay frock from off a dervise in the crowd, covered myself up, and escaped from being the prime minister at Ispahan. Let us now try to find our fourth brother, Ittai, and return, though ragged, to our father's house."

The first man they met showed the leading path, and pointed out the way. Arrived, they saw the fields so much improved, it was scarce possible to recognise the place. The man of talents, however, climbing a ladder which was reared against the wall for some reason, looked in, and perceived Ittai dancing at the celebration of his son's birthday. "Oh, brother!" he exclaimed, "here we are; we have never found Asheri." "That is a truth, indeed," replied a little figure from behind the screen, "for I have never moved for fifteen years from this very spot." "Is that the *beautiful* creature we were taught to expect?" cried out the man of pleasure. Ittai set wide his door, and a burst of brilliancy illuminated the dwelling. Virtue, Love, and Friendship—three forms under one radiant head—dazzled their sight; and, "Keep your distance," said the well-tuned voice: "Asheri abhors men who deny the existence of what all must wish, but none will ever find in pleasure, fame, or power. *Asheri* dwells in heaven, visiting in *disguise* even the favoured mortals who, like Ittai, send up their pious aspirations *there*, and live contented with their lot below." The brothers waked as from a dream, resolving to forget all their projects of felicity in *this* life; which they closed in company with Ittai; and each half hoped he saw a *gleam* of *Asheri*, as this world gradually receded from their view, and soft futurity advanced to meet them.

Streatham Park, April 3, 1816.—Mrs. Piozzi gave me this (the foregoing) paper in the Library. After telling several amusing anecdotes, she mentioned one of Sir R. Jebb. One day somebody had given him a bottle of *castor* oil, very pure; it had but lately been brought into use. Before he left his home, he gave it in charge to his man, telling him to be careful of it. After the lapse of a considerable time, Sir Richard asked his servant for the oil. "Oh, it's all used!" replied he. "Used!" said Sir Richard; "how and when, Sir?" "I put it in the *castor* when wanted, and gave it to the company." The way of telling this story by Mrs. Piozzi added to the humour, and renders all description useless. —*Sir James Fellowes.*

HER CHARACTER OF THRALE.

As this is *Thraliana,* I will now write Mr. *Thrale's* character in it. It is not because I am in good or ill-humour with him or he with me, for we are not capricious people, but have, I believe, the same opinion of each other at all places and times.

Mr. Thrale's person is manly, his countenance agreeable, his eyes steady and of the deepest blue; his look neither soft nor severe, neither sprightly nor gloomy, but thoughtful and intelligent; his address is neither caressive nor repulsive, but unaffectedly civil and decorous; and his manner more completely free from every kind of trick or particularity than I ever saw any person's. He is a man wholly, as I think, out of the power of mimickry. He loves money, and is diligent to obtain it; but he loves liberality too, and is willing enough both to give generously and to spend fashionably. His passions either are not strong, or else he keeps them under such command that they seldom disturb his tranquillity or his friends; and it must, I think, be something more than common which can affect him strongly, either with hope, fear, anger, love, or joy. His regard for his father's memory is remarkably great, and he has been a most exemplary brother; though,

when the house of his favourite sister was on fire, and
we were all alarmed with the account of it in the night,
I well remember that he never rose, but bidding the
servant who called us to go to her assistance, quietly
turned about and slept to his usual hour. I must give
another trait of his tranquillity on a different occasion.
He had built great casks holding 1000 hogsheads each,
and was much pleased with their profit and appearance.
One day, however, he came down to Streatham as usual
to dinner, and after hearing and talking of a hundred
trifles, " but I forgot," says he, " to tell you how one of
my great casks is burst, and all the beer run out."

Mr. Thrale's sobriety, and the decency of his conversation, being wholly free from all oaths, ribaldry and
profaneness, make him a man exceedingly comfortable
to live with ; while the easiness of his temper and slow-
ness to take offence add greatly to his value as a domestic man. Yet I think his servants do not much love
him, and I am not sure that his children have much
affection for him ; low people almost all indeed agree
to abhor him, as he has none of that officious and cordial
manner which is universally required by them, nor any
skill to dissemble his dislike of their coarseness. With
regard to his wife, though little tender of her person, he
is very partial to her understanding ; but he is obliging
to nobody, and confers a favour less pleasingly than
many a man refuses to confer one. This appears to me
to be as just a character as can be given of the man
with whom I have now lived thirteen years ; and though
he is extremely reserved and uncommunicative, yet one

must know something of him after so long acquaintance. Johnson has a very great degree of kindness and esteem for him, and says if he would talk more, his manner would be very completely that of a perfect gentleman.

(Here follow Master Pepys' verses addressed to Thrale on his wedding-day, October, 1776.)

People have a strange propensity to making vows on trifling occasions, a trick one would not think of, but I once caught my husband at it, and have since then been suspicious that 'tis oftener done than believed. For example : Mr. Thrale and I were driving through E. Grinsted, and found the inn we used to put up at destroyed by fire. He expressed great uneasiness, and I still kept crying, 'Why can we not go to the other inn? 'tis a very good house; here is no difficulty in the case.' All this while Mr. Thrale grew violently impatient, endeavoured to bribe the post-boy to go on to the next post-town, &c., but in vain; till, pressed by inquiries and solicitations he could no longer elude, he confessed to me that he had sworn an oath or made a vow, I forget which, seventeen years before, never to set his foot within those doors again, having had some fraud practised on him by a landlord who then kept the house, but had been dead long enough ago. When I heard this all was well; I desired him to sit in the chaise while the horses were changed, and walked into the house myself to get some refreshment the while.

In 1779, June, after his recovery from the first fit of paralysis, she writes : —

His head is as clear as ever; his spirits indeed are

low, but they will mend; few people live in such a state
of preparation for eternity, I think, as my dear master
has done since I have been connected with him; regular in his public and private devotions, constant at
the Sacrament, temperate in his appetites, moderate in
his passions,— he has less to apprehend from a sudden
summons than any man I have known who was young
and gay, and high in health and fortune like him,

TRANSLATION OF LAURA BASSI'S VERSES.

MESSER CHRISTOFORO, who shewed us the Specola at
Bologna, and made his short but pathetic eulogium on
the lamented Dottoressa, pointed with his finger (I
believe he could not speak) to her much admired and
well-known verses on the gate :—

" Si tibi pulchra domus, si splendida mensa,—quid inde ?
   Si species auri, argenti quoque massa,—quid inde ?
   Si tibi sponsa decens, si sit generosa,—quid inde ?
   Si tibi sunt nati; si prædia magna,—quid inde ?
   Si fueris pulcher, fortis, divesve,—quid inde ?
   Si doceas alios in qualibet arte ;—quid inde ?
   Si longus servorum inserviat ordo :—quid inde ?
   Si faveat mundus, si prospera cuncta,—quid inde ?
   Si prior, aut abbas, si dux, si papa,—quid inde ?
   Si felix annos regnes per mille,   quid inde ?
   Si rota Fortunæ se tollit ad astra,—quid inde ?
   Tam cito, tamque cito fugiunt hæc ut nihil,—inde.
   Sola manet Virtus ; nos glorificabimur,—inde.
   Ergo Deo pare, bene nam tibi provenit—inde."

I brought them home of course, and tried to translate them; but ventured not the translation out of
my sight till now.

    26th October, 1815.

TRANSLATION OR IMITATION OF LAURA BASSI'S VERSES.

Thy mansion splendid, and thy service plate,
Thy coffers fill'd with gold ; — well ! what of that ?
Thy spouse the envy of all other men,
Thy children beautiful and rich,—what then ?
Vig'rous thy youth, unmortgag'd thy estate,
Of arts the applauded teacher; what of that ?
Troops of acquaintance, and of slaves a train,
This world's prosperity complete,—what then ?
Prince, pope, or emperor's thy smiling fate,
With a long life's enjoyment,—what of that ?
By Fortune's wheel tost high beyond our ken,
Too soon shall following Time cry—Well ! what then?
Virtue alone remains ; on Virtue wait,
All else *I* sweep away ;—but what of that ?
Trust God, and Time defy : eternal is your date.

*

A FRIGHTFUL STORY.

HERE (at Florence) our little English coterie printed a book, and called it the "Florence Miscellany,"—you have seen it at my lodgings,—and here, one day, for a frolic, we betted a wager who could invent the most frightful story, and produce by dinner time.* The clock struck three, and by five we were to meet again.

Merry brought a very fine one, but Mr. Greatheed burned his, and the following

" FRAGMENT OF A SCENE NEAR NAPLES "

carried off the palm of victory.

He tore her from the bleeding body of her husband, and throwing her across his horse, spurred him forward, till even the imaginary noises, which for a while pursued his flight, began to fade away and leave him leisure to reanimate his brutal passion. He alighted in a distant and deserted place, and by the faint light which the new moon afforded some moments ere she sunk below the horizon, examined his companion, and found her—dead. A crowd of horrid images possessed his mind, but that which prevailed was the fear of discovery. He regained his seat, intent upon escape,

* A somewhat similar compact or competition produced " Frankenstein " and " The Vampire."

but the horse trembled, and refused to stir. Ruggiero resolved to lose no time in fruitless contentions with his steed, but fly away as fast as it was possible. He ran for a full hour, then found himself entangled by some unseen substance that hindered him from proceeding.

The mountain, which had for thirty years been silent, then gave a hollow groan. Ruggiero knew not that it was the mountain: but a column of blue flame shot up from the crater convinced him, while gathering clouds and solemn stillness of the air announced an approaching earthquake. Ruggiero's joynts began to loosen with the united sensations of guilt and fear; surrounded on all sides by torrents of indurated lava,—which he recollected to have heard flowed from Vesuvius the year that he was born, when both his parents perished in the flames, and he himself was saved as if by miracle,—his feet stood fixed by difficulty, whilst his mind ran rapidly over past events. The mountain now swelled with a second sigh, more solemn than before. The hollow ground heaved under him, and by the light of an electrick cloud which caught the blaze as it blew over the hill, he happily discovered a distant crucifix, and seeking with steps become somewhat more steady to gain it. Tears for the first time eased his heart, and gave hope of returning humanity. Ruggiero now prayed for life only that he might gain time to request forgiveness; and after a variety of penances courageously endured, he lives at this day, a hermit on Vesuvius, — religion making that residence delightful, the sight of which, when guilty, chilled him with horror, — and he scruples not to relate the story of his conversion to those who, passing that way, are sure to partake his hospitality.

This story was never seen since that day by any one.

DELLA CRUSCA VERSES.

AMONG many other undeserved praises I received at generous Florence, I select these from Mr. Merry, whom we called Della Crusca, because he was a member of their academy:

> " Oh you ! whose piercing azure eye
>   Reads in each heart the feelings there;
> You ! that with purest sympathy
>   Our transports and our woes can share ;
> You ! that by fond experience prove,
>   The virtuous bliss of Piozzi's love ;
> Who while his breast affection warms,
>   With merit heightens music's charms ;
>
> " Oh deign to accept the verse sincere
>   Nor yet deride my rustic reed ;
> But pitying wait my woes to hear,
>   For pity sure is folly's meed :
> The good, the liberal, and the kind,
>   Possess a tolerating mind :
> Nor view the madman with a frown
> Because of straw he weaves a crown."

These were sincere verses indeed ; for he wanted me not to join the Greatheeds and Parsons and Piozzi, who were all persuading him to go home, and not fling any more time away in prosecuting his dangerous passion for Lady Cowper; while the Grand Duke himself was his rival. I answered his application, poor fellow! in the concluding verses of our " Florence Miscellany." They wanted it larger; so I said :—

The book's imperfect you declare
And Piozzi has not given her share;
What's to be done? some wits in vogue,
Would quickly find an epilogue;
Composed of whim, and mirth, and satire,
Without one drop of true good nature;
But trust me; 'tis corrupted taste
To make so merry with the last:
When in that fatal word we find
Each foe to gayety combined.
Since parting then — on Arno's shore
We part—perhaps to meet no more;
Let these last lines some truths contain,
More clear than bright, less sweet than plain.

Thou first; to sooth whose feeling heart
The Muse bestowed her lenient art;
Accept her counsel, quit this coast
With only one short lustrum lost:
Nor longer let the tuneful strain
On foreign ears be poured in vain;
The wreath which on thy brow should live,
Britannia's hand alone can give.

Meanwhile for Bertie Fate prepares *
A mingled wreath of joys and cares;
When politics and party-rage
Shall strive such talents to engage,
And call him to controul the great,
And fix the nicely balanced state:
Till charming Anna's gentler mind,
For storms of faction ne'er designed,
Shall think with pleasure on the times
When Arno listened to his rhymes;
And reckon among Heav'n's best mercies,
Our Piozzi's voice, and Parson's verses.

Thou too; who oft hast strung the lyre
To liveliest notes of gay desire;
No longer seek these scorching flames,
And trifle with Italian dames;
But haste to Britain's chaster isle,
Receive some fair one's virgin smile,
Accept her vows, reward her truth,
And guard from ills her artless youth.
Keep her from knowledge of the crimes
That taint the sweets of warmer climes;
But let her weaker bloom disclose
The beauties of a hothouse rose:
Whose leaves no insects ever haunted,
Whose perfume but to one is granted;

---

* Mr. Greatheed. She describes him as completely under the
influence of his wife, the charming Anna.

Pleased with her partner to retire
And cheer the safe domestic fire.

While I — who, half-amphibious grown,
Now scarce call any place my own —
Will learn to view with eye serene
Life's empty plot, and shifting scene:
And trusting still to Heav'n's high care,
Fix my firm habitation there:
'Twas thus the Grecian sage of old,
As by Herodotus we're told,
Accused by them who sate above,
As wanting in his country's love:
" 'Tis that," cried he, " which most I prize,"
And pointing upwards, shewed the skies.

ODE TO SOCIETY.

I.

SOCIETY ! gregarious dame ! *
Who knows thy favour'd haunts to name?
Whether at Paris you prepare
The supper and the chat to share,
While fix'd in artificial row,
Laughter displays its teeth of snow:
Grimace with raillery rejoices,
And song of many mingled voices,
Till young coquetry's artful wile
Some foreign novice shall beguile,
Who home return'd, still prates of thee,
Light, flippant, French Society.

II.

Or whether, with your zone unbound,
You ramble gaudy Venice round,
Resolv'd the inviting sweets to prove,
Of friendship warm, and willing love ;

---

* See Vol. I. p. 262. Moore has substituted *Posterity* for *Society.*
His reports of conversations are both meagre and inaccurate. Thus
(vol. iii. p. 196) he says: " In talking of letters being charged by
weight, he (Canning) said the post-office once refused to carry a
letter of Sir J. Cox Hippesley's, it was so dull." Canning said
" so heavy "; the letter being the worthy baronet's printed letter
against Catholic Emancipation.

Where softly roll th' obedient seas,
Sacred to luxury and ease,
In coffee-house or casino gay
Till the too quick return of day,
Th' enchanted votary who sighs
For sentiments without disguise,
Clear, unaffected, fond, and free,
In Venice finds Society.

III.

Or if to wiser Britain led,
Your vagrant feet desire to tread
With measur'd step and anxious care,
The precincts pure of Portman-square; *
While wit with elegance combin'd,
And polish'd manners there you'll find; ⎫
The taste correct—and fertile mind :   ⎬
Remember vigilance lurks near,   ⎭
And silence with unnotic'd sneer,
Who watches but to tell again
Your foibles with to-morrow's pen ;
Till titt'ring malice smiles to see
Your wonder—grave Society.

IV.

Far from your busy crowded court,
Tranquillity makes her resort ;
Where 'mid cold Staffa's columns rude,
Resides majestic solitude ;

* The residence of her old rival, Mrs. Montague.

Or where in some sad Brachman's cell,
Meek innocence delights to dwell,
Weeping with unexperienc'd eye,
The death of a departed fly :
Or in Hetruria's heights sublime,
Where science self might fear to climb,
But that she seeks a smile from thee,
And wooes thy praise, Society.

V.

Thence let me view the plains below,
From rough St. Julian's rugged brow ;
Hear the loud torrents swift descending,
Or mark the beauteous rainbow bending,
Till Heaven regains its favourite hue,
Æther divine! celestial blue !
Then bosom'd high in myrtle bower,
View letter'd Pisa's pendent tower ;
The sea's wide scene, the port's loud throng,
Of rude and gentle, right and wrong ;
A motley group which yet agree
To call themselves Society.

VI.

Oh! thou still sought by wealth and fame,
Dispenser of applause and blame :
While flatt'ry ever at thy side,
With slander can thy smiles divide ;
Far from thy haunts, oh! let me stray,
But grant one friend to cheer my way,

Whose converse bland, whose music's art,
May cheer my soul, and heal my heart;
Let soft content our steps pursue,
And bliss eternal bound our view:
Pow'r I'll resign, and pomp, and glee,
Thy best-lov'd sweets—Society.

DIDO EPIGRAMS.

We were speaking the other day of the famous epigram in Ausonius:—

" Infelix Dido, nulli bene nupta marito,
   Hoc moriente fugis, hoc fugiente peris."

Two lords, in vain, unlucky Dido tries,
One dead, she flies the land; one fled, she dies.*

" Pauvre Didon ! on t'a réduite
   De tes maris le triste sort ;
   L'un en mourant cause ta fuite,
      L'autre en fuyant cause ta mort."

is reckoned a beautiful version of this epigram.

---

* To the same class of *jeux d'esprit* as this epitaph on Dido, belongs one made on Thynne, " Tom of Ten Thousand," after his assassination by Konigsmark, who wished to marry the widow, the heiress of the Percys. Thynne's marriage had not been consummated, and he was said to have promised marriage to a maid of honour whom he had seduced.

" Here lies Tom Thynne of Longleat Hall,
   Who never would so have miscarried,
   Had he married the woman he lay withal,
   Or lay with the woman he married."

There is, however, a very old passage in Davison, alluding to the same story:—

> " Oh, most unhappy Dido !
>   Unlucky wife, and eke unhappy widow :
> Unhappy in thy honest mate,
>   And in thy love unfortunate."

When Lady Bolingbroke led off the Crim. Con. Dance, about thirty-five years ago, the town made a famous bustle concerning her ladyship's name—Diana. She married Topham Beauclerc, and when her first husband died, some wag made these verses :—

> " Ah ! lovely, luckless Lady Di,
>   So oddly link'd to either spouse :
> Who can your Gordian knot untie ?
>   Or who dissolve your double vows ?

> " And where will our amazement lead to ?
>   When we survey your various life ?
> Whose living lord made you a widow,
>   Whose dead one leaves you still a wife."

Can you endure any more nonsense about Dido ?

" Make me (says a college tutor) some verses on the gerunds *di*, *do*, *dum*, as a punishment for the strange grammatical fault I found in your last composition."
" Here they are, Sir "—

> When Dido's spouse to Dido would not come,
> Then Dido wept in silence, and was Dido dumb.

Will it amuse you to read some of the unmerited

praises I picked up in this charming society? When we all stood round the pianoeforte, and I felt encouraged to reply to Bertola's complimentary verses, which were certainly improvised; when he sung:

" Esser mi saran fatali
    Cento rivali e cento;
Ma più che i miei rivali
    La tua virtú pavento.

" Non in sen d'angliche mura
    I tuoi be' lumi al dì se schiuse;
Tu nascesti, de un dio me lo giura,
    Ove nacquero le Muse."

To which I replied : —

Delicati al par che forti
    Son li versi di Bertola;
Dolce suon che mi consola
    Mentre lui cantando và;

Ma tentando d'imitarli
    S'io m'ingegno,—oh, Dio! invano:
Dall' inusitata mano,
    Il plettrino cascherà.

We were in a large company last night, where a beautiful woman of quality came in dressed according to the present taste, with a gauze head-dress, adjusted turban-wise, and a heron's feather; the neck wholly bare. Abate Bertola bid me look at her, and, recollecting himself a moment, made this epigram improviso :—

Volto e crin hai di Sultana,
    Perchè mai mi vien disdetto,
Sodducente Mussulmana
    Di gittarti il *fazzoletto?*

of which I can give no better imitation than the following :—

While turban'd head and plumage high
    A Sultaness proclaims my Cloe;
Thus tempted, tho' no Turk, I'll try
    The handkerchief you scorn—to throw ye.

This is however a weak specimen of his powers,
whose charming fables have so completely, in my
mind, surpassed all that has ever been written in that
way since La Fontaine. I am strongly tempted to
give one little story, and translate it too:

Una lucertoletta
Diceva al cocodrillo,
Oh quanto mi diletta
Di veder finalmente
Un della mia famiglia
Si grande e si potente!
Ho fatto mille miglia
Per venirvi a vedere,
Mentre tra noi si serba
Di voi memoria viva;
Benche fuggiam tra l'erba

E il sassoso sentiero :
In sen però non langue
L' onor del prisco sangue.

L' anfibio rè dormiva
A questi complimenti,
Pur sugli ultimi accenti
Dal sonno se riscosse
E dimandò chi fosse?
La parentela antica,
Il viaggio, la fatica,
Quella torno a dire,
Ed ei torne a dormire.
Lascia i grandi ed i potenti,
A sognar per parenti;
Puoi cortesi stimarli
Se dormon mentre parli.

Walking full many a weary mile
The lizard met the crocodile
And thus began—How fat, how fair,
How finely guarded, Sir, you are!
'Tis really charming thus to see
One's kindred in prosperity,
I've travell'd far to find your coast,
But sure the labour was not lost:
For you must think we don't forget
Our loving cousin now so great;

And tho' our humble habitations
Are such as suit our slender stations,
The honour of the lizard blood
Was never better understood.

Th' amphibious prince, who slept content,
Ne'er listening to her compliment,
At this expression rais'd his head,
And—Pray who are you ? coolly said.
The little creature now renew'd,
Her history of toils subdu'd,
Her zeal to see her cousin's face,
The glory of her ancient race;
But looking nearer, found my lord
Was fast asleep again—and snor'd.
Ne'er press upon a rich relation
Rais'd to the ranks of higher station;
Or if you will disturb your coz,
Be happy that he does but doze.

Here, then, are Abate Ravasi's verses,— which he
called his

PARTENZA.

Ah ! non resiste il cuore
 A vedermi lasciar,
 Io sento a palpitar
Ei manca, ei muore.
E in mezzo a tal dolore

Co' tronchi accenti,
Co' flebili lamenti,
Altro non sa dir l' animo mio,
Ch' addio, gran donna! eccelsa, donna,
    addio!

RÓNDO.

Ne' viaggi tuoi rammentati
  D' un fido servidor;
  Nell' Inghilterra ancor,
  Non ti scordar di me.
  Ch' io, dovunque vado,
  Sempre verràmmi in mente,
  Che donna si eccellente
  Non trovasi di te.
Conservami l' amico
  L' amato tuo consorte,
  Dilli che anche la morte
  Potrà violar mia fè.

VERSES ON BUFFON.

WHILE we were daily receiving some tender adieux from our Milanese friends, the famous Buffon died, and changed the conversation. He was blind a few days before his death, and occasioned this epigram:

> " Ah ! s'il est vrai que Buffon perd les yeux,
> Que le jour se refuse au foyer des lumières :
> La nature à la fin punit les curieux,
> Qui pénétroient tous ses mystères."

The Abate Bossi translated it thus:—

> " Ah ! s'è ver che Buffon cieco diventa,
> Se alle pupille sue il dì s' asconde ;
> Natura alla fin gelosa confonde
> Chi entro gl' arcani suoi penetrar tenta."

> Buffon's bright eyes at length grow dim,
> Dame Nature now no more will yield ;
> Or longer lend her light to him
> Who all her mysteries revealed.

This last of course was done by your own little friend ; who was careful to preserve a power over her own language, although beginning almost to *think* in Italian, by such constant use.

FLORENCE MISCELLANY.

Dedication (writer not specified).

WHAT a whimsical task, my dear friends, you impose
To contribute a fine Dedication in prose !
Our Piozzi, methinks, is much fitter for this,
For she writes the Preface, and can't write amiss.
But my thoughts neither beautiful are nor sublime,
So I wrap them in metre, and tag them with rhime,
Like theatrical dresses, if tinsel'd enough,
The tinsel one stares at, nor thinks of the stuff,
  We mean not our book for the public inspection,
Then why should we court e'en a Monarch's protection?
For too oft the good Prince such a critic of lays is,
He scarcely knows how to peruse his own praises.
Ourselves and our friends we for Patrons will chuse,
No others will read us, and these will excuse.

Preface, by Mrs. Piozzi.*

PREFACES to Books, like Prologues to Plays, will seldom
be found to invite Readers, and still less often to convey
importance. Excuses for mean Performances add only
the baseness of submission to poverty of sentiment, and

* See Vol. I. p. 133.

take from insipidity the praise of being inoffensive. We
do not however by this little address mean to deprecate
public Criticism, or solicit Regard; why we wrote the
verses may be easily explain'd, we wrote them to divert
ourselves, and to say kind things of each other; we collected them that our reciprocal expressions of kindness
might not be lost, and we printed them because we had
no reason to be ashamed of our mutual partiality.

Portrait Painting, though unadorn'd by allegorical
allusions and unsupported by recollection of events or
places, will be esteem'd for ever as one of the most
durable methods to keep Tenderness alive and preserve
Friendship from decay: nor do I observe that the room
here where Artists of many Ages have contributed their
own likenesses to the Royal Gallery is less frequented
than that which contains the statue of a slave and the
picture of a Sibyl. Our little Book can scarcely be less
important to Readers of a distant Age or Nation than
we ourselves are ready to acknowledge it: the waters of
a mineral spring which sparkle in the glass, and exhi-
larate the spirits of those who drink them on the spot,
grow vapid and tasteless by carriage and keeping; and
though we have perhaps transgress'd the Persian Rule
of sitting silent till we could find something important
or instructive to say, we shall at least be allow'd to have
glisten'd innocently in Italian Sunshine, and to have
imbibed from it's rays the warmth of mutual Benevo-
lence, though we may have miss'd the hardness and
polish that some coarser Metal might have obtain'd by
heat of equal force. I will not however lengthen out

my Preface; if the Book is but a feather, tying a stone to it can be no good policy, though it were a precious one; the lighter body would not make the heavy one swim, but the heavy body would inevitably make the light one sink.

On Tuesday evening, the 26th December, 1815, (writes Mr. Fellowes) we met at the Vineyards, our conversation led to the House of Commons, and my father expressed a wish that I had been a member, adding that he believed I should have followed that line with more pleasure than physic. Mrs. Piozzi assented to this, in her usual good humoured complimentary manner. I made an observation about illusion, &c., and something was said about Spain, and the beauties of the language, and I read the following Spanish verses to her, which pleased from their simplicity and neatness:

> " La otra noche soñaba,
> Que feliz sueño,
> A decirte lo iva,
> Pero no quieso.
> Permita el Amor,
> Que algun dia tu sueñes,
> Lo que soné yo."

On the following morning I received from Mrs. Piozzi these lines : —

> " The amorous Spaniard's glowing dream,
> Joined with our doctor's soberer scheme,

Caused in my brain confusion;
Yet when before my closing eyes,
I saw Saint Stephen's chapel rise,
Say; was that all illusion?

"Oh, if the stream of eloquence,
I saw you gracefully dispense,
Was fancied all and vain:
Daylight no more I wish to see,
But drive back dull reality,
And turn to dream again.

" Mr. Linton takes this imitation of the verses you
showed me last night.   H. L. P."

During her stay in Italy (writes Sir J. Fellowes)
in this delightful society, upon the banks of the Arno,
which was duly enlivened by brilliant wit and classic
taste, the conversation often turned upon more serious
subjects, and one day it was proposed to write an impromptu upon the fatal monosyllable *now*, the present
moment passing away even before the word is written
that explains it. This pretty quatrain was produced
by Della Crusca, who had been asserting that all past
actions are nihilitic, and that the immediate moment
was the whole of human existence:

" One endless Now stands o'er th' eventful stream
Of all that may be with colossal stride;

And sees beneath life's proudest pageants gleam,
And sees beneath the wrecks of empire glide."

To this H. L. P. replied : —

" 'Tis yours the present moment to redeem,
And powerful snatch from Time's too rapid stream;
While self-impell'd, the rest redundant roll,
Slumb'ring to stagnate in oblivion's pool."

LINES WRITTEN JULY 28TH, 1815.

Is it of intellectual powers,
Which time developes, time devours,
Which twenty years perhaps are ours,
     That man is vain?

Of such the infant shows no sign,
And childhood shuns the dazzling shine,
Of knowledge bright with rays divine,
     As mental pain.

Still less when passion bears the sway,
Unbridled youth brooks no delay,
He drives dull reason far away,
     With scorn avow'd.

For twenty years she reigns at most,
Labour and study pay the cost;
Just to be rais'd is all our boast,
     Above the crowd.

Sickness then fills th' uneasy chair,
Sorrow, and loss, and strife, and care ;
While faith just saves us from despair,
                    Wishing to die.

Till the farce ends as it began,
Reason deserts the dying man,
And leaves to encounter as he can
                    Eternity.

ON A WEEPING WILLOW PLACED OVER AGAINST THE SUNDIAL AT BRYNBELLA, NOV. 28TH, 1802.

Mark how the weeping willow stands,
    Near the recording stone ;
It seems to blame our idle hands,
    And mourn the moments flown.

Thus conscience holds our fancy fast,
    With care too oft' affected ;
Pretending to lament the past,
    The present still neglected.

Yet shall the swift improving plant
    With spring her leaves resume ;
Nor let the example *she* can grant,
    Descend on winter's gloom.

Loiter no more then near the tree,
    Nor on the dial gaze ;
If but an hour be giv'n to thee,
    Act right while yet it stays.

When Pleasure marks each hour that flies,
    And Youth rejoyces in his prime,
It may be good, it may be wise,
    To watch with care the flight of time.

But now; — when friends and hours are seen
    To part, and ne'er return again ;
Who would admit of a machine
    To mark how few there yet remain ?

I am asked to produce some *étrennes* for dear Mrs.
Lutwyche. Will these verses do, accompanied by a
bouquet ? —

The charms we find Maria still possess,
Deciduous plants like these but ill express :
Your emblem in a brighter clime we see,
No season robs of flow'rs — the Orange Tree.

HER LAST VERSES.

TIME, DEATH, AND H. L. P.

MORS (*loquitur*).

Tell her, old Time of foot so fleet,
Once caught, she can't our strokes avoid :

H. L. P.

I know it ; but when next we meet,
'Twill be to see you both destroyed.

LETTERS.

LETTERS.

THE two brothers to whom the first batch of the following letters are addressed, were members of a county family settled for more than two centuries at Hempsted in Gloucestershire. Both were eminently distinguished by the extent and variety of their antiquarian and literary acquirements, as well as highly esteemed for their social qualities. It is sufficient to mention their principal work, the "Magna Britannia," which they undertook in copartnership. The younger, Samuel, afterwards Keeper of the Records in the Tower and a V.P.R.S., was presented to Johnson and favourably received by him; but the acquaintance commenced only a few months before Johnson's death.

The present proprietor of Hempsted Court and rector of Rodmarton (the family living) amply sustains the hereditary reputation of his family, being the author of several works of learning, ingenuity and research.

A selection of letters from Mrs. Piozzi to the same

gentlemen, of an earlier date, appeared in " Bentley's Miscellany," in 1849.

To the Rev. Daniel Lysons.

4 o'clock in the morning of
Saturday 10, 1794.

DEAR MR. LYSONS,—Here are we returned home from a concert at one house, a card assembly at a second, a ball and supper at a third.   The pain in my side, which has tormented me all evening, should not however have prevented my giving the girls their frolic, and enjoying your company myself; but servants and horses can't stand it *if I can,* and even Cecilia consents not to be waked in four hours after she lies down.   Excuse us all, therefore, and believe me ever truly yours,

H. L. PIOZZI.

To the Rev. Daniel Lysons.

Denbigh, N. W., Wednesday,
7th January, 1795.

DEAR MR. LYSONS,—I write to you, knowing that you are stationary, and you will tell your brother that we are coming back to Streatham Park, where our first pleasure will be to see and converse with our long absent friends, among which I hope long to reckon you both.   Many strange events, but I think no good ones, have taken place since we parted ; yet, although many accidents have happened, I see not that the fog clears or dissipates, so as to give us any good view of the end yet. Those who live nearer the centre may perhaps obtain better intelligence, and see further than we do; and more light may break in still before the fourth or fifth of February, when we shall request *your* company, or *his*, or *both* for a day's comfortable chat. What do the Opposition say concerning their projects for peace with a nation that continues, or rather renews, predatory hostilities, while the armistice (themselves were contented to grant) remains in full force?

Has no caricatura print been made yet of a Frenchman shaking Nic Frog by the hand in a *sinister* manner, at the same time that the other arm is employed in cutting his throat? They are terrible fellows, to be sure; and if they take Pampeluna, the King and Queen of Spain will have to run away from Madrid, as the Stadhtholder and his lady from Holland, I suppose; so you will do well to finish your Environs of London* quickly while *that* lasts.

How do your amiable neighbours, the Miss Pettiwards? You will have dear Siddons amongst you soon, I hear, for they have taken Mr. Cologon's pretty villa. Write once more, do, before we meet, and say you will come to Streatham Park soon, and make a world of chat with my master, and Cecy, and, dear Sir, yours ever, very sincerely,

H. L. PIOZZI.

Pick me up some literary intelligence if any can be

* Mr. Lysons was engaged in a topographical work entitled "The Environs of London."

found.   I hear Miss Burney that was — Madame D'Ar,-blaye — is writing for the stage.

To the Rev. Daniel Lysons.

Denbigh, Sunday night, 15th February, 1795.

DEAR MR. LYSONS, — A thousand thanks for your letter, and literary intelligence.   I suspect the tragedy &c.* will prove a second Chattertonism; this is an age of imposture.   What became of the philosopher in St. Martin's Lane, who advertised a while ago that he gave life and motion to stone figures, that moved and turned in every direction at the word of command?   I never saw it in the paper but once; 'twas a curious advertisement.   So is Mr. Kemble's *in another way;* he has proved himself no conjuror, sure, to get into such a scrape, but Alexander and Statira will pull him out, I suppose.†   Poor dear Mrs. Siddons is never well long together, always *some* torment, body or mind, or both. Are people only *sick* in London (by the way), or do they *die?* not of any one contagious disorder, but of various maladies.   I suspect there is disposition to mortality in the town, sure enough, for never did I read of so many deaths together; these violent changes from cold to heat, and from heat to cold, occasion a great deal of it.

For the Princess of Wales, I think little about her just now, and still less about that horrid Mr. Brothers;

* The celebrated Ireland forgeries.
† He was obliged to make a public apology for indecorous behaviour to a lady, afterwards his sister-in-law.

but it will be a dreadful thing to see the King and Queen of Spain setting out upon *their* travels, as appears by no means improbable, if the French are in possession of Pampeluna. The Spaniards can fight nothing but *bulls;* we shall have that royal family unroosted, I verily believe, and in a few months too. The capture of Holland will seem a light thing in comparison of so heavy a calamity when it comes to pass, for all the riches of Mexico will then drop into the wrong scale.

> " But we will not be over-exquisite
> To scan the fashion of uncertain evils,"

as Milton says; but keep out famine by liberality, and contagion by cleanliness, as long as ever we can ; loving our gallant seamen meantime, and rewarding them with all the honours and profits old England has to bestow.

I should like to read your Fast sermon ; we shall have a very good one *here,* for among other comforts Denbigh possesses that of an excellent preacher and reader. Pray tell how the day is observed in London and its environs : I shall be curious to hear ; and do assure you with the greatest sincerity that letters from you and your brother are most desirable treats. He is cruel, though, and keeps close *Mum.* Pray are the Greatheeds in town ? what do they say of Mr. Kemble's conduct? and what of their countryman Shakespeare's extraordinary resuscitation? It seems to me a sort of tub to the whale, a thing to catch attention, and detain it from other matters. When we see Mr. Lloyd of Wickwor, whom we here justly call the philosopher, I shall find what *he* thinks of the discovery. Give my kindest regards to your very amiable neighbours, Miss Pettiwards; they must take *double* care of their mother now, if possible, for all the people past a certain age seem to be dropping off.

'Tis very wicked in me to send you these sixpenny-worths of interrogations every time I feel my ignorance of what passes in the world painful to myself, or disgraceful among those whom I wish to entertain; but whoever is rich will be borrowed from: so Adieu! and write soon, and accept my master's and Cecilia's best compliments from, dear Sir, yours most faithfully,

H. L. PIOZZI.

To the Rev. Daniel Lysons.

Brynbella, 9th February, 1796.

You really can scarcely believe, dear Mr. Lysons, how much entertainment and pleasure was given us by your agreeable and friendly letter, in which however you do not mention your brother, but I doubt not he is well and happy. You do not mention the high price of provisions neither, though sufficient to make everybody *un*happy; but this mild season, and good plenty of coals, I trust, contribute to keep people quiet, assisted by our new laws against sedition. I have found a wise book at last—Miss Thrale sent it me—on Monopoly and Reform of Manners; printed for Faulder. It should be given about, I think, like Hannah More's penny books, and got by heart for a task by servants, apprentices, &c., and much finer people, though *they* are too fine by half.

The Chinese embassy * will not tempt three guineas out of my pocket, say *what* they will, and say it *how* they will. Æneas Anderson has convinced me that it was an empty business at best.

Your account of Shakespear's being forged and fooled after so many years' peace and quietness, most exactly tallies with what my heart told me upon reading the queen's supposed letter to him in our newspaper. I have seen no other, but was struck with the word *amuse*. She would have said *pastyme*. The other phrase was hardly received in France (whence we got it) so early as the days of Elizabeth. The dates, however, are decisive, when you tell me she is made to promote the *amuse*ment of a man then known to be dead. The Earl of Leicester was ranger here of Denbigh Green, you know; and my ancestor, Salusbury of Bachygraig, opposed his innovation when he sought to enclose the common for his use. The tyrant followed him up, though, till he got his life; and not contented with that, brought his first cousin, Salusbury of Llewenney, — my *mother's* ancestor, — to death likewise, by way of revenge; all which shall serve as my pretext for a good piece of the Green whenever it is ordered for cultivation. Meantime, let me request an early narrative of Vortigern's success. I think they will pluck his painted vest from him, but we shall see.

* The work on Lord Macartney's Embassy to China, price three guineas.

It has been long matter of surprise to me that
the less-instructed part of our common audiences in
London never miss being right in their judgment of a
play, or even of the language; for as to incidents, those
are as obvious to one set of men as to another, if probable or not.   But what I mean is this: when Lady
Macbeth tells them that the grooms of Duncan's chamber
she will with wine and wassel so *convince*, &c., they
think it (as it certainly is) perfectly right, and in character with the times; but let Cumberland or Jephson
use the same phrase, and say they will *convince* a knot
of friends with *drink*, a loud shout of laughter would,
without any instigation, burst from the upper gallery;
every single member of which, talked to apart, would
appear to know very little, if anything, concerning the
history of their native tongue.   For these reasons it is
scarce a fair wager how this new tragedy is received,
without they bring it out in Shakspear's name, which I
do think would save it harmless, so long as they believed the imposition.

Meantime, I see by the newspapers people continue
to insult the king, throwing stones at him as he passes.
Methinks the very word *stone* should be offensive to all
his family : one mad fool of the name persecuted Princess
Sophia, as I remember, with offers of marriage; and this
coachmaker or coal-merchant, or what was the anagram-
matical gentleman who signed *Enots*, *he* seems to have
escaped by testimonials to his character from the rich
Democrates.   I think they are all Gall *Stones*, and I
heartily wish we were rid of them.

What becomes of the Beavor family? I never write to Mrs. Gillies, because I know she hates letters; but my true esteem of her brave brothers does not lessen by absence. Mrs. D'Arblaye's new novel is not advertised yet. Somebody told me Lady Eglinton is turned writer now she has married the son of Doctor More; but perhaps it was a joke. Will Miss Farren's coronet *never* be put on? I thought the paralytic countess would have made way for her long ago.

Dear, charming Siddons keeps her empire over all hearts still, I hope; if an Irish plan takes place in her arrangements this spring, we shall not despair to see her at Brynbella. Tell her so with my true love.

There is a new pamphlet supposed by Jones, the Hutchinsonian, to say that our Saviour's Coming (but not the end of the world) is at hand. I cannot recollect the title of it, but do buy and send it to Streatham Park with any other *little* thing worth notice, but no three-guinea books. I wonder who wrote the small tract about Monopoly; 'tis monstrously clever, and clever *only* because *it's true*. So is my conclusion of this letter, saying that I am most sincerely, dear Sir, yours,

H. L. Piozzi.

My master * unites in compliments.

---

* It is curious that she could call her second husband by this name, so well calculated to revive the memory of her first.

To the Rev. Daniel Lysons.

Brynbella, 9th July, 1796.

DEAR MR. LYSONS,—This is a letter of mere request, to beg remembrances from old and distant friends. Do pray write now and then, and make me up a good long letter of *small London chat:* you can scarcely think how welcome *living* intelligence is to those who have chiefly the *dead* to converse with, and I work hard at *old* stuff all morning, and sigh for some *evening* conversation about literature and politics, and the common occurrences of the day.

Esher, or *Asher,* in Surrey, is a place I cannot find in your Environs. It was my grandmother's property, and she sold it to the Pelhams; *her* mother lies buried there with a painted or coloured monument if I recollect rightly, though 'tis many years since I saw it. Mr. Piozzi used to promise me a drive thither, but we never went.

Hume says that Cardinal Wolsey retired to that seat when the king withdrew his favour from him; and Mr. Fitzmaurice, from whose library I borrowed the book, queries the place, and doubts whether he ever was there; although Stowe tells—for I remember it—how Wolsey alighted from his horse in the road between Asher and Richmond, to receive the ring which Henry sent him, and threw himself on his knees in the dirt from thankfulness that he was not *wholly* out of favour. I wish you would set me right. Likewise I want to know where the spot once called Castle-risings now stands.

Edward II.'s queen Isabella was confined there to her death, but lived very grand, I trust, for she had 3000*l.* a year, a sum equal to a royal jointure *now*, I suppose. Hume says it *was* ten miles from London, and it must be nearer *now.*

Do Mr. Walpole's works sell, and is his *Love Story* that you once read to me in them? I liked the letters to Hannah More mightily.

If Mr. Bunbury's *Little Gray Man* is printed, do send it hither; the ladies at Llangollen are dying for it. They like those old Scandinavian tales and the imitations of them exceedingly; and tell me about the prince and princess of *this* loyal country, one province of which alone had disgraced itself; and now no Anglesey militiaman is spoken to by the *Cymrodorion*, but all completely sent to *Coventry,* for nobody wants them in Ireland.

The mysterious expedition of Buonaparte will I hope end at worst in revolutionising the Greek Islands, and restoring the old names to Peloponnæsus, Eubœa, &c. I should be sorry he ever got to India, but waking the Turks from their long sleep will not grieve me. The Knights of Malta make a *triste figure* at last; I suppose Mr. Weishoupt's emissaries were beforehand with the *hero of Italy,* as they call him.

My husband is particularly disgusted with the people that exalt Buonaparte's personal courage and valorous deeds. "He goes nowhere unless he is called," says Mr. Piozzi; if he wanted to show his *prowess,* why did not he *come here,* or to Ireland? we would have shown him sport; but like Caliban, those fellows *will be wise henceforward and sue for grace,* and worship the French no more, unless they are still greater blunderers than even *I* take them for, who am ever, dear Sir, yours faithfully,

H. L. P.

To the Rev. Daniel Lysons.

Brynbella, Tuesday Evening, 1797.

I THANK you very sincerely for the entertaining letter I received the other day. Indeed, my dear Sir, you can scarcely imagine how much a cargo of London chat enlivens our conversation here in the country, where those deceased topics of the town revive and flourish which were withering away upon their native seed-bed. When you have anything fit for transplantation, pray send hither, where there is more soil than trees in almost every sense. Burke's pamphlet and his answerers are in *full bloom* with us *now;* but *you* have forgotten them, I trust, and are busy about what is in succession. Miss Thrale has promised me Watson's Apology. Could you, as you walk about and examine books upon stalls, find me a second, or third, or *thirteenth*-hand History of Poetry, by Warton, or of Music, by Hawkins; I should be much obliged to you; but it must be under a guinea price. I have the good editions myself at Streatham Park. Your book of " Ladies' Dresses " must have received curious addition, by what I see and hear of the present fashions; but cutting off hair is the foolishest among the foolish. When they are tired of going without clothes, 'tis easy putting them on again; but what they will do for the poor cropt and shorn heads, now there are no convents, I cannot guess.

Do people rejoice now wheat falls in price? they made heavy lament when it was high, — or do we only sigh for peace that we may be at leisure to meditate mischief?

And so I see that both Ministry and Opposition have at last *agreed* in *one* point; they join against the *Lapdogs:*

> " So when two *dogs* are fighting in the streets,
>   With a third *dog* one of these two *dogs* meets;
>   With angry teeth he bites him to the bone,
>   And this *dog* smarts for what that *dog* had done."

These verses are somewhat too *soft* and *mellifluous* for the occasion, being Fielding's, but I half long to address a doggrel epistle to Mr. Dent *; he would be as angry as Mr. Parsons, no doubt, and I understand *his* wrath is very great. What becomes of Ireland, I wonder, now *his solemn mockery is ended.* It was a forged bill, you see, and the public did well to protest it.†

If Mrs. Siddons was to work at Drury Lane all winter and run about all summer, she would have had no

* Who gained the nickname of Dog Dent by this piece of legislation.

† " Vortigern " was acted and damned on April 2, 1796. The last audible line was

"And when this solemn mockery is o'er,"

which Kemble was accused of uttering in a manner to precipitate the catastrophe.

enjoyment of Putney; and the young ones, for whose sake she is to work and run, would never have delighted in an *out of town* residence. Cecilia is coming to the scene of action, London, where *I* think there were enough just such half-hatched chickens without her and Mr. Mostyn adding to the number; but then they do not care what I think, so 'tis all one. The Bishop of Bangor likes Wales no better than she does, I suppose, but he ought not to have said so; because an old bishop should be wiser than a pretty wench, and much will be endured from *her*, very little from *him*, especially in these days; he is got into a cruel embarrassment.

Tell something about our Princess of Wales and her domestiques, and of our infant queen-expectant, pretty creature! I should somehow like to see that baby excessively. My hope is that every English heart will devote itself to the service of so much innocence and sweetness.

I depend upon an excellent account of " Almeyda;" * the epilogue is charming. Only one fault; 'tis an epilogue would do for any play. I call such things verses *to be let.* Prologues and epilogues should, to be perfect, be appropriate, referring to what has been presented, or is to present itself before the audience. This, however, is playful and pretty, and so far as I know or can remember, quite original.

Adieu, dear Sir, and bid your brother not quite forget

* Miss Lee's play.

me. The arm of an old vestal virgin kept under ground since Agricola's time, is cold compared with the hand of his and your faithful servant,

H. L. PIOZZI.

To the Rev. Daniel Lysons.

Brynbella, Sunday.
(post-mark, 1796.)

DEAR MR. LYSONS, — You have at last written me so kind and so entertaining a letter, that no paper on my part shall be wasted in reproaches; I thank you very kindly, but you should never suppose me informed of things which *you* cannot help hearing; but they escape *me* easily enough. I *do* hear of the Arch Duke's successes however, and of poor Italy's disgrace; I *hear* of peace too — when shall we *see* it? Mr. Ireland is a pleasant gentleman indeed, and his last act his *best* act in my mind; absolution follows confession; I have done being angry with him now. There is a note in Mr. Malone's pamphlet * for which I would give half a dozen publications of fifty pages each *concerning the times;* it contains my sentiments so exactly that I may easily commend the writer's good sense and sound judgment. The mysteries of Carlton House surpass those of Udolpho: may they end as those do, in mere nihility. I will not quarrel with you for making no reply to my questions about "Camilla," † because I have read it myself, and

---

* Against the Ireland forgeries.
† Madame D'Arblay's novel.

because these are really not times for any man of the living world to waste his moments in weighing of feathers; he, however, who neglects to read Burke's last pamphlet, loses much of a very rational pleasure.

I turn the page to talk of yours and your brother's discoveries *, of which I honestly wish you much joy. There are medals at Capo di Monte with a pagan triumph on one side, and on the other the monogram of Christ; but connoisseurs told me those were Constantine's, who was, you know, enrolled among the heathen gods; but I can give no account of its connection with a temple to Neptune, and what a little temple it is! only thirty feet long; are you sure it *is* a temple after all? We had a base-born Constantine in Britayne, had we not, about Honorius's time? he made his son Cæsar if I remember well; was he in Dorsetshire? or was this long room mere private property, and Neptune nothing but an ornament — as he is now. I should like to know if the ℞ was concealed or plainly set in view. Christians wore them of divers kinds I believe in places of persecution, much as the Royalists in France carried the effigies of Louis Seize about them in unsuspected forms; and the ill treatment of those who professed our religion did not cease *immediately* in remote parts of the empire, although it ended in the capital after the outspread Labarum had swept its foes away. Perhaps, too, the mark was not unknown to Constantine, when he saw it somehow

* Of Roman antiquities at Woodchester, on which Mr. Samuel Lysons based two valuable publications.

miraculously displayed with the Greek words expressive of *In hoc Signo vinces* under it; perhaps (but these are too bold conjectures) it had been a private sign among Christians before, and was exalted only — not first recognised — at the grand battle between him and Maxentius. The 24th chapter of St. Matthew and the 30th verse, give one an idea that it shall again appear; as the *sign* of the Son of Man is there spoken of as *preceding* our Saviour's second coming. There are medals with another monogram upon them resembling the arbitrary mark of a planet, with a triumph on the other side and a hand held out from the clouds; if they mean Constantine, 'tis awkwardly expressed, because he refused to triumph after the ancient manner.

I doubt whether Ætius thrice consul, to whom the groans of the Britons . . . was a Christian; Placidia we know was. Could *he* have had any share in your marine worship? When the sea drove them back to the barbarians who by dint of numbers forced them forward on the sea, perhaps they tried what pleasing old Neptune might do for them; some heathens in the Roman army might recommend the measure. Numberless are the connections between Christian and pagan ornaments in Italy. I saw a Madonna in the Vatican with Cybele's tower on her head, and other insignia of that goddess, from the workman's confusion, as it appears, between Mater Dei and Mater Deorum; and there is an altar in the church where Sannazarius reposes at Naples, decorated with the story of Jupiter and Leda. But I have left no room for Mr. Piozzi's compliments: he talks of being at Streatham Park early next spring, where I hope to thank you for many a kind letter received before that time. Write soon, *do*, and believe me ever with just esteem,

Dear Sir, yours and your brother's obliged
and faithful servant,

H. L. P.

To the Rev. Daniel Lysons.

Brynbella, Thursday.
(No other date, and no post-mark.)

DEAR MR. LYSONS, — Accept a renewal of inquiries, literary and domestic; but 'tis for yourself I inquire; your brother, we know, is well and busy with his subterranean discoveries. What statues has he found? they will be very valuable; and tell me for mercy's sake what this *Apology for the Bible**** means: we live in fine times sure when the Bible wants an apology from the bishops. How is Mr. Burke's book received? and what will his regicide peace be? I see no sign of peace except in the books: for they make them ready to battle in all parts of the world, and we shall have the Turks upon us directly if we chase French ships into their very harbours so. No matter! my half-crown for Flo shall be willingly contributed, though I do think *seriously* that the Dog Tax and Repeal of Game Laws will have an exceeding bad effect on the country, where

* Bishop Watson's celebrated answer to Paine and Gibbon.

gentlemen will want inducements to remain when hunting and coursing and shooting are at an end. Horses will lower in price, however, and little oats will be sown at all. I think democracy in all her insidiousness could not have contrived a more certain principle of levelling, and republicanism in all her pride could not plan more perfect gratification than that of seeing the young farmers' sons cocking their guns in face of a landlord upon whom no man feeling any dependence, he will shelter himself among the crowds of London, and prefer being jostled at Vauxhall by his taylor, to the being robbed of innocent amusements by those who were bred on his land, and fed on his bounty.*

Our Chester paper even now reproaches the rich with their donations of bread and meat, which are already styled *insults* on the *poor's independence;* and Mr. Chappelon, who has been here on a visit, protested he was glad to get *alive* out of Norfolk, because he had presumed to *give* his parishioners barley and potatoe bread baked in his own oven. I wish you would write me a long letter, and tell me a great deal about the living world; and something of the *dead* too, for I see Mr. Howard's epitaph, but cannot guess who wrote it.

Vortigern will, I trust, be condemned almost without a hearing, so completely does the laugh go against it. This is the age of forgeries. I never read of so

---

* If indignation makes verses, it does not supply syntax; and this sentence, which I have not attempted to correct, bears a strong resemblance to that of the county member who described Sir Robert Peel as "not the sort of man that you could put salt upon his tail."

many *causes célèbres* in that way as of late; but poor
dear Mrs. Siddons saves Ireland awhile, I suppose, by
her ill health, and keeps Miss Lee from fame and fortune which she expects to acquire by " Almeyda." Does
Madame D'Arblay's novel promise well? Fanny wrote
better before she was married than since, however
that came about. I understand nothing concerning the
young baronet that lost so much at backgammon.
Those tales are seldom true to the extent they are
related: much like the stories of mad dogs, which
chiefly exist in newspapers; but I fear Lady West-
meath's Divorce Bill, like Mrs. Mullins, will carry conviction of *her* infidelity all over the world. We knew
her and her lord at Bath. very well. I try every time
I write to get some intelligence of the Beavor family,
but without effect.

Selden says marriage is the act of a man's life
which least concerns his acquaintance, yet, adds he,
'tis the very act of his life which they most busy
themselves about. Now Heaven knows, I never did
disturb myself or him by Dr. Gillies's marriage, though
it affected me exceedingly; his amiable lady and
her family being of my most favourite acquaintance,
and they are all lost to me somehow. Mr. Rogers'
name has crost me but once since we left London
either: it was when he gave evidence in favour of
that *anagrammatic* Mr. Stone*, who wrote his name

---

* On Stone's trial, the author of " The Pleasures of Memory "
proved a conversation with him in the streets, tending to show
that he made no mystery of that which was charged as treason-
able.

backwards, as witches are said to do; who deal in deeds of darkness, and sing

"When good kings bleed we rejoice," &c.

How does your book of fashionable *dresses* go on? it must, I think, receive some curious additions by what one hears and *sees;* for a caricature print of a famous fine lady who leads the Mode has already reached poor little Denbigh.

To the Rev. Daniel Lysons.

Brynbella, 5th Jan. 1796.

DEAR MR. LYSONS, — After making repeated inquiries for you of all our common friends, I begin to find out that the best way is to ask yourself. Dear Siddons was always a slow correspondent, though a kind wellwisher; and she has so much to do in good earnest, that we must forgive her not sitting down to write letters either of fact or sentiment; for a little of both these I apply to *you,* and beg a little chat for information of what is going forward. Tell me, in the first place, concerning your own health and your *wicked* brother's, who forgets his old correspondent very shamefully; after that, let the sedition bills or the Shakespear manuscripts take post according to the bustle made about them in London. Make me understand why Mr. Hayley writes Milton's life, and why Doctor Anderson publishes Johnson's. Those roads are so beaten they will get dust in their own eyes sure, instead of throwing any into the eyes of their readers; at this distance from the scene of action I cannot guess their intents. Tell what other new books attract notice, and what becomes of the Whig Club now 'tis divided like Paris into *sections*. I fancy France will be divided into sections at last, — a bit to Royalists, another bit to Republicans; and perhaps the very name of a nation so disgraced by crimes and follies will be lost for ever. No matter! I long to see Burke's letter to Arthur Young: *his* predictions have the best claim to attention of any living wight.

Oh pray what becomes of the man who set mankind a staring this time last year? he is in a madhouse, is not he? We had a slight earthquake about eight or ten weeks ago, and such extraordinary weather as never did I witness; very providential sure that it should continue so warm and mild and open while bread remains at such an advanced price. Yesterday the prospect was clear and bright as spring; nor have we seen ice hitherto; but storms enough to blow the very house down, and I fear prevent our West India fleet from ever arriving at its place of destination. A beautiful prismatic halo round the moon in an elliptic form very elegant on Christmas Day, was said by our rural philosophers to be a rare but certain præcursor of tempest, and so it proved: I was, however, glad to have seen a meteor so uncommon.

Has your brother examined any of the gold from our new mine in Ireland? The bishop showed us some, and Mr. Lloyd, I think, sent specimens to Sir Joseph Banks

—it is supposed purer, and less drugged with alloy than what comes immediately from Peru — could we but get enough of it. Meanwhile *I* had half a ticket in the Irish Lottery with Mr. Murphy, but can hear nothing either of my fortune or my partner. Take compassion do, and send us a long letter. Mr. Piozzi adds his best compliments to mine, with wishes of a happy New Year. The pianoforte is not quite neglected, though he has lost Mrs. Bagot, who sings such sweet duets. Cecilia and her husband are well and merry; my other daughters write me word from Clifton that they like Mrs. Pennington and attend her benefit balls, which I am glad of. You will expect no news from me, but I shall be very desirous to receive your thanks for obliging *inquiries.* *They* are all I have to send, except the truest regards of Brynbella to Putney; and pray tell me that those agreeable Miss Pettiwards are well who have probably quite forgotten by this time, dear Mr. Lyson's

Ever faithful humble servant,
H. L. PIOZZI.

To the Rev. Daniel Lysons.

Brynbella, 3rd Sept. 1802.

AND now we are come home at last after an eight months' absence, and a 500 miles' tour, 'tis high time to congratulate dear Mr. and Mrs. Lysons on the happy event of which the newspapers informed us, whilst in a *far country,* though none more pleasing than Gloucestershire. We passed a fortnight or three weeks at Cheltenham, where I remembered the pretty planted walk finishing with a tall spire, when I was there a *child* in company of my mother and my aunts; and I *think* I remember the *Smith's* epitaph in the church-yard, because when reading "Camden's Remains" many years after, it came in my head how much cleverer *that* is, which *he* preserves, and in the same style. John English's inscription on his monument was however *too deep* for me then to be struck with, 'tis almost *too deep now*. The marking capitals to denote the name of Jesus in that strange way, neither anagram nor acrostic, is exceedingly curious; I warrant you have a true copy of it, and perhaps will give me one. Write to me, dear Mr. Lysons, and *tell* me something. Tell me particularly about the new comer to Rodmarton's — Health, Strength, and Beauty. The excellence of *so* new a comer will be comprised in those three words; and if the truth were well known, the first implies the other two completely.

Here am I without anything to feed on but my own thoughts; our house is painting and ornamenting, and they have thrust the few books I possess, all into one closet on a heap. My thoughts are fuller than they were though; by the addition of your brother's kindness in showing me the stone at Somerset House, from which if I could *learn* but little, for want of more skill in languages, I can please my busy fancy well enough, perhaps better than if sullen truth intruded and catched imagination by the bridle. For example, my recollection says that among the hieroglyphicks, I saw a *crow* perpetually, and I *do* think, that this same *crow* came originally out of the same nest as old Odin's *reafan* that King Regner Lodbrog's three weird sisters worked for Hialmar, a standard of victory (ladies *still* present consecrated *colours* to the troops you know), and a raven then was the lucky impress in *every* part of the world, which had not perhaps wholly forgotten its being dismissed from the ark as a bird chosen for purpose of fixing future nations in permanent happiness. The Egyptians least of *all* forgot that great event, and when I see in the library at Somerset House a vase brought from the *Musquito shore* adorned with *Grecian* fretwork, I cannot wonder at any marks of affinity between old Coptic and Scandinavian ideas.

Besides does not *Justin* say?—I told you *true* that I could not get at a book; does not *some one* say how Ptolemy that finished the Cut from Nile to the Red Sea, and whose *deification act* is said to be now in our antiquarians' room in the Strand, joined with Gallo Greeks and Galatians against Antigonus? The *Gauls*, wherever planted, considered a crow as their coat armour, if we may call it so; and lost all courage for that very reason, when the fatal bird perched on a Roman's helmet, called Corvinus from that day by his own countrymen, who readily adopted *all* neighbouring superstitions. I do believe the croaking raven * meant victory in hieroglyphic language, and am impatient now till clear translation shows the analogy, and makes some

* Hardly in Macbeth, act i. sc. 3.

explanation. If the *British Critic* was to see *this* stuff, he would say my letters were in *rhyme* I suppose, as he says "Retrospection" is written in blank verse. Lord bless the people, what things do come into their heads ! *Mine* is at present very full of Kader Idris : I never saw it till this summer, and a grand sight it is. We crossed South Wales, and bathed in the sea at Tenby; Mr. Piozzi kept clear of confinement at least, though he complains of being very tender-footed. He unites with me in true regards and *compliments;* or more properly in sincere *un*complimentary good wishes to you and yours; and bears me witness, that I am always very truly, dear Mr. Lyson's

Faithful servant,

H. L. P.

Pray write me a long letter.

To Samuel Lysons, Esq.

Wednesday, 10th Feb. 1808.

DEAR MR. LYSONS,—I have not written to you a long time, and now I cannot *help* writing. I loved your brother so much, and wished him happy so sincerely, his change of life affects me, and my feelings will not permit me to tell *him* so. Tell him yourself, my good friend, and assure yourself that the account of his wife's death in the papers gave me a sensation beyond what my acquaintance with her called for. But she was pretty when we last met, and she was young, and it seems so odd and melancholy to look in the grave for those one used to see at the tea-table ! Well ! you who live among the records of past life will bear these things better; my spirits are much depressed by Mr. Piozzi's miserable state of health, nor can the gaieties I hear of draw my attention from the sorrows that I *see*. Mrs. Mostyn has politely taken a week's share of them just now while her sons are absent, and the London winter not begun. *Our* winter commenced in November, and when it will end I know not. The mountains are still covered with snow, and such tempestuous weather did I never witness.

The political wonders have increased since the suspension of our correspondence so much, that we are all tired of wondering at them; but this new discovery of a nest of Christians in Travancore must be considered as curious by everybody who reads of it. Tell me the price of Buchanan's book and its character; I see nothing but extracts, and those imperfect ones; and tell me some literary chat, remembering our distance from all possibility of adding a new idea to our stock, except by the voluntary subscriptions and contributions (to use an hospital phrase) of the nobility, gentry, and others. Hospital phrases, indeed, best suit the dwellers at Brynbella; but Doctor Johnson — never wrong — was right, *pre-eminently* right in this: That chronic diseases are never cured; and acute ones, if recovered from, cure themselves. The maxim has been confirmed by my experience every day since to me first pronounced, and I dare say the late unfortunate event in your own family affords it no contradiction.

Has your brother many children left him by his lady,

and is he living at Hempstead Court? He had better get to London, and lose his cares in the crowd.

Dear Mr. Lysons, do write to me, and in the meantime pity me and my poor husband, whose sufferings one should believe, on a cursory view of them, wholly insupportable; but God gives the courage, with the necessity of exerting it.

Adieu, and believe me, ever faithfully yours,

H. L. PIOZZI.

I hear all good of Mrs. Siddons.

To Samuel Lysons, Esq.

Brynbella, 22 Aug. 1813.

MRS. PIOZZI presents her most respectful compliments to her old friend Mr. Lysons, as Governor of the British Institution, with an earnest request that he will protect her portraits from being copied, as she was strictly promised before she could consent to lend them. It would break *her* heart, and ruin the value of the pictures to posterity, and now some artist living at No. 50, Rathbone Place, who spells his name so that she cannot read it, unless 'tis Joseph, writes to her, begging he may copy the portrait of Doctor Johnson, when she was hoping all the four were by this time restored to their places at old Streatham Park. Mrs. Piozzi wishes Mr. Lysons joy of his brother's marriage, but hopes he himself is not now at Hemstead Hall, as she knows not where to apply.

To Samuel Lysons, Esq.

Brynbella, 17 Feb. 1814.

DEAR MR. LYSONS,— I was desired by some disputants to obtain correct information, and felt immediately that I could be *sure* of it from none but yourself. The question is, What authority can be produced, for an account given in some public print, of a frost on the River Thames, equal, or nearly equal to this last, in the second or third centuries? Do me the very great kindness to let me know; and *where* you read the fact, whether in Holinshed, Stowe, Speed, or Strype's Annals, and from what record the incident is taken, it having been averred that no records could then have been kept. I mean in 260 or 270 A. D.

Having now discharged my commission, I take the opportunity, though *late*, of wishing you and your brother a happy new year, and full enjoyment of the felicities which people seem in such strong expectation of. Your living world is so remote from *us here*, and the intelligence so limited, that I know absolutely nothing of what is going forward. My correspondents always begin their letters with, You have *heard so much* of, &c., &c., that I am precluded hearing *at all*. Come now, do send me a kind letter, and tell me if Madame D'Arblaye gets 3000*l.* for her book or no *, and if Lord Byron is to be called over about some verses †

---

* "The Wanderer, or Female Difficulties," published in 1814.
† The verses beginning:

"Weep, daughter of a royal line."

he has written, as the papers hint. And tell me how the peacemakers will accommodate the Pope, and the little King of Rome too ; and the Emperor of Germany beside, whose second title was King of the Romans, and how all this and ten times more is to be settled, before St. David's Day. Wonders! wonders! wonders! Why Katterfelto and his cat never pretended to *such* impossibilities. What says your brother to *these* days? He used to feel amazed at the occurrences of twenty-one years ago; but if everything we saw so tumbled about *then*, can be so easily and swiftly arranged *now*, much of our horror and surprise might have been saved.

The fire at the Custom House must have been very dreadful ; I hope you suffered nothing but sorrow for the general loss. Devonshire Square is a place, the situation of which is unknown to me, but I have friends there, who I should grieve for, if they came to any harm.

Adieu, dear Mr. Lysons : if I *live*, which no other old goose does I think through this winter, we shall meet at old Streatham Park, and I shall once more tell you truly, and tell you *personally*, how faithfully

I am yours,

H. L. Piozzi.

MISS WYNN'S COMMONPLACE BOOK.

THE following extracts from some of Mrs. Piozzi's letters to a Welsh neighbour, are copied from Miss Williams Wynn's commonplace book : —

1797.—'Tis really not unworthy observation, how the vital part of every country has been struck at during the last ten years. Loyalty and love of their *Grand Monarque* was a characteristic of Parisian manners. *Their Sovereign has been executed.* Religion and the fine arts comforted the Italians for loss of liberty and of conquests. Their ceremonies are now insulted, their models of excellence taken forcibly away. Our English John, safe in his wooden walls, counted the treasures of the Bank and feared no ill while ships and money lasted. Our guineas are turned to paper, our fleets mutiny, and our boobies here in London run to crown the dead delegates with flowers, forgetting how we were all terrified when the Thames was blocked up, the trade stopt, and an actual civil war at Sheerness, not twenty miles from the capital.

1799.—Your heart would melt to hear the horrid tales from Italy.! Poor Conte di Frow, late Turinese

Ambassador, comes now and then to disburthen his heart and vent his sorrows on us, and, lamenting more his King's misfortunes than his own, tells how that hapless Prince knelt on the ground in vain before the unfeeling general of the French forces begging a brother's life, while that commander, lately a low attorney of some country town, showed him humbled to his brother officers, and made the scene a matter of encouragement to France to persist in her resolves against crowned heads. *This was Sardinia's King.* The royal family of Naples suffered little less, &c. &c. Dear Mr. Piozzi's countrymen tell him that the oxen, &c. in the North of Italy have been so put in requisition, that large tracts of land lie waste for want of cultivation, whilst civil war of opinions among the inhabitants, some holding fast by the old way, and some embracing the new notions brought amongst them by the French, make that once lovely country a theatre of agony, and produce such dearness of provisions, that at Genoa a dog's head was sold for five shillings during the siege, and friends, enemies, soldiers, traders, alike perished more by hunger than by the sword.

1813. — Compliments of the season. It is a very old fashion. Our ancestors used to send mistletoe to each other. The Romans presented dates and dried figs to their friends, and the modern Italians make up elegant boxes of sweetmeats for the same purpose. *We* keep our oaks as clean as we can from all parasitical plants. We leave the sugar plums for children, and send empty wishes of a merry Christmas and a happy

New Year,— even that good custom is going out apace. Well, Ovid's line to Germanicus was the prettiest:—

" Dii tibi dent annos, à te nam cœtera sumes."

Buonaparte doubtless thought such a speech would suit him some months ago, but he must renounce all hope of being *Germanicus.*

.   .   .   .   .   .

1814.— Your partiality will encourage me to a long chat with you concerning the atmospheric stones which have attracted much of my attention. I do believe that Diana of the Ephesians was no other than one of these, and it was thought, you know, that she fell down from Jupiter, but I have heard a Camb-man maintain that it was possible that the *moon* might produce them —an idea best befitting to a *lunatic.* Dr. Milner's joke on such immechanical notions is the very best I know — the ready-furnished house. They must, I think, go *up* before they fall down, and certainly there are more volcanoes at work than we are watching, which fill the air with substances of an attractive kind, which, for the most part, assume conical shapes, as Nature when alone appears particularly to delight in. The Dea Pessinuntia, or Cybele of classic mythology, was, I fancy, a mere meteoric composition. They washed her with much silly reverence, you remember, and Heliogabalus's black stone, which he drove into Rome with four white horses, was nothing better, only the form happened to be perhaps a more regular and perfect cone. He was a Syrian, you know, and this, dropping from heaven as they believed, served excellently to represent their Bel, or Baal, or lost Thammuz, the *Sun*, in short, of which divinity he was *priest*, as a pyræum of aspiring flame.   .   .   .

Let me hope that you will not pursue geology till it leads you into doubts destructive of all comfort in this world, and all happiness in the next. I am not afraid of *Gibbon*. Whoever has a true taste of Cicero's sweetness and Virgil's majesty, will not take *his* modern terseness of expression or neatness of finish, so completely French, for perfection.   .   .   .   .   With regard to our own nobility and people of fashion getting into these horrid scrapes of swindling and stock-jobbing*, and the Lord knows what — they fright *me* to read of them.   We need no longer say with Capt. Macheath,

> ."" I wonder we han't better company
> Upon Tyburn tree."

The executive Power should really address them now in the official phrase of

My lords and gentlemen!

Meanwhile Alexander deserved much of the bustle we made about him.   When a child, it seems, his grandmother, the great autocratix Catherine, took an English boy out of a merchant's counting-house at Petersburgh and put him about the young Czar as a playfellow and to teach him our language.   When she had done with him he was sent off of course, and Alexander confessed

* This evidently alludes to the fraud for which Lord Dundonald was unjustly punished.

that his companion was forgotten. One day, however, in the crowds of London, the Emperor recognised a face that he knew, and made the man come up and say in what way he was *now*, and how he could be served; after which interview no time was lost, till the Prince Regent had not promised only, but actually provided, this old companion of his new friend with a place in the Treasury of 500*l.* a-year. Such actions are like those related in novels, and acted on the stage. . . . .

I refused every invitation for the shows in the Park, and saw the red glare over London so plainly from my own gate, that every moment added to my rejoicing that I was no nearer the crush and the crowd when so many *unnamed* human creatures perished. Miles Peter Andrews, the rich and gay, sent out two hundred cards of invitation to see the festivities from his windows, verandah, &c., but Miles Peter Andrews (his friends say) *went off* before the fireworks; so his heir removed the body and received company *himself*. You and I have read of a golden age, a silver, and an iron age: is not *that* we live in, the marble age? so smooth, so cold, so polished. . . . . . .

Meantime 'tis really curious to hear the different opinions of those who live at the Fountain Head of information. London at this moment exhibits bills stuck up on every post, with Murder in large letters on it, soliciting the apprehension of a felon who has killed his sweetheart, and the lawyers all declare that the annals of Newgate are *disgraced* (comical enough) by the proceedings of the common people

these last three years. . . . Per contra, as shop-
keepers would express it, you may see the *good* people
(I visit many of those who style themselves the *Evangelicals*) congratulating me and each other on the
diffusion of religious knowledge and consequent virtuous
behaviour. Jews, say they, are converting, slaves releasing, and heathen nations obtaining instruction by
means of missionaries warm in the cause of piety, and
useful in researches for bettering the general condition
of mankind. Preachers, no longer supine, *vie* with
each other in eloquent persuasion of their hearers. Who,
twenty or thirty years ago, would have run after any
one of those who now adorn our pulpits? and are, as
far as I can observe, very coolly listened to. Such is my
survey of London in 1814.

1817.—The improvements in London amused me
very much, and such a glare is cast by the gas lights, I
knew not where I was after sunset. Old Father Thames,
adorned by four beautiful bridges, will hardly remember
what a poor figure he made eighty years ago, I suppose,
when gay folks went to Vauxhall in barges*, an attendant
barge carrying a capital band of music playing Handel's
water music — as it has never been played since.

I saw Mr. Wanzey yesterday evening. His account
of the procession at Rome, consisting of Christian slaves

---

* "One evening, at Mrs. Doyley's, when the party had been
talking of the glories of Waterloo bridge, then just opened, a
gentleman turned to the lady of the house and said, 'You and I,
Mrs. Doyley, remember the time when London had but one
bridge.' Miss Grimston was present."—*Note by Miss W. Wynn.*

liberated by Lord Exmouth, was very Interesting.* They walked up the long street, Strada del Popolo, in uniform, and up to St. Peter's Church, attended by all the priesthood singing Litanies, Thanksgivings, &c.; then depositing their standards at the foot of the altar, prostrated themselves before the cross, and returned blessing the English, and crying, as soon as they had passed the church doors, "Vivan i bravi Inglesi! Viva la santa religione, &c."

We are *party* mad here. I do not mean politically so, but the people run to numberless *parties* of a night. No illness or affliction keeps them out of a crowd. A lady at my next door almost had her party on Sunday night, and her husband invited a large company to dinner on the Tuesday following. "Nay," said Dr. Gibbs, "I doubt whether Mrs. —— will *live* beyond Tuesday. She is very ill indeed." At three o'clock the husband sent to put off his company, and at eight o'clock she died. He sent his cards out that day fortnight, and had his party again. So runs our world away. The men play at macko and lose their thousands all morning; one gentleman was seen to pay seven guineas for the cards he had used in four hours only.

1818.—Mrs. Lutwych will have the loss not only of

---

* "It is very strange that the vulgar mistake of writing adjectives with capital letters occurs frequently in these letters. I have copied some of her oddly affected orthography. She is always *set o'laughing*. Through a long negociation she speaks always of the Piano *e* forte which they are buying for Boddylwyddan."— *Note by Miss W. Wynn.* Was it a vulgar mistake at the time?

a good husband and certain friend, but she will lose her greatest admirer too, which few people could boast of in conjugal life, besides herself and me. Alas! alas! but we must lose or be lost. Her death would have broken his heart. The most painful sight of all is a sick baby, for there is such a vegetating power, such a disposition in the habit to drive that death away which grown people often seem half to invite, that it shocks one; and I hoped poor Angelo would have been the staff of my age. You can scarce think how low-spirited all these things make me. I am glad the sea is at hand to wash care away. This weather is melancholy, and so is all one hears — of riots and conspiracies, and people that call aloud for murderers, as the Jews did for Barabbas. The trifling spasms which assailed me this morning will do very little indeed—nothing, I trust, towards releasing me from this busy world, described by many as daily improving. P. S. You wonder at my saying the people call aloud for murderers, but my paper says there were placards distributed in Court while the trials went forward, saying, We want a Bellingham.

1819.—Llewenney Hall pulled down too! and its forests *Alta cadit quercus;* but schools are made of the bricks, and *Teachery,* as I call it in a word of my own inventing, goes on at a famous rate; yet one does not remember it is ever said in the Old or New Testament, " If you *study* My ways, and *learn* My commandments ;" but " if you *walk* in My ways, and *observe* My commandments *to do them,"* which was surely never so little practised as now. Well, the work of reformation runs forward apace. Female associations are forming every day and everywhere. They come into your kitchens, instruct your servants, tell them how their masters and ladies run to perdition, give them books against tyranny, and tell them they are all slaves.

Your vraie amie octogenaire,
H. L. P.

1820.—I certainly feel sorry for his death; and if I do *not* feel *alarmed*, who am three or four years older, it is because even the grim Lion Death may be rendered familiar by stroking, and never suffering him long out of sight. . . . . . . Will you hear the story of my *present* neighbour? Zenobia Stevens, of a good family not far off, had a lease of ninety-nine years under the Duke of Bolton, and *lived it out.* When she went herself and gave it up, her kind landlord begged her to keep the house during her life, and offering her a glass of wine, " *One*, if your Grace pleases," was her prudent reply, " but as I am to ride twelve miles on a young colt these short evenings, I am afraid of being giddy-headed,"

MISCELLANEOUS LETTERS.

To Sir James Fellowes.

Bath, 17th January, 1815.

ACCEPT a thousand compliments; I found the pasquinade after a long search as it was given me on the inauguration of Buonaparte.

> " Romani! vi mostro un bel Quadro,
>   Il santo Padre và coronar un Ladro ;
>   *Un* Pio per conservar la Fede
>   Lascia la Sede,
>   *Un altro* Pio per serbar la Sede
>   Lascia la Fede."

> Romans! behold a picture new,
>   The Holy Father crowns a thief ;
>   Our group exhibits to your view
>   Wonders which far exceed belief.

> Pius the Sixth his seat could leave
>   To save alive our Christian faith ;
>   His successor that seat to save,
>   Abandon'd *her* to certain death.

H. L. P.

The sense is kept, and the point blunted in the translation, but so it is in all translations.

To Sir James Fellowes.

Bath, April 10, 1815.

I RETURN your paper, dear Sir, and thank you for the additional conviction it has given me, that argument and eloquence can be found in Free States only, — decision and promptitude in Despotic Governments alone. While we are talking, they will *act* however, and our pelf will put the puppets in motion.

Do you remember the French Fable of Dragon à plusieurs Testes, and Dragon a plusieurs Queues? I will look for it. Meanwhile I wish Buonaparte was pulled down. Too long he has made the world his pedestal, mankind the gazers, the sole figure, he!

Mrs. Dimond is just come in, and invites me to her box to see Mr. Betty.

The Star containing Lord Liverpool's and Castlereagh's speeches on the Prince's message.

To Sir James Fellowes.

Bath, 10 April, 1815.

MY DEAR SIR,—This is a copy of the memorandum I took when the Bishop of Killala (Stock) showed me the fact in Mezeray's History of France.

"When Hugh Capet was first set in the seat of power, he consulted an astrologer, who told him his descen-

dants would *scarcely* wear the crown above 800 years.
' Will it' (says the King), ' make any difference to the
dynasty, if I consent, not to be crown'd at all ?' ' Oh
yes !' was the reply. ' They will then sit at least 806
years.' " .... and so they *did :* for if you add 806 to
the year 987 when Hugh Capet was inaugurated, it gives
you the year 1793 when his descendant Louis XVII.
was murdered in prison. Les Horoscopes étoient fort à
la mode en ces Tems là. The bishop said it was 816
I remember, and I took the memorandum in haste : if
it was really so, their time was not expired till two
years ago. 'Tis an odd circumstance at any rate : *an
odder still,* that you should prefer my version of Adrian's
lines, to those of better poets.

> " Animula vagula, blandula,
> Hospes comesque corporis,
> Qvæ nunc abibis in loca !
> Pallidula, rigida, nudula,
> Nec ut soles dabis joca."

> Gentle soul ! a moment stay,
> Whither wouldst thou wing thy way?
> Cheer once more thy house of clay,
> Once more prattle and be gay :
> See, thy fluttering pinions play ;
> Gentle soul ! a moment stay.*

* Thus translated by Pope :—
> " Oh, fleeting spirit, wandering fire,
> That long has warm'd my tender breast,
> Wilt thou no more my frame inspire ?
> No more a pleasing cheerful guest ?

The conversation we had that *serious* evening last week on the most serious of all subjects, put the verses in my head which you will read over leaf, with your accustomed partiality to, Dear Sir,

> Your very much obliged,
>
> H. L. P.

I had some of the lines lying unremembered in my mind ever since the year 1809, but I believe never written out.

> Heart ! where heav'd my earliest sigh,
> First to live, and last to die ;
> Fortress of receding life,
> Why maintain this useless strife ?
> Weary of their long delay
> Time and Death demand their prey :
> Worne with cares, and wearied, thou ;
> Willingly their claim allow :
> Soon shall Time and Death destroy'd
> Drop in th' illimitable void,
> Whilst thou thy petty powers shalt ply,
> An atom of eternity.
> For when the trumpet's lofty sound
> Shall echo thro' the vast profound ;
> When with revivifying heat
> All nature's numerous pulses beat,

> Whither, ah ! whither art thou flying,
>   To what dark, undiscover'd shore ?
> Thou seem'st all trembling, shivering, dying,
>   And wit and humour are no more."

Touch'd by the Master's hand : shall come
Thy unforgotten pendulum ;
No longer feeble, cold, and slow ;
Retarded still by grief or woe ;
But firm to mark th' unfinish'd hour,
That shall all grief and woe devour.

To Miss Fellowes.

Monday Night, 24 April, 1815.

MY DEAR MISS FELLOWES,—I send you the strangest
thing I ever saw ; an adaptation of the mystical beast
described in the thirteenth chapter of St. John's Apocalypse, to the name of Napoleon Buonaparte, in Spanish.
It has been done in England various times, and in
various manners ; but that it should be done as it *is
here* in a country of bigotted Romanists, is indeed sur-
prising. If you send it to Sir James, send it very
carefully, for it cannot be got again, and he alone deserves it ; perhaps 'tis better, keep it for him. My
letter contains nothing but some verses he liked when
he heard them read last night : I send it open that you
may read the lines if you please, and say you like them
too. Farewell ! If I find I *can* go to Sidmouth this
year, it must be for the two months, September and
October : and I must be here again to begin November.
What folly and madness, at my age, to be talking of
pleasure I am to receive six months hence !! But I
must talk what the Spaniards call *disparates* while

H. L. P.

A FABLE FOR APRIL, 18:5.

A modern traveller, they say,
Crossing the wilds of Africa,
Saw a strange serpent at a distance,
  Moving majestically slow :
  With fifty heads at least in show,
  Not placed together in a row,
    As if to yield assistance;
But here and there, and up and down,
Some with and some without a crown,
Foaming with rage and grinning with vexation
Against a dragon which behind a brake
Waited without much fear the attack,
  And swell'd with indignation.
His lofty head disdain'd the ground,
  His neck was long and pliant;
Could stretch to earth's remotest bound,
  Or lick the scraps that lie on't.
    Of ugly tails a tortuous train
      Still twisted in his rear ;
    But whilst to follow they were fain,
    He viewed their motions with disdain,
      In that alone sincere.
To watch these mighty monsters greeting
    Our traveller climb'd a lofty tree ;
    Where safe and clearly he could see
    All that befell their meeting.
    But whilst the various heads combin'd,
    From every hedge resistance find ;

Till hope's grown fat and anger cooling
Each his companion ridiculing,
The sly insinuating snake
Slipt his long body through the brake.
Defied his followers to find him,
And tuck'd his servile tails behind him.

To Sir James Fellowes.

Blake's Hotel, Monday, July 31st, 1815.

My dear Sir James Fellowes's friendly heart will feel pleased that the spasms he drove away, returned no more : altho' you were really scarce out of the street before I received a cold short note from Mr. Merrik Hoare, who married one of the sisters, to say that Lord Keith, who married the other, wished to decline purchasing : so here I am no whit nearer disposing of Streatham Park than when I sate still in Bath. Money spent and nothing done : but bills thronging in every hour. Mr. Ward, the solicitor, has sent his demand of 116*l.* 18*s.* 3*d.* I think, for expences concerning Salusbury's marriage. I call that the *felicity* bill : those which produce nothing but infelicity, all refer to Streatham of course. But you ran away without your epigram translated so much apropos :

" Créanciers ! maudite canaille,
Commissaire, huissiers et recors ;
Vous aurez bien le diable au corps
Si vous emportez la muraille."

Creditors! ye cursed crew,
Bailiffs, blackguards, not a few:
Look well around, for here's my all:
You've left me nothing but this wall,
And sure to give each dev'l his due,
This wall's too strong for them or you.

I must make the most of my house now they have left it on my hands, must I not? *may* I not? and, like my countrymen at Waterloo, sell my *life* as dear as I can. Oh terque quaterque beati! those who fell at the battle of St. Jean, when compared to the miseries of Cadiz and Xeres; and oh, happy Sir James Fellowes! whose book, well disseminated, will save us from these horrors, or from an accumulation of them; when the Cambridge fever shall break out again among the Lincolnshire fens, if we have unfavourable seasons. The best years of *my* temporal existence — I don't mean the happiest; but the best for powers of improvement, observation, &c. — were past in what is now Park Street, Southwark, but then Deadman's Place; so called because of the pest houses which were established there in the Great Plague of London. From clerks, and *blackguards not a few*, I learn'd there that Long Lane, Kent Street, and one other place of which the name has slipt my memory, were exempt from infection during the whole time of general sickness, and that their safety was imputed to its being the residence of tanners. I am, however, now convinced from your book, that it was seclusion, not *tan*, that preserved them. And do

not, dear Sir, despise your sibyl's prediction: for that
God's judgments are abroad, it is in vain to deny; and
though France will support the heaviest weight of them
till her phial is run out; our proximity, and fond inclination to connect with her, may, and naturally *will*
produce direful effects in many ways upon the morals,
the purses, and the health of Great Britain.

Do you observe that there is already a pretender
started to the Bourbon throne? You cannot (as I can)
recollect in the very early days of the Revolution, that
Abbé Sieyes declared he had saved the *real Dauphin*
from Robertspierre, and substituted another baby of
equal age to endure the fury of the homicides. Some
of us believed the tale, and some, the greater number,
laughed at those who *did* believe it. But an intelligent Italian, since dead, assured me that the last Pope,
Braschi, believed it; and marked the youth, in consequence of that belief, with a Fleur-de-Lys upon his
leg. Whether the young man described in the newspaper as seizing the Duchess d'Angoulesme, is that
person or another: or whether some fellow under the
influence of national insanity, imagines himself the
Dauphin; he is likely enough to disturb them and
divide their friends. Such times by the violence of
fermentation produce extraordinary virtues; but your
incomparable Don Diego Alvarez de la Fuente would
never have had his excellence of character properly
appreciated, had you not been the man to hand his
fame down to posterity. Æneas would have been forgotten but for Virgil.

I am not yet aware that any suspicion of promoting contagion during the fearful moments you describe, lighted on the Jews: the propensity they show to deal in old clothes makes it very likely that they should now and then propagate infectious diseases among their Christian persecutors, but I hope those days are coming fast to an end; when France has been disposed of, *their turn will come.* You will find a kind word or two for them in the first chapter of my second volume (of " Retrospection ") but the last chapter in the first volume is my favourite, and should be read before the short dissertation on the Hebrews for twenty reasons. I hope you like my preface, and find it *modest enough,* tho' the critics had no mercy on my *sauciness.*

Well ! now the rest of this letter shall be like other people's letters, and say how hot the streets are, and how disagreeable London is in the summer months; and how sincerely happy I should have been to pass the next six or seven weeks at Sidmouth, but that,—— Oh, such speeches are *not* like other people's letters at all : but that,—— I have not (with an income of 2000*l.* a year) 5*l.* to spend on myself, so encumber'd am I with debts and taxes. Leak says he must pay 40*l.* Property Tax, now, this minute. He is a good creature, and will be a bitter loss to his poor mistress, whenever we part; although the keeping him, and his wife, and his child, is dreadful, is it not? Since, however, in mental as in bodily plagues, despondency brings on ruin faster than it would come of itself:

> " What yet remains ? but well what's left to use,
> And keep good humour still, whate'er we lose."

Give my best love to dear Miss Fellowes, compliments to Mrs. Dorset if with you, and true regards to your venerable and happy parents, beseeching them all to remember that they have a true servant in, Dear Sir, your infinitely obliged,

H. L. P.

The battle with Anderdon will be fought to-morrow. I make sure of losing the *field;* my generals are unskilful.   Direct Mrs. Piozzi, Bath.

To Sir James Fellowes.

Monday Morning, Blake's Hotel,
7th Aug. 1815.

MY DEAR SIR JAMES FELLOWES,—When in the library at Streatham Park yesterday, I just looked into an old book of my writing, now completely out of print, and found these long-forgotten lines.   The date 1792.

> Shall impious France, though frantic grown,
> Drag her pale victims from the throne.
>   Shall royal blood be spilt:
> Yet think neglectful.Heav'n will spare,
> And by conniving seem to share
>   In such gigantic guilt?
>
> No, tardy-footed vengeance stalks
> Round her depopulated walks,
>   Waiting the fateful hour;
> When human skill no more can save,
> But hot contagion fills the grave,
>   And famine bids devour.

Rise, warriors, rise ! with hostile sway
Accelerate that dreadful day,
    Revenge the royal cause :
Exerting *well-united* force,
Tear all decrees that would divorce
    True liberty from laws.

Is it not very odd I should so predict what is sure
enough likely now to befall *them*, and yet never predict
what has befallen myself? But I do not even now repent
my journey. The offer to my daughters was not only
made, but in person *repeated;* so my conscience is clear
of blame if we sell,—there are, however, those who
think nothing but an acre of land will in two or three
years be worth a guinea.

The funds do fall so strangely, and so fast. Should
these explainers of the prophecies prove the wise men
we take them for, and should the call of the Jews be at
hand—*their* taking out such monstrous sums would
break us down at once; but the Turkish empire must
give way before that hour approaches; and rapidly as
the wheel does run down the hill, increasing in velocity every circle it makes, I can't believe that things
are coming so very forward, but that poor H. L. P.
may, by the mercy of God, escape those scenes of tur-
bulence and confusion.

Your book*, however, helps to alarm me. I had no

---

* " Reports of the Pestilential Disorder of Andalusia, &c. &c.;
with a Detailed Account of the Epidemic in Gibraltar, in 1804,
&c. &c." London : 1815.

notion that such pestilence had been so near, and you
can have but little notion how little we were impressed
by newspaper accounts of what you yourself not only
witnessed but endured. From all future ills that
Heaven may protect *you*, is the sincere wish and prayer
of yours and your charming family's

Truly obliged,

H. L. PIOZZI.

To Sir James Fellowes.

Bath, August 24th, 1815.

I COULD not recollect poor dear Garrick's verses yesterday, when we were talking on the subject: although
they were made in the library at Streatham Park and,
by Johnson's approbation and consent, substituted instead of Murphy's, which he thought pedantic.

" Ye fair married dames who so often deplore
That a lover once blest, is a lover no more;
Attend to my counsel, nor blush to be taught,
That prudence must cherish what beauty has caught.

" Use the man whom you wed like your fav'rite guitar.
Though there's music in both, they are both apt to jar;
How tuneful and soft from a delicate touch;
Not handled too roughly, nor played on too much. *

* " The soul of music slumbers in the shell,
   'Till waked and kindled by the master's spell;
   And feeling hearts, touch them but rightly, pour
   A thousand melodies unheard before."—ROGERS.

" The sparrow and linnet will feed from your hand,
   Grow tame by caressing, and come at command ;
   Exert with your husbands the same happy skill,
   For hearts like your birds may be tamed to your will.

" Be gay and good-humoured, complying, and kind,
   Turn the chief of your care from your face to your mind,
   Attractions so pleasing, resistless will prove,
   And Hymen shall rivet the fetters of Love."

Murphy's Song : —

" Attend all ye fair, and I'll tell ye the art,
    To bind every fancy with ease in your chains;
   To hold in soft fetters the conjugal heart,
    And banish from Hymen his doubts and his pains.

" When Juno accepted the cestus of Love,
    At first she was handsome, she charming became ;
   It taught her with skill the soft passions to move,
    To kindle at once, and to keep up the flame.

" Thence flows the gay chat more than reason that
    charms,
    The eloquent blush that can beauty improve ;
   The fond sigh, the sweet look, the soft touch that
    alarms ;
    With the tender disdain — that renewal of love.

" Ye fair ! take the cestus, and trust to its power,
    The mind unaccomplished, mere features are vain ;
   When wit and good humour enliven each hour,
    The Loves, Joys, and Graces will walk in your train."

To Sir James Fellowes.

Monday, 28 August, 1815.

RETROSPECTION, too much crowded with figures; anticipation, in *every* sense, a *blank!* and thus it is, Dear Sir, that the world runs away. Mrs. *Flint* and *Dun* (where you bought the bitter horehound,) *hard* as one of her names, and dreadful as the other, told me our lost fortune on Saturday night; I send it you, enclosed to Miss Fellowes, who will accompany it with pleasanter tydings I hope. Do the friends, for whom you are sacrificing health, make you large compensation by trying to be happy themselves? I hope they do. If *more* inducements are wanting, they will surely think on *that.*

I have been plagued with a gumboil, a mouth abscess. Punishment upon the peccant part for all that rattling nonsense it poured out on Fryday morning, when you met Miss Williams here; but we had been talking gravely before, and my mother used to repeat a Spanish refrain, which *you* know, I dare say, but I do not, expressing: from a companion that knows but one book, and can relate but one story, Good Lord deliver me; and sure enough monotony will always tire, whether the talk be of mutton or of metaphysics.

> "One charm display'd, another strike our view,
>   In quick variety for ever new,"

as some among our Streatham wits used to say, was *her* forte.

Well! but Leak thinks, I see, that necessity will compel me to dispose for ever of *that* place, and Lady Williams invites me strongly to quit *every* place; and purchase a beautiful cottage, near my own native sea, with sublime mountain scenery, and good convenience for bathing, twenty or thirty miles from Brynbella (where, by the way, there is a baby born,) and two or three hundred miles from London or from Bath. The place is to be hired, or sold with its faery furniture, and you would laugh to see little Bessy Jones's fear, lest I should accept the offer, and as *she* says, bury myself completely alive. She knows well enough what North Wales is in winter.

Shall I try the book of names first, and without further care concerning money, after the debts are paid, venture on No. 8 Gay Street? I should like that better. This East Indian war, however, will keep the Property Tax on most certainly, perhaps increase it, and that will affect all our purses.

The Cambrian heiress passed an hour here this morning. She is really a very rational girl, and her father says Cobbett's last performance is beyond all measure inflammatory.

We shall surely have a *storm*, literal or figurative, and the first would do least harm; but here's the bit of paper quite exhausted, without a word of the portrait. My letters give the truest portrait after all, and this is a *miniature* of

Dear Sir James Fellowes's
exceedingly obliged servant,
H. L. P.

To Sir James Fellowes.

Bath, Wednesday, 27th September, 1815.

WHY Dear Sir James Fellowes! Peter the Cruel was surely *your* ancestor instead of *mine.* After the thousand kindnesses of you and your charming family, hombres y hembras, had heaped on your ever obliged H. L. P., to run out of the town so, and never call to say farewell. Ah! never mind; I shall pursue you with letters, and they shall be more serious than you count on. I took your Spanish Bible *myself* to Linton's (the man in Hetling Court), on Monday morning; and thither the Wraxall shall follow, when I have finished cramming it with literary gossip. Your name on the first page secures it for the present.

Now do not wrong mè by suspicion of low spirits. All the absurdity consists in making you an offer of such trifling remembrances; but with regard to *my life,* which has already past the portion of time allotted to our species, forgetfulness of danger would be fatuity, not courage. You would not think highly of a soldier, who, hearing the enemy's trumpet though at a distance, should compose himself to take another nap; but what would *he* deserve, who should be found sleeping on an attack?

I have lived to witness very great wonders, and am told that Bramah the great mechanic is in expectation of perfecting the guidance of an air balloon, so as to exhibit in an almost miraculous manner upon Westminster Bridge next Spring. I saw one of the first,—the *very*

first, Mongolfier, I believe,—go up from the Luxembourg
Gardens at Paris; and in about an hour after, expressing my anxiety whither Pilâtre de Rosier and his friend
Charles were gone, meaning of course to what part of
France they would be carried, a grave man made
reply: " Je crois, Madame, qu'ils sont allés, ces Mes-
sieurs-là, pour voir le lieu où les vents se forment."

What fellows Frenchmen are ! and always have been.
I long for your brother's new account of them, and if I
could turn the figures from seventy-four to forty-seven,
I would certainly go and see them myself: in a less
hazardous vehicle than an air balloon.

Abate Parini made a pretty impromptu on that we
saw go up at Paris, and I translated it, here it is :—

" E LA MACCHINA CHE PARLA.

" Eccomi dal Mondo e Meraviglia e Gioco,
    Farmi grande in un punto, e lieve io sento,
    E col fumo nel grembo ed a piedi il fuoco,
    Salgo per aria e mi confido al vento.

" E mentre aprir nuovo cammino io tento,
    A l'uom, cui l'onda, e cui la terra è poco,
    Fra incerti moti e l'anco dubbio evento,
    Alto gridando la natura invoco.

" Oh Madre delle cose ! arbitrio prenda
    L'uomo per me de questo aereo regno ;
    Se cio fia mai che più beato il renda:

"Ma se nuocer poi dee, l'audace ingegno
  Perda l'opra, e'l consiglio; e fa ch'io splenda
  D'una stolta impotenza eterno segno."

THE MACHINE SPEAKS.

In empty space behold me hurl'd,
The sport and wonder of the world:
Who eager gaze, whilst I aspire
Expanded with aerial fire.

And since man's selfish race demands
More empire than the seas and lands;
For him my courage mounts the skies,
Invoking nature as I rise.

Mother of all! if thus refin'd
My flights can benefit mankind,
Let them by me new realms prepare,
And take possession of the air.

But if to ills alone I lead,
Quickly, oh quick let me recede;
Or blaze a splendid exhibition,
A beacon for their mad ambition.

And now after all this prattle, adieu!

                                    H. L. P.

To Sir James Fellowes.

Bath, Tuesday Night, 3rd Oct. 1815.

WITH regard to public matters, I think Maximilian, the witty Emperor of Germany, was not far from right when he said that *he*, like Agamemnon of old, was Rex Regum; the King of France, Rex Asinorum; the King of England, Rex Diabolorum (though he had not heard of the Irish mutineers of *our day*); the King of Spain Rex Hominum. I hope they will verify the appellation and behave like men and gentlemen. Of dear Cervantes' merit, you must know *most*, and those who do so, must *most* value him. I believe there is no writer in Europe as popular — no not Shakespear himself, who is justly the idol of his own country — while the Spanish hero is hero of *every* country — no nation that does not swarm with prints, and resound with stories of Don Quixote — and 'tis very likely I am quoting my own book when I say so, but there is no remembering the crowded figures clustered together in " Retrospection." We will talk of the name book when I am grown rich; it will do nothing for me till I don't want it, and *that* day I purpose to see on the 25th of next July, if not hindered by Los Hatos, and cramped in my noble exertions. Nine months, is it not, to July? Well! I have carried many a heavy burden for nine months, and why not a load of debt? 'tis a new sort of burthen, but Leak writes me word that Gillow's bill has many charges in it that cannot be supported, so if he can heave off a *hundred* weight, things will run better,

and 'tis only following your example about the vexatious
tooth—bearing, and forbearing, and wearing the misery
out.

Our theatre is open, and I saw the new opera dancers
from Mrs. Dimond's box. La Prima Donna is the
smallest creature I ever saw, that was not a dwarf; her
husband a Colossus of a fellow, and the waltze they
dance together, just the very oddest thing I ever saw
in my life. We were talking here one morning, if you
recollect, with Miss Williams, of these Baylerinas, and
the ideas they intended to excite. The present set excite *no* ideas except of dry admiration for the astonishing difficulties they perform, and some serious fears lest
they should break their slender limbs in the performance. Holding out one leg and one arm in a parallel
line, is destructive of all grace; and when, after spring-
ing up to a prodigious height, they come down on the
point of one toe — nothing can exceed our wonder at
its possibility, except one's joy that they escape in
safety. Music and dancing are no longer what they
were, and I grow less pleased with both every hour —

" Year chases year, decay pursues decay,
    Still drops some joy from with'ring life away."

But do not let us teize dear Miss Fellowes to write ;
it only worries *her*, and whilst I am conscious of it,
cannot delight *me*. While secure of a friend's affectionate regard, I abhor dunning them for letters; when
my heart tells me that their kindness is growing cold,
and feels weary of keeping up an uninteresting corre-

spondence, 'tis then that silence is a mute that strangles.

I am enchanted to think of your brother and sister's felicity: they are the most amiable, and most deserving of happiness, that can be found; and how wise they were to discover the value of happiness in time, and fling no more of it away!

We have an old beauty come here to Bath—you scarce can remember her—one of the very *very* much admired women, Lady Stanley. Poor thing! she went to France and Italy early in life, learned *les manières* and *les tournures*, and how gay a thing it was to despise her husband, who was completely even with her —

> " In youth she conquer'd with so wild a rage,
> As left her scarce a subject in her age:
> For foreign glories, foreign joys, to roam,
> No thought of peace, or happiness at home."

Her fortune, however, as an independent heiress, she held fast; and her wit and pleasantry seem but little impaired; but the loss of health sent her here, and she wonders to see mine so good, so indeed do I; but we were no puling family; my father, both my grandfathers, and three uncles, all died suddenly, which renders me more watchful of course. Never mind; Pope says,

> " Act well your part, there all the honour lies."

> " Nos sumus in scenâ quin et mandante magistro
> Quisque datas agimus partes; sit longa brevisve,
> Fabula, nil refert."

I hope you will come to Bath soon, and give me some good advice. I *do hope* you will: nobody will be more observant of it, as nobody ever could esteem it more than does dear Sir James Fellowes's ever obliged and faithful

H. L. Piozzi.

You have made all *your* friends *my* friends. Pray tell them what a grateful heart *that is*, which they have been so kind to.

To Sir James Fellowes.

Bath, 10th Oct. 1815.

Such letters would make *anybody* well. I will implicitly follow the advice of my *incomparable* friend, and I will not advertise Streatham Park till you approve the measure. Alas, dear Sir, my wish is to conciliate, not provoke them. Lord North's maxim, "Amicitiæ sempiternæ, inimicitiæ placabiles," * is the best in the world; and they will perhaps one day tell you that I have always followed it. Meanwhile, I will not swear that the cross winds of domestic life have forborne to injure my tackling, and if I can now get home under jury masts, how thankful ought I to be! Apropos to *jury* masts, what can be the meaning of such an awkward word? I have not a dictionary in the room, but I dare say they mean mâts de *durer*. Masts that will just serve and *last* but for a short time. Now if I am the worse for the musket shot of this warring world, how reasonable is it to expect that *you* should

---

* Popularly rendered : " Enmities in dust ; friendships marble."

have suffered, who have been so exposed to its heaviest artillery! Let us never have done rejoycing that you are returned to the bosom of your family, and permitted to enjoy *their* happiness which you have unremittingly prefered to your own.

I was selfish, *once*, and *but* once in my life; and though they lost nothing by my second marriage, my friends (as one's relations are popularly called) never could be persuaded to forgive it; was not it always so? Your Spanish Bible, in the eighteenth chapter of Saint Matthew's Gospel, shows us how to obtain pardon by applying to the *right place and person*, not to our *cruel* fellow servants. . . . . .

So here is reciprocation of confidence, and a confession no one but your kind self could deserve — or indeed comprehend . . . . . .

Where the mad warrior fights for fame,
   And life beneath him lies;
'Tis love of praise that bears the blame,
   And those that blame are wise.

When female levity and youth
   Run wild a thousand ways;
Each stander by, with equal truth,
   Arraigns the love of praise.

But praises when by virtue given,
   To virtue are assign'd;
They light like harbingers from Heav'n,
   And cheer the trembling mind.

'Tis then with pride resembling shame,
    We bask beneath their rays;
And virtue with an humbler name,
    Becomes the love of praise.

Adieu then! and retain for Mil Años y mas your
kindness for poor

                                        H. L. P.

I remember an awkward Irish Miss once, when it
was the fashion to give sentimental toasts, making us
all look silly, because the men laughed so, who loved
rough merriment, when in reply to their request of a
sentiment, she made answer, "What we think on most,
Sir, and talk on least." Mrs. Hoare and I both would
feel that to be Streatham Park.

To Sir James Fellowes.

                            Tuesday Night, 24th Oct. 1815.

No anecdote, nor no verses, no, nor even your praises,
which so highly I value, can give equal pleasure to the
account you send me of your health. May God Almighty, long, very long, preserve it for all our sakes;
and inspire you with gratitude for its restoration, as he
has inspired you with skill to preserve it.

The day was so bright, and at one time so fine, I
was impelled to make the rhymes you will read enclosed. Collins promises me the "Travel Book" on
Thursday, which I shall correct for you, and make as

clean, and as little unworthy of your acceptance, as I can.

Doctor Fellowes is certainly right; I took my account of Katherine's cruelty, from Govani's, whose "Memoirs des Cours d'Italie" I left in Wales. Are these verses in your margin? they should be there.

> "Elle fit oublier, par un esprit sublime,
>   D'un pouvoir odieux les enormes abus;
> Et sur un trône acquis par le crime,
>   Elle se maintint par ses vertus."

> Her dazzling reign so brightly shone,
>   Few sought to mark the crimes they courted;
> Whilst on her ill-acquired throne
>   She sate; by virtue's self-supported.

The Anecdotes of Doctor Johnson were begun at Milan, where we first heard of his death, and so written on, from milestone to milestone, till arriving at Leghorn, we shipped them off to England.

Mr. Thrale had always advised me to treasure up some of the valuable pearls that fell from his (Johnson's) lips, in conversation; and Mr. Piozzi was so indignant at the treatment I met with from his executors, that he spirited me up to give my own account of Doctor Johnson, in my own way; and not send to them the detached bits which they required with such assumed superiority and distance of manner, although most of them were intimates of the house till they thought it deserted for ever. I think we must not tell your dear father that his friend Bennet Langton was one of them. If we do, he will not say as Dr. Johnson did,

" Sit anima mea cum Langtono."

But my marriage had offended them all, beyond hope of pardon.

Now judge my transport, and my husband's, when at Rome we received letters saying the book was bought with such avidity, that Cadell had not one copy left, when the King sent for it at ten o'clock at night, and he was forced to beg one from a friend, to supply his Majesty's impatience, who sate up all night reading it. Samuel Lysons, Esq., Keeper of the Records in the Tower, then a law student in the Temple, made my bargain with the bookseller, from whom, on my return, I received 300*l.*, a sum unexampled in those days for so small a volume.

And here, my dear Sir, is a truly-told anecdote of yours and your charming family's gratefully attached,

H. L. P.

Pray present them my verses.

To Sir James Fellowes.

Sunday, 15th October, 1815.

No, no; it was Jael that killed Sisera, who was a warrior, not a woman. The termination in *a* does not in Hebrew feminize a name, any more than the termination in *o* renders a name masculine in the Greek. סיסרא, Sisera, was the proper name of the general of a hostile army sent to subdue Israel, and reduce them forcibly to acknowledge as *Deity* the very same abominations they are adoring even now, as our friend the general knows, further to the eastward. Tabor is still an insulated mount; it was called Itabyrius by the profane writers; but *indeed* to be a good bible scholar is better far, and *will carry further*, than being the best Greek one; and if the Spanish version does justice to that magnificent piece of lyric poetry—for such it is—which you read in the fifth chapter of Judges, called the Song of Deborah and Barak, you will be enchanted with it. Lowth's praise of it is sublime indeed; and Kurstness, or Pelicanus as they call him, says boldly: "Now let your Homer or Virgil find a passage equal in eloquence and beauty to the last eight verses of that incomparable ode."

I believe the challenge cannot be answered; but if you really *do* value my taste in literature and my opinion in the choice of books, assure yourself I would give all Lord Spencer's library for his best bible; reflecting, with Locke and Paley, that of *that work* God is the author, Truth is the subject, and its tendency Eternal Life. Should such at length become *your* preference, too; it *might* not, possibly, but it is too presumptuous to say so; yet it perhaps *might* not be in *this world only*, so soon to be hid from our eyes – that dear Sir James Fellowes should have cause to recollect with complacency his partial friendship for poor

H. L. Piozzi.

The vulgar menace of I'll be after you with a *su-*

surraré means, as far as it means anything, I'll follow you up with a writ of *certiorari* *, to call up the *records*, that justice may be done *impartially*.

To Sir James Fellowes.

Bath, 19th Oct. 1815.

THE next best thing to shaking a friend by the *hand* is seeing his *hand*writing. .I am happy to read yours, and most earnestly hope you will keep close to the house till better days. The ladies will have sad weather to travel in. General Garslin did me a great deal of honour, and deserved some amusement in payment for his trouble in finding the house.

If it were not for flattery, I should break my heart yet, old bills not counted on coming against me so: but I don't care, as the children say; I shall out of my plagues, and out of my prison too, next July.

Meanwhile, dear old Doctor Lort, the Greek professor, was godfather to the gentleman you mention, and his surname went to the bishop at the font as a Christian name. You will find Doctor Lort mentioned under the article Daphne, as I remember.

But I have had a nice dish of flattery dressed to my taste this morning. That grave Mr. Lucas brought his son here, that he might see the *first woman in England*—forsooth. So I am now grown one of

---

* She is substantially right. It is a writ for the removal of the proceedings, civil or criminal, from an inferior to a superior jurisdiction.

the curiosities of Bath, it seems, and *one of the Anti-quities.*

This evening a chair will carry me to Mrs. Holroyd's, to meet two other females, whom Richardson taught the town to call old tabbies, attended, says he, by young *grimalkins.* Now that's wrong; because they are young tabbies, and when grown grey are *gris malkins,* I suppose. Is not this fine nonsense for the first woman? Prima Donna! in good time!

If I could detain your man to say one grave serious word, it would express my content that your dear father is arrived to take care of my inestimable friend, Sir James Fellowes, whose health is of such consequence. Mind what he says, and believe me, most sincerely your obliged servant, H. L. P.

October 27, 1815.

"Mrs. Piozzi," remarks Sir J. Fellowes in a memo-randum on this letter, "dined with our family party to-day. Speaking of Hogarth, she mentioned a clever impromptu, addressed to Mr. Tighe, who was intent upon some Greek book when dinner was ready: —

" ' Then come to dinner, do, my honest Tighe,
And leave thy Greek, and η β π.
eat a bit o' pie.' "

To Sir James Fellowes.

30 October, 1815.

If dear Sir James Fellowes still continues under dis-cipline, this anecdote of Hogarth and of his little friend may amuse him. My father and he were very intimate, and he often dined with us. One day when he had done so, my aunt and a groupe of young cousins came in the afternoon,—evenings were earlier things than they are now, and 3 o'clock the common dinner-hour. I had got a then new thing I suppose, which was called Game of the Goose, and felt earnest that we children might be allowed a round table to play at it, but was half afraid of my uncle's and my father's grave looks. Hogarth said, good-humouredly, "*I* will come, my dears, and play at it with you." Our joy was great, and the sport began under my management and direction. The pool rose to five shillings, a fortune to us monkeys, and when I won it, I capered for delight.

But the next time we went to Leicester Fields, Mr. Hogarth was painting, and bid me sit to him; "And now look here," said he, "I am doing this for you. You are not fourteen years old yet, I think, but you will be twenty-four, and this portrait will then be like you. 'Tis the lady's last stake; see how she hesitates between her money and her honour. Take you care; I see an ardour for play in your eyes and in your heart: don't indulge it. I shall give you this picture as a warning, because I love you now, you are so good a girl." In a fortnight's time after that visit we went out of town. He died somewhat suddenly, I believe, and I never saw my poor portrait again; till, going to Fonthill many, many years afterward, I met it there, and Mr. Piozzi observed the likeness when I was showing him the fine house, then deserted by Mr. Beck-

ford. The summer before last it was exhibited in Pall
Mall as the property of Lord Charlemont. I asked Mrs.
Hoare, who was admiring it, if she ever saw any person
it resembled. She said no, unless it might once have
been like me, and we turned away to look at something
else.

With regard to play, I have been always particular in
avoiding it, so that I scarce know whether the inclination ever subsisted or not. The scene he drew will
certainly remind any one of poor H. L. P., and no one
but yourself knows the story.

But I must tell you how well your dear father is,
and how heartily I made him laugh this morning at
one of my comical stories, true as the day, which I heard
a silly lady in my own country two or three years ago
ask me quite suddenly before a room full of company, to
tell her; " for," says she, " you know Mrs. Piozzi does
understand everything ; what bone her son broke at the
battle of Talavera." This was *too* hard a question ; but
the lady went on: " No, no," continued she, " not hard
to Mrs. Piozzi. Louisa, you lost the letter very pro-
vokingly which had the fine word in it ; and now you
laugh, you ill-natured thing, because I can't recollect it,
but Mrs. Piozzi will know in a minute." Turning to
me : " It was one of your fine words, I say, and very
like fable-book." " I have," said I, " heard that Mr.
Morgan's horse fell upon him, and perhaps broke the
fibula, or small bone of his master's leg." " There,
there ! " cries out the lady ; " I told you Mrs. Piozzi
would know it at once."

To Sir James Fellowes.

Sunday, 26th November, 1815.

WE all remembered you at the Lutwyches last Thursday, where the galanterie of the master of the house was quite the prettiest thing presented on the occasion. With one dying marigold these lines:

> " The gift of him whose heart can't vary,
> How paradoxical! Behold!
> Having no gold to give my Mary,
> I here present *this marygold.*"

They received my fleurs and fleurettes very obligingly, and shewed my worked fly, finely mounted as a fire-screen. Well! all that is politeness, is it not? a strong polish, over which everything glides and rolls and appears to make no impression, but if you look closely you will discern afterwards a lasting stain. Time's daughters (the days of the year) like the daughters of man, are deceitful; while young and in their papa's house, they flatter and promise the pleasures of next July to one confiding lover, a prize in the lottery to another: but see them come out, wrinkled and roughened with what each of them calls unforeseen vexations; their votaries turn away, not as they should do, to mansions beyond their control; but looking back, make love to a younger sister, and trust another day.

Yesterday did better; Mrs. Holroyd's party: we were a choice set indeed. But she had unluckily asked talkers to play the part of hearers, while Mrs. Lysons sung, and Mrs. Twiss * read. So one said the selection of songs was a dull one; another thought it was foolish to be listening to "Macbeth" in a room, when we had so lately seen it represented with every additional assistance on a stage. I persuaded her to take up Milton, and try what could be done with the second book; her sister read the fourth book, I remember, at Doctor Whalley's, about five or six years ago, and Sir William Weller Pepys made this impromptu while she was speaking, repeating it the moment she had done:

> " When Siddons reads from Milton's page,
>   Then sound and sense unite;
> Her varying tones our hearts engage
>   With exquisite delight:
> So well those varying tones accord
>   With his seraphic strain;
> We hear, we feel, in every word,
>   His angels speak again."

To Sir James Fellowes.

1st December, 1815.

THE customary season of good wishes; which, like your Spanish oranges, are in warm hearts a fruit of every season, dear Sir James Fellowes has anticipated, in expressing a kind hope that my next year may prove more happy than the last. Recollect meanwhile that

* The wife of Francis Twiss, (author of the " Complete Verbal Index to Shakspeare,") and mother of the late Horace Twiss. She was the sister of Mrs. Siddons, and very like her. She read beautifully, as I well remember, having been domesticated with the family as a private pupil of Mr. Twiss for two years.

my last year began with making your acquaintance, and
I hope ends with having gained your friendship.   Will
a good house in Gay Street (should I ever live to enjoy
it) mark 1816 as agreeably?   I say not.   Accounts
from Streatham Park, however, are neither good nor
bad.   The place is a mere drag upon my mind, a drain
upon my purse ; and no Marquis of Stafford yet appears,
nor do I feel as if anything were likely to be done ·
there, good or bad.

The best joke going here, and most like your *hors de
combat,* was made on the bustle with which Mr. Parish
presented Princess Talleyrand to a large company at his
house; where some wag observed that the lady had
gone through many adventures, and now was come to
the *parish.*

To Sir James Fellowes.

Now eighteen hundred and fifteen
Will quickly write herself — has been.
For tho' success was never seen
Brilliant as ours in bright fifteen ;
Old Time will rear his lofty skreen,
To part us from the year fifteen.
If, then, this frail though nice machine
Can last till death of dear fifteen,
Let those few hours that lie between
Throw no disgrace on past fifteen !
Free from reproaches, coarse or keen,
Be sung the dirge of dead fifteen !

While peace extends her olive green
O'er the pale wounds of poor fifteen.
Nor let th' enticing air and mien,
The promis'd freshness of sixteen,
Lead us to tempt, howe'er serene,
Eternity ! Offended queen.

Vineyards, Wednesday Night,
6 December, 1815.

I HAVE been dining with your dear family, as happily as we *could* dine without our kind absentee. I think you will find the effects of your father's fine Malaga in the above impromptu from

H. L. P.

For mercy's sake burn this stuff; it seems strange even to myself, after tea.

To Sir James Fellowes.

Bath, Monday Evening,
11 December, 1815.

VERY ill pleased with myself for sending such an empty scrap when my heart was full, but it was because your servant waited at the door for it ; and very ill disposed to delight in your determination upon the choice of life, as Doctor Johnson calls it in his "Rasselas." I sit down now to write you as long a letter as I like, and fairly send it to the post. My dear Sir James Fellowes confesses that I have spoiled him for the frivolous conversation of beaux and belles; if I say all I think, I shall disgust you from the project of practising medi-

cine in a thronged metropolis, where those that employ
a physician pretend not to know how far his skill is
worthy of confidence, and those that reject him, have
no means of guessing wherein lies his deficience; who
choose a doctor, as girls choose a husband, because some
other head, as empty as their own, was casually filled
with a fancy,—that of his being fashionable. Is there
any other rudder used in present life but the mode?
Is there any other book read but "Rhoda?"* And is
not that admired because it shows every body what they
like best? — their own faces in the' glass. I beg pardon, your brother's little work is well spoken of by every
body; but Walter Scott has certainly fallen in the
plains of Waterloo: I was always half afraid that Arctic
Phœbus would set in a fog.

We had a pretty evening at the Lutwyches, where
I repeated your pretty speech and spoiled it from
complete nervousness, the word best calculated to disguise ill-humour: and which induced a strangling or
choking at the dinner table, which politeness, however, smoothed down so well that nobody was aware
on't, but your dear sister, who called aloud for water.
Shall I put it in the "Biographical Memoires" that
both my husbands lived and died in the persuasion
that I should expire suddenly, or by accident? It is
true that they *did* think so, and that I think so too. Let
it serve as one among many inducements to live in a

* "Rhoda" a novel, in four volumes, published by Colburn.
Her remark on it resembles one made by Madame de Sévigné on
the play of *Les Visionnaires.*

state of preparation. Well! if I die to-morrow, Gil-
lowes' people have now had 1700*l.* of the 2380*l.* which
their bill came to: and Leak says we may cut the bill
down to 2070*l.* if we could pay it quick, and save the
interest: so I sent him 200*l.* now of the January dividends, and must owe *him* 170*l.* instead of owing *them*
380*l.* I don't like the arrangement, though an advan-
tageous one; but I like nothing else better, as in the
case of your London practice; apropos to which I will
add one good thing: you will see women to more advantage than in a ball room; attentive to a sick parent,
brother, or sister, and you will say:

> " Oh woman! in our hours of ease
> Capricious, coy, and hard to please;
> When grief and anguish wring the brow,
> A ministering angel thou."

Those are Walter Scott's lines, and very pretty sure.
While you accept my criticism, and quote my " Synonymes," I will not complain (though but just three
years behind your father) of the tædium vitæ. By
the way, I am engaged to dine at the dear Vineyards on
the 14th of February, and you are engaged to be at the
Lutwyches on the 15th of this December.

I met your mamma in the street, and said, " Well!
Ma'am! Sir James Fellowes has not forgot me
though among so many charmers." " Forgot *you! !* "
replied Mrs. Fellowes, " I would not give a pin for him
if he forgot *you.*" So you see I have a friend at court.

Poor old Dr. Harrington is going, and I now wish
him gone. When the bright visions painted by the

pencil of youth, or those no less dear to us formed by the firmer hand of maturity, on the canvass of human understanding, grow dull, and dirty, and dingey, like those landschapes of Titian done when he was ninety years old, 'tis more kind to let them drop quietly in pieces, than sew them coarsely together, and bid for them as a rarety. I wish he would pack up and be gone.

Dr. Holland helped to lower my spirits too : all my Venetian friends killed or beggared by this vile revolution. How melancholy!

So Farewell! and for a short time, dear Sir : come soon and chase the gathering clouds away.

> " Mon premier est le premier de son espèce,
> Mon second n'eut un premier jamais :
> Mon tout, je n'aime guère le vous dire."

H. L. P.

But adieu !

Dr. Myddelton had been troubled with cramps and spasms, but shook them off, and used the slipper bath. When in it one evening he cried, " Oh, my head," and died without another word or groan.

> " Nil mihi rescribas, attamen ipse veni."

To Sir James Fellowes.

5 November, 1815.

I SEND my dear Sir James Fellowes the " Synonymes " that he may finish with the best thing I ever wrote; I send likewise my defence of *his* favourite "Retrospection:" they were very civil to the Synonymy, and there was a fine eulogium on the string of words, calling over the meaning of crush, overwhelm, ruin, in the first volume. I have marked very few passages, but hope you will like many.

I have no other way of showing the regard with which I shall for ever remain,

Your obliged friend,

H. L. P.

How kind you are and how partial! and what an unspeakable loss shall I have when you enter on a London life and London practice. Dr. Holland, who writes about the Ionian Islands, is going to London to practise, and exchange the *Cyclades* for the *sick ladies;* he has been a lyon here for three whole days. I caught the *Queue du Lion,* and passed one evening in his company, but a whole menagerie would make me no compensation for exchange of sentiment in friendly converse. Oh! do make haste to Bath, and let me lament my fate to you personally. Is that being grateful to Heaven, though, when one year's valuable friendship has been granted, at a time when so few years can be expected by poor

H. L. PIOZZI.

" Let us leave the best example that we can." I have, however, much to say to you about the Biographical Memoires, which are really in some degree of forwardness.

Adieu! Going to dine with the Lutwyches, Sunday, 10th December, 1815.

Bath, Wednesday,
13th December, 1815.

My dear Doctor Thackeray's kind partiality followed
me so long and so far upon my journey through life,
I think he has enough left even now not to be weary-
ing of hearing how I do, and what I do in a situation
very new to me indeed, but rendered supportable by
the countenance and conversation of pleasant friends
and agreeable acquaintance. The accounts I hear from
Wales, too, make me very happy and thankful, and
convince me that my tenderness was bestowed on
worthy creatures who seem to make themselves much
beloved in their neighbourhood. Oh how that neighbourhood is changed! Oh how many sighs shall I
have to leave on every house as I pass it, if it should
please God that I can come down next July, unen-
cumbered by debts and no longer haunted by vexations
which have tormented me for two long years! But you
are country gentleman enough to know that a high
paling round a park of two miles extent, besides front-
ing a large house made by my exertions as if wholly
new *, and then furnishing it in modern style su-
premely elegant, though I thought not costly, cannot
be done but by enormous expense, and, in fact, sur-
veyors, carpenters, and cabinet makers, have driven
poor Hester Lynch Piozzi into a little Bath lodging,
where Miss Letitia Barnston found her, two rooms and

---

* She is speaking of Streatham.

two maids her whole establishment; a drawing of
Brynbella, and by the fair hand of Mrs. Salusbury, her
greatest ornament.

Meanwhile our town, like yours, takes turn for the
fine dancers or fine actors when they have a week to
spare; and as for private talent, there never were so
many young people so skilled in music as now. I
heard a child of ten years old, perform on the forte
piano last week like a professor. The winter seems as
if it would be a long one, it began early, and many old
people sink under the rapid changes. Doctor Harrington, however, kept his eighty-ninth birthday a
while ago, and listened with delight to his charming
compositions. The last catch and glee are said to be
the best he ever produced, and sure he lives a proof
that air and exercise are not the preservatives of life
which we account them, as he always visited his
patients in a chair half a century ago, as he now visits
his acquaintance, and always with his mouchoir at his
face to keep away every breath of wind; when walking
in the abbey with his son-in-law last summer, "Come,"
said he, "let us choose a spot for my old bones," and
recollecting himself suddenly —

> " These ancient walls, with many a mouldering bust,
>   But show how well Bath waters lay the dust."

If you have not heard that impromptu before, you will
like it. Adieu, dear Sir! and make my best regards
to Mrs. Thackeray, with love to the lasses who were
nice babies. Do you remember Selina, she would be
Mrs. Piozzi herself? Now write me a kind word, do,

and say you will be glad to see me next July, but how unlikely is there should there be anything left of your poor

HESTER LYNCH PIOZZI.

To Sir James Fellowes.

MY DEAR SIR,-- Come to Laura Chapel next Sunday, and listen to my favourite preacher, when he winds up the whole year. 'Tis a hackneyed theme, but from him I cannot help expecting somewhat new, at least somewhat particularly impressive. My desire of your happiness must end in steril good wishes, handed down from generation to generation, dirtied and tarnished by too much wear and tear. Is not it melancholy to have fresh feelings, and none but worn-out words to express them in ?

To experience every sentiment of the truest and most disinterested friendship, and to say only that I am, dear Sir, your most obliged servant,

H. L. PIOZZI.

Bath, 30th December, 1815.

To Sir James Fellowes.

6th January, 1816.

GOOSEY LINTON is a good goosey, and deserves apple sauce when apples are dearest. I see no mistakes at all, and if you find any, I will rectify them.

The Travel Book and the anecdotes there will show you perplexities of a new and untoward nature ; for though I had witnessed much theological talk, controversy was wholly strange to me; and now dear Sir James Fellowes will see, as he has often *felt*, what a wretched thing the happiest human life would be, were this all : but who, without pain's advice would e'er be good; and who, without death but would be good in vain ? The old undertaker's motto, "Mors janua vitæ," is after all our best consolation.

That every comfort may attend your staying hither and your going hence, after mil años y mas, is the unceasing wish of your much obliged, &c.,

H. L. P.

My *jour de naissance* is coming round in a few days, now; and as Pope says,

> " With added years of life brings nothing new,
> But like a sieve lets every blessing through :
> Some joy still lost, as each vain year runs o'er;
> And all we gain, some sad reflection more.
> Is this a birthday ! 'tis, alas, too clear
> 'Tis but the funeral of the former year."

Yet will I not (like Dr. Johnson) quarrel with my birthday. To have been born into this world is our only claim for some sort of place in a better; and surely to have gained attention and friendship from Doctor Collier in my early days,—the hour of female attention being scarce arrived, and from Sir James Fellowes in my latter scenes,—when that bright hour was over, might well compensate for those long, busy, intermediate acts, even of a more tragic drama than I was engaged in, through a fatiguing past indeed; sometimes very sweetly supported, many times very cruelly thwarted, by my companions on the same stage; and now, if all is to be soon over, Valete et plaudite.

H. L. PIOZZI.

Here is a dreadful storm; the sea runs very high, no doubt. I could not get out to-day.

Ask the young ladies if they can describe to you the colour of the wind; if they can tell you the tint of the storm!

'Tis an enigma. Adieu.

11 January, 1816.

(Jour de Naissance, 27th January.)
Tuesday night, 16th January, 1816.

My dear Sir James Fellowes will like a long independent letter about a thousand other people and things. When I am one of the family cluster we can think only of you. Yet poor old Dr. Harrington must be thought of; he will be seen no more. Was it not pretty and affecting that they played his fine sacred music so lately, and by dint of loud and reiterated applause called him forward as he was retiring, to thank him for their entertainment? He returned, bowed; went home, sickened, and   ! This was a classical conclusion of his life indeed; like the characters at the end of Terence's plays, who cry *Valete omnes et plaudite!* But I would wish a less public exit, and say *Vale!* to my nearest friend, *Voi altri applaudite* to the rest.

Apropos, did you ever read Spencer's long string of verses, every stanza ending with Wife, Children, and

Friends? I can neither find nor recollect them rightly; but too well does my then hurt mind retain my answer to a lady (one of the Burneys) who quoted a line expressive of contempt for general admiration, going on to this passage, which I *do* remember : —

"Away with the laurel, o'er *me* wave the willow,
   Set up by the hand of wife, children, and friends."

My reply was "No ; for," said I,

"Should love domestic plant the tree,
      Hope still would be defeated ;
   Children and friends would crowd to see
      The neighbouring cattle eat it.

"Deciduous plants will lose their leaves
      With winter's provocation ;
   And ev'ry sigh that sorrow heaves
      Will sap the slight foundation.

"Till in a sea of follies tost,
      Foes to each fine emotion ;
   Our drooping willow 's driven and lost
      On Life's tempestuous ocean.

"While true to time-worn worth, we view
      The verdant laurel rising ;
   Firm-fixed, and of unchangeful hue,
      Each wintry blush despising.

" Around the late-reposing head
 This faithful foliage hovers ;
Points out the merits of the dead,
 And many a failing covers.

" And should the berries e'er invite
 Some envious nibbling neighbour,
A blister'd tongue succeeds the bite,
 And best repays their labour."

Did you believe I could ever have expressed myself
with so much bitterness ? but if people will break the
heart even of an apricot, sweetest and most insipid of
all fruits, the kernel will yield a harsh flavour.

Poor Doctor Harrington, like myself, has found the
kindness that sweetened his existence always from without doors, never from within.

My cough is no longer a bad one, but the hoarseness
does not go off ; and when I tried to tell old stories last
night to amuse, I found the voice very odious ; so
Sir James Fellowes is best off now, that has me
for a correspondent. Don't you remember, in some
of my stuff, how Johnson sayd if he was married to
Lady Cotton, he would live a hundred miles away from
her, and make her write to him. " Once a week,"
added he, " I could bear a letter from the creature, but
it is the poorest talker, sure, that ever opened lips."

Well, if you asked the pretty girls to tell you the
colour of the wind, and explain to you the tint of the
storm, they would say the storm rose, I imagine, and

the wind blew. We used to spell the colour so in very old days.

Meanwhile, the geological maps of what is to be discerned under ground, are fine things certainly; but I feel so completely expectant of going to make strata myself, that the science does not much allure me, although I am *deeply* concerned in it at seventy-five years old. Dear me! 'tis a silly thing to try to extract sunbeams from cucumbers, like Swift's projector in " Gulliver's Travels."

Princess Charlotte has at length made her choice, it seems, of Le Prince de Saxe-Coburg, a handsome man, and she thinks so. Without that power of making impression, beauty in either sex is a complete nihility; find me a better word, and that shall be turned out by her who wishes to keep the best in every sense for you.

Your faithful

H. L. P.

To Sir James Fellowes.

Bath, 17 January, 1816.

I TOLD dear Sir James that his next letter should cost him nothing, and sure nothing can equal the event it tells. But Sévigné's pen alone could describe it; could excite your wonder so, and produce no disappointment.

A lady, then, well-born, well-looking too, my near neighbour, marries a gentleman, an officer, a general officer. Where, say you, is the wonder? She is thirty-six years old. She marries General Doukin, senior; his

military cloak and old cocked hat have won her.
Needs any man despair? He called her in to dinner
the very day his wife, thirty years younger than he,
was carried out a corpse. She told her son and daughters that it would be so, and so it will be. The bride-
groom in his ninety-first year.

Miss Wroughton is arrived. She says her mother is
ninety-seven years old. I bid her be careful of *les es-
pouseurs*, and told her of General Doukin. She says
her mother has the full use of her understanding, and
is of course out of any such danger.

Among all the afflictions which vex our human frame,
the most dreadful (says Dr. Johnson) is the uncertain
continuance of reason.

God preserve yours unclouded and serene for at least
half a century more. As no man ever employed it to
more benignant purposes, so no man ever merited longer
possession of felicity; great as can be wished to her
best friend in her best moments by your faithful

H. L. P.

Doctor Harrington kept his wits to the last minute,
and laughed when they told him the story I have told
you.

To Sir James Fellowes.

Bath, Sunday, 21 Jan. 1816.

MR. GREENFIELD preached a very fine *Oraison funèbre*
upon poor old Harrington to-day, and used my very
expressions; was not it odd enough! Not odd at all,

say you, that Mrs. Piozzi should like his compositions, if that is the case.

But I have something less pleasant — bills following me from ——. Small shot, indeed, but mortifying in the extreme. I told your . . . I was like some famous boxer that was knocked down by a farthing candle artfully slung at his head, while yet bleeding and bruised to death almost, from a victory newly won. Dr. Goldsmith, whose feet " every path of vulgarity trod," told us once of an ale-house wager. A man betted that he would produce a person who should perform this operation on some well-known hero of the fist ; who, not being apprised of the frolic, and panting for breath and refreshment, felt this sudden hit upon his temporal artery, and dropped down, demolished by a farthing candle. *

Now do not you believe me sensible to my own anxieties, careless of yours. I hope you know me better ; but a moment's variety will contribute to amuse your mind and repay you some of the pleasure — no, not pleasure ; how can this stuff give any but a momentary recollection — that you have a friend, and that that friend is

H. L. P.

To Sir James Fellowes.

Bath, 25 January, 1816.

I HAVE suffered much from nervous irritation, but your kind father is so good to me. I did not tell him

* This story of Goldsmith's is mentioned by Boswell.

that I apprehended aphthæ, but the lady who was afraid
of her own hearth-rug could not be more fanciful than
I have been.

> " Strong and more strong her terrors rose,
> Her shadow did the nymph appal;
> She trembled at her own long nose,
> It looked so long against the wall.

Now for what the newspaper calls miscellaneous
articles. Your father bids me drink the Bath water,
and I did do so yesterday, and was more alive than . . .
and I tried the Bishop of Salisbury's party last night,
but made a poor figure,—so hoarse. A mute Piozzi
is a miserable thing indeed, but health will mend.

The bishop is very agreeable; and though he is a
nobleman now and a courtier, remembers old times and
old jokes, and how he and I sat down together on
a dirty bench in St. Mark's Place, Venice, to hear a
Dominican friar, while harlequin jumped about unheeded on the other side of the square.

Your . . . . must see the new book, though the best
thing in it is telling how the foreigner comes to an inn
at Dover, and finding a member of the Bang-up Club
loitering about the yard, cries, " Here, Ostler, hold my
horse." " Know your road work better, you . . . ."
replies the other, and challenges him. Escaped from
this misery, he meets a lady going to a party, her head
heaped in the fashionable way with flowers. " Sell me
some roses, pretty dear! " cries the new-arrived foreigner,
laying hold of them. " Insulting fellow! " cries the girl;
" I'll have you punished for an assault." A passer-by re-

lieves him from this difficulty, and they strike up a friendship and go together to the inn. " Pray, Sir, who have I the honour to be so much obliged to?" says the stranger. " I, Sir, am captain of the band of pensioners." The Spaniard looks in his English dictionary (Johnson's) for so hard a word; and finds Pensioner, a man hired for the destruction of his country. " Oh! for pity leave me directly," cries he; "I am in company with a chief of banditti. What will become of me? Get out of my apartments."

Well! now I will have done with all this buffooning nonsense, and with the truest regard,

H. L. P.

To Sir James Fellowes.

Saturday, 3 February, 1816.

I HAVE some very curious things at Streatham, more curious than you think for; one pair of frightful old Etruscan jars, for example, given me by a monsignore, Ennio Visconte, a Milanese nobleman then resident at Rome, and a first-rate connoisseur.

" These," said I, " are indeed antiques." " Antiques!" replies the man; " why they were antiques when in Cicero's cabinet. Antiques! why they were antiques in Romulus's time; they are coeval with the Babylonish captivity." With proper blushes I accepted them, and there they are.

I have a pair of old blue and white porcelain bottles, too, which were brought into my family by an old Salusbury in the year 1400; and my grandmother, used to frighten my father from improper matches, by holding them in her hand, and protesting she would break them; "for," said she, "they came by the Red Sea before the passage round the Cape of Good Hope was discovered, and do you think they shall ever be possessed by Miss Such-a-one?" When, however, she learned that he had united himself with his cousin Cotton of Combermere's daughter, she said: "Well, then, now I will kiss my old bottles, and keep them for John's eldest child." They are yet in her possession, 1816.

To-morrow I shall break quarantine, go to church (in a chair), and give God thanks for all his mercies.

Your ever obliged and grateful

H. I. P.

To Sir James Fellowes.

Bath, 29 February, 1816.

Such a kind letter as your dear father put in my hand this day, and I, bankrupt even in acknowledgment, can only curtsey and say, Thank you, Sir. In return for your confidence, however, I shall tell you a secret; and that is, that I am engaged to dine at No. 13 on Tuesday next, 5th March, and your mamma says we are to drink sweet wine, I suppose till we see double.

My heart has been so bruised of late; it did promise me to think all of the next world and no more of this;

but Doctor Halley said, you know, that in the centre of this globe there was a great spherical magnet pulling and attracting us down to earth; from which pieces, which he calls Terrellæ, broken off from the grand loadstone but partaking its powers, are scattered up and down in order to hold us fast. Your happiness is one of these Terrellæ to me, and I wish to remain here till I see it completed, for which reason not a word will I utter about provocations, only to say they had nothing to do with the small shot.

My next letter from dear Sir James will be dated Streatham Park. Thus will he

> "Ope the hospitable gate,
> Ope for friendship, not for state.
> Friends well chosen enter there,
> Confidence and truth sincere;
> Love, in mutual faith secure,
> Transport generous and pure;
> Sparkling from the soul within,
> Never boasted, always seen."

Is it not a shame to fancy you have time to read a letter? yet vanity, that vile passion, says you will read it.

And now let me finish with the most serious and solemn wishes for every possible happiness to you and yourself, and yourself's half. I like the expression, 'tis sincere and new; new I suppose because it is sincere. So God bless you, my dear and highly-valued friend.

Yours, &c.

H. L. P.

To Sir James Fellowes.

Bath, 1 March, 1816.

ON St. Taffy's day does ——'s little Welsh friend renew her wishes of happiness. The thought of its being so near, and the delightful certainty of your going to my house at Streatham Park to be happy, puts me in the best good-humour possible. And since —— has written again without insolence or peevishness, I have contented myself, in reply to his inquiries after my health, with saying that my cough is gone, and that I hope he is recovered from his nettle-spring rash, which seems to burst out annually, as I had an odd letter from him in the same style ten or twelve months ago.

We are raving mad here about the property tax. Will it be abolished or no?

General Doukin is married and Mrs. Wroughton dead, characters well known in Bath. They are nearly of an age, but the lady's is the more prudent step, sure, after ninety.

Did Leak show you the bason I was baptized in so many years ago? it is in the china closet next the drawing-room door, with a bit of dirty paper in it which Mr. Piozzi made me write, I think but am not sure, lest it should be confounded with the other things.

Did you never go to Hampton Palace, Hampton Court I mean, and see a poor, half-starved, snuffy-nosed old woman showing the now nearly empty rooms, and saying in a shrill though sleepy tone: "And here's

Prince George of Denmark over the chimney." Then, with a sigh: "Over the chimney Prince George of Denmark," hoping her task near over.

Now don't you be thinking of her when I show my little show, as Mrs. Siddons was caught recollecting some of my silly jokes, and burst out o' laughing in the most mournful part of Aspasia's character, to the amusement of Kemble and annoyance of all the actors at rehearsal.

Adieu, dear Sir, and burn this nonsense, for the sake of your faithful, obliged,

H. L. P.

Give my truest regards to your brother, and tell the lady you love best, how sincerely I am disposed to love her; and write to me from Streatham Park. Oh! that is the letter I long for.

To Sir James Fellowes.

18 April, 1814.

My home for fifty years will I hope procure me, by disposing of it, a temporary residence for the remainder of my short term; and what more ought to be wished by one who will soon take up a narrower space? I am glad Squib * is so sanguine. Did you see real Squib, the father? he is a very good-looking man.

There is an old story of Balbus †, when Quæstor at

* The well known auctioneer of Saville Row.
† The anecdote is recorded in a letter to Cicero from Apicius Pollio.

Seville, throwing an auctioneer to the lyons in his menagerie, because a female friend who was selling up her possessions complained to him, that the auctioneer was so ugly and deformed, he frighted all buyers away. Our people will lose no bidders by that fault; but is it not odd that the world, with all its fluctuations, should have undergone so little change? Always vexations, disappointments, and inadequate anger for what can hardly be helped, though the mode of expressing that anger is altered by the different situations of society.

Always a friend or two perhaps in the world like Sir J—— F——; always luckless ladies enough, like your faithful, obliged,

H. L. P.

To Sir James Fellowes.

Here is the 9th of May; and now if S— J—— F—— renews his kind invitation very pressingly, I will have the honour to wait on him and his lady in the Whitsun Week, having a mind to break up, as children say, for the holy days, and run to see the Waterloo Bridge, the Western Exchange, and other London wonders; then return, shut my front windows, and protest myself (with the strictest truth) in the country.

Hope, says Lord Bacon, is a good breakfast, but a bad supper; and with regard to this life, he is right; no other supper would sit easy, however, during the long night of the grave.

Do you feel interested in Southey's or Canning's Attack and Defence? I am pleased to see them turn with so much vigour on their enemies.

The prettiest new book, however, is "Chalmers on Modern Astronomy," which he reconciles to Scripture in a manner he seems to fancy unexampled, but it is not so. The work is worth reading, nevertheless, and I have a notion you would like it.

Let me hear that you are very busy. Business for men of leisure, and leisure for men of business, in due proportions I mean, would really add to mortals' happiness here below more than mortal man can imagine.

Adieu; and believe me, yours most faithfully,

H. L. P.

To Sir James Fellowes.

Wednesday, 22 May, 1816.

My dear Sir James has broken the Mum at last; and I will now tell him how we are hesitating between a convenient house on the Queen's Parade, or pretty No. 8, Gay Street, which is particularly inconvenient for the servants below stairs. Either of them ought to content me well enough after how I have been living — a common expression, but infamous bad English.

Apropos, Charles Kemble has been here acting; and in some part of a comedy written by Murphy, said, " We are like Cymon and Iphigĕnīa in Dryden's Fables." The ladies stared, but the scholars said he was right; and I said it were better be wrong than so pedantic, for 'tis always called Iphigēnīa in common use. Mr. Lutwyche held with the wise men, and he, you know, is a good prosodist. I quoted Pope's " Homer," 9th book,

"Laodice and Iphigĕnia fair,
And bright Chrysothemis with golden hair."

"Oh!" said Mr. Mangin, "Pope is no firm authority; he calls the wife of Pluto Prŏserpine, as in colloquial chat, when writing his fine ode on St. Cecilia's Day. But old Milton disdained such barbarism; he calls her Prŏsērpĭna, as in the Greek." We all appealed to Falconer; dear Sir J—— was too far away. I know not the success of our appeal yet.

Well! here are fine apple blossoms, pink and white, as any lady can make herself, and here is peace, too, and I think plenty.

When we were all looking at the fireworks in 1748 from temporary buildings, fragile enough I suppose, Dr. Barton merrily exclaimed, "Do you call this a good peace, which brings so many heads to the scaffold?"

Adieu, dear Sir, and believe me ever, yours faithfully,

H. L. P.

In reference to the intended sale of Streatham, my health will be better when the whole business is decided. At present I have neither taste nor smell; and as Prior says,

"No man would ask for my opinion
Between an oyster and an onion" (pronounce inion).

To Sir James Fellowes.

Bath, Saturday Night, 3rd August, 1816.

I AM so glad to leave this town, with the agreeable taste of what was most agreeable to me in it, that I shall never have done thanking you, dear Sir, for your very kind letter, and shall direct this straight forward to Adbury House. After church to-morrow the chaise runs us to Rodborough, another two days more will finish the journey, and I shall see Salusbury's babies.

The lady in the straw. Query, why do we say lying-in-women are in the straw? I think it was originally an allusion to the Blessed Virgin Mary, who had no other accommodation.

Lady F—— is very obliging, she will like Grims-thorpe so much; I am glad you are going, and shall be most glad when you return. I pass some happy days together in Gay Street: the plate is already on the door with my name, and you will say, " I see she has bra-soned it." * The old ebony chairs from Streatham Park will meet you in the entry, and it will make the house look like home, and if you advise me to, so I will make it my home, buying the lease and furniture. If I really should return from Wales, bright and brisk, and if (to speak in earnest) it should please God that I should,—Oh how many shoulds!—live this longest of all long years through, and like to begin another in the same place, why then I will purchase the whole concern. Nor will Salusbury have reason to regret, as 1000l. may be better by that time in stone than in stock, &c.

* " Until to some conspicuous square they pass,
  And blason on the door their names in brass."—*Don Juan.*

When Lord Stowell married and set up house with the Marchioness of Sligo, the brass plate with his name was placed under the brass plate with hers. " So," said Jekyll, " I find you are already obliged to knock under." Lord Stowell reversed the position of the plates. " Now," said Jekyll, " you are knocked up."

S—— is the wise man I always thought him, and forbearing to make one among the shoal of self-impelled fish, that rush to the opposite shore, they know not why, is a new proof of it.

Madame D'Arblaye, cydevant my dear friend Miss Burney, says there are 50,000 English at Paris now. Suppose on an average each spent only a guinea a-week, what a sum is quitting the country for a year? and they will not stay a shorter time if economy is their point — 2,600,000*l*. 50,000 millions (an't it) and 600,000*l*.

Should not some stop be put to the folly? And we the while making subscriptions which they avoid, and you feeding the poor whom they neglect!

How I shall delight in seeing Adbury House and environs! and hearing the cottagers blessing my worthy friends. Assure yourself, dear Sir, such blessings are your best purchases. Meanwhile, the workmen must have their share, and what is very odd, one hates them at first, and for a long time indeed; but I remember Piozzi and I felt a strange vacancy in our minds, when they were all gone. 'Tis so in everything. We had an oak tree in a little island no bigger than itself, and surrounded with water, which an oak tree abhors. We dried the pond up, and the tree pined away.

But here comes Miss Williams, loaded with presents for me to carry to her family; and not another word can I say, and not another moment have I to say it in.

To Miss Fellowes.

THIS letter to dear Miss F., begun at Blake's Hotel, London, will be ended at Streatham Park. Your brother, and the kind General (Garston), have called, and will meet me at the old house. I hope he will be there to receive me, or how shall I present myself to the lady?

London looks very dull, very dull indeed; I augur ill of the times, and feel glad to be going where love and happiness attend me. Saturday I saw one of my daughters, who rejected all connexion with the place for herself and Co.; and now every true friend I have in the world, dear Sir J—— first in command, must and do approve of my putting everything to open sale. I have surely suffered enough, and you and your good father know I have suffered within less than what people call, an inch of one's life.

To Sir James Fellowes.

Streatham Park, 2 April.

WELL! I have presented myself, and the lady (who is much nearer to a very pretty woman than I expected) received me with great kindness. Lady Abdy and Miss Abdy are here and charming.

We dine with them next Thursday, when Sir —— goes to the Drawing Room, and we return here at night, and leave them Saturday morning, to dine with business people at London.

The men are here making catalogues, and calling out for my dear Miss ——'s ever faithful,

H. L. P.

This note was written in King Street, 6th Jan. 1816, 10 P.M.

THANKS, a thousand and a thousand more, my dear Sir. Your kindness is without limitation, and your pity very soothing to a mind, which once could fly so high, but wounded as it has been, flutters now and beats the ground, when trying to rise up and (like Floretta's gold-finch) to sing in circles round your head, as gratitude demands from your incessantly obliged,

H. L. P.

> Buenos noches,
> Felicissima notte,
> Bon soir,
> Gute nacht,
> Good night,
> Vale.

On her return from London she thus writes:—

To Sir James Fellowes.

Bath, Wednesday, 10 April, 1816.

MY dear S—— and Lady —— will like to hear that I got safe through the thunder and lightning on Sunday evening by taking shelter at Salt Hill, from whence I ran hither, over a road watered as if by a water-cart, the next day, and arrived at my smoky hut on Monday night, eighty-eight miles in twelve hours.

I found Lady Keith's card on my table at Blake's Hotel on Saturday night, and returned the visit on Sunday, leaving the kindest letter I knew how to write. I did more, I left orders with Leak and Squibb, to take their money if they offered, but if they did not offer, to hurry on the sale of the pictures at Streatham, and put me out of pain as soon as possible.

This morning I went into a public auction here in Milsom Street, and saw sold a varnished-up performance of Peter Neef, for thirty-four guineas; this gave me spirits, so did the story of these Bank restrictions, which they say will operate immediately in making money plenty.

I am a miserable financier, but you will understand me, as Miss Streatfield's maid said I should, when she asked me to lend her lady *Milk and Asparagus Lost*. I did immediately comprehend her meanings and sent her the "Milton's Paradise Lost" you saw in Streatham Park Library. Perhaps my Bank restrictions may be as awkwardly worded.

Adieu! this vile paper tears my worn out pens, and my worn out patience quite to pieces, or I would send more, though kinder I could not send.

H. L. P.

To Sir James Fellowes.

Bath, 30 May, 1816.

MY DEAR SIR,— . . . . I will be careful about sea bathing. Dr. Gibbes bid me beware of the re-action, but what can one do towards keeping such thing at a distance? Cowper says, you know, and truly and sweetly :

> " Fate steals along with silent tread,
> 　Most dangerous when least we dread ;
> 　Frowns in the storm with angry brow,
> 　But in the sunshine strikes the blow."

Now, don't you believe me low spirited ; few people ever had such uniformly good spirits. Did I tell you I had saved Murphy* from the general wreck ? and that Mr. Watson Taylor wrote after me to beg him for 157*l.* 10*s.* ; but I am no longer poor, and when I was, there ought surely to be some difference made between fidelity and unkindness. When B———s (Burneys) were treacherous and Baretti boisterous against poor unoffending H. L. P., dear Murphy was faithful found, among the faithless faithful only he :

> " He, like his muse, no mean retreating made,
> 　But follow'd faithful to the silent shade."

Equally attached to both my husbands, he lived with us till he could in a manner live no longer ; and his portrait is now on the easel, with that of Mr. Thrale, coming to Bath ; my mother, whom both of them adored, keeping them company.

Let us, however, bid you farewell, assuring you how much I am, yours,

H. L. P.

* Portrait by Sir Joshua Reynolds, painted for the library at Streatham.

To Sir James Fellowes.

Bath, Tuesday, 9 July, 1816.

NOT yet forgotten by dear Sir James Fellowes, his old friend hastens to inform him that she *does* mend, slowly, and heavily; but yet she feels climbing up, rather than sliding down, the hill.

So Sheridan is going, and Mrs. Jordan gone: in want both of them, though perhaps not actually of want either of them: shocking enough! and Mary Mayhew dying, and Miss Katherine Griffith dead. *Equo pede pulsat* the old enemy Death:

> Le Pauvre en sa cabane où le chaume le couvre
> Est sujet à ses Loix :
> Et la garde qui veille à la porte du Louvre,
> N'en défend pas nos Rois.

The Misses here are all reading "Glenarvon,"* "a monstrous tale of things impossible," at least one hopes so. I have finished it at last, though not comprehended it: and can only say with King Lear:

> "An ounce of civet, good Apothecary,
> To sweeten my imagination."

Your dear father and mother, meanwhile, are happier than the very poets could dream for them; if Miss —— would but get quite well; I think this world has no more to give them. You, dear Sir, must present them my truest regards, and accept every good wish from yours ever,

H. L. P.

* A novel by Lady Caroline Lamb; the two principal characters were supposed to be intended for Lord Byron and herself.

I feel sorry the Parliament is broken up; for, laugh as one may, in that House does reside the united wisdom of the nation. " Wisdom," says Solomon, " crieth in the streets, but no man heareth." I think in London streets the horn blowers and the flowers in blow contrive to drown his voice.

To Miss Fellowes.

Bath, 18 July, 1816.

YOUR letter, dear Miss Fellowes, came to my hand late last night. I do not, this morning, believe this the *last* day of our foolish and wicked world, but I think it the *worst* day I ever saw at this season of the year. All are uneasy about the ruin it is causing, and though nothing impels English people into church but a famous preacher, many feel alarm at the effect this extraordinary weather will have on the hay and corn.* Meanwhile our friends here at pretty T——i would be happy but for the necessity of fires in July, and the oddity of living enveloped with cold mist, unable to enjoy their beautiful spot, or see fifty yards from it.

Death still holds a court for himself here in New King Street; whence poor old Colonel Erving will be carried to Walcot in a day or two: I shook hands with him on Monday morning, and passed him in a chair, going out. On Wednesday morning, much earlier than that hour, he was a corpse; without any previous illness,

* On the 18th July, 1860, the weather and its apprehended consequences were the same.

except mere old age. Dr. Fellowes remembers him in America.

Have you read " Glenarvon," and its key? I hope some newer fooling has taken up the Londoners' attention by now. We Bath folks are content to admire Lady Loudon and Moira's beautiful Asiatic, not having Lady H——'s atheist to stare at *; but any thing will do. But I am detaining you with questions concerning people and things, by this time wholly forgotten among your folks.

Distance between friends produces that certain vexation: one talks to them on worn-out subjects always, and that is the grand cause of letters being generally insipid, unless they tell of one's health: and I think yours and mine have been long absent from their owners; yours only mislaid I hope; but lost, and of no value to those who find it, is the once very strong and active constitution of your truly faithful and obliged friend,

H. L. P.

To Sir James Fellowes.

Bath, Monday, 22 July, 1816.

HERE's terrifying weather indeed. Such a thunderstorm on the 18th as I have seldom seen in England. B. J——'s observed the fire ball in the street, and

---

* The late Mr. Allen, who lived with Lord and Lady Holland as a member of the family, was called Lady Holland's pet atheist.

report soon told us the frightful effects left behind it at
poor Windsor's here in James Street. You must remember to have copper, not iron, bell wires; nothing
else saved the lives of those pretty children: I live to
the fields you know, and escaped all the wonders, nor
could quite believe till Mrs. Windsor shewed me her
floor, burned in places, her wall pushed in, and her
plate-warmer in the kitchen perforated very curiously
indeed; and all this on a cold rainy day.

Worse storms tear the atmosphere to pieces in Italy
every summer evening, yet I never but once heard of
any life lost or endangered: but then they have no
newspapers, so much may happen without one's hearing
of it.

Miss W——s showed me a letter from Lady ——e
that says, M—— M——w is getting quite well, by
taking the juice of red nettles!! I never heard of red
nettles before; and make no doubt but a few pebble-
stones boyled in milk, would be just as efficacious. But
Hope is drawn with an anchor always, and common
sense is never strong enough to weigh it up.

The mischief is, we seldom drop or cast it in the
proper harbour; it would then keep steady, and deserve
the name the Romans gave it, *anchora sacra* . . . .
I shall probably not live to see you in the happy character of father; but remember my words, or rather
those of old Archbishop Leighton; when speaking of
education, he said, "Fill you the bushel with good
wheat yourself; because then fools and foes will have
less room to cram in chaff."

Nothing better has ever been said upon the subject. Adieu! you well know how to get more such stuff when you wish it, from dear Sir, your old and faithful friend,

H. L. P.

To Sir James Fellowes.

Bath, Wednesday, 18 September, 1816.

. . . . The best scraps I could pick up, you will read over leaf. They were written in imitation of the Greek verses by Metrodorus, or Posidippus (which was it?) for " Life against Life." I read them long ago, translated in the "Adventurer;" but cannot recollect what number they are in, besides that I possess not the book.

FOR LONDON.

Can we through London streets be led
Without rejoycing as we tread?
The city's wealth our eye surveys,
The court attracts our lighter gaze;
Whilst charity her arm extends,
And sick and poor find host of friends.
Wit sparkles round our rosy wine,
And beauty boasts her charms divine:
Musick prolongs our festive nights,
And morning calls to fresh delights;
A London residence then give,
For here alone I seem to live.

AGAINST LONDON.

Can London streets by man be trod
Without repenting on the road?
Where nobles, whelmed in shame or debt,
And bankrupts swell each sad gazette;
All licensed death our frame attacks,
And to his aid calls hosts of quacks;
False smiles on beauty's face appear,
And wit evaporates in a sneer.
Dangers impede our days' delights,
And vermin vex our sleepless nights;
From London, then, let's quickly fly
In rural shades to live or die.

After a good dose of London, and then A——y, I
think you will read these verses *con amore.*

Yours, dear Sir, ever,

H. L. P.

To Sir James Fellowes.

Bath, 25 September, 1816.

THE promptness with which I answer dear Sir J——
F—— is the surest proof of my rejoicing in his
letters. . . . . We had a delightful day at F——,
where Mr. H—— F—— and I had no little talk upon
the subject you recommended to my consideration, and
which is surely now the most interesting of all subjects.
My private opinion is, that the person who leads the
Hebrews on, against their old oppressor, the Sultan, is
one of the false, the Pseudo Christs, against whom our

Lord warns his disciples; first, in the 24th chapter of St. Matthew, 4th and 5th verses; then in the same chapter, 23rd and 24th verses. The first of these impostors arose very soon after Christ's Ascension, Barchochebas by name, and he vomited fire, and led astray multitudes. Dositheus was another; I think " Retrospection " mentions one or two, and we had Joanna Southcote within these two or three years in England. She seems to have been one of those mentioned in the 26th verse of the same chapter, saying, " Behold he is in the secret chambers," but, says our Saviour, "Go not forth." The same injunctions are repeated in St. Mark, the 13th chapter, 6th verse; and the 8th chapter of St. Luke gives a similar prohibition. This person, however, may be the great Antichrist, or Antechrist, though I do not believe it. The Protestants, you know, have attributed that character uniformly to the Papal Power; but Romanists, following the opinion of Father Malvenda, a Spanish Fryar, who flourished in 1600, and was an admirable Hebraist, believe that Antichrist is to be a Jew, of the tribe of Dan, that he will reign three years and a half, and shew many miracles. When Jacob pronounced his prophetic blessing on his sons, he says, " Dan shall be a serpent in the way," and a dragon was always painted on their standard. Jeremiah says, " the armies of Dan shall devour the earth ;" and when St. John, in his Apocalypse, saw the angel sealing the twelve tribes of Israel, 'tis observable that Dan is omitted. Conjectures concerning Antichrist are, however, quite innumerable. There is a folio volume in

our Bodleian Library at Oxford, written to assert that
Oliver Cromwell was the person, and Mr. Faber, you
know, said it was Buonaparte, or gave us reason to
believe he thought so.   St. Paul's description of him in
his 2nd chapter of his 2nd epistle to the Thessalonians
as preceding the general judgment, does always appear
to me as if designed to pourtray *one single man*, whoever he may be; but Bishop Newton and all cool ex-
positors seem to think the Papacy was intended; and
your brother, as an orthodox Protestant divine, is of
that opinion.

Meanwhile it does strike all reflecting people, that
great changes are about to take place; things advance
with a velocity best compared to the rapidity of a wheel
down hill, increasing at every step.   I own myself convinced of the approach of

> " That great day for which all days were made ;
> Great day of dread, decision and despair,
> When nature struggling in the pangs of death
> Shows God in terrois and the skies on fire."
>
> > YOUNG.

Whether this catastrophe is to happen forty or fifty
years hence, is, however, of no consequence to *me* as an
individual.   My last day must come long before.

The nonsense verses for and against London were
written when I was very sick of it, so the last were
best of course.   You must read Gray's " Connections
between Sacred Writ and Classic Literature ;" it is a
very fine performance and much admired.

Yours while

H. L. P.

To Sir James Fellowes.

30 September, 1816.

. . . In January 1817 such will be my fortune; and who in their wits, circumstanced as I am, can wish for more? Your dear mother laughed when I told her I was buying plate, linen, &c. to begin the world with, like a boy just come of age.

But life is a strange thing, and has been often compared to a river. "Labitur et labetur," &c.

> Leave the lofty glacier's side,
> Leave the mountain's solemn pride:
> Down some gently sloping hill
> Let's pursue this silent rill,
> Noiseless as it seems to flow,
> Wrapt in some poetic dream:
> Watch the windings of the stream.
> In such varied currents twisting,
> Still escaping, still existing:
> Let us find life's emblem here:
> Haste away! The lake is near.

Wales inspired these verses, which, of course, Sir J—— F—— never saw: but he can make life valuable as delightful. God keep the lake far distant from *him* for a thousand sakes. . . . .

Dr. Robert Gray, who wrote the new book that every one is reading, wrote the lines under our sun-dial at Brymbella:

" Umbra tegit lapsas, præsentique imminet horæ;
Dum lux, dum lucis semita virtus agat."

" Ere yet the threat'ning shade o'erspread the hour,
Hasten, bright Virtue, and assert thy power."

The well known George Henry Glasse* said there was
a fault in the prosody, and wished to correct it, as thus:

---

* The Rev. George Henry Glasse, author of several volumes
of sermons, and some translations from the learned languages.
Amongst Mrs. Piozzi's papers, were found notes of the following anecdotes concerning him. On Miss Blaquieres bidding
him write some verses for her, he said, " he had nothing to write
upon." " Then," replied the lady, " write upon *nothing*," he immediately obeyed : —

" And wilt thou, Nymph, compel my lays,
And force me sing thy rival's praise?
Why, then, in *this* thing let's agree,
That I love *no* thing more than thee."

On passing through a turnpike gate to officiate at a neighbouring
parish, he claimed exemption from paying the toll; the turnpike-
man, who was intoxicated, insisted upon payment, making use
of abusive language and swearing many oaths; upon which Mr.
Glasse paid the toll demanded, saying at the same time that he
should have it returned or the man should be fined for every oath he
had sworn; this Glasse carried into effect. Shortly afterwards he
received a letter from the turnpike-man, fining him for not reading
the swearing list once a quarter in the Church, agreeably to the
Act of Parliament then in force.

His life terminated strangely and lamentably. He had been to
the city to raise a sum of money to pay his debts, or (some say) to
enable him to escape from his creditors to the Continent. On his
return in a hackney-coach, he left his pocket-book containing the
money in banknotes on the seat, and on discovering his loss, committed suicide. The day following, the pocket-book with its contents

" Umbra tegit lapsam, præsentique imminet horæ
   Hospes, disce ex me vivere, disce mori."

" Ere yet the unreturning shadows fly,
   Go mortals ; learn to live, and learn to die."

Tell me which you prefer ; I like the English of the
last best, myself; but the first, of course, remains round
the little marble pillar set up by Mr. Piozzi, and very
much admired for its elegance. Oh! what a beautiful
house and place it is! Salusbury did make me the
compliment of not cutting down a weeping willow we
planted, because I had made verses on it.

To Sir James Fellowes.

Bath, Monday, 7 October, 1816.

I HAVE got no new books to read ; Mr. Whalley recommended me some verses, a long poem indeed, but
to me very unintelligible. Modern writers resemble the
cuttle-fish that hides himself from all pursuers in his
own ink. That is not Doctor Gray's case, however: I
think you will like his performance exceedingly. The
weather is as gloomy as November, and the poor gleaners
can get no corn out of the stubble ; it rots and grows,
and threatens ruin both to small and great.

was brought by the driver to the hotel at which he had stopped.
Neptune Smith was more fortunate. He flung himself into the
sea after casting up his betting book, from a conviction that the
balance was against him ; was fished out, found that he had cast
up his book wrong, and lived many years to exult in his nickname.

Miss Hudson says a famine will bring us to our senses: I say it will deprive us of the little wits we have left. The delirium proceeding from hunger will have fatal consequences, because vulgar minds will feel sure that 'tis somebody's fault, and woe to the mortal they pitch upon.

Send a consoling word, dear Sir, for my fancy sees very bad visions. The world always does see most to endure, when most blind, says old Fuller: perhaps that is now the case with yours faithfully and gratefully,

H. L. P.

To Sir James Fellowes.

Bath, 11 October, 1816.

In adversity, in prosperity, ever dear and kind friend, my Wraxall opens well. What signifies knowledge locked up, either in man or book? I think if Lady Keith has a fault besides her disregard of poor H. L. P., that is hers.

Oh! here is a new book come out, that I know not how she will like, or how the public will like. Do you remember my telling you, that in the year 1813, when I was in London upon Salusbury's business, before his marriage some months, a Mr. White sent to tell me, through Doctor Myddleton, that he possessed a manuscript of Johnson's, and wished me to ascertain that the handwriting was his own. I invited both gentlemen to dinner,—we were at Blake's Hotel,—and Dr. Gray, afterwards Bishop of Bristol, met them, and I saw that the MSS. was genuine. It was a diary of the little journey that Mr. Thrale, and Mr. Johnson (such he was then), and Miss Thrale and myself made into North Wales, in the year 1774. There was nothing in it of consequence, that I saw, except a pretty parallel * between Hawkestone, the country seat of Sir Richard Hill, and Ilam, the country seat of Mr. Port, in Derbyshire. But the gentleman who possessed it, seemed shy of letting me read the whole, and did not, as it appeared, like being asked how it came into his hands, but repeatedly observed he would print it only it was not sufficiently bulky for publication. He said he could swell it out, &c.

We parted, however, and met no more; but when I came first into New King Street, here, Nov. 1814, a poor widow woman, a Mrs. Parker, offering me seventeen genuine letters of Doctor Johnson, which I could by no means think of purchasing for myself, in my then present circumstances: I recommended her to apply to Mr. White, and she came again in three weeks' time, better dressed, and thanked me for the twenty-five guineas he had given her; from which hour I saw her no more, nor ever heard of or from Mr. White again.

Since you and I parted at Streatham Park, however, a Mr. Duppa has written me many letters, chiefly inquiring after my family; what relationship I have to Lord Combermere, to Sir Lynch Salusbury Cotton, &c.,

* This "pretty parallel" is what I had in my mind when speaking of Johnson's notice of Lord Kilmorey's place, Vol. I. p. 78.

n d comically enough asking who my aunt was, and if she was such a fool as Doctor Johnson described her. I replied she was my aunt only by marriage, though related to my mother's brother, who she did marry; that she was a Miss Cotton, heiress of Etwall and Belleport, in Derbyshire. Her youngest sister was Countess of Ferrers, and none of them particularly bright, I believe, but as I expressed it, Johnson was a good despiser.

So now here is Johnson's Diary, printed and published with a facsimile of his handwriting. If Mr. Duppa does not send me one, he is as shabby as it seems our Doctor thought me, when I gave but a crown to the old clerk. The poor clerk had probably never seen a crown in his possession before. Things were very distant A. D. 1774, from what they are 1816.

I am sadly afraid of Lady K.'s being displeased, and fancying I promoted this publication. Could I have caught her for a quarter-of-an-hour, I should have proved my innocence, and might have shown her Duppa's letter; but she left neither note, card, nor message, and when my servant ran to all the inns in chase of her, he learned that she had left the White Hart at twelve o'clock. Vexatious! but it can't be helped.

I hope the pretty little girl my people saw with her, will pay her more tender attention.

To Sir James Fellowes.

October 14, 1816.

YOUR brother Dorset has lent me Bubb Dodington's Diary, and I have done nothing but read it ever since. 'Tis a retrospection of my young days, very amusing certainly, but anecdote is all the rage, and Johnson's Diary is selling rapidly, though the contents are *bien maigre*, I must confess. Apropos, Mr. Duppa has sent me the book, and I perceive has politely suppressed some sarcastic expressions about my family, the Cottons, whom we visited at Combermere, and at Lleweney. I was the last of the Salusburys, so they escaped. But I remember his saying once, " It would be no loss if all your relations were spitted like larks, and roasted for the lap dog's supper."

It would certainly have been no loss to me, as they have behaved themselves; but one hates to see them insulted.

This letter is written in the dark, you will hardly be able to read it, but if words are wanting, supply the chasm with the kindest. They will have best chance to express the unalterable sentiments of

H. L. P.

Your brother Dorset and I disagree only in our opinions concerning Buonaparte, of whom he thinks much higher than I do; although as Balzac says of the Romans :—

" Le ciel benissoit toutes leurs fautes,
Le ciel couronnoit toutes leurs folies.''

We must, however, watch the end; for, till a man dies, we can neither pronounce him very great or very happy; so said at least one of the sages of antiquity.

Adieu!

To Sir James Fellowes.

Bath, Fryday, 1 Nov. 1816.

WHEN my heart first made election of Sir J. Fellowes, not only as a present but as a future friend, I felt rather than knew, that he would never forget or forsake me. Everything I see and hear confirms my saucy prejudice.

Such a Sunday evening I passed in Marlborough Buildings *, where I used to meet friends, so beloved, companions so cheerful, sent me home to Bessy Jones † with a half-breaking heart; and in every vein Johnson's well-founded horror of the last.

The family left Bath next day, for Paris, where they have taken a house for a year! Poor Boisgeler is dead, you know. One could not care in earnest for Boisgeler, but at my age, 'tis like losing the milestones in the last stage of a long journey.

We shall, however, both of us, have a cruel loss in the Lutwyches. How happy, how elegant is the epitaph on poor Mary. Beautiful, though not too shewy; just as it should be. I am afraid to trust myself with translating or even praising it.

H. L. P.

* At the house of the Lutwyches.
† Her maid.

To Sir James Fellowes.

Bath, Nov. 29, 1816.

ANOTHER letter you shall have, dear Sir, and that directly.

Cobbett has been galvanizing the multitude finely, I am told, in his last paper. "Be scum no longer," says he, "be no longer called scum, I say." Did I ever tell you a story of which this reminds me, concerning the blind Lord North's father, old Guildford; who delighted in affecting coarse expressions, and used to say to his friends when he met them, "Oh, such a one, how does the pot boil?' Some democrat, who probably disliked the rough address, when Wilkes and liberty set London maddening, called to Lord Guildford across a circle of ladies round the tea-table, and cried exultingly, "Well my good lord, how does the pot boil now?"

"Troth, Sir," replied the peer, without hesitation, "just as you gentlemen would wish it to do,—scum uppermost."

I am so afraid this tale is not new to you, any more than baptizing the bells. We have two in England, you know, that were christened Thomas. The Oxford one I forget all account of; but when the devil was set up to look over Lincoln Cathedral, the wise folk found baptizing the bell was an efficacious method of sending him off. Some of their conclave, however, being incredulous, "Let us," said they, "baptize the bell by name of the doubting apostle, and that will do," so he is Tom o' Lincoln.

I fancy the phenomenon you allude to at Valencia, where they are, I trust, not much improved in philosophy, was a real meteor. The atmosphere is loaded with vapour, certainly, in a way not wholly natural; and has been all the summer, if summer it may be called. Adieu!

This letter has been written all by scraps and snatches; people coming in without ceasing, and stealing the wits from my head, the pen from my fingers, every moment. Let it at least do its duty in presenting my best regards and compliments to ——'s acceptance.

> Paper therefore fly with speed,
> Let thy friend make haste to read,
> To be read, is all thy meed,
> Hark! the bell is ringing!

Can such stuff come from any creature but

H. L. P.

To Sir James Fellowes.

Bath, 27 Dec. 1816.

THANK you, my dear Sir, for the kind wishes that I restore you from my heart a hundred fold.

It was odd enough, and pretty enough, that the happiest day of the year should have been the finest; but indeed I never saw such a 25th of December, and what blowing weather followed! But we must expect it now to be slippy, drippy, nippy; after which, showery, bowery, flowery; then hoppy, croppy, poppy; oh! and autumn wheezy, sneezy, freezy; as good, sure, as Fabre

d'Eglantine's Nivose, Pluviose, Ventose, &c. I wonder
if any of that nonsense will be remembered!

There is a good French joke now at Paris, concerning
the King's illness; for say the Jacobins,

> " Si Louis s'en allait,
> Charles dix paraitrait."

Meaning that

> " Charles *dis*-paraitrait."

'Tis well they are so merrily disposed.

Mrs. Lutwyche writes in capital spirits, but your own
dear father's heart is as light as a Frenchman's, though
solid like John Bull. We had a world of chat to-day
when he brought me your letter about Lord and Lady
Mount Edgecombe, being parted like Mr. Sullen and
his wife in the comedy; east, west, north, south; far as
the Poles asunder. They have been married just nine
months. She wedded twice before, and now they cry,
" O terque quaterque beati!" I suppose.

Mrs. Dimond offers me a place in her box to-night,
whence will be seen Massinger's horrible "Sir Giles
Overreach," played by Mr. Kean. If he can stretch
that hideous character as he does others, quite beyond
all the authors meant or wished, it will shock us too
much for endurance, though in these days people do
require mustard to everything. Actors, preachers, whoever keeps within the bounds of decency,— may not we
add patriots? are all censured for tameness, and considered as cold-hearted animals, scarce worthy to crawl
on the earth.

Meanwhile, the thoughts of your Adbury establishment charm me, and I feel sure that my dear friend will never fall into this new and fatal whimsey, of fatting beasts, while men are wanting food. It is a senseless thing to see calves, and sheep, crammed till they cannot walk, but are driven into the town for show, in their carriage, like Daniel Lambert in his easy chair, when the mutton and veal so managed is not eatable, and the very fat useless to tallow-chandlers for want of solidity. I really wonder nobody takes the matter up as seriously censurable.*

We are subscribing here at a great rate, to imitate the Londoners. I told Hammersley, that the donation of 50,000*l.* to 50,000 poor, put me in mind of Merlin, the German mechanick, who, when people were terrifying each other about the invasion, some five and thirty years ago, proposed to let them come, and then meet them with a guinea each, and beg of them to go home—never reflecting, till heartily laughed at, that they would come again next week for another guinea a-piece. Surely these are senseless methods of preserving tranquillity.† The people want nothing but employment

---

* It was remarked by Lord Macaulay that prize oxen were only fit to make candles, and prize poems to light them.

† They are not much unlike what were proposed by sundry opponents of the Volunteer Movement at its commencement. Some years ago, during a popular rising in Yorkshire, a well-known banker wrote to the Home Office, that if the malcontents did not receive a cheque (meaning check) he would not answer for the consequences. The obvious answer was, that he was the best man to apply the proposed remedy.

and pay, and then they will love the hand that helps
them, while feeding them by subscription leaves them
not a whit obliged, but in some sort, and scarce unjustly, offended; while the donors are impoverishing
themselves.

Well! all this you know better than I do, but Doctor Fellowes charged me to give you some tydings of
my own health, because I confessed to him that I had
been taking dear No. 1, and he probably thought that
if the sails would not turn with a common wind, it was
a proof somewhat was the matter with the mill; but
with all my comforts it would be graceless to complain.

Adieu, dear Sir; may your next year be happy! all
spring, showery, bowery, flowery. I really do believe
it will be the happiest year of your life, it will make
of the most dutyful and affectionate son upon earth,
the wisest and tenderest father. Do not, however, forget, that in 1815, you promised long and faithful friendship to her who knows the value of all your good
qualities, and who will be, while life lasts, perhaps still
longer, your sincere, as obliged,

H. L. P.

To Sir James Fellowes.

Bath, 4th January, 1817.

'Tis well for me, dear Sir, that my letters meet so
kindly partial a reader; for I have a notion they often
repeat themselves. Doctor Johnson, and men less wise
than he, say we forget everything but what passes in
our own mind. Those ideas are among the most fleeting
of mine.

That I had not seen the great actor (Kean) in Sir Giles Overreach when last writing to Adbury, is however perfect in my remembrance; he did it very finely indeed. A clear voice and dignified manner are not necessary to the character, and personal beauty would take off too much from one's aversion. I was well entertained, and caught no cold at all.

My New Year's Day party went off to everybody's satisfaction. Next morning brought verses with " Attic wit " and " graceful Piozzi " in them, and praises of the music, which I praised myself for enduring. With good manœuvring, however, I kept them from singing Italian, and everybody was the better pleased; but I had rather talk of your trees.

Miss Williams says you must make the children of your cottagers bring in the Hawthorn berries at so much the lapful, and put them in a large tub or pot, and place them in sand, — a layer of berries and a layer of sand, — to be put out at the proper season. Acorns, too, might be gathered, she says, every autumn, and save you buying dwarfish and ricketty things from imposing nursery and seedsmen. Her care for your pocket is very comical indeed, but those fine plantations at her brother's country seat haunt the poor dear soul's fancy everlastingly; and she remembers and knows that 5l. would have paid the whole cost; for in old Judge Williams' time there were not, as now, things of every kind to be bought. They planted their own beech mast and fir apples; and certainly the trees are worth ten times as much to posterity.

Miller, the great botanist of fifty years ago, told me that an acorn grounded, as he expressed it, on the same day with a seven year's old oak, would be taller and stronger than his competitor in seven years time. I told Mr. Thrale so, but he was in haste to be happy ; and now the trees he bought,—younglings,—are nothing, as you saw, while Bodylwyddan Woods are quite in a thriving state.

So here's a wise letter, and that always resembles a dull one ; but let dullness have its due : and remember that if life and conversation are happily compared to a bowl of punch, there must be more water in it than spirit, acid, or sugar. Besides that, I am convinced 'tis variety alone can delight us either in a book or a companion.* "Rather than always wit, let none be there," says Cowley, who had himself enough for two people, and I know not why, but my heart feels heavy somehow.

Dear ! dear ! what a fragile thing life is ! A young man was riding full gallop down this street † yesterday; and fell down dash at the very spot where Miss Shuttleworth was killed. He is not dead this morning, poor fellow ! but in a sad way, I fear. This street always was like Virgil's Tartarus, and now 'tis like the high road to it. Coal carts scrattling up the hill often used to make me think—

> "Hinc ex audiri gemitus, et sæva sonare
>   Verbera ; tum stridor ferri, tractæque catenæ."

---

* "On ne plait pas longtemps si l'on n'a qu'une sorte d'esprit."
—*Rochefoucauld.*
† Gay Street, Bath.

Well! no matter; our exits and entrances are apparently innumerable, and no two alike. Here comes Miss W—— daggled like a duck-shooting spaniel on a dirty November day, and catching her very death with cold, to tell me that S— J—— F——— must not put the seeds of his pine cones, that I call fir apples, into sand. They must be dried in napkins, &c. &c.

So now adieu, my dear Sir. I have got a member of parliament by happy fortune to free my nonsense, and cover with his frank my compliments to ——.

I asked my servant how your letter was brought me, for it came in the midst of my little bustle on the 1st of January. "Indeed, Ma'am," replied the man, "I can't tell, but it seemed to arrive promiscuously."

Once more farewell, and believe me ever yours,

H. L. P.

To Sir James Fellowes.

Bath, Sunday, 4 January, 1817.

Ah! he was a wise man who said Hope is a good breakfast but a bad dinner. It shall be my supper, however, when all's said and done, and the epilogue spoken upon poor H. L. P.

This snow will do infinite service, but I want something to string my spirits up to concert pitch. The parties are going forward through frost and snow, but I come home from them, when I *do* go, a little duller than at setting out. One reason is they will sing to

me, the men will; and oh! how much rather would I
hear a dog howl!

Your friend —— was very kind, sate and chatted
with me very good-naturedly, and did not sing.

Here is a thin quarto book come out concerning Miss
McEvoy; you should see it. The Shropshire boy was
not a better deceiver, if the wise men who attest these
wonders do indeed give credit to them. For my own
part, I think the world is superannuating apace, and I
suppose sees double like drunken people, and horses
that are going to lose their eye-sight. Such an age of
imposture was sure never known. Joanna Southcote, the
Fortunate Youth, and Miss McEvoy, all in four years!
With stories of the —— of —— that put belief out
of all possibility. Poor Wales, too, a principality without a prince, whenever the king dies.

Mrs. Lutwyche has written from Rome: says her husband can walk now seven miles o' day. They spend their
time in seeing sights under the direction of far-famed
Cornelia Knight*, and rejoycing in the society of the first
society of the first city in Europe — never mentioning
the famine and distressful state of the inhabitants,
which Sir Thomas and Lady Liddel protest is beyond
endurance, Capua alone having lost 12,000 human
creatures from hunger and consequent disease within
the last two years, and this corresponds with Dr. Whalley's account of Northern Italy.

What is one to believe? Now dispose of my compliments, loves, and respects, and *Addio!*

* Author of "Marcus Flaminius" and other works.

To Sir James Fellowes.

Bath, 16 January, 1817.

On the seventy-sixth anniversary of my life, according to your good father's reckoning, the first thing I do after returning God thanks, is to write to dear Sir James.

Kemble is here, and has called on me; I was shocked at the alteration in his face and person. Poor fellow! But the public were, or rather *was*, very contented, and huzzaed his Coriolanus gallantly. I was glad for twenty reasons; Brutus and Sicinius being precisely the Hunt and Cobbett of 2000 years ago, it was delightful to hear how they were hissed.

Our hills exhibit a heavy snow, but it does not lie in this warm town.

These are days when nothing can be deemed impossible. I think the people in Thibet are right for my part, who kneel down when a female baby is born, and pray that she may have a physician for her husband. He would at least keep her from such exploits, as Mrs. M——, who frighted me so by going out to dinner into the country the 11th day after delivery; the very hearing of it half killed me, who was then in Wales. Miss W—— walks about this horrid weather with a weight of clothes which would kill any one whose ancestors had not worn armour, and then strips for the evening party, covered (if covered) only by trinkets just fit for the eldest Miss ——. Such is the world, and such are its inhabitants. Do not suffer yourself to be too

sorry that I am so near out of it. If my setting sun
leaves one long red streak behind, to lengthen the twilight and keep back dark oblivion, shall I not be happy
and thankful? whilst I am recollected as your true and
trusty old friend,

H. L. P.

Verses on the 16th of January, 1817, the seventy-
sixth anniversary of her life.

> Whilst all on Piozzi's natal day
> Their tributary offerings pay,
>   Of due congratulation;
> Let not my faithful muse forget
> To pay her just, her willing debt,
>   Upon the glad occasion.
>
> Nor, lady! deem she here presents
> Those cold unmeaning compliments
>   Made only for the ear;
> Hers is true tribute of the heart,
> Expressed, indeed, with little art,
>   But honest and sincere.
>
> Then deign t' accept the votive lay,
> Incited by this festal day
>   We hail with such delight.
> To friendship sacred, and to song,
> Let joy the happy hour prolong,
>   And stay their rapid flight.

Nor shall my interested prayer
Invoke for you one added year
    Than every way may please ;
I wish their number limited
To those which come accompanied
    With happiness and ease.

Yet frequent may the Day return,
And distant that which we shall mourn
    Returns no more for you ;
With silent pain the mental eye
Pierces thro' deep futurity,
    And turns her from the view.

At length, by years alone opprest,
When summon'd hence to join the blest
    In their celestial sphere ;
Resign'd you'll quit us at the last,
Viewing without regret the past,
    The future without fear.

But friendship whispers to the heart,
That tho' condemn'd on earth to part
    From those it lov'd before :
Its ties unbroken still remain,
And former friends shall meet again,
    To separate no more.

To Sir James Fellowes.

Bath, 23 January, 1817.

DOES —— ever read novels ? The second and third volumes of a strange book, entitled " Tales of my Landlord " [" Old Mortality "] are very fine in their way.

People say 'tis like reading Shakespear! I say 'tis as like Shakespear as a glass of peppermint water is to a bottle of the finest French brandy; but the third — I think it is the third—volume, is very impressive for the moment, without spectres or any trick played, except the sensations of Morton when going to be executed, and the gay conversation of Claverhouse immediately following, which is a happy contrast indeed.

I will, however, detain you no longer than to say — not how much, for it would not be said in an hour — but how very sincerely I remain, your obliged and faithful friend, whilst

H. L. PIOZZI.

To Sir James Fellowes.

Bath, Saturday night, 8 February, 1817.

I HAVE disengaged myself from the party this evening was to have been lost in, for the pleasure of thanking dear Sir James for the very friendly letter brought me to-day by his happy father, who was going down the town to sign his name among the honest men who promise to rally round our excellent Constitution. All this looks well, as you say; but I so hate to recollect the times * when England was divided between factions much re-

---

* 1680. See Macaulay's History, vol. i. p. 256.

sembling ours, and calling one set petitioners, and the other set *abhorrers* — of the petitions, I suppose.

France is no happier, no richer than Great Britain; all Europe is enveloped in these frightful fogs.

Your friend and I had a very nice conversation about political economy. The people certainly feel offended at seeing one man receive 12,000*l.*, another 20,000*l.* o' year in return for no apparent service done; but I am not sure they are injured at all, unless the possessor carries his wealth and spends it in a foreign country. Were we to roast all the race-horses, and give the corn which feeds them to the poor, making "Hambletonian" into soup, &c., what would become of the grooms and the jockies and their helpers and hangers-on? They would know how to till the ground no better than their masters; and we should have so many more thieves, professed, that are now merely amateurs and dillettanti. Servants out of place are among the worst members of society; and a gentleman once told me that none of the wretches sent to Botany Bay were so truly untractable as that class. "They can do nothing," said he, "but wait at table where there is no one to sit down at it, or stand behind a carriage and cry *Go on* with an air, when no lady listens and no carriage can be found, —

> "'Where the gilt chariot never marks the way,
> Where none learn Ombre, none e'er taste Bohea.'"

Mr. Robertson has received his money by now. If everybody was really and bonâ fide to use their fortunes with economy, what would become of his 120 pipes of wine and of his correspondence abroad? But he hopes to sell some to the sinecurists, I doubt not, while their valets and livery servants drink an inferior sort. Ah me! Government is a long and sometimes a tangled chain, but tearing but one rusty link will rather weaken than brighten it.

Veniamo ad altro, as Baretti used to say. Boswell and he were both of them treacherous inmates, but their books are very pretty, very interesting, and very well written.

The best writers are not the best friends, and the last character is more to be valued than the first by contemporaries; after fifty years, indeed, the others carry away all the applause.

Apropos, Madame D'Arblay is said to be writing a new work; and the " Pastor's Fireside," by Miss Porter, comes in for a large share of praise, after the " Tales of my Landlord." But my paper comes to an end, my candles burn down to the socket, my fire is gone almost out, and I have not yet said, though I hope you have felt, that everything will diminish before either absence or silence can lessen the regard of your obliged and sincere

H. L. PIOZZI.

To Sir James Fellowes.

Bath, 5 March, 1817.

WELL, my dear Sir, Salusbury came to his time, but is obliged to run away so, we have hardly had a moment for necessary chat. I rely on you to tell him what clothes he must wear, what fees he must pay, and to whom. As a prudent mortal, he would willingly have

escaped such costly titles : but I really do not think it
right to refuse honours from a sovereign when offered
them ; I am not yet so much a modern democrate.
" Stick to the crown, though it hang upon a thornbush,"
was old Sir William Wyndham's precept, and we have
heard none better. Mr. Dorset Fellowes is Mr. Salusbury ready-made friend; he will kindly — in intro-
ducing him to you — assist, dear Sir,

Your ever obliged and faithful

H. L. P.

To Sir James Fellowes.

Bath, Sunday, March 9th, 1817.

Your melancholy letter, my dear Sir, reminded me
of an autograph I once saw of Alexander Pope, saying
to Martha Blount: " My poor father died in my arms
this morning. If at such a moment I did not forget
you; assure yourself I never can.—A. P."

I felt something like the same consolation as she
must have done.

M—— is deeply affected . . . loses sleep. I have
not seen the D—— P——; everybody makes too sure;
we are all *such* hopers. Get —— well, and away for
Adbury, where pleasure, and fair weather, and what is
well worth both, agreeable entertainments, await you.

This season requires attention in you farmers, and
the times require attention from *you* as an English gentleman,— the character perhaps most to be respected of
any that Europe has in it.

Stocks rise every hour, but let us not for that reason over-hope ourselves; there are heavy clouds hanging about, and every nation has a right to expect storms: we have not yet had our share.

Farewell, my dear friend, and shew your superiority to disappointment as you have shewn it in a thousand instances to ill-fortune in other forms and shapes — acquiring every one's esteem, and the ever unrivalled regard and value of your obliged servant,

H. L. P.

To Sir James Fellowes.

Bath, Sunday, 20 March, 1817.

AT present we are close on Passion Week, a period forgotten in town, I believe, where a gay man once asked me whether Christmas Day was always on a Fryday? "because," said he, "they call it Good Fryday, don't they? and they neither dance nor play at cards." Such a question could not be asked in Spain or Italy. This moment Miss —— calls for my letter and expresses uneasiness about the dear D——r. I hope her affection magnifies the distress; but at our age we must break: and if the last tickets *do* linger in the wheel, why people will give more than their value for them, though often blanks at last.

These reflexions are forced on me by a visit from poor dear Mr. Chappelow, a friend of thirty years' standing, who comes here to take a last leave of poor

H. L. P.!

To Sir James Fellowes.

Begun Sunday, March 20, 1817.

I WAS going to write you a letter this morning, but Miss —— called, and I sent it away half written. My spirits have been much lowered by poor Mr. Chappelow's visit, but this is a season for mortification, and a stronger *memento mori*, saw I never.

Your dear father has sons and daughters round him, but my wretched old friend, a batchelor ecclesiastic, with nobody to tell him that he is getting superannuated, affords indeed a melancholy spectacle.

Mrs. Broadhead, too, dying in the Crescent *, plump and gay three months ago, now pale and wrinkled like one's white handkerchief after Mrs. Siddons' benefit; *mondo! mondanio!* as Baretti used to say.

Well! here's Monday, the first of Passion week, and I do hope the people's hunger for amusement will be suspended here till Easter holidays.

Pretty little Mrs. G., the doctor's wife, must go abroad, or die at home of weakness and atrophy. Parry's colossal form (tenacious of life) permits not his departure, but detains him here, helpless, hopeless, senseless, except to agonising pain; gout, stone, and palsey, upon one man. Dreadful! and suspended so (like Mahomet's tomb) between life and death.

No matter, those whose lives are longest forget what past in their maturer years, remembering best the early

* This lady is, I believe, living still.

days of youth. Mr. Chappelow, my superannuated visitant, recollects marrying Doctor Parry when he first took orders. Those whose date is shorter, laugh at the parts that are past. The boy despises the baby; the man contemns the boy; a philosopher scorns the man, and a Christian pities them all. When we approach the confines of immortality, however, the best is to look forward; for retrospection is but a blotted page to wiser and better folks than dear Sir James Fellowes's ever obliged and faithful

H. L. P.

To Sir James Fellowes.

Bath, Monday, 14 April, 1817.

I THANK you, my dear Sir, for your kind letter. You are very good-natured to think about my health, who am, as it appears, neither racked with pain, like our poor friend at T., nor panting with an asthma, like the dear Doctor, about whom I observe Miss —— to be visibly uneasy, though by no means well herself.

That we must either outlive those who are most valued by us, or go ourselves, and quit the stage to them, seems hard to remember, though the first lesson that we learn : what we fear to lose rises in value. Distance has such an effect, that even the apprehension produces consequences. " When you were near me," says Pope, " I only thought of you as a good neighbour; at a hundred miles from me, my fancy formed you beautiful; and now ! (they had crossed the seas remember) you are a goddess, and your little sister approaching to divinity." *

This was said in sport, but there is truth in most jests. We look on those approaching the banks of a river all must cross, with ten times the interest they excited when dancing in the meadow. Yet let them cross it once, and get fairly out of sight, how soon are they out of mind!

My proximity to the river's brink, all overcast with fog, and now and then disturbed by fume and vapour, shews me very imperfectly the schemes and monstrous projects of our time, and shews me them in disproportions too. They are not regularly formed gyants, like Polypheme, but one-eyed as he was; and weak, although gigantick, from being so badly put together.

The rise of our friends is unnatural, and " nothing now is, but what is not," according to Macbeth's opinion.

A gentleman far from here, who has large concern in the iron-works of a neighbouring county, called fifteen of his principal people together the other day, and told them he was no longer able to give them piece-work—such is the phrase—because his rents were so ill-paid; but he would present them with a pound note each every Monday morning, till they were to resume their old employment, as he wished might soon be the case for all their sakes. God bless your honour, was the immediate reply: with thanks and expressions

---

* " 'Tis distance lends enchantment to the view."—CAMPBELL.

of (as he believes) sincere attachment. They said, however, that the bargain could not be formally acceded to, till letters arrived from Manchester, but that they would wait on his honour the following Wednesday, and settle matters. Wednesday came, and so did the fifteen workmen, but with altered countenances. Friends had taught them not to be bamboozled, was their word ; so their employer might keep his money, and they would throw themselves upon the parish. A measure instantly adopted, to the distress of the parish, and triumph of their Manchester acquaintance!

So dry a season after a long season of wet, is good for the ground, I dare say; but we shall be all pulverized by and by, if no rain falls. I am already weary on 't, and feel apprehensive lest the haymaking should be hurt by an abundance of what we are now sighing for, &c.

H. L. P.

To Sir James Fellowes.

Bath, Fryday night, 16 May, 1817.

WELL, well! 'tis fine saying We will do this and we will do that when death is so near, saying, "No, you shall not," to us all. Poor Callan the upholsterer, my landlady in Westgate Street, went perfectly well to bed, called up her daughter at 4 o'clock, Mrs. Booth, told her she should die in half an hour, and kept her word to a second.

The corporation yesterday, all well and merry, marched down the South Parade in some silly procession, I know

not what, endeavoured to cross the river in the ferry-
boat, upset the machine, and sixteen of them were
drowned, at noonday, in sight of the walkers up and
down.   Mr. Marshall, curate of the abbey, 'scaped by
miracle, resolving to walk round and meet them, in spite
of their entreaties to make one of the frolickers.

A stranger thing never befell, because the river is so
shrunk by our long series of dry weather, I am sure
your brother Thomas could cross it on foot; and you
know there is a rope, too, which by some marvellous
fatality none of them clung to.

So there is no need of ice-islands to drown, or of
dreadful diseases to kill us, when it pleases God to call
either the great Alexander, or your little friend,

H. L. P.

To Sir James Fellowes.

Wednesday, 28 May, 1817.

MISS —— tells me, dear Sir, that she has room in
her letter to squeeze in a note from me; but what is to
be said in the note, who can tell?   We talk here of
the insurrection at Brazil, or of the girl that drowned
herself yesterday morning, or the ten times more wonderful tale of the Welsh girl, who returned by her own
good will to the house of a man who was proved seven
years before to have beaten and starved her almost to
death.   Oh! that beats all the stories that I ever heard
or told.

H. L. PIOZZI.

To Sir James Fellowes.

31 May, 1817.

It is very fine, my dear Sir, and I am well persuaded on 't, that your kindness for poor H. L. P. is not to be damped by climate, nor I hope diminished by distance. Yet there is no harm in the journeys being put off, though I should really like to hear what Dr. Whalley does mean by these improbable tales of starvation upon the continent.

I fancy his servants shut him up, and told him only what they wished him to hear.

The story of Eliza Davies is, however, most disgraceful to this land of liberty and opulence. If such atrocities can be committed in London, what may not happen in Russia or even in Portugal?

We have been all engaged in care for a girl who drowned herself in our canal here, but whose only cause of concern was her inability to squeeze some rich friend out of 500*l.*; he sent her 50*l.*, but that she scorned. What is come to the people? Lunacy? One would think so, to hear these wonders.

The Dean of Winchester's account of Bennet Langton coming to town some few years after the death of Dr. Johnson, and finding no house where he was even asked to dinner, was exceedingly comical. Mr. Wilberforce dismissed him with a cold " Adieu, dear Sir, I hope we shall meet in heaven!" How capricious is the public taste! I remember when to have Langton

at a man's house stamped him at once a literary character.*

Johnson's fame, meanwhile, lives even in the lightest
and slightest shreds of his wit and learning.

We have a caricature print here now of Sir John
Lade going through all the stages of profligate folly, and
drowning himself at last, with Dr. Johnson's verses beginning

> "Long expected one-and-twenty,
> Lingering year, at length is flown,"

written under, exactly as I printed them in his letters
to me, only I omitted the name, as a civility to the
family which showed me nothing but spite after Mr.
Thrale's death.

Well ! I will be prudent, and recover the bruises my
purse has suffered by sitting still as a mouse. Was I
once at Adbury, temptations to go further would be
irresistible, so I will take good advice instead of kind
invitation, and keep quiet.

A glass of Bath water before dinner, or half a glass of
Mr. Divie after†, will keep my inside tolerably good-
humoured, I hope, though dining from home is still
unpleasant to me, and *la bile* is my utter aversion,—

> "For that is bitter with a witness,
> And kinder souls delight in sweetness, &c."

Your good mother is recovering gradually but cer-

---

* The Earl of Norwich, who ranked as the wit of Charles the
First's court, was voted a bore at the court of Charles the Second.
† Divie Robertson was a wine merchant at Bath.

tainly. The dear Doctor is, as he terms himself, true heart of oak.

They are always the same true and partial friends to dear Sir James's ever obliged and faithful

H. L. P.

To Sir James Fellowes.

Bath, Thursday, 26 June, 1817.

I CANNOT sufficiently rejoyce, my dear Sir, or be half thankful enough for the intelligence your kind charming sister has this moment given me, of your resolution to run no further in chase of hot weather than the Queen's Drawing Room of this day. Poor Salusbury! I think if he escapes fever it is sufficient felicity. Such a journey in such a June! and the thermometer standing at 82° in my cool marble hall. I have the headache myself, caught perhaps by reading Mrs. Carter's letters, which tell of nothing else, and yet all our pale blue ladies here, are saying how fine they are. Come, there is one good thing in them: she says to Mrs. Montague:—

" Your scheme of omitting the house, and improving the plantations, is founded on a motive equally good and wise. Time would sink the proudest palace you could raise, into ruins; but eternity will secure to you the wealth which is applied in the encouragement of honest industry and relief of distress."

I like the intention of the sentence here quoted, excessively; but 'tis awkwardly expressed, because masons and bricklayers want money and encouragement as much as gardeners and planters, no doubt; yet am I all of her mind, to prefer improvements on land, rather than sink sums which may be wanted, in building houses and stables, which never repay the owner and too often remain for ages —

> " Remnants of things that have pass'd away,
>   Fragments of stone — rear'd by creatures of clay."

Poor old Lleweney Hall! pulled down after standing 1000 years in possession of the Salusburys, made over to Lord Kirkwall's father in the last century, and now demolished by fine Mr. Hughes, of the Parys Mountain, would cure any one of pride in houses, or in ancestry.

Land is the only thing which can pretend to duration, though you see our funds keep up very finely, 'spite of ill-willers; and what a piece of work has been made with these housebreakers, and street ruffians, to convert them into gentlemen, and try them for high treason!* The Dean of Winchester says, one of the jury was penny collector to Lord C.

Here is heavenly weather, however, and if anything can put or keep people in good humour with those above them, a copious harvest is of all most likely.

You will see my fair daughters at the Drawing Room, of course. They hurried home for it I fancy, for S. has written to me, expressing her regrets at leaving

* The Thistlewood conspirators.

Paris, " where ladies have nothing to do with *ménage de famille*, and can entertain themselves their own way." Yet I believe she has, of all women, least to regret on that side her head.

> " Like a City wife or a beauty,
>   She has flutter'd life away ;
> She has known no other duty,
>   But to dress, eat, drink, and play."

This for your privacy — as Gloster says.

Ah dear Sir! what a loss I should have had by your journey to the Continent. I shall now not care a straw about missing Adbury this year, for there Adbury stands, and there resides its master; and like the Irish lover, who says, " Arrah ¦my dear Sheelah, (or Shalah)! If I was once within forty miles of you, I would never desire to be nearer you in all my life, and still in the same little island," when he was transported to Botany Bay.

Your dear father and mother are so well and so happy at Sidmouth, they half persuade me to go and see them there; and when all debts are paid, the 500*l.* bought in again, which I sold out in March, and a certain sum *dans la poche,* who knows what may be done by dear Sir James Fellowes's ever obliged and grateful

H. L. PIOZZI.

Miss Fellowes assures me this stuff shall cost you nothing, or you should have had more on't at least, by way of making out the bargain; did you care about Caraboo?

To Sir James Fellowes.

Bath, 1 July, 1817.

No, my dear Sir, I will not stir from home till after the 25th of July, which day made me happy thirty-three years ago, after the suffering so many sorrows, and here will I keep its beloved anniversary, always remembering

> " St. James's Church and St. James's Day,
> And good Mr. James that gave me away."

Adbury will be beautiful the last week of my favourite month, and London will be empty the first week of August, so that will just suit me; for the small shot, as we used to call trifling debts, will be all discharged by then; my 500*l*. brought back again into the three per cent. consols, and myself at liberty to come and thank Sir James for his kindly repeated invitations.

The bustle we made about Caraboo * was very comical indeed. Those who thought her an impostor dared not say so. Such was the persuasion of the people to believe her a decided Oriental, though she never had the skill to write her odd characters in the Eastern manner, but beginning from the left hand clearly proved herself a novice, though she had made up a good alphabet enough, composed of Persic, Arabic, and Hebrew letters. I put my opinion of her into bad verses, as you shall see, more spiteful to Murray, who refused my book than worth your reading for any other merit; but if you

---

* A woman of bad character, who passed herself off at Bath and Bristol as Caraboo, Princess of Jarasu.

have not seen the new poem, you will not laugh as I
wish you to do : —

Our bright maid of Bristol by all men admired,
Till ev'n admiration itself grows half tired;
While praying, or swearing, or swimming, or fencing,
All merits in one happy female condensing;
The more I examine his wonderful book,
The more I'm persuaded she's Moore's Lallah Rookh.
In her black cotton shawl which no heart can resist,
While the morn, like her character, melts into mist,
Addressing old Titan with tender devotion,*
Or shrinking averse from the treacherous ocean;
The ship which produced her, the swain who forsook,
All bring to my memory Moore's Lallah Rookh.
Should Murray once wind her, no pelf would he spare,
Indulging her taste in each Turkish bazaar;
The Mukratoo rabble † oh how he would scare 'em!
And long live the lady, the light of his haram!
The rich feast of roses he knows how to cook,
Who gave three thousand pounds for Moore's fam'd
    " Lallah Rookh."

My dear Sir James will perceive that his old friend
has not forgotten her old follies,

    " Ev'n in our ashes live their wonted fires,"

as Gray says, and we go on to the last, jogging in the
same dusty road.

  * Caraboo pretended to worship the sun.
  † If a man offered to touch her she cried out, Muckratoo.

Apropos, I don't believe London will be empty enough for me till September. I will not go to encounter invitations and parties on the one hand, slights and cold looks on the other. Everybody shall be away when I present myself at Blake's Hotel, unless, perhaps, poor Lady Kirkwall; and if she can get her annuity paid, she will put herself in some cool place, I hope, after such heating work of both body and mind.

After all, you and your family are safe in Hampshire, and summer is before us. This hay weather is bad indeed; and I did think we waited too long for the rain; we shall now have more than we want. *S'intende acqua*, says the Italian gardener, who had been praying for rain, *ma non tempesta*.

We hear that the lady, whose good-nature the little gipsey imposed upon, is so struck with her ingenuity, that she protests they shall never part again. By the same rule, Rundell and Bridge ought to make the swindler, who cheated them of 24,000*l.* the other day, head clerk of their house, if they can catch him.

Would you laugh to see me in a white hat and ribbands! The black * was wholly insupportable during the violent heats, and thunder always gives me a sullen headache.

Con mille rispetti. Addio.

Yours ever truly attached,

H. L. P.

* She never left off her black silk dress after the death of Piozzi.

To *Sir James Fellowes.*

Blake's Hotel, 23rd Aug. 1817.

LONDON is most embellished since I saw it last, but the Regent's Park disappoints me: had it been as I fancied, a place appropriated to the Regent, with rangers, &c., the boundaries of London northward would have been ascertained, and a beautiful spot, like Hyde Park, have contributed to the health and ornament of the metropolis; but buildings there are, it seems, hourly increasing, and it will end in an irregular square at last, of which there are enough already. The bridges are very fine, and will make my old habitation, Southwark, a gay place in due time, I dare say.

Here is a little sunshine after the rain, and the pale white-faced wheat will be got in somehow. But no golden ears, no rich coloured grain imbrowned the views in Berkshire, as I came along. The " cold unripened beauties of the North " must have a melancholy appearance to foreigners from warm climates, to whom the verdure of fields and snugness of comfortable cottages would make this year but broken amends, I am confident.

Can you tell what's good for the bite of a dead viper's tooth.* Oyl, I trust, and emollients; yet 'tis a slow remedy. I feel ashamed to think how much the posthumous poyson has disturbed me. Write a word of consolation, and Adieu.

* Alluding to Beloe.

P 2

To Sir James Fellowes.

Blake's Hotel, 29 August, 1817.

I HAVE been living with poor dear Lady K—— and her mother; up to their very eyes in love and law, distressed as nothing human ever was distressed, and will I suppose (in Dr. Johnson's phrase) be at last delivered as nothing human ever was delivered. Siddons and they are the only people I have seen, but the things are charming, and the places so improved that, without hyperbole, I actually passed through Southwark — the borough I canvassed three times, and inhabited thirteen years—without knowing where they had carried me any more than if I had been found in Ispahan.

The gas-lights, and steam-boats, and new bridges are all incomparable, and will serve us for chat at the castle, when your Honour has counted your money, the grand pacifier of all quarrels, although the fountain whence spring so many disputes. But adieu! I must dress to dine what I call out of town, the top-house in Baker Street.* Make my best regards and sincerest good wishes acceptable to Lady F——, and believe me hers and yours while

H. L. P.

To Sir James Fellowes.

Bath, 3 September, 1817.

JOY to my dear Sir James Fellowes. *Mil años y mas*, and through the whole thousand, friends to value him no less than I do.

The cock and hens will be beforehand with me, how-

* At Mrs. Siddons'.

ever, in my congratulations; Smith assures me they are
beautiful and healthy; and were to be on their journey
yesterday; when I concluded mine. We had lovely
weather; a negative day as I call it,—no sun, no rain, no
wind, no dust. Driving through the Devizes, I recollected an old epigram which I wrote there, some centuries ago, when Sir Fletcher Norton was —— Oh, but I
dare say 'tis in a blank leaf of your " Wraxall;" if it is
not, you shall have it another day.* Meanwhile, as sublime effusions are the fashion, what think you of my
verses lamenting the fate of my own sisterhood? when
Bagshot, Hownslow, &c. were first taken into cultivation, and beginning :—

Goosey! goosey! gander!
Whither will you wander
When your commons all are gone,
That you plum'd yourselves upon?
Sure I think they'll leave no places
Where to wash our feathery faces,
All the world's become our foes
From this hurry to enclose.
Could a ray of hope spring from one's
Interest in the House of Commons,
I'd exhaust my last poor quill
To avert th' impending ill.
But the troop of Foxites there
Make the mournful goose despair:
And for t' others there's no chance,
While they rate their geese as swans.

* See Vol. I. p. 330.

P 3

But you are tired of this stuff, or at least I am : the harvest is worth talking about, and a very good harvest I now believe it will be.   But to see haymaking, wheat carrying, and barley full ripe, all at once, is new ; so far as I have looked on life, and the staff of life.   One newly-turned up field exhibited shocks of corn on one side of it, manure on the other, the plough at work in the middle.   A curious combination !

The Mount at Marlborough was too dewy in the morning, and it was quite dark when I got in over night, we had chatted so long, and so comfortably : it would have been a famous thing to have run up a hill which I ran up in the year 1750, the maid calling after me, "Miss! don't you jump over the hedges."   Cardinal du Perron, you know, did purchase an estate for double the money another man would have given, because he leaped a famous leap on those grounds seventy years before : I did not, however, understand that he could have leaped it again. *

Miss Williams is in trouble; her beau very ill indeed, and keeps bed; Mr. Cam attending him : by her odd account it seems Hæmorrhoids, Hæmorrhage, or some undescribable mischief.   She is zealous, however, about your dairy, &c.   My description of it set all her head to work.   I have friends here going to Ireland : it would make your very ducks and drakes laugh to see her diligence (ill-employed) in persuading me to instruct

* The Archbishop of Armagh, meeting the Earl of Carhampton, boasted that his legs carried him as well as ever, "Ay, my Lord, but not to the same places."

them which way they should go; for cheapest, best, &c. How can she multiply her cares so!! But she would think us no less absurd, for making enquiries now, A. D. 1817, concerning the Ægyptian Mary, who died in the desart beyond Jordan in the year 430: having never seen a human face for forty-seven years, living on raw roots and herbage, with no change of clothing from the dress she wore at the moment her conversion took place. She was then a notorious profligate, yet wished to attend the festival of Fête Dieu, but felt herself supernaturally repelled by the pressure of an unseen hand, and a voice crying Unworthy Mary. She retired, so warned, from the cathedral, resolved to break off all connection with a world she had behaved so ill in, and after making solemn vows of penitence, tried the church door again, which opened to her of its own accord. This apparent approval of Heaven sent Mary to perpetual solitude and sorrow: to alleviate which in her last moments, Zosimus the hermit was sent to administer the last consolation a Christian can receive. She took the eucharist though speechless from exhaustion, and when the hermit came next day, he found only a lifeless corpse, with the pathetic words "Poor Mary" traced in the burning sand. Has not Murillo done the story justice? Better, oh, better far, than the poor quill of yours and Lady Fellowes's ever,

H. L. P.*

---

* Mrs. Piozzi, on her return to Bath from Adbury, where she had paid us a visit, having admired my fine picture by Murillo, sent me the above account, taken from the Popish legend.—*J. F.*

To Sir James Fellowes.

Bath, September 8, 1817.

WHAT an unreasonable friend is dear Sir James Fellowes! as unreasonable as partial, I think; and that is enough. On the same day that we obtain attestations of all the Tales told in the "Golden Legend," and that will not be soon, he may expect another strange letter, just like the last, from his much obliged H. L. P. My story is abridged from a French abridgment of the old book. Authority enough, as it is not only to be found in "L'Advocat's Biography," but in Danet's "Account of Christian Antiquities." I would not, however, swear to the truth of any tale told in the dark ages. The world sees most visions (says Fuller) when she is most blind, and the ophthalmia of those days, inflamed by persecution on the one hand, and hope of immediate beatitude on the other, presented objects of strange distortion doubtless; while the difficulty of committing anything to paper, multiplied and magnified every deviation into a miracle. Such are the accounts religiously believed by Romanists of St. Francis retiring to the desart, making himself a wife of snow, &c. and while under these dreadful mortifications, receiving in vision from our crucified Saviour's own immediate touch — a separate mark or stigma, is it not? upon each hand and foot. Your picture seems as if stretching round to touch the side of the saint as I remember, and 'tis related how his wounds dropt blood, though later than Ægyptian Mary's legend by nearly seven centuries.

Alas! the while: that such delusions were thought necessary to prop our faith, or propagate Christianity brought down from heaven by the God of Truth himself. Romanism, however, cannot, even now, divest itself of love for pious frauds, and hatred to all sects except their own. See how they are working themselves into power! reminding one of the old fable in our babies' books: where the poor axe lies helpless in the wood, lamenting his incapacity to serve his friends or get his own living, for want of a handle, and you (says he) cruel creatures! wont give me even a twig. After a long time spent in such intreaties, one of the young ash, a sapling, takes compassion, "and here, my lad," he cries, "thou shalt have this branch of mine, make thee a handle;" he does so, says the fable, and cuts down the whole grove. What else did he want it for?

Ah! old Sir Fletcher Norton, that I wrote the epigram upon, was no sapling; no truly, he was made of sterner stuff. But the present state of things has spoiled my epigram, like that which was drowned (as Boswell said) when the grand piece of water was made at Blenheim, and

"The arch, the height of his ambition shows,
The stream, an emblem of his bounty flows,"

was no longer a joke.

And now here is just such a letter as the last; and in yours a confirmation of my own just surprize at your talk of partridge shooting, when such loads of corn were yet unhoused. Soon, however,

> " Shall the staunch pointer brave the sultry heat,
>   And tread the stubble with unfeeling feet."

And till then you must carefully preserve your album
of fowls immaculate.   The ginger wing will not I hope
be hereditary: if it is, I shall get somebody to thrust
Mr. Kenrick down the throat of his own alligator, as
they do infants in China.   The weather is truly delightful, and good for workmen at home, as for harvest
men abroad.   Enjoy it, dear Sir, and never forget Lady
Fellowes's and your own true servant,

H. L. P.

Do you recollect the little Simon Paap, a dwarf whom
you and I went to see, and he said he would have the
honour to drink a bottle with Sir James Fellowes, comically enough? and produced a tiny vial out of his
pocket that he called his pocket pistol?   He is here
now, and the people go to see him.   Bessy Bell was
glad to shake hands with her handsome husband, I
doubt not: but as I flatter myself she has still some
regard for her poor mistress, I shall beg you will not
withdraw yours from her.

Farewell! and present me properly to Lady Fellowes.
I am glad she likes my notion of the fine Murillo.   She
will be much amused with Caraboo.

To Sir James Fellowes.

Bath, September 25, 1817.

How kind the —— have been! never forgetting their
little friend at No. 8, but sending me crouted cream, &c.

They thought a little soothing would do me good, I suppose, after Mr. Beloe's venomous attack.

No matter; here is a copious and beautiful harvest, and many happy hearts in consequence, Salusbury's beyond all. I don't know when I can recollect the barley in Wales housed by the last week in September, and we are painting, and repairing, and emulating London, all we can, nothing doubtful but that the second and third cities of England will soon follow the first, being paved with iron and lighted with air.

Mrs. Mostyn, for whom I was, as you know, anxious, is said to be well, and disposed for a journey to Italy. Those who return from thence say the English are in high favour, owing chiefly to Lord Exmouth, whose liberation of Catholic slaves at Algiers struck the Roman people as an act worthy Christians, and scarce to be credited of British heretics.

Mr. Wanzey tells me a thing scarcely to be credited of Romish bigots; no less than that the Protestants have hired an apartment near the Colonna Trajana; where our English liturgy is read every Sunday by some of the numerous clergymen belonging to our Church, who are loitering about that city unprohibited, unnoticed, unoffended.* Such connivance who could have hoped for in 1785? Mr. W—— says that our country-

---

* James Smith used to tell a story, on the authority of Sir George Beaumont, that the English applied to the Pope to bless a cemetery so that they might lie in *consecrated* ground, and that his Holiness replied, all he could do for them was to *curse* any spot they might select for the purpose, so that they might lie in *desecrated* ground.

men spend 1000*l.* per diem in Italy; in Rome only, if I am not mistaken.

How good and wise, meanwhile, is ——, staying at his own beautiful house, and embellishing it every hour.

I have seen the lyons old and young, but was surprised to witness the oddity of a female setting-dog suckling her young enemies. The whelp is not half as tame as some cubs shown at Bath last year, that played with the children of the town and with one another just like kittens. I pulled those about myself, but this little rascal was surly.

Waterloo Panorama, however, and the learned Italian dog Manito, must be visited. I think next week will have exhibited all the wonders London can produce at this time of year, and then my horses' heads will turn homewards on the 1st day of the new month, September.

To Sir James Fellowes.

Bath, 8 October, 1817.

Don't buy the book, dear Sir.* That method only propagates the mischief. You know me too well not to believe me completely callous to literary abuse. But this man (who I never saw but once in my life, eighteen years ago) tells the public that Mr. Piozzi pulled down

---

* The Sexagenarian, by Beloe. His statement, false in every particular, more than quadruples her Welsh rent-roll.

my old family seat at Bachygraig, and that when he was dead I searched the Alps for a young mountaineer to inherit my estate of 4000*l.* per annum. Now, in the first place, Mr. Piozzi paid off a mortgage that was on the Welsh estate with 7000*l.* of his own money, not mine. He then repaired and beautified old Bachygraig at a great expense, rebuilt and pewed the church, made a fine vault for my ancestors, and built Brynbella to live in, because the family mansion lay down low by the river side.

He begged my name for his brother's son, and when the French invaded Italy, sent for him hither, an infant unable to walk or talk; lived till the lad was fourteen years old, and died, never naming him in his will, but leaving all to me. Why, I must have been worse than Mr. Beloe himself, to do any otherwise than I have done.

Yes, yes, when people will talk of what they know nothing about, see what nonsense follows.

To Sir James Fellowes.

Bath, Wednesday, 6 November, 1817.

THE Queen has driven us all completely distracted; such a bustle Bath never witnessed before. She drinks at the pump-room, purposes going to say her prayers at the Abbey Church, and a box is making up for her at the theatre.

Your S——l W——'s life appears to affect the D——r more than I hoped it would. Women bear crosses

better than men do, but they bear surprises worse.
Give me time, and I'll go gravely up to the guillotine;
but set me down suddenly within view of a battle, I
shall be a corpse before the first fire is over through
fear, whilst my footman shall feel animation from the
scene, and long to make one in the sport.

> " Heres, si scires unum tua tempora mensem ;
>   Ut rides dum sit forsitan una dies,"

was said to men who always count upon an escape;
women provide for certainties as well as they know how.

But here's my translation, which probably I have
shewn you long ago, yet I somehow think not either:

> If you thought you should live but a month, how you'd cry,
> Yet you laugh though you know you to-morrow may die.

Here are worse pens, and papers, and handwriting
than those I am always most happy to see, but the post
shall not pass my door with his bell whilst I go can-
vassing for franks; no, indeed, and my health is quite,
in the matron phrase, as well as can be expected. So
adieu, and believe me yours faithfully,

H. L. P.

To Sir James Fellowes.

Bath, Fryday, 28 November, 1817.

Mr. —— brought me so kind a message begging a
letter, that I can't help complying.

Everybody's spirits are mending on our Queen's return. The people are running up and down again ; and

those who have any names — many, too, of those who have none—leave them at her Majesty's door.

To a mere spectator the appearance of things is dismal. The burst of grief * is, however, pretty well gone by; but if it was a proof of our virtue, as Mr. Grinfield said it was, why so let it be accounted.

His assertion, indeed, that no profligate country ever regrets a prince or princess for their moral qualities, is more pleasing than strictly true. When was ancient Rome more sunk in vice than when all its inhabitants poured forth to meet and lament over the ashes of Britannicus! Their theatres about that time, too, did certainly exhibit *ballets d'actions* equal to our own; and by the accounts I hear of Covent Garden and its gay *salon,* we are even trying to go beyond them if possible.

The description brought me by a friend was so eloquent it reminded me of Milton's devils building and lighting up with gas their pandemonium : —-

> " Nigh on the plain in many cells prepar'd
> That underneath had veins of liquid fire
> Sluic'd from the lake ; mechanic multitudes
> With wondrous art founded the massy ore,
> Severing each kind, and scummed the bullion dross.
> Others as soon had formed within the ground
> A various mould, and from the boiling cells
> By strange conveyance fill'd each hollow nook.
> Till sudden from the soil a fabric huge
> Rose like an exhalation. From the roof

* Occasioned by the death of the Princess Charlotte.

Pendent by subtle magic many a row
Of starry lamps and blazing cussets, fed
With naphtha and asphaltus, yielded light
As from a sky."*

When I repeated the lines, he swore that Milton had
invented the gas-lights, and given the first draught of
our grand theatres in London.

This letter I shall take to ——, so that they may
put it in their pockets with a heavy load of compliments
and offers of service from Sir James's oldest friend,

H. L. P.

To Sir James Fellowes.

Bath, Monday, 15 December, 1817.

DR. GRAY, whose name and character you know,
laments the loss of his mother, because, says he, she
died so unexpectedly,—at ninety-one years old! He
had left her in high health and spirits but three weeks
before. Such is this world, its inhabitants, and their
ideas. He has sent me his Connexions, and two sermons
on the princess's death, protesting that he will or will
not publish them as I approve or condemn. The subject
is not treated in a commonplace manner, you may be
sure, when touched by his hand. Poor princess! she
has really stood like an Academy figure to be viewed in
various lights. The shadows in his sketch are eminently
deep and broad, an impressive Rembrandt.

Veniamo ad altro. That one friend should send me

---

* Paradise Lost, book i. The quotation is singularly happy,
and is one among many instances of her knowledge and readiness.

sermons to criticise, while the theatrical folks try to court me out of an epilogue, does look as if they thought I was not quite superannuated.

Of the clusters in the Pump-Room, who swarm round Queen Caroline as if she were actually the queen bee, courtiers must give you an account: of the ecclesiastical history you will soon hear a great deal, but I'm not sure whether it will interest you. Everybody writing at the same time on the same subject does no harm. The same ideas may be delivered out with attractions that may lure minds of a different make; and you will kindly rejoyce that I came out alive from the Octagon Chapel, where Ryder, Bishop of Glo'ster, preached in behalf of the missionaries to a crowd such as my long life never witnessed; we were packed like seeds in a sun-flower.

At the Guildhall two days after, when pious contributors were expected to come and applaud, Archdeacon Thomas suddenly appeared, and protested against the meeting as schismatical. So he was hissed home by the serious Christians, Evangelicals as they sometimes call themselves,—half the population of Bath at any rate,—and his friends felt uneasy; till yesterday the Duke of Clarence, some say the Queen, some say both, consoled him by their particular notice. All which you will learn better from Colonel C——, who, for ought I know, presides at the presentations.

Adieu, dear Sir, with assurances of my being ever gratefully and faithfully your obliged

H. L. P.

To Sir James Fellowes.

Bath, 23 January, 1818.

WHEN and in what year will the women find out that company makes one gay only as it brings out that gayety which was in the heart before? A great coat makes a man warm, I suppose, not by virtue of any warmth in the coat, but as it keeps the natural heat of the body from flying away. Yet parties are all the rage, and I shall have one next week, and put my wisdom to sleep the while.

Doctor Gibbes has been very good to me, very kind and attentive. Illness commonly catches me by the throat, you know, and makes a mute of me for a while, punishing the peccant part. In a few years those things will be made easy: Miss McEvoy sees with her finger tips, and Miss Somebody* embroiders with her shoulder and elbow; no need of hands and arms for the old purposes, say the improvers of the world. Have you read " Frankenstein or the Modern Prometheus?" I have never seen such an audacious, and I might add, such an ingenious, piece of impiety. But Faber says, you know, that the world is to end in 1866; so the old gentleman below stairs must work double tides for these next fifty years, and he has a good assistant in Mr. Hone, who is surely well paid for his work.

Meanwhile the virtuous few, as it is the fashion to call them, are instructing the poor, and keeping schools for young people in the country. Lady Williams writes me word that one of her sisters, a managing woman,

* Miss Biffin.

who is in the habit of looking into her own affairs,
took one of these instructed maidens for her cook three
weeks ago. The dinners did well enough, and she went
into her kitchen to say so one morning; when the
whole family seemed collected round and expressing
such attention in their gaping countenances, the door
opened unawares to them all; and " enter the King and
Laertes," cried the cook, in an attitude of recitation, her
back towards the lady, whose only difficulty was to say,
who was most astonished? Well, dear Sir! here is a
world of nonsensical babble such as you used to like,
and when you go to London (if you *do* go) you must
make me amends, and tell me all about the succession,
after it has been well contested in the House of Parliament. But we shall meet before then at dear No. 13,
and I shall see Lady Fellowes in her new character of
nurse-a-baby, and we shall have a full table and a merry
day; fine weather of course *this* year, in which even
the North Pole is become passable, and everything
cheerful may be expected, when such mountains of ice
have been thawed I think. So adieu! and continue to
be the kind and partial friend, though you will not be
the correspondent, of your obliged and faithful servant,

H. L. P.

To Sir James Fellowes.

Bath, Monday, 2 March, 1818.

THE best joke going here is about the man who
killed his wife the other day: they printed his name

Haitch, if you remember, but after he had cut his own throat, they wrote him down Mr. Aitch: no wonder, for when the windpipe was divided, you know, how could he retain his Aspirate?

St. David's Day has been a rough one, and your brother Dorset forces me on the reflection that it was a Saturday's moon. But what reflections or what conjectures can they form who shall lose time and space — at least the old-fashioned methods of reckoning them — by being under the pole, seeing the sun always at the same altitude, finding neither east nor west, neither latitude nor longitude, contemplating their own figures represented as in a mirror on the opposing cloud, and viewing their old acquaintance the rainbow no longer an arch but a circle?

Will they come home pretending not to have shuddered at such appearances? and will they feel more terror of being titter'd at for speaking of such things as extraordinary? — Oh yes, I dare say they will, — than wonder at the strange phenomena! There was a time in my life when I would have been happy to have gone and come back safe as a cabbin boy rather than not make one in such an expedition; and am now actually eager to hear of their setting out, that I may have some chance of hailing their happy return. Meanwhile my health is not to be complained of; but whenever I catch cold, my eyes suffer somewhat unusually.

This stuff is written with one candle and a green shade over it, which makes me incline to be sullen, and say what vile pens these are, when, perhaps, 'tis one of the well deserved warnings knocking at the door of dear Sir J. F.'s faithful and grateful servant,

H. L. P.

To Sir James Fellowes.

Bath, 17 March, 1818.

I AM much flattered, my dear Sir, by the fault you find with my letter being too short. Yet I'm disposed not to lengthen this unreasonably, for fear your mind should be engaged when it arrives. May that engagement prove prosperous! and let me make haste to tell you what happened to me the other day, lest you should not have leisure to laugh at it. Our Regent having sent for specimens of curious marbles to the north coast of Africa, Mr. Smith has discovered — not the marbles (one never finds what one is looking for), but a better thing, — the possibility of getting at the long sought for city, on the Zaire or Congo River, which they have tried so vainly to bring to light.

I who heard of this discovery in the morning, said hastily to Captain Digby, who sate next me, "So Tombuctoo is found at last!" "Ah, ah!" says a man on the other side me, — "what was that fellow hiding for? Forgery, I suppose; and what names those scoundrels give one another with their slang — Tom Buckle to!"

Well! and there is a ship disinterred (to use a fashionable phrase and not a bad one); for the ship has been buried in the earth many centuries no doubt,

forty miles from the nearest sea, somewhere in Caff-
raria. *Toujours l'Afrique* (say Frenchmen), *nous
aurons donc de la fricassée* (*l'Afrique assez*); but
those who are not in jest are of opinion that the Cape
of Good Hope was once detatched from the continent,
an island like Terra del Fuego at Cape Horn.

"Thus do men run to and fro, and knowledge is
much increased," as, says the Prophet Daniel, it will be,
when this world is near its conclusion. I know not
how far distant that event may be, but every thing is
doing, and everything is happening, that we are told
will happen, and that we are sure will be done, in the
concluding centuries of terrestrial existence. Yet people
are in such haste to accelerate their own perdition,
that a clergyman has hanged himself at the Castle
and Ball this morning, — I don't know his name; and
if I did, your brother D. knows that "The Wonder, or
A Woman keeps a Secret," has been performed with
success at No. 8, Gay Street, within this last fortnight.
So adieu, dear Sir, and write oftener, if the letter
only contains the words — Steady and all well.

The foreigners say we English ruin the uniformity of
our handwriting by taking a new pen every tenth line.
I say, the not doing it every time you turn the paper,
makes one's letter look like a masqued figure of day and
night. This is written in the dark. Farewell and be
happy as is wished you by your ever, &c.,

                                                  H. L. P.

To Sir James Fellowes.

Bath, 21 March, 1818.

Tho' my muse is grown old,
And her life blood all cold,
    Still trembling from any surprise a ;
Warm congratulation,
With true admiration,
    Must welcome our pretty Eliza.

Excuse this nonsense: my head is full of the lauda-
num I took last night, more perhaps from fear than
from feel of the same nephritic affection that made me
miserable this time last year. The poppy, however,
which nature sows amongst the corn to show us that
sleep is as necessary as bread, did its duty, and here
am I, better than when R——— saw me lying on the
couch yesterday evening pretty late, when he brought
me the happy news — Adieu, dear Sir. God bless you
and yours, prays most fervently, Your

H. L. P

To Sir James Fellowes.

Bath, April, 1818.

WHILST I was trying to reconcile myself to the uneasy state of being wholly forgotten by dear Sir J. F.,
I met his excellent father in Collins's Library, looking
wonderfully well; but saying you had toothache and
faceache, and I don't know what beside. So I resolved
to write you a long letter as the only opiate which cannot injure the nerves.

Q 4

And now shall it be books or people that we talk about? Of books, let us both begin and end with Gisborne's new publication upon Natural Theology, a tiny work, but replete with good sense, sound learning, and pious reflections. I shall buy and perhaps interleave it, apropos to poor me and my quondam possessions. You see Doctor Burney, who purchased his father's portrait and dear Garrick's at my sale, now drops down dead, and the library, pictures, &c. are purchased (if my information is correct) by the British Museum!

When will the ladies be more or less strict in their manner of dressing? A genteel young clergyman in our Upper Crescent told his mamma, about ten days ago, that he had lost his heart to pretty Miss Prideaux, and that he must absolutely marry her or die! La chère mère of course replied gravely, " My dear, you have not been acquainted with the lady above a fortnight, let me recommend it to you to see more of her." " More of her ! " exclaims the lad ; " why, I have seen down to the fifth rib on each side already."

Will this story help to cure the toothache ? It will serve to convince Captain J. F. and yourself, that as you have always acknowledged the British belles to *exceed* those of every other nation, you may now say, with truth, that they *outstrip* them.

I am very sorry to see the death of Sir Richard Musgrave in the papers. He was much my admirer forty years ago, and what was more to his credit by half, he wrote the History of the Irish Rebellion and all its horrors, a work one word of which has never yet been contradicted.* It will now obtain its due celebrity I hope, and, indeed, it ought to grace the library of your lovely country seat. Shall you go thither soon? The swallows and cuckoos will meet you in May, and I really expect a hot baking summer after all this soaking rain. Warm weather would give us a famous harvest, and your children will be delighted with the butterflies before they leave our land.

Salusbury says I must come to Brynbella and see his young plantations — animal and vegetable — next July; and if health goes no worse than it has been, I shall just hope to be no nuisance,--a difficult matter, the difference in his lady's age from mine considered. The babies will be interesting at any rate. We have a nest of babies here, — females all, I think, — to whom our old friend Matilda Hook was a complete nothing: the eldest, a small creature, taking off Mr. Kean in Shylock and King Richard, convulses every audience with delight. I am going this evening, Saturday, 25th, and shall give you an account when I come home, and then you will have a long letter instead of a good one.

Well, dear Sir! here am I come home, after being more astonished than delighted. Clara (Fisher), who played Richard III., did it extremely well. She is just such a little thing as Simon Paap, the dwarf, that you and I went to see, and I daresay is a dwarf; but 'tis an amusing exhibition upon the whole. If you have seen

---

* On the contrary, it is considered a very one-sided production.

the children in London, however, where the size of the
house and the actors are so contrasted, the effect must
be twice as powerful, and nothing remains to be said
on the subject by your tedious correspondent and
affectionate, &c.

H. L. P.

To Sir James Fellowes.

6 May, 1818.

I SHALL be glad when the modish world permits you
to exchange the sight of emerald trinkets for that of
green fields, and lapis lazuli tables for a clear blue
sky.

I grieve for Bullock, however, who first found out the
quarry of Verd antique marble in our county of Anglesea.   Apropos, that little island has no little to
boast: three times has she ruled over the three kingdoms of nature.   Once when Druidic superstition swelled
every sea breeze with her howlings, and Mona's thickly-
planted woods covered her cromlechs from the sight of
Agricola.   Once again, when destruction had laid her
plains bare of timber; herds of black cattle feeding on
the mountains, supplied the London markets for more
than five centuries; and are mentioned in some of the
coronation feasts.   The present day, by this dear Bullock's ingenuity, discovered treasures of marble in her
rocky bosom, and exhibits specimens of Ægyptian green
not to be surpassed by anything which antiquity has
bequeathed us.

I was ranting on in the same strain before Miss
W—— when she exclaimed: " Ah ! roast him ; is that
odious Bullock dead at last, that cheated my brother,
Sir John, giving him 500*l.* for a bit of land, that to be
sure *we* thought not worth 50*l.* but which that fellow
knew contained these blocks of green stone, dyed by
the copper,—nothing else in the world." Well ! if it was
so, Anglesea is still the queen of mineral nature, in
right of her mines. Venus, too, is she not ? Sprung
from the sea, and showing her brazen face in every part
of the world.

Sir Joseph Banks will consider Bullock as a loss to
all students in natural history. I am glad you attend
his Sunday nights: they used to be delightful ; and I
hope he does not grow too much enfeebled by age, but
makes them still worth your care.

You used to say how I preached the end of the world,
but here was a learned Dr. Hales stood up in our pulpit
at Lama, last Sunday, and said sixty-two years more
would complete its duration. This was, in the modern
phrase, committing himself, and the laughers all stuffed
their handkerchiefs into their mouths, and the man
went on explaining his calculation and minding them
ne'er a whit.

The actors are more easily abashed ; Mr. Young
looked full of distress when he saw Lady St—— tit-
tering in the stage box at his well played Zanga, and
the beautiful girls, her daughters, counterfeiting sleep.
But derision is a thing no powers, except those of piety,
can endure. At her approach, wit darkens, and, as

Milton says of Eve, in her presence, Wisdom's self loses discountenanced, and like Folly shews.

Those large fields of ice starve the people's hearts, and they think insensibility a merit, I suppose. Distinction it is not, for they all do it.

I did not English, or rather Anglicise, any of the mottoes, but have been long of your mind, that G. H. Glasse's is the best. He was an extraordinary man, " le galant le plus pedant, et le pedant le plus galant, qu'on puisse voir." Science, which acted as a sceptre in the hand of Johnson, and was used as a club by Dr. Parr, became a lady's fan when played with by George Henry Glasse. I wish you had known them all three that you might applaud the fancy. You often do approve the odd fancies of your truly attached

H. L. P.

To Sir James Fellowes.

Bath, 20 May, 1818.

My dear Sir James Fellowes's last letter was so long and so kind, that I could wish for another chat with him ; did not the idea intrude of his being all engaged with these quality weddings, and that he would wish my large sheet of paper, perhaps, back in my own writing-box. Well! no matter ; there are some people one never can get quit of, — say the great folks, and you perceive I am one of them. Meanwhile we were making impromptu charades and nonsensical trifles the other day, when one of the company said suddenly :

"Why is Mrs. Piozzi like a kaleidoscope?"

REPLY.

The brilliant colours that appear
Shine, like her wit, distinct and clear;
While Fancy's fleeting magic power
Combines to charm each varying hour:
Giving to trifles light as wind
The lustre of her fertile mind,
Imparting pleasure and surprize,
Delighting still our hearts and eyes.

Good-natured at least, was not it? But we have not the fine thing here, constructed by Brewster *, uniting camera obscura with the other catoptric devices. Oh! how I should like to see that, and the exhibition, in your company. You really should write me some account of it. This weather will bring wealth to the farmers, and felicity to the apple vats. A Devonshire lady, Sir Stafford Northcote's wife, who knows your brother Henry, says there is promise of more cyder this year than has been known for many summers, and as to hay and wheat there can surely be no want.

The Queen's approaching death gives no concern but to the tradesmen, who want to sell their pinks and yellows I suppose; though something should be settled concerning the guardianship of her poor old husband's person. Our Demagogues are to make a grand push for triennial parliaments, they say. People are in such haste to be happy; they play *short* whist, *short* com-

* Sir David Brewster, Principal of the University of Edinburgh, &c.

merce, &c. but after all these complaints of bad har-
vests, I did not expect them to cry for *short commons;*
so that's one of my silly jokes. Is it a joke that Buonaparte is dying dropsical? Ay, ay: sweetly sung the
old French poet who said of such folks:

> " Tant que la Fortune vous seconde,
>   Vous êtes les maîtres du monde,
>   Votre gloire nous éblouit:
>   Mais au grand revers funeste
>   Le masque tombe, l'homme reste,
>   Et le héros s'évanouit."

> Bright with fortune's dazzling favour
> Seconding each bold endeavour,
>   Warriors tame our souls to fear;
> But reverses spoil their feigning,
> Down drops mask; the man remaining,
>   While the heroes disappear.

Well! 'tis no great matter whether they are turned
off the kaleidoscope or no, if we listen to Dr. Hales,
the great theologian, under whose quarto volumes on
Chronology, poor Upham's shelves are bending. He
stood up in Mr. Grinfield's pulpit last Sunday fortnight
(as, perhaps, I told you), and said confidently that the
world would end that day sixty-two years. It was the
anniversary of our Lord's Ascension; and perhaps it may
be so. You will find innumerable reflections on that
event, in King's "Morsels of Criticism," which I have
loaded, if not deformed, by numberless notes — manuscript, but legible enough, for I looked them over

since Hales's sermon, as I thought they would amuse you. 'Tis almost a pity you should suffer them to be sold after my death.

Sir Joseph Banks's evenings must this year be more interesting than ever, though I *do* fear the North Pole expedition will be a long time in finishing, and the people here are so desirous always to put extinguishers on their own entertainment. The ice field attached to our Ultima Thule, Fulda or Fulah, is now said to be a mere newspaper story.

Yours faithfully,
II. L. P.

Adbury must be in high beauty just now—when do you go thither? I hear much of an exploding mineral in Derbyshire, that is to supply our deficiency in volcanic matter; and my curiosity is all alive about it: what mineral can they mean?

To Sir James Fellowes.

Bath, June 1. 1818.

MY shamefacedness, and my desire of talking about twenty other things, kept me from showing you the verses I sent —— in answer to her exaggerated compliments, and kept me too from reading you some which she made impromptu on my complaining of the loss of youth and its accompaniments, beauty, admiration, &c.

" Oh talk not to me of the days that are flown;
  Tho' Youth's cheerful blossoms decline,
Even Autumn and Winter their treasures can boast,
  While Virtue's pure sunshine is thine.

" In each season of life there are blessings in store ;
    Then still, my dear friend, be it ours,
To rejoice in the fruit our life's harvest may give,
    Nor repine at the loss of its flowers."

To this I replied : —

> Where Winter chills the leafless grove,
> Silent to mirth and dead to love,
> Should robin from some slippery spray
> Tune up his long-remembered lay,
> Each passenger would cheer the bird,
> In Summer's concert scarcely heard.
>
> When Jura's icy mountains rise,
> Let one green spot salute our eyes;
> Amid the lofty glaciers lost
> As if forgotten by the frost;
> Each Briton smiles, extends the hand,
> And cries, Oh charming Switzerland !
>
> My talents thus your eyes allure,
> And please, reduced to miniature ;
> 'Tis thus you sooth my fond regret,
> For times I never can forget ;
> And thus your praises, partial friend,
> Excite the spirits they commend.

Miss O'Neill will be visible here with the naked eye,
as men say of a new star or comet, on the 13th June
next, Saturday se'nnight. I shall make her panegyric
an excuse for another letter. The first *début* on these
boards is Belvidera, which I have seen Siddons play to

Dimond's, Brereton's, and to Kembles Jaffier, well recollecting how she spake and acted every passage,
particularly her soft but striking " Farewell! remember
Twelve!" which was sure to electrify the house; but I
must say " Farewell! remember five!" which when
the clock has struck, the postman will wait for no
more from yours ever faithfully,

H. L. P.

To Miss Willoughby.

Monday, 15th June, 1818.

My dear Miss Willoughby was very kind in writing so
soon, but do not call me unkind in writing so late; I
waited to see Miss O'Neill. She is a charming creature without doubt, and charms, as it should seem, without intending it, calling in no aid from dress, or air, or
studied elegance, such as in old days one expected to
find in a public professor or dramatic recitation; but
like Dryden's Cleopatra,

> " She casts a look so languishingly sweet,
> As if, secure of all beholders' hearts,
> Neglecting, she can take them."

Comparing such an actress with Mrs. Siddons, is like
holding up a pearl of nice purity, and asking you if it
is not superior to a brilliant of the first weight and
water. You are fortunate in finding a cool place during
these unlooked-for heats of a summer season long forgotten in our country. My house is, as you know, on
the hill's side; but down in Green Park Buildings,

one can't help thinking how a fairy would feel if held down at the bottom of a bowl, from which the hot punch had just been poured away.

But I am going to Wales, if these elections will have left me any untired horses. Meanwhile, our pretty friend, Mrs. Webbe, had a very nice party some time ago, and her brother presided so kindly. I fancy he is a good sort of man, but loves a wonder; and told me the other day of a gentleman who expected to sit in the House of Peers as Earl of Huntingdon. A gay dream, I suppose; but Mrs. Fox will know if there is any truth in the tale.

Well! I do hope your favourites, the Wards, will rise in the profession. He is indefatigable; and though I felt him feeble and sinking in some parts, some scenes I mean, of that never-ending Jaffier, he sustained many scenes admirably; the one with Renault was inimitable, and 'tis long, indeed, since I have seen such a beautiful Pierre as Conway. Mr. Ward is so correct, too, so never-wrong. The poet has always justice done him by a scholar-like speaker; on the whole, I was very well entertained.

Miss Stratton, one of them, is really very pretty: she went in hysterics at Belvidera's distress, so did Miss Glover. I said we should all *melt* into tears, but the joke was good for nothing, the house was no hotter (where I sate) than any other house entered of late by dear Miss Willoughby's ever faithful, humble servant,

H. L. PIOZZI.

To Sir James Fellowes.

Thursday, June 18th, 1818.

I⊤ was sweetly done of you, indeed, dear Sir, to put the little warm bottle, and the warm kind invitation into your brother's pocket so. God forbid that I should outlive that quantity of Cayenne pepper, and want more!! An old Welsh squire did certainly keep on breathing till brandy was not sufficiently exciting for him without Cayenne pepper, but I think he was turned of ninety.

Well! Miss O'Neill might have moved him even then. Our ladies are all in hysterics, our gentlemen's hands quite blistered with clapping, and her stage companions worn to a thread with standing up like chairs in a children's country dance, while she alone commands the attention of such audiences, as Bath never witnessed till now. The box-keepers said last night that the numbers Kean drew after him were nothing to it. She performs every evening for seven days together: but Clifton is near, if she does break a blood-vessel or two.

A Dublin bookseller expects to end his days Earl of Upper Ossory, 'tis said; and a young lieutenant of a man of war hopes to sit in the Upper House with the old, and to me dear, title of Huntingdon. Oh, the last earl was one of my truly partial friends! but Count Flahaut's*

---

* Count Flahaut married the only daughter of Viscount Keith by his first wife. Miss Thrale was his second, by whom he left an only daughter, the Hon. Mrs. A. J. Villiers.

claim has proved of more importance than them all, by digging out this obsolete law.

Formerly, as I have read, whenever a Scotch gentleman meditated a journey southward, he used to have the crier's bell rung up and down Edinburgh for many weeks beforehand, to ascertain the parcels and packages he considered himself as bound to carry for his neighbours, and to settle the expences, &c., but *tempora mutantur;* and Mr. Scrase told me once that he had made gentlemen's wills when they left the county of Sussex about Brighthelmstone : describing the leave-takings, &c., as if the people had been setting out for a discovery of the North Pole.   Mr. Scrase was eighty-six years old when I first knew him in 1765 : a man of great abilities then, and of delightful conversation.   But what he most delighted to converse about, was the famous Farinelli.   Indeed, of all public performers, I believe Farinelli was the only one whom no successor ever pretended to equal.

To Sir James Fellowes.

Bath, 1st July, 1818.

THE heat has certainly exhaled my faculties, and I have but just life enough left to laugh at the fourteen taylors who, united under a flag with Liberty and Independence on it, went to vote for some of these gay fellows, I forget which ; " but the motto is ill chosen," said I ; " they should have written up *Measures not Men!* "

Sir Thomas Lethbridge, however, gave in last night ; oh how unlikely, how impossible, was it for him to hope for a seat, who had sent the popular favourite, Sir Francis Burdett, to the Tower*,—I wonder he would try !

Doctor Gray says in his last kind letter, that we quarrel with no time but the present. Hope still anticipates pleasure for a future day; and those that are past, delight us by recollection. He longs to see me and Mrs. Mostyn, he says, to talk about old Streatham Park. His sisters and nieces, two old ladies and two youngish ones, are come to settle here at Bath, and he begs me to introduce them into society; but 'tis the wrong time of year : I tried to make them a party for to-morrow, but cannot muster twenty faces, everybody has left town ; in a week more, I shall leave it too.

---

* He moved the committal of Sir Francis, whose language, he said, "made his hair stand on end." Excited by an ironical cheer, he added, "it really had that effect." In allusion to this unlucky declaration, he was saluted with cries of *porcupine* and encountered by pictures of that animal wherever he went during the election.

Wales will be quiet at least, and people expect health and pleasure from change of air, which having once delighted us, we talk of its enjoyments when no longer capable of enjoying them.

No matter! the farce must go on till the curtain drops, and if everybody left off their disguisings as they grew old, why age would appear with still more deformity than at present. Have you interested yourself concerning the discovery of Ossian's originality, so long doubted, so strenuously denied? The concatenation arose in my mind from his expressive words: — "Age is dark and unlovely, it is like the glimmering light of the moon when it shines through the broken clouds; the blast of the north is on the desolate plain, and the traveller shrinks on his journey."

I feel sometimes ready to shrink from mine to North Wales; and your good-natured brother said, he wished I should change my destination, and go no further than Sidmouth. I told him *this* was my last long frolic; and that next year (if I am to see A. D. 1819) I would try to spend the summer of it in Devonshire; and so I will.

Meanwhile you will have a stormy Session of Parliament, made still more so by the Catholic Question being brought forward. Forcing religion into the dispute, will set all in a state of effervescence; for although, poor thing, she is disregarded in common moments, and left like a football covered with mould and dust, give that football but a kick, and set the sport going, all the youth of the village will mix in the game, and some eyes will be beat out and some blows exchanged, before they lay the poor football to sleep under the old wall again, little as they really care for it.

Well! but you must not pay ninepence for this letter without my insertion of a joke you will like, perhaps, because it is mine; of the man who comes into a coffeehouse at Ilchester during the heat of our election contest, and asks for the news. " Ah, Lord, Sir!" replies the waiter, " we are badly off for papers. The popular candidate has got the day; the poor old 'Times' has been torn to pieces in the scuffle, a sea captain has catched up our only 'Pilot,' because he could see neither 'Sun' nor 'Star'; and no 'Courier' can be got for love or money. They are all on the road to Bath." Adieu! and don't wholly forget yours ever,

H. L. P.

I have lost a day as well as my wits I find. This is the 2nd not the 1st of July. Bessy and I set out for our own country on Friday, 10th; so if you will not write soon, the direction must be Brynbella, near Denbigh, N. Wales.

To Sir James Fellowes.

No. 8, Gay Street, Tuesday Night,
15th September, 1818.

WHEN I was about seven years older than your Tommy, we had a permitted holyday : and two of my uncle, Sir L. S. Cotton's, children, with poor Miss Owen and her brother, came, and one of our gambols was to dance round him or her who sat in the middle, and teize them till they quitted their post, when another took it, and underwent the same worry.

When George Cotton however (afterwards Dean of Chester) was seated, no arts, no tricks, no force could make him move; so that Jack Owen came and whispered me: "If you'll help, we will make him jump up, stout as he is. Let you and I set fire to Mrs. Salusbury's papers here in the closet, and make a noise. George will run away I warrant you, and look foolish enough." I took the hint, and cried fire at the very top of my voice. Out ran my mother and her company from their tea or cards, in the next room, frighted beyond all telling, . . . " and Dear Mama, don't be angry," cried I, " it was only to get George out of his place."

Query, is Cobbet any wiser? You have finished his nonsense by now.

I have got a sort of French Thraliana: fragments of letters written by Madame ——, Louis XIV.'s brother's wife, to our Queen Caroline, grandmother to George III. of England. I can hardly unpack my trunks for the avidity I feel to read this (to many) uninteresting stuff: to me more than delightful.

Madame's account of her visit to a Female Benedictine Convent, where she saw a nun of the royal family amuse herself by shooting at a target and firing pistols at a mark, is very curious; and shows one how difficult it is to dispose of leisure hours; for this lady had very few hours indeed that by the rules of the convent she could call her own; and this was her way of getting rid of them: the most extraordinary method that ever met my eye in reading through seventy years, Time's short preface to the " Volume of Eternity."

I can add no more but that, I am, Dear Sir,

Yours and Lady Fellowes's ever obliged

and grateful and faithful,

H. L. P.

To Sir James Fellowes.

Bath, Michaelmas Day, 1818,
like the 1st of May.

NOTHING kills the Queen, however. It is really a great misfortune to be kept panting for breath so, and screaming with pain by medical skill: were she a subject, I suppose, they would have released her long ago; but diseases and distresses of the human frame must lead to death at length, as the smallest brooks of the most inland country will sink in the sea at last. Sleep gave me up to his brother, says some old writer, and then

> " Soles occidere et redire possunt;
> Nobis cum semel occidit brevis lux,
> Nox est perpetua una dormienda." — *Catullus.*

Pretty lines certainly for a heathen poet. Will these do in imitation?

The sun that sets, with light refin'd
   Returns to gild the plains;
When man's short day has once declin'd,
   Perpetual night remains.

And recollecting that some old bishop who cured himself of the dropsy by reading "Quintus Curtius," pointed out a pleasant remedy, I sent to Upham for Coxe's newly written "Life of John Duke of Marlborough," in hopes Blenheim would do as well as the Battle of Arbela, and so it did; I am very well again, now.

The glance I gave into "Thraliana" showed me these verses, better adapted to my present age than to that in which they were written. In hope of amusing you I write them out, and pray read them to pretty Lady Fellowes —

"J'aurai bientôt quatre-vingt ans;
  Je crois qu'à cette heure il est temps
    De dédaigner la vie;
  Aussi je la perds sans regret,
  Et je fais gaïement mon paquet,
    Bon soir la compagnie.

"Lorsque d'icy je partirai,
  Je ne sçais pas trop où j'irai,
    Mais en Dieu je me fie:
  Il ne me peut mener que bien,
  Aussi je n'apprehends rien:
    Bon soir la compagnie.

" J'ai gouté de tous les plaisirs,
 J'ai perdu jusqu'aux désirs,
    A present je m'ennuye :
 Lorsqu'on n'est plus bon à rien
 On se retire, et on fait bien,
    Bon soir la compagnie."

And now, after a thousand repetitions of a thousand kind compliments to Lady F., and kisses to her darling babies, I shall take a thin pen, and write out my version of President Lamoignon's lines not much amplified —

Arriv'd at grave and grey fourscore,
'Tis time to think on life no more;
Time to be gone ; and therefore I
Can quit this world without a sigh :
Without or sorrow, care, or fright
Can bid the company good night.

When hence we part, 'tis hard to say
Whither we rove, or which the way;
But He who sent me here can show
My doubtful footsteps where to go;
So trusting to His truth and might,
I'll bid the company good night.

I've tasted here of every joy,
But time can taste itself destroy ;
It teizes me to see how soon
Quite good for nothing I am grown ;

When such the case, 'tis surely right
To bid the company good night.

Adieu! and accept this Michaelmas goosery with
your accustomed kindness for

H. L. P.

To Sir James Fellowes.

Bath, Thursday, 15th October, 1818.

My dear Sir James Fellowes, like his own western
sun, delights to warm and gild the evening of a stormy
day; but I have no commissions that I remember.
Divic Robinson has sent the wine, and I have sent him
the money, so that's all over. When you feel your own
purse too heavy, take it to Mortlocks, 290, in Oxford
Street: and carry Lady Fellowes a beautiful specimen
of South Wales china, and tell *him* how I am panting
for my ice pails and large dishes to use this day sen-
night.

The horrid story of Mr. Bowles shooting his own
favourite nephew, heir to his estate, I believe, will make
me shudder at a partridge all this autumn. 'Tis a sad
thing one cannot buy these birds like ducks and geese.
But the thoughts of meeting at Mr. and Mrs. Greatheed's
again, and meeting at Adbury! Oh I must not indulge
such extravagant fancies, and Lady Fellowes must not
encourage them. She is too good to us all. Was the
young Lady of Grey's Cliffe with the Greatheeds? No
girl that ever I saw could compare with your brother's

daughter for beauty and apparent intelligence at her age, but I suppose she will not maintain her superiority for twenty years; if she does, the poets will weary all readers with verses written in her praise. Apropos to poets, I think Lord Byron's " Pegasus " is moulting his wings; one hears nothing of him or his muse. Madame D'Arblay writes and comes, and cries, and goes to live at London with her son. She is very charming: she always was; but I will never trust her more. The first time one is betrayed by semblance of friendship, may be the fault of another; the second time, 'tis one's own fault; and to be twice made April fool by the same trick after ten years old, is too late.

Did you like the last volume of the " Tales of my Landlord "? I prefer a pretty novel little spoken of, called " Civilisation." If I did not recommend it to Lady Fellowes, I ought to have recommended it. Dr. Whalley says 'tis written by Hannah More, and the girls call it a preaching novel, and resolve not to look at a page of it. The British Museum is the thing worth seeing in London, and I missed it. English people make every curiosity so difficult of access, that you may live among us half a century, and see nothing. Foreigners throw the doors open, and take no present going in or out. Our fees at palaces, and our card money under the candlesticks, are certainly a remainder of old ill manners; nor can I reconcile to myself, or to my notions about good breeding, the trick of prescribing to our visitants the stake they shall play for in our house. I feel as well disposed to say what cap they should wear,

or what ribbonds they should buy.   Let them buy and
wear what they will.

All seem disposed to liberate Buonaparte.   The dash-
ing people, because he will make a dash; and they
will like to see the old firework, after a pause, burst
out in a new wheel, or throw up a showy serpent
for us to stare at.   The grave folks expect him to
fulfil Faber's new prediction of great things yet to be
accomplished by the Francic Emperor, and all consider
the sovereigns as very fruitlessly employed in en-
deavouring to shut the Temple of Janus.   Meanwhile
there is an old metaphysical work, which I cannot take
pleasure in reading, published by Hartley, ancestor
to David Hartley, in the year 1749.   Eighty-first pro-
position says: "It is probable that all civil governments will soon be overturned."   His eighty-second pro-
position has these words : "It is highly probable, and
to be expected, that all Church government will in
course of less than a century be completely dissolved."
Nobody minded him at the moment, I suppose, except
a few pens which were preparing to answer him, but
his calculation must now be allowed to have been a
good one.   France led the fashion, and all the world
is following it.   Did I tell you of the conquest I made
in Wales of the Bishop of St. Asaph, Luxmore?   He
says now : " What is become of that little Mrs. Piozzi ?
who shone here among us like a meteor for a month or
two, and then away; when will she return, do you
know ? we are very dull without her."   And so they
are sure enough; no music, no cards, nor no conversa-

tion, except the petty quarrels which infest all counties distant from the metropolis, round whose central globe we roll at different distances, and Denbighshire is Saturnian in every sense of the word: their sorrows, as well as their joys, are so stupid. One would think Doctor Young had passed his life among them, when he says :—

> " Without misfortunes, what calamity !
> And what hostility without a foe ! "

Adieu ! and do not make it long, Dear Sir, before you come and cheer the hearts of Russell Street and Gay Street : and don't run away with your brother Dorset. I shall try to borrow him of his good-natured lady for my flash next Thursday, 20th, being evermore

Yours and all your family's
obliged and faithful,
H. L. P.

To Sir James Fellowes.

Bath, October 29th and 30th, 1818.

THE ravens of my dear Sir James Fellowes are pheasants: brilliant in colour and tasteful to perfection. Your letter made me recollect the verses. The planting scheme enchants me. Robert shall give you account of my diligence :—

> " And as the crescent acorns swell,
> These oaks to future time shall tell,
> How friendship like themselves can shoot
> To Heaven its height, through Earth its root."

My mind has yet some youth in it, as you say, who know it best. The battered case, however, has had some blows lately.

I am perpetually stopped in these last stages of my long journey for want of horses, and shall be late home of course; so like all travellers, I read the tombstones in the next churchyard, and without further allegory, how the deaths do increase round one!

Miss Fellowes called on me this morning. She is in high looks, and does not perhaps entertain those apprehensions about poor dear Mamma, which *you* cannot avoid being sensible of: but do not be too selfish. People of her age cannot long be detained here: no, nor of mine either. Cowley says:—

> " It grieves me when I see what fate
> Does on the best of mortals wait,
> Poets or lovers let them be,
> 'Tis neither love nor poesy
> Can arm against Death's weakest dart
> The fertile head, or honest heart.
> For when our life in the decline
> Touches th' inevitable line,
> In Death's strong hand a grape-stone proves
> Fatal as thunder is in Jove's."

Meanwhile let us die but once, and not double the pang by cowardice, or poyson the dart by wilful sin, but meet the hour with at least as much deference to God's will, as every Turk shows to that of the Gran Signor. " It is the Sultan's pleasure," says he, " and so ends the matter,—here's my head."

I have set my acorns. 'Tis the oddest thing in the world that the wind blew me an ash and a sycamore key into this little garden a year ago, and George put them in the ground, and they prospered.

So you will have a Piozzi forest some day, but take care and claim them, and let nobody but yourself get a twig; and if I live till they are old enough, they shall be marked and ticketted.

H. L. P.

To Sir James Fellowes.

Bath, 1st December, 1818.

WELL! now I will not wait for a letter from Adbury, though I do desire it above all things in the world; for you will like to hear how the Persians * behaved at an English family dinner, and I am dying to tell dear Sir James Fellowes how much I was entertained.

It is truly astonishing to see how they have mastered our language, and caught up our European manners. Men who have sate on carpets for thirty years, and eat with chopsticks, are really a little better bred than the rest of the company, manage knives, forks and chairs, with grace and propriety, and what they ought not to do (for they are Mussulmen) take their glass like an

---

* Meerza Saefar and Meerza Saulih (the two Persians mentioned in these letters), two of the most distinguished personages sent into this country three years ago by Abbas Meerza, the reigning Prince of Persia. They speak English fluently, and are quite familiar with our manners and customs, and are at no loss to defend ably their opinions. They are dressed in the costume of their country. I saw them at Bath, Nov. 29, one in a scarlet and gold pelisse, the other blue.—*J. F.* 1818.

English country squire, and flirt with the girls famously.
I tóld them, however, that —

> "The glowing dames of Persia's royal court
> Have faces flush'd with more exalted charms;
> The Sun that rolls his chariot o'er their heads,
> Works up more fire and colour in their cheeks:
> Arriv'd 'mong these, the prince will soon forget
> Our pale unripen'd beauties of the North."

Well! I really was very ill bred myself; studied these
men all day, and turned them over like the leaves of
a book, to get what information could be obtained.
What pleased me best was the confirmation of my own
conjecture concerning the names of Cyrus and Darius.
The last means sovereign, as I always believed, and
the first is synonymous with Cosroe. My fear of being
mistaken ever since I gave you my " Retrospection," has
haunted me night and day. Error is such an insinuating thing, it works through every book like water
through a filtering stone. Let us go, and say with
Horace: Satis lusistis, satis bibistis, &c. We must go,
that's certain, and 'tis the only thing that *is* certain.
Και α πεθανε ends all the cases Dr. James quotes from
your old friend Hippocrates.

Meanwhile ladies leave cards, and starving females
write romances. The novel called " Marriage " * is the
newest and merriest. How marriage should be a new
thing, that is at least as old as Adam, the author

---

* By Miss Ferrier. It received a high compliment from Sir
Walter Scott in the preface to one of his novels. It was followed
by the "Inheritance " by the same writer.

may tell: but 'tis a very comical thing, and would make Lady Fellowes laugh on a long evening.

Here is the first frost on the first day of winter: quite right. The next three months, of which this is one, ought to be drippy, slippy, nippy.

Pluviose, Nivose, Ventose: all that stuff is very prettily put together in the " Clavis Calendariæ." I wonder you never looked at mine, crowded with notes—I would say deformed: but you would only answer Pish! The author, an Irishman, has borrowed most liberally from " Retrospection," and never said thank you, Mrs. Piozzi: but no matter, 'tis a very useful book, and not unentertaining. But I must write to Doctor Gray, and thank him for his very, very kind letter. One would think I was like Sir Epicure Mammon in Ben Jonson's " Alchemist," who fancying he had found the philosopher's stone, was enumerating the felicities it would purchase, and cried out in a rapture :—

> " I will have grave divines to flatter *me*,
> Poets I will not heed."

Adieu, dear Sir, and assure yourself that although no poet, nor grave divine, your friendship is the most valued possession of

Yours and your family's ever obliged and faithful,

H. L. P.

To Sir James Fellowes.

Jan. 6, 1819.

Mr. MANGIN is come from Paris, and says my "Synonymes" are all the rage there; and they have got a print of me, and asked him if it was like *cette dame célèbre.*

To Sir James Fellowes.

Bath, 12 Jan. 1819.

So although dear Sir James Fellowes is screwed up, as in a vice, by bad verse and worse prosing, poor H. L. P. cannot squeeze a letter out of him. Well! so it is with Salusbury—not a word from him either. The ladies are better correspondents by half; they will at least tell one, poor souls, how sick they are.

Meanwhile, here is my annual foolery at hand almost; it really seems but the other day since our last celebration. But

"Thus perish years, as moments from our view.
Some mourned, some loved, all lost; too many, yet too few."

I have, however, added to my stock of ideas, since 1819 came in, the sight of a man flying on the slack rope, and of another man professedly fire proof. I have likewise seen red snow brought from within the Polar circle, and have seen the man who witnessed a phenomenon often read of with wonder, a circular rainbow. Curiosity is supposed exclusively to belong to youth; but 'tis foolish to leave this world without knowing what's done in it, especially as eternity will be past in that which is to come.

Doctor Charles Parry, who shewed me the Arctic rareties, and traced his brother's track for me on the enormous map we looked over, is very indignant at their needless haste to return home without doing their errand in any wise; though these two or three occurrences render their voyage interesting. They will certainly go again next summer, and make another visit to the new nation, who never saw ship, or even canoe, like the people predicted to Ulysses in Homer. They indeed called an oar when they saw one, a corn-van; but these poor creatures never saw corn, or encountered an enemy.

They contemplated the " Alexander " and " Isabella " long before they could believe them inanimate and worked to motion by mortals like themselves; and when, embracing the masts, they found them dead wood, they burst into a horse laugh and continued holding their sides — our people guessed not why, but I think it was at the mistake of their reporters, who had miscalled them male and female gyants — and probably added some false wonders of their own; for truth is native of no clime hitherto discovered — but by Gulliver.

And now do, dear Sir James Fellowes, come home to us — and see good mamma — who pined after you last time, sadly. You said you had two old women at Adbury — weeder women I believe, who wanted you there. I am sure you have two old women here who want you as much, or more. The weeds of conversation weary

me to death with "Dear Maam,—I hope you caught
no cold at the last party; Lord bless me! how hot the
rooms were! Well! I do hate hot rooms above all
living things, &c., &c."

Oh come back for very pity—*reddes dulce loqui*—and
do not make me force my partner's hand incessantly
thus, for a fragment of comfortable chat. The Bishop
of Meath is your best substitute: he is very good-humoured, and writes verses, and shews me what he has
written. Apropos, poor Lady Crewe is dead—an object
of deformity! The greatest beauty of her time: at
least, the most admired woman; "Whose mind kept
the promise was made by her face;" as Charles Fox
said and sung. But palsy shook her frame, and cancer
gnawed it. Oh may such a death never reach yours and
your dear family's ever,

H. L. Piozzi.

Farewell! remember, not 12, but 26.

To Sir James Fellowes.

Bath, Jan. 17, 1819.

Indeed, my dear Sir, it is very comical in you to
fancy my letters so superior; but as a mountebank said,
who I heard haranguing the crowd upon Berwick-upon-
Tweed: "People of a good taste likes my deceptions,
and so says I, *despitur;*" meaning *decipiatur* of course,
wherever he had gained his classic knowledge.

Our fire-eaters continue their tricks, and are said to
get a great deal of money. That they do really and

bonâ fide swallow boyling oyl into their stomachs and arsenic, eating a good supper and sleeping sound afterwards—who can believe? There must be a quick substitution effected by legerdemain of a glass *without* poyson, for the glass we see *with* poyson; just at the moment *Ma'amselle* prepares in appearance to receive its contents down her throat.

As new a thing, though not as strange perhaps, was exhibited the other day by and before Lords and Commons, themselves convened in Parliament, without either King or Chancellor, but, *substitution* again. And now for the Catholick Question justly so called, for its consequences will be *universal,* and you will find the most difficult question possible decided by mere prejudice not investigation. The Romanists, I see, expect a very favourable issue to their cause, which will come on, we are told, soon as the petitions are decided. But you would rather hear about the red snow, and I would rather tell about it.

What Doctor Charles Parry showed me was preserved in very large transparent phials, hermetically sealed. It was blood red, and I saw a little sediment. Did it? Oh, no! did it fall red from the clouds? said I. "We cannot tell," was the reply. "My brother saw no snow fall while he was in that district, but he gathered what he gave me—not from the surface but at two feet deep in the drifts. It lay at least four or five feet on the earth, and was of the same colour down at the very bottom." They saw white snow in plenty upon the distant glaciers. The wise men in the ships attributed

the sanguinary hue to aerolite stones which fall in large
quantities; and the new discovered Esquimaux (for Esquimaux they are) make knives and saws such as they
do make, poor creatures, of this sky-dropt iron, having
no other metal of any sort or kind.   I was talking to
your brother Dorset concerning the astonishment of
our late-found northern friends, at seeing the "Isabella"
and " Alexander" with their attendant boats; and observed how well Dryden must have studied human
nature, when he gave his beautiful description of Cortez's
first arrival in Mexico.   "Oh," said he, "write to James
and remind him of the excellent adaptation you have
made; the lines are little known."   Here 'tis then: —

> " 'We went obedient, Sir, to your command,
>   To view the utmost limits of the land;
>   To that sea shore, where no more world is found,
>   But foaming billows breaking on the ground;
>   There for a while my eyes no objects met
>   But distant skies that in the ocean set,
>   Or low-hung clouds that dipt themselves in rain
>   To shake their fleeces on the earth again.
>   At last, as far as I could cast my eyes
>   Upon the sea, somewhat methought did rise,
>   Like bluish mists, which still appearing more,
>   Took dreadful shapes, and mov'd towards the shore.'
>
> 'What shapes did these new wonders represent?'
>
> 'More strange than all your wonder can invent:
>   The object I could first distinctly view,
>   Were tall straight trees that o'er the waters flew:
>   Wings on their sides instead of leaves did grow,
>   Which gather'd all the breath the winds could blow:
>   And while their bodies cut the yielding seas,
>   Low at their feet lay floating palaces.'
>
> 'Came they alive, or dead upon our shore?'

'Alas! they liv'd too sure; I heard them roar.
They turn'd their sides, and to each other spoke;
I saw their words break forth in fire and smoke,
Sure 'tis their voice that thunders from on high,
Or these the younger brothers of the sky.
Deaf with the noise, I took my hasty flight,
No mortal courage could endure the sight.'"

It is, as your brother observed, very remarkable, that the idea of a savage should thus have possessed a court poet; but besides the exquisite beauty of Dryden's Virgilian diction, there is a truth as to the sentiment, that fills one's soul with wonder at the comprehensiveness of such a mind. Ay, ay, when pyramids crumble to dust like the bodies of kings they were meant to cover — good poetry and power of language will remain: till well written inscriptions shall outlast their monuments. But I am growing enthusiastic, and feel glad the paper is so near full, that I may be forced to leave off. Whenever dear Piozzi caught me ranting in this manner, he used to say — "*Ah, ha, vien l'estro adesso.*" So adieu!

To Sir James Fellowes.

Bath, 9 Feb. 1819.

If any thing could give astringency to my ink, and make me write a constrained letter to dear Sir James Fellowes, it would be the feel of my mind with regard to your late situation, and the feel of my own mouth, which has been so uneasy to me, that fears of carcinoma haunted me three days and nights at least, while the silence I was obliged to use became no character but that of your Algerine mutes, that strangle and say nothing.

Common sense at length suggested that it was only relaxation — so I used your white stuff, and honey of roses; and now

"My mouth praises God with joyful lips."

Oh anything, sweet heaven! but a cancer. I should then indeed have to follow my angelic mother — *eheu! non passibus equis*—down the last dark and slippery hill.

If, however, the passage was unpleasant to your mamma and mine, what will become of these strange creatures whose indefinable sins pollute the page of every newspaper?   .   .

What a universal styptic is gold, if a bold hæmorrhage of truth does chance to burst out !   Oh, well and wisely said Sir Robert Walpole, that everything had its price.*   Why this colonel is like Sir Edward Mortimer in the " Iron Chest."   .   .   .

But here is a pamphlet come out, I guess not by whom written †, called " Historic Doubts concerning Buonaparte : " you must give it a reading.   It has at least the grace of novelty to recommend it, and will, I dare say, run rapidly through many editions — 'tis so cheap.   .   .   .

So here is a real commonplace letter like every-

* What Sir Robert Walpole is commonly reported to have said was, " All men have their price."   What he really said was, " All *these* men have their price ; " alluding to the so-called patriots of the Opposition.
† By Dr. Whately, the present Archbishop of Dublin.

body's letter, written among perpetual knocks at the door by people who know not how to dispose of the hours between breakfast and the moments when they may without self-condemnation pretend impatience for dinner, better than by throwing a few of them away upon dear Sir James Fellowes's ever obliged and faithful H. L. P.

In the midst of all this I find my paper full, and wonder when I found time to fill it; but my pen, like a horse at Newmarket, moves most swiftly when it carries least weight — 'tis plain. Adieu then, and remember me to kind Lady Fellowes and lovely Mariuccia, for so we should call her in Italy.

To Sir James Fellowes.

Bath, 25 Feb. 1819.

THE languor you describe as possessing your mind, my dear Sir, while it urges you to restless activity of body, no one can better understand than myself, who used to walk incessantly, squeezing the flag-stones of our South Parade here, with my *feet*, in order to obtain relief for my *head* when struggling against "Thick coming fancies that robbed me of my rest." Well! 'tis a foolish thing ever to be uneasy at all.

Our longest life is but a little short parenthesis in the broad page of time, which is itself a mere preface or prologue to eternity. Let us, however, write the brief period neatly, and leave our visiting ticket to the world, such as may not disgrace us.

I have asked for St. David's Day, and we will have a good dinner and a Welch harp.

Mrs. Stratton says she would give us authors, actors, &c.,—a merry day at her house, but that if she did, it must be " un table fort libre mais peu de couverts," as she keeps no professed cook. Never mind, replied H. L. P., we care only for the salt.

When all is over, I will tell you how it ended : meanwhile, the best Bath news is that good old General Leighton is now become Sir Baldwin, with three or four additional thousands a year. You remember old General Leighton : he stooped excessively from a cold caught bivouacking somewhere in our service. He is a true Salopian, who, though well acquainted with both hemispheres, delights in talking only of Shrewsbury. He will now end his life where it began, nine miles from his favourite spot — a pretty spot enough, but its power over a soldier of fortune like General Leighton, or a full minded man like my friend the first Dr. Burney, is really to its credit.

When the last-named friend had occasion to kiss his Majesty's hand two or three times within two or three years, I remember the wags saying, " Why Burney takes the King's hand, sure, for Shrewsbury brawn ; he puts it so often to his lips."

To Sir James Fellowes.

Bath, March 13, 1810.

THE salt you get, dear Sir, must be all out of the old salt cellar, with the cypher of H. L. P. upon it. Our gay dinner is not to be held till the 19th of this month, next Fryday, at Mrs. Stratton's. I shall then invite the company to my own house on some day, when Warde and Conway are disengaged.

Your dinner shall be a good one: for you remember Boileau's epigram on just such a feast:—

> " Damis! vous donnez la famine,
>   Votre table a trop peu de plats ;
>   Peu content de votre repas,
>   Enseignez moi donc où on dine."
>
> Too few good dishes is a fault,
>   Bad too many without salt ;
>   Among your other *bons mots*, pray
>   Tell me where we dine to-day.

But here we are chatting and laughing, and in comes your brother Dorset to tell me . . . and he wished me to take charge of his Ariadne, but my room will not hold her. It came into my head as he was talking, that the deserted ladies, who cannot get their lovers to marry them after promises, &c., all follow her classical example, and make alliance with Bacchus as soon as their Theseus is gone: at least, I see some who are doing so here at Bath, and I suppose Divie Robertson, the wine-merchant, would be glad they were still more in number.

Dear me! how sick, how thrice sick, am I of these parties! so falsely called society: for one idea in common with them I possess not. Yet one must live among people one cannot care about, in order to serve those who really amuse and delight one.

Mr. Warde will, through Miss Willoughby's interest and mine, produce a gallant show of hands to-night, to use an election phrase. Did I ever tell you an old joke of Garrick's, when I sat in his lap at the celebration of our peace with France, signed at Aix-la-Chapelle? in the year—what was it? 1748, I think. "A bad peace surely," said our favourite actor, " that brings so many heads to the scaffold." He did not like my reminding him of his saying so, because it made him look old. But here comes company and here come beggars. I have not five minutes nor five guineas left, they plague me so :—

> All considering me as their prey
> All assisting tow'rds my decay.

I was near escaping them yesterday by choking myself at dinner, but only a very little soreness remains; and with what wits I have left in my head let me protect myself.

Yours, &c.,

H. L. P.

To Sir James Fellowes.

Bath, Day of the Vernal Equinox, 1810.

I CAN now tell you that Mrs. Stratton's dinner went off delightfully; the salt shining and spar-like, unbruised, unbasketted, very good indeed. I wish mine may be as good and brilliant next Fryday, the 26th, when my very best dependence will be on you, my ever best friend. We must sit down, though, as near to five o'clock as possible, because of Sir Walter James, who hates to dine later, and who has begged himself in with a condescendance I little expected.

You and he will find Warde most of a scholar, Conway the man of high polish, general knowledge, and best natural abilities. If you don't like them, it will vex me.

Apropos to authors, actors, &c., I have had an offer since I wrote last, not of marriage—as Ninon de l'Enclos boasted when touching her eightieth year,—but of a better thing, money for Murphy's portrait. The rich Mr. Taylor, George Watson Taylor, who bought Johnson's picture and Baretti's at the sale, solicits it with beg and pray. He once offered me, if you remember, 157*l.* for it, so I can't, in honour or conscience, ask him more ; but if he would take my Cypriani Magdalen, who is eating her head off at old Wilson's European Museum, along with Mr. Murphy's head by Reynolds, and give me 200*l.* for both together, the bargain would be very good for both of us, and I should take a good wide step towards buying the 6000*l.* which dear Piozzi left to his relations in Italy, and which I always have promised Salusbury to make up for him in the Consols three per cent., after which transaction my money is my own ; and whatever I may feel disposed to give or spend, it shall be without self-reproach. There are 5000*l.* in now, you know.

Your friends, the Greatheeds, have had a famous acquisition made to their fortune by death of this Mr. Collyear. I wish it might drive them to Bath; for if I recollect rightly, you said they were once more restored to chearful endurance of that life their son's death made a scourge to them.

My friends the Mangins, who were kind to me when you were, and in whose welfare I take the tenderest concern, — have suffered from the danger of their little boy as much almost as could be inflicted; and though my life has been so drawn into length, and so many scenes of sorrow have crossed my path, I am yet to learn whether the death of a young man like Bertie Greatheed, or that of a promising baby, strikes deepest; bursting a bubble with all its colours varying each to a tint more lovely than the last, does certainly require religious fortitude to support.

Yet what is infant life *but* a bubble? *

Poor Salusbury and his wife are hanging over the couch of their second son, I understand, and the thought throws a gloom over your

H. L. P.

Come on Fryday 26th, next Fryday, and disperse my cares away.

Do you remember Milton's solemn invitation to a man to be merry with him? —

---

* " Ere sin could blight or sorrow fade,
    Death came with timely care,
  The op'ning bud to heaven convey'd,
    And bade it blossom there." — *Louth.*

" This day deep thoughts resolve with me to drench
    In mirth, that after no repenting draws ;
    Let Euclid rest, and Archimedes pause,
    And what the Swede intends, and what the French.
    To measure life learn we betimes, and know
    Tow'rd solid good what leads the nearest way,
    For other things mild heav'n a time ordains,
    And disapproves that care, tho' wise in show,
    That with superfluous burden loads the day,
    And when God sends a cheerful hour, refrains."

To Sir James Fellowes.

Bath, Monday, March 28th, 1819.

MY dear Sir J. F. sometimes says, when he has a
mind to make me very happy, Your last letter was the
best I ever received from you, Mrs. Piozzi. 'Tis my
turn now.

Your last letter is the very best I ever read from the
hand I have long looked to for substantial friendship.
It assures me of your remaining at hand, not, as many
would say, to save my worne out frame from death, but
to protect my remains—the poor remains of the Piozzi ;
her never forfeited honour, and secondly, at unmeasura-
ble distance, her literary fame : to ascertain the possibility likewise of passionate love, subsisting with
uncontaminated conduct, and enthusiastic friendship
without prospect of interested gratification. *Veniamo
ad altro.*

The last series of those half novels, half romance
things, called " Tales of My Landlord," are dying off a
pace ; but if their author gets money, he will not care

about the rest *; having never owned his work, no
celebrity can be lost, nor no venture can injure him. 'Tis
thus Joanna Baillie might have done. I well remember
when her plays upon the " Passions " first came out,
with a metaphysical preface. All the world wondered
and stared at me, who pronounced them the work of
a woman, although the remark was made every day
and everywhere that it was a masculine performance.
No sooner, however, did an unknown girl own the work,
than the value so fell, her booksellers complained they
could not get themselves paid for what they did, nor
did their merits ever again swell the throat of public
applause. So fares it with *nous autres,* who expose ourselves to the shifts of malice or the breath of caprice.

My justly admired Conway meanwhile drives all
before him at Birmingham, after ill usage enough here
at Bath ; and now I tell him, he must beware the tryals
of prosperity. May no others ever assail you, dear
Sir !

Doctor Gibbes was here five minutes ago, laughing
at these liver cases †,—so everything is called now:

" Whence this distress of head ?
Whence comes my nose so red ?
Our doctors all have said,
　　　　　　　　　　　　From liver.

* This was not the first time the same reproach was gratuitously
levelled at the author —

" Let others rack their meagre brains for hire,
Enough for Genius if itself inspire."

† It was the fashion to call all doubtful or undefinable complaints
liver, as it is now the fashion to attribute them to suppressed gout.

" Why all this heat of skin ?
Why so much pain within ?
What makes me get so thin ?

     My liver.

" Why gout in feet and toes?
Carbuncles on my nose,
When all this only shows

     'Tis liver.

" Miss Rosa has a pimple
Where once she had a dimple,
And she believes, Oh, simple !

     'Tis liver.

" Why, my torn frame to tease,
Bites of bugs, gnats, and fleas ?
All these excrescences

     Come from my liver."

These are not my verses — Dieu m'en garde; but
they are very comical, and would, as Mr. Piozzi used to
say, make the very chickens laugh. If they amuse
Lady F. in her present state for five minutes, they are
five good stanzas. So adieu ! and believe me ever her's
and your's, while .

      H. L. PIOZZI.

Doctor Gibbes's mother, seven years younger than me,
is struck with palsy, which has taken away much of her
articulation. Friends, companions, contemporaries. Ah
poor Floretta !

   T 2

To Sir James Fellowes.

Bath, 30th March, 1819.

My dear Sir James Fellowes will kindly rejoyce to hear that Mr. Watson Taylor has already paid in the 200*l*. to Hammersley's : a letter from Pall Mall informs me so this moment. I must pack Murphy's portrait up very nicely to send off.   .   .   .

How you did laugh at my funny story of original painting ! * But the conversation between you and Mr. Wickens concerning your school days, led me to it; and my bag of tales, alias bagatelles, never seems exhausted when in pleasant company. The string ties tight round the neck of the sack, if I don't like my companions, and that of its own accord, and the people are left wondering why any one should fancy that Mrs. Piozzi is agreeable.

It is astonishing how soon irony or allegory may be mistaken for truth; I mean in how few years. Epsom Wells were fashionable early in the last century; but some people there disobliging Doctor Radcliffe, " Oh ! "

* Sir James Fellowes' note on this letter is : — "I had met Mr. Wickens a few days before at Mrs. Piozzi's. As we were brother Rugbeeans, the conversation took place about the mode of punishing the boys in Dr. James's time, when Mrs. P. related the story of Vandyke, who, when a boy, first evinced his genius in a remarkable manner by painting the exact likeness of the master upon the person of a schoolfellow about to be flogged, which so astonished and amused the pedagogue that he burst out a laughing, and excused the boy the punishment that awaited him. Mrs. Piozzi's manner and humour in relating this anecdote of Vandyke was remarkably comical."

said he, "I will put a toad in their well presently," meaning he would bring the water into *disrepute*, I trust; but going to Epsom a few summers ago, a lady told me very seriously, that Doctor Radcliffe had ruined that fine well by putting a *toad in it*.

Did I ever tell you that Sir Walter James was the person who first suggested to me the idea of making a Lyford Redivivus, and teaching all the people what their Christian names meant? It certainly was so, and he recollected our conversation on the subject, when reminded of it the other day at No. 8. I shall show him the manuscript some morning.

The celebrated Dr. Farmer as a man particularly well informed on the subject of old English literature and as a man of learning, was master of Emanuel College at Cambridge when I became acquainted with him as an undergraduate of Peter House; at a dinner party toasts were called for, and most of the men present gave the names of ladies whose names chanced to begin with the letter B. Dr. Farmer made the following impromptu : —

" Is it not strange that Cupid should decree
    That all our favourites should begin with B ?
    How shall we solve this paradox of ours ?
    The bee flies always to the sweetest flowers."

Once more adieu, and twenty times more adieu !
H. L. P.

To Sir James Fellowes.

Bath, Monday, 5 April, 1819.

. . . . . . Mr. Taylor wrote me a fine coaxing letter, sent by a man who came to pack and carry, and to bring me a request that I would authorise Wilson to give him up my beautiful Magdalene. I sent him the annexed, unsealed, and enclosed it in this billet to Taylor:

" Mrs. Piozzi despatches her writ of authority to the European Museum, with many compliments to Mr. Taylor, and wishes him joy of his pictures. A sort of low-spirited feel hinders her saying any more now, but she really means on some future day to pay her personal respects in Harley Street.

" Mrs. Piozzi sends compliments to her old friend, Mr. Wilson, begs he will put her fine portrait of Mrs. Rainsford in the character of a Magdalen safely into the hands of George Watson Taylor, Esq., who has at length courted her out of it, and of what she parts from with more reluctance, her famous portrait of Arthur Murphy by Sir Joshua. They will, however, be where they ought to be. Mrs. Piozzi thought Mr. Taylor would have left Murphy till *she* too was where she ought to be, but he was not willing to wait till the last of the old coterie dropt into the grave which has devoured so many of them. Mr. Wilson is to consider this note as authority to deliver the Cipriani Magdalen into his hands, from his faithful servant, &c.,

" H. L. PIOZZI."

Now do not you, my dear Sir James Fellowes, fancy me superannuated, because I do not write neatly as usual. The paper is, I think, actual blotting-paper, such as " Retrospection " is printed on exactly, and so thin. Your idea of Pan among the bacchanals (Devil among a bag of nails) is incomparable. 'Tis the only solution of so strange a sign; and Scaliger says that his Satanic Majesty, when visible to his adorers, commonly does assume the port and person of Azazel, Hebrew for the goat.

You must not suffer my Scaligerana to go into any hands but your own; 'tis covered with marginal notes, a single small 8vo. or rather 12mo. volume. He wrote his thoughts in French and Latin, but ever classically, ever acutely exprest. What he says of the God Pan is confirmed every day now we are so well acquainted with the Hindoo superstition. They certainly worship the scapegoat of Hebrew ritual; and Milton, who was ignorant of nothing that could be known in his day, alludes to him under the name of Azazel, who unfurls the standard of Lucifer in the first book of " Paradise Lost." Pan is employed too, but I cannot find him; his comprehensive appellation is a Greek word for all I know. The Orientals we are living amongst consider him merely as generative power: the conservative and destructive intelligences form their triad of Brahma, Vistnou, and Mahadeva, in unison with the Hebrew Azazel; and I think the Rabbins believe the seducer of Eve was either Azazel or Sammàel; the latter, probably, as he combined best with the serpent-nature; and he too is worshipt, you know, under the name of Cneph; and there were Ophites among the Greeks, for Homer's Menelaus has a serpent on his shield, probably because he was devoted to the demon Deity adored under that form ; and the creatures that destroyed Laocoon were superhuman we remember.

I used to be fond of mythological studies, but have neglected them of late, unless casually reminded. Damascius, however, says Ζωναι meant the serpent which girds the globe; the Zodiac, I trust, or ecliptic line denoting the sun's path. Sun worshippers were serpent worshippers, Ophites; and this being a serpentine line, the line of beauty and perfection, confirms the fancy. Zone is a girdle still. The Globe, Wing, and Serpent are now become common ornaments; and when I saw a fine mirror once so adorned at the house of a rich clergyman, and explained them to him, he stared like a thing astonished; but you will be tired, and so am I, the implements are so bad with which I profess myself ever faithfully and gratefully yours,

H. L. P.

Make my proper — that means my best — regards to dear Lady Fellowes.

To Sir James Fellowes.

Bath, April 10, 1819.

BUT a strange thing, and not much less comical, is the solicitude Lady Burdett and her family have evinced,

of making acquaintance with me. I guess not where
the inducement can lie, for of me they know nothing
but my avowed aversion to their principles. It would,
however, be ridiculous to refuse, so I shall dine with
them on Thursday next. The rest of the week will be
past at the theatre, where Shakespeare's most agreeable
characters are exhibited; Fauconbridge and Marc Antony, for which my favourite Conway seems to have been
born.

Did I ever shew you a horrible story of my own writing (*antè*, p. 32) done upon the spur of a moment, for a
wager, at Florence? Lord bless me! that hideous tale
of the Modern Prometheus was done, it seems, by Miss
Godwin, in some spirit of competition between her and
some physician *—nobody says who—and Lord Byron.
His " Vampyre" is a filthy and a fearful thing, but her
" Frankenstein" carries away the palm of horror and impiety. What times are these! The growth of crime is
beyond all telling; " It lames report to follow it," as
Shakespear says, " and undoes description to do it." I
suppose the warm weather, and our prosperous state of
finance, are in fault. Indigence does certainly check
many vices, which opulence brings out. The snake of
man's plant, like that of the dung-hill, lies torpid
during winter, a hot summer day unwreaths his folds,
till frost fixes him once more in a torpid state. Ross's
account of the crimson cliffs would have been very en-

---

* Polidori, the author of the popular story of " The Vampire,"
which is based on Lord Byron's.

tertaining had we not anticipated the whole in conversation at Charles Parry's, who permitted me to see his bottle of red snow, and the Greenlander's jacket, with drawings of those wild creatures the new found nation teems with. They are much below the people that Drake found; who were so seized with wonder at the music made by a scraper from on board the ship, that one man thrust an arrow in his leg, not doubting but that melody could cure it. These half-starved animals minded no fidler, but sought to break the instrument, like babies. I fear the new adventurers will miss them. They certainly do lie out of the proper track.

Adieu! to-morrow's post may bring me news from Adbury: till then, and ever, farewell.

Mr. Watson Taylor was in such a hurry*, and my desire of 200*l.* was so impetuous! Well! as the old prologue written by Prior says, " 'Tis best repenting in a coach and six." So I shall die rich, if that is any comfort, and I shall die the sooner, too (which is a good thing), if I get neither the dear Pellegrins, or the dear No. 1. Adieu, then, once more, and make ——, like young Edward Mangin, acknowledge a true friend in the portrait of

H. L. P.

* To buy her portrait of Murphy, by Reynolds.

To Sir James Fellowes,

Sunday Night, 18 April, 1819.

WHAT a world! or rather what inhabitants of a beautiful place in which our study is to make deep ruts for each other to stumble in. And you not enraged at these sedition-mongers that we read of? What would the foolish creatures have? Let government be constructed how it will — we must be governed; or the strong will press down the weak. Make up your mess like Venice treacle, a dram of this, a scruple of that — but government must govern when it *is* made up; for after all you only take from one department,—kings, lords, commons, and the mob, to give a little more, or a little less, to the others. Limited monarchy, limited aristocracy, we understand, but limited government is a contradiction in terms.

Ah me! we shall have a grand inundation of worse than nonsense, I see plainly. After the Nile's overflow, you remember, the old Ægyptians turned in droves of swine, to root, and trample, and wallow in the mud; nor till the ensuing year was it observed, that their endeavours had fertilized the soil they sought to ruin.*

I shall not live to see the end of all; and if after a powerful fermentation, some pure spirit does at length come over the helm, it will be for you, not me, to praise its purity. Meanwhile, I do not in any wise resemble the old Cavalier, who predicted return of royalty,

* Burke overlooked this when he denounced the "swinish multitude."

when Cromwell had just destroyed it; and a republican friend reproached him with, "Ah, Sir! you Tories are always building castles in the air." "Why where the plague *should* we build them?" said the other, "when you Whigs have got all our *land* from us."

But here's enough for to-night: my spirits were running over with joy about my picture, or I could not have gone so far. I waked very early, far from well this morning, and forbore to go to church; but as all my droppers in agreed that I looked beautifully well, 't were pity to contradict them; and since the stocks are falling, for me to complete my purchase, when Newton and when Elliott pay their money, I will make matters up with myself, though your friend Bertie Greatheed used to say, when we lived in habits of intimacy, "Dear Mrs. Piozzi 's never so agreeable as when she is heartily vexed." And I trust you found it so too, since the fancy that you took for my conversation on the first day of the year 1815, was certainly kindled in a most ragged and tindery state of my poor worne-out soul. Well! all 's over, and if I wait longer than to-morrow morning before I claim my prize, let me lose it!

Adieu, and keep sweetest Maria from wit and learning, as long as ever you can; for though Floretta did resolve to hold fast both to the end, you may recollect that one had been a burden, the other a plague, to her through long protracted life. Mine has been rendered really very comfortable by your continued kindness and partiality to your much obliged

H. L. P.

To Sir James Fellowes.

MY DEAR SIR,—I am in possession of nothing; nothing, at least, that I value, except Tudor's opinion of our good Dr. Fellowes's case, which will perhaps bring him to Bath three or four days sooner. His proud Salopian tenants have no taste to parting with the last ornament of their drawing room ; so I will keep possession of my temper, and wait sullenly, but civilly, till the 3rd of May.

Dr. Gibbes says he is hurried to death, the people are so ill; he saw me half in hysterics at Young's King Lear, and he came the next morning to feel my pulse, kind creature ! " But you profess to like my chat," said I, "and never come to make me a nice long visit." " Just for the same reason," replied he, " that I never drink claret,— I have not time to sit down to it." Did I tell you what a flattering letter I received the other day from Mr. Comber, who wrote the pretty verses Miss Williams did so rave about ?

" Tell me no more of Ninon's wondrous charms,
  Which on life's verge, set kings and courts in arms ;
  Piozzi's sparkling wit and brilliant fire
  All hearts can charm, and dulness self inspire :
  Long may the spirit animate the clay !
  When sever'd from it, rise to endless day."

I do not, however, mean to tell only what verses I receive, here are some, no better than these, which I have written : expressive of the indignation I feel to see our theatrical managers here, sacrificing my favourite actor to Mr. Warde's ill-humour. You remember Martial's epigram :

" Rumpitur invidiâ quidam, carissime Juli,
     Quod me Roma legit, rumpitur invidiâ.
Rumpitur invidiâ quod turba semper in omni
     Monstramur digito, rumpitur invidiâ.
Rumpitur invidiâ quod sum jucundus amicis,
     Quod conviva frequens, rumpitur invidiâ.
Rumpitur invidiâ quod amamur, quodque probamur
     Rumpitur quisquis—rumpitur invidiâ."

The word swelling is more elegant in English, how-ever, than bursting, ain't it ? so I turned the whole, as follows, alluding to their orations; for both of which, see Shakspeare's Julius Cæsar, which they plaid (*sic*) so admirably :

     Swelling with envy, Brutus now appears,
     Because the town lends Anthony their ears.
     Swelling with envy views his pers'nal graces
     When girls point handsome Conway as he passes.
     Swelling with envy, sees him in retreat
     At gay thirteen perhaps;—or number eight.
     Such as so swell, would sting too, if they durst,
     But since they swell with envy—let them burst.

Well! envy is a vice, say the "Synonymes," and theft is a crime. The increase in both is marvellous; ay, and portentous too, if we speak seriously; but no wonder, while the words " Office for the Deist," stare boldly in each passenger's face who treads the Strand; and books against the Trinity are publicly advertized, even by those we call ministerial papers. Yes, yes, you may do as you please with people at Quarter Sessions, &c., but it is only medicating the stream, while an enemy has already poysoned the source — and *that won't do.* We may as well expect fine grapes from the Upaz tree.

My dear Sir James Fellowes asks me for commands. I have none: his talk, his shadow, and his medicine, comprise all that is wanted by his much obliged servant,

H. L. P.

Make my best compliments to all the dear coterie.

To Sir James Fellowes.

Tuesday, May 4th, 1819.

CONGRATULATE me, dear Sir; I have got my picture, and every visitant that has dropt in to-day has seen me jumping round it for joy; Miss Williams most delighted among them. The likeness strikes every one. Oh! I stewed the Shropshire leeks down to nice Welsh pottage at last, and they were wondrous kind. The master of the house, poor fellow! screaming with gout. Tell the young ladies they must find out this French enigma :—

> Enfant de l'art, enfant de la nature,
> Sans prolonger la vie j'empêche de mourir ;
> Plus je suis vrai, plus je suis imposteur,
> Et je deviens plus jeune à force de vieillir.

Art's offspring, whom nature delights here to foster,
  Can death's dart defy, tho' not lengthen life's stage;
Most correct at the moment when most an impostor,
  Still fresh'ning in youth, as advancing in age.

I have got a new book lent me, not new either, but
very interesting. The "Letters of Lady Hartford and
Lady Pomfret," written at the beginning of last century. They are very pretty, so pretty that I think I
must burn them, lest you should prefer them to mine,
as Cleopatra drowned Mariamna's picture, lest Mark
Anthony should think it handsomer than her. The
best of the collection are signed H. L. P. however,
Henrietta Louisa Pomfret, so that must be my consolation.

Kind Conway has promised me a proof mezzo tinto of
his likeness in the character of Jaffier by Harlowe; he
says yours by Pellegrini is alive with resemblance.
What will Salusbury say when he comes first to dinner
at aunt's house? who he considers as a superannuated
old goose, while she is petted and flattered, and fed
with soft dedication, all day long.

The Catholick question is too serious a subject for
light correspondents like me, so I shall say nothing
about it, this year; and if I were to see another year,
it would be too late.

My fête for the end of January, 1820, will be splendid indeed: I have asked people from all parts of the
world, and some have promised from the farthest Thule.

I daresay Parry's Arctic Expedition will be more

entertaining than that of Captain Ross; but my heart bleeds for the loss of Jack Sacheuse the Eskimaux. It was so foolish to let the poor creature burn up his inside with spirits, and that was all that destroyed him. Adieu. . . .

H. L. P.

To Miss Fellowes.

13 June, 1819.

My dear Miss Fellowes, when she reads that beautiful panegyrick on Mrs. Siddons, will readily acquiesce in her old friend H. L. Piozzi's decision; that she is indeed the brilliant diamond of that interesting profession, of which Miss O'Neill is the elegant and pleasing pearl. Conway asks me if we are all here seized with the O'Neill fever? My reply was that he need not fear what a sprig of jessamine could do towards turning our brains, while under the dominion of himself, the towering tulip: this, in allusion to a sale of those flowers in the beginning of last century, when the root of one, called Semper Augustus (his own name) sold for 700*l*.*

Meanwhile Siddons must stand for the moss Provence rose; which when her colours are confessedly faded, and her bloom gone by, still yields a sweet perfume, and

* See a note to " Retrospection," 2nd vol., 8th chapter. In this note she states that the collection sold for 9000*l*.; and in the margin she has written : " When the folly revived again, it was cured by a painter's daughter producing her tulip at the Florists' Feast, with the long-desired vainly (till that day) hoped-for streak. She won the prize and told the secret: she had painted it. The flowers were exhibited under glasses."

her dried leaves are sought for to give scent to royal cabinets.

I'm going to the Marquis ——. Good night, dearest Madam !

H. L. P.

To Sir James Fellowes.

Bath, Fryday, 18 June, 1819.

No need to try distant countries now for a sight of les beaux Restes de l' Antiquité. We have them in Russell Street, and in such numbers that I am informed they actually incommode each other. Before my desired visit to dear Adbury, they shall display their beauties to my sight, for 'tis a dull thing not to know what lies so near one.

The thought of your going abroad in search of novelty lowers my spirits when I think of it, yet I believe you will go too ; and it will not be a right thing to do, because the departure of every wise and reflecting mind will be a national loss when vice and folly make their final stand, as soon they will do. Let the sun shine and the harvest come in copiously; that hour may be deferred, but it is not distant; and you have a post to maintain. While you read this you say, Ay, ay, she would have a loss, and so she wants to make me believe I should be missed at Court. Not so.

My literary character, to-day perhaps of some small trifling import to the shallow stream of prattle, would then be driven down by the torrent of talk; and poor H. L. P. wrecked in the storm's first fury. . . . . .

What a letter! but if one ever should prove the unworthy subject of conversation, 'tis better be told truth of, than lyes. Dear Mr. Mangin said to me last week, that his mother saw me once at the theatre sparkling in diamonds, the winter of 1764. " She wrote it down," said he, " when she came home, observing how beautiful you were." " I never possessed a diamond in my life," was my reply, " never was in a theatre from my first wedding day, till my daughter born in 1764 went with me; and never was considered through the early periods of my life as even tolerably pretty."

Adieu, and continue your kind partiality, disregarding the fabulous history of yours ever,

H. L. P.

The person Mrs. Mangin saw was Polly Hart, Mr. Thrale's mistress, whose picture he wore on his box, &c.

To Sir James Fellowes.

Bath, Tuesday, 6th July, 1819.

MY DEAR SIR, — The Doctor and Miss Fellowes, who I met yesterday dining at the Lutwyches, told me I might send a letter to you by him, and my heart feels glad of the opportunity. Samuel Lysons' death — a famous antiquarian, and keeper of the records in the Tower — lowers my spirits a little; not from tenderness, though 'tis shocking to me that a young man should die so suddenly, but because he had an odd humour of collecting things other people would wish annihilated; and I remember his making a breakfast for the Greatheeds, Kembles, and Mr. Piozzi and me once, many years ago, when he oddly pointed to some shelf in his chambers, crying, "There, there they are; I gathered up every paper, every nonsense that was written against you at the time of your marriage; every thing to ridicule either of you that could be found, and there they are." "Thank you," said I, and the conversation changed.

As we went home, I recollect John Kemble saying, "Lysons made it his business to come and tell him every disagreeable thing he could think on concerning himself; every ballad, every satirical criticism he could hear of." What a taste! and now he is dead, one cannot help feeling *feels* about it.

But his brother Daniel is a cool-headed man and has children, and will not like making enemies — will he?*

I am half and but half uneasy—pacify my nerves, dear Sir, with assurances of your care, that no harm shall come to your ever obliged and faithful

H. L. Piozzi.

Love to the dear ladies, and good wishes for a young and beautiful beau.

---

* I have examined the collections in question, and am convinced that Mrs. Piozzi was mistaken when she wrote this letter, which is quite irreconcilable with her frequently expressed esteem for both of the brothers.

To Sir James Fellowes.

Bath, Wednesday, 7th July, 1819.

THE valorous fellows in the North are very noisy indeed, and exhibit Milton's meeting of rebellious spirits with too much exactness; but all this gas, literal and figurative, is as likely to do mischief as good, and will take fire with a spark in an instant.

Mr. John Dimond told me just now that Covent Garden Theatre had escaped blazing almost by miracle. The head of the retort flying off, the whole space under the stage was rendered suddenly combustible; and had not the man who approached with a light, had the wit to throw that light behind him, the whole would have consumed directly.*

Gala on my eightieth birthday.

When I return home I shall calculate whether I can get to dear Adbury, and thence to London.

To Sir James Fellowes.

Weston-super-Mare, 27 August, 1819.

I FEEL delighted, dear Sir, that you have not forgotten me. Some ladies that I met upon the sands last night said Sir James Fellowes had mentioned my name at gay and fashionable Bognor. This little place is neither gay nor fashionable, yet full as an egg, in-

---

* It was on this occasion that the stage manager came forward to beg the audience not to be afraid of fire, as he could drown the pit in five minutes.

sipid as the white on't, and dear as an egg o' penny. I
inquired for books; there were but two in the town
was the reply, a Bible and a Paradise Lost. They
were the best, however. No market; but I don't care
about that. When Miss Burney asked Omiah, the.
savage, if he should like to go back to Otaheite, "Yes,
Miss," said he; "no mutton there, no coach, no
dish of tea, no pretty Miss Horneck; good air, good sea,
and *very good dog*. I happy at Otaheite." My taste
and his are similar.

The breezes here are most salubrious; no land nearer
than North America, when we look down the channel;
and 'tis said that Sebastian Cabot used to stand where
I sit now, and meditate his future discoveries of New-
foundland. Who would be living at Bath now? the
bottom of the town a stew-pot, the top a gridiron, and
London in a state of defence or preparation for attack,
or some strange situation, while poor little Weston is
free from alarms, on Juvenal's principle, *Cantabit va-
cuus coram latrone viator*. I offered a cheque on
Hammersley at the hotel here. "Yes, Madam, by all
means," says the landlady; "but pray who is the gentleman? does he reside in Bath? or is he a Bristol merchant?" Our banker little dream'd that such questions
could be asked concerning him; and indeed it reminded
me of the character in Congreve, who when spoken
to of Epictetus, inquired whether he was really a
French cook, or only one who wrote out particular re-
ceipts.

Miss W——, everybody tells me, is breaking up very

fast, but some must come into the world, and some must go out on't, while it lasts. The comet is gone by without hurting anybody, and when Mr. Hunt's voice is stopt by a rope, there are those who believe we shall be quiet—and so we may, perhaps,—at Manchester.

We have swarms of babies here, and some bathe good-humouredly enough, while others scream and shriek as if they were going to execution. Bessy's boy is among them, completely hydrophobous.

I am going on a water-party next Monday with a very agreeable young man, Mr. Rogers. There are few people here that I know; one lady, however, challenged me as an acquaintance of her brother's just seventy years ago, when he was a little boy at Weston's school, and used to come home for holidays with Sir Robert Salusbury Cotton, father of this Lord Comber-mere, to our house in Jermyn Street, now part of Blake's Hotel.

Adieu, dear Sir, *portez vous bien.* Present me to Lady Fellowes, and tell your children they have an humble and an attached servant in

H. L. PIOZZI.

To Sir James Fellowes.

Weston-super-Mare,
Tuesday, 21 September, 1819. '

I OWE you a long letter, and my dear Sir James Fel-lowes knows that I am always desirous to balance my accounts, how much more when the sun is in Libra! It is indeed an especial mercy that I should be above ground cracking jokes, and making quibbles at fourscore years old; and the people do make such a wonder of me, that by and by they will deceive me into a marvellous good opinion of myself.

My fearlessness in the water attracts the women to the rocks, where it seems such fine sport to see Mrs. Piozzi swim. Poor H. L. P. ! she will certainly end in a fish, an odd fish ; but 'tis long since any could have said of her, *Mulier formosa supernè.*

Mr. Thrale used to teach Lady Keith with a frog in a large bason, and be so rough with her if she alleged terror, that we swam in our own defence, for he swore he would follow with a horsewhip if we dug a hole in the water, as he justly called it. Dear —— will follow us without any threatenings. She can scarcely fail of being a beautiful woman. Shall we wish her to be a wit, after reading the story of Floretta and the epitaph on my mother ? When I said, "Why did you name her person before her mind, Doctor Johnson ? " " Just because everybody can judge of the one, and hardly anybody can judge of the other," was the truly wise reply.

Hayley and I were never friends, you know ; Lady Sophronia's character and that of Dr. Rumble in some of his never-read writings, only lost our good will, and got no admiration from any one. The epigram on him and Miss Seward were among the things Sammy Lysons used to read with a world of humour. I much wonder what became of that man's literary gleanings. Dear

Conway's kind offer of buying them instantly for me, should they be set for sale, would have won my heart if he had not gained it before; but I hope the danger is over now.

Meanwhile I was right in saying that such small knaveries or follies will merge in the grand knavery of these Russells* and Burdetts, who really should be more careful than they are of their own interest; and when they are galvanising the otherwise inert populace, should mind and not exert too strong a power, as the modern phraseology terms it. The monstrous engine they are by steam and vapour raising against Government will fall upon and crush us all under its weight. Sin in Milton acted as they do precisely, for—

> " . . . . . She opened; but to shut
> Excell'd her power: the gates wide open stood,
> That with expanded wings a banner'd host
> Under spread ensigns marching, might pass thro'
> With horse and chariots rank'd in loose array:
> So wide they stood, and like a furnace mouth
> Cast forth redounding smoke and ruddy flame.
> Before their eyes in sudden view appear
> The secrets of the hoary deep — a dark
> Illimitable ocean — without bound,
> Without dimension, where length, breadth, and height,
> And time, and place are lost."

Fools! teaching, as you say, English boys to sing Ça ira! when they don't know nor can guess what it means. They do know, however, what it means to deny their

---

* Alluding to Lord John Russell's and Sir Francis Burdett's advocacy of Reform in Parliament.

Redeemer's divinity, and find out how Jesus Christ was only an honest man ; yet some of them, of these horrid Unitarians, do believe that he will come to judge the world too. I guess not why, but suppose they settle it on the old classic system of Minos, who put his chancellor's seal in commission, did not he? and called Rhadamanthus and Æacus to his assistance on great occasions. Oh! they are a precious set, certainly.

We had a gentleman here yesterday who attracted much notice. He was young and handsome, had ten lovely children, most of them females, by a beautiful lady, who, being of this new persuasion, seduced her husband to own her opinions, and half break the heart of his good father, the learned and pious Sir Abraham Elton, eighty-six years old. Well, a Mr. Rogers was telling me all this yester-morning, and added that young Elton was a fine actor once in private theatricals, but that he was a serious man now, forbore to play at cards, or dance, or see a play ; and was supposed to write Hunt's speeches for him, and send essays to the office in London where Deism and French philosophy are taught, under direction of Mr. Carlisle: but oh! what was my sense of horror at 5 o'clock the same dreadful yesterday, to hear that this man was raving round the town in fruitless pursuit of his two sons — one fourteen, the other sixteen years of age, both good swimmers — both certainly and irrecoverably drowned ; the mother saved from suicide only by the immediate intervention of a medical man, a Welshman, a Mr. Price. To-day they have left the place.

My plan is to walk and bathe, and enjoy the salutary breezes of poor little Weston, and then home to my nest at No. 8, Gay Street; no London or Adbury this year. When returned home, I shall call on your Divie Robertson for a double portion of his fine wine, because the Salusburys of Brynbella will come to me at Christmas.

Adieu! I have scarce room to say how faithful a servant you and your fair lady and dear babies possess in their and your ever obliged and grateful

H. L. P.

To Sir James Fellowes.

No. 8, Gay St., Bath,
Sunday, 24 Oct. 1819.

CONGRATULATE me, dear Sir James Fellowes, on my return from a place where, as I told you, the name of Hammersley was unknown. They said if he was a Bath shopkeeper or Bristol merchant, they would take his drafts, not else: so far behind Denbigh or St. Asaph. They had, however, heard of Mr. Carlisle *, and were not sure but he was right, for there were many opinions. Mine is, that Lord Byron's book (Cain) will do more mischief than his; and you see there is a cheap edition advertised, in order to disseminate the poyson. Why, the yellow fever is not half as mischievous. You are sadly wanted in Spain just now. A lady told me

---

* The publisher of Paine's "Age of Reason" and other infidel works.

since I came home, that the plague was wanted here to thin our numbers and correct our vices. Were ever such opinions broached before? were ever such ideas of right and wrong entertained in this country till now? I certainly have lived long and never heard them. Lord Fitzwilliam's dismissal * fills every mouth.

Why, we shall be divided soon, like the Hebrew alphabet, into radicals and serviles. But here come Sir Henry and Lady Baynton, and a boy that was just born when I saw him last, now an elegant lad—*bien manière* — and so like his pretty mamma, I quite admired him. Mercy on me! how the generations of mortal man do spring up! to dance the dance of life from top to bottom of the long room.

" The three black Graces, Law, Physick, and Divinity,
   Walk hand in hand along the Strand and dance *La Poule ;*
   Trade leaves her counter, Alma her latinity,
   Proud and vain with Mr. Paine to go to school.
   Should you want advice at law, you'll little gain by asking it :
   Your lawyer's not at Westminster, he is busy *Pas de Basquing* it.
   Should you wish a tooth to lose and run to Wayte for drawing it,
   He can't possibly attend—he's *demi Queue de Chat'ing* it :
   Run neighbour, run ; all London is quadrilling it,
   While order and sobriety dance *Dos-à-dos.*"

These are clever Mr. Smith's clever verses, the man who wrote the Rejected Addresses, and were sent me by one of the fashionables.

．   ．   ．   ．   ．   ．   ．   ．

They are making bonfires of Bibles in the North, I'm

* From the lord-lieutenancy of Yorkshire.

told, but your great folio in three monstrous volumes will escape I hope. The Reformers shall burn *me* before they fall upon that; there is no talk of their disturbing Bath with their Reformation.

I hear wondrous tales of Doctor and Mrs. Whalley; half the town saying he is the party aggrieved, and the other half lamenting the lady's fate. Two wiseacres sure, old acquaintances of forty years' standing, and both past seventy years old! . . .

The Salusburys come to me on the 20th of December: we will set about quadrilling it the last week in January, when you and your lady will surely do honour and give grace to the eightieth birthday of dear Sir James Fellowes's ever obliged friend and true servant,

H. L. P.

To Sir James Fellowes.

Bath, Monday, 17 Jan. 1820.

YOUR wonderful friend, my dear Sir James Fellowes, will be most wonderfully disappointed if she cannot boast your appearance at her last concert, &c.; her last foolery! such a foolery! but you will come, and so will Lady Fellowes, and your sister is sure of it, and so is your H. L. P. The frost breaks gently, and I hope when spring returns, we shall have compensation for this cruel Siberian winter. It has killed the poor half crazy lady that our friend Miss Williams lived with; she died last night suddenly of the cramp in her stomach, and I know not how the brother and Miss

Williams will manage, either to part or live together:
because the sister was a sunk fence you know, and if
they do not marry or separate, why the people will cry
ha! ha! Well, 'tis a blest thing to be fourscore, and I
would not be younger for the world I am going to quit.
My health and spirits are good, and my friends are very
good to me, and I can be as kind to them as I please,—
defying scandal and the "Morning Post."

These verses were brought me to-day. Mr. Mant,
who wrote them, heard some uninvited lady exclaim,
"Lord! will this Mrs. Piozzi never have done singing
and dancing!" he instantly replied: —

> "Sweet Puritans! don't frown severe
> On dear Piozzi's dance and cheer;
> Groaning beneath your loads of sin,
> She does not bid *you* enter in ;
> But mindful of youth's happy day,
> When innocence was glad and gay
> (Now well assur'd that joy alone
> Can to the pure of heart be known),
> She bids the ignorant of wrong
> Her dance attend—a jovial throng ;
> And friends long-lov'd she calls to see
> The scenes of liveliness and glee.
> Nor least will they that gladness prize
> Who only come to sympathise :
> Induced by arguments so weighty,
> She dares to give a ball at eighty."

Well, verses are fine things, and

Praises are pretty things, 'tis true :
 Yet, to a well turned mind, the pain
Of making them, indeed, our due,
 Is the best pleasure we can gain.

And I would rather see how my book stands at Hammersleys than any poetry of my own or my neighbours. People of letters are never people of figures, it is said; yet I have always been taught that two and two make four ; and when it appears that they make only *three,* I feel very nervous and very cross. We have got a new actress to supply the loss of Miss O'Neill—I like her best in a room though. Adieu! and hasten to Bath as Mr. Piozzi used to say—*non c'e tempo da perdere* — if you would wish to see untorn to pieces for cards of admission, yours and your dear family's ever grateful and faithful

H. L. P.

To Sir James Fellowes.

Tuesday Evening, April 4th, 1820.

 . . . The fête was a long promised foolery, and can never happen again, and did do exactly what I meant it should ; it procured me the power of making Conway's benefit equal to Warde's, notwithstanding Miss Wroughton's party, &c. He has left our town and our stage now, and I shall trouble my head no more with theatrical affairs, except to remunerate charming Mr. Loder's loyalty, who would not be seduced from my orchestra to that of Mr. Ashe: let ladies, and beauties, and pecuniary inducements go which way they would. *Au reste,* your sister says she is bilious, and must go to Cheltenham. I feel very sorry, but the dear doctor's constitution seconds him through all acts of heroism. He was screaming with gout to-day: gout in his foot, the roughest and most regular fit he has experienced these seven years. The torture of all those horrid operations, he swears, was nothing of pain to what he now suffers: so true is it that God Almighty does not trust the rod of reproof out of his own hand, nor suffer mortals to inflict upon each other, what natural illnesses, gout, stone, and the pangs of parturition impose on us all every day in the course of nature. I am glad it is so; for our new masters, *le peuple souverain,* would, I fear, prove rough dispensers of punishment, and kind behaviour does not seem to excite the courtesy, expected by those who so willingly make that Row-Tow to Messrs. Hunt, Cobbet and Co., which they scorned to bestow on the Emperor of China.

Well! kings are out of fashion certainly, but queens are in. The Hymenoptera of Linnæus included all animals that possessed stings, I am told; and if George IV. delights in study of reptiles and insects, he may soon be master of the subject. A popular government suits best where there is thin population. Spain will do well enough under an oligarchy of the great nobles, besides that your old friends the Castilians will wish to be under the rule and sway of Hidalgos, whether King or Cortes; indeed, I wish them success, and think Ferdinand will have more leisure to embroider trimmings for the Blessed Virgin's petticoat, when relieved from the cares of state.

What did they do with Godoy? did they strip him of his ill-gotten wealth? I either never heard, or have forgotten. A young lad, nephew to Miss Williams, who has been some years abroad for his health, says the whole Continent is even yet warm in its passion for Buonaparte, whose return they still hope to hail in due time : —

Thyrsis when he left me swore
In the spring he would return ;
What then means that violet flow'r?
Or the bud that decks the thorn?
'Twas the lark that upward sprung,
'Twas the nightingale that sung.
Idle notes untimely green,
Why such unavailing haste?
Summer suns and skies serene
Prove not always winter past.
Ease my fears, my doubt remove,
Spare the honour of my love.

REPLY.

Thyrsis will return no more,
Simple maid, expect him not ;
Ere the autumn well was o'er
Were his summer vows forgot :
But since wintry snows and rain
Not a trace of them remain.

Cease repining, simple maid !
  Thorns may blossom, birds may sing
Love's a flow'r when once decay'd
  Knows of no returning spring.
Haste, and seek another swain,
  Trust ; and be deceiv'd again.

You have heard how the Duke of Marlborough was received here with hoots and hisses, and the arrest of his carriage and horses.   Lord Charles Churchill who . attended scarcely could protect him, and he ran for refuge to a rich half-crazy lady in the Crescent, from whence he came to a poor half-superannuated lady, No. 8, Gay Street, who he called his earliest friend, said how kind I had been to him when a sick little boy at Streatham, fifty years ago : how I had given him a little Shetland pony to ride, and so I did sure enough, but had forgotten it.   Poor wretched man !   We dine together to-day.   The weather is not amiss, as it appears, only a want of rain.   Adieu ! make my best attentions acceptable to Lady Fellowes and Mrs. Dorset and Mrs. J. Fellowes . . . from, dear Sir, your ever obliged and grateful and faithful

                                        H. L. P.

This moment brings me an agreeable letter from Mrs. Mostyn.   She and her youngest son are very gay at Florence, acting English plays, &c. . . . all among lord and lady performers of course.

To Sir James Fellowes.

13 April, 1820.

My dear Sir James Fellowes is but too partial to me, and to my letters : the verses are not mine, but certainly very pretty. Mr. Eckersall amazed me with the assurance of our Court's having been solicited by that of Austria to give the violet more room to grow; better say at once, Let the man out, a vigorous bag fox for Europe to hunt down another day. Rebellion, not ill-organised within our island, and growing discontents about the queen, &c., are too cold for our present taste of horrors. We long for lawful bloodshed; war and property tax, a battle in every newspaper, an enriched commissary in every fashionable street, like a country squire we once knew, who could not taste his brandy latterly, without it was warmed, he said, by Cayenne pepper.

Miss Fellowes is not well, and fancies Cheltenham will mend her. The Lapland winter we have endured has chilled the vital principle in many. My Oxfordshire tenant, wishes, no doubt, it had effected the same purpose in me. I can never get my money from that fellow without help of an attorney, which I dislike as expensive, or a quickening letter from Lord Keith, which I detest as offensive, because he once, if you remember, contested the property, and I hate making Chinese Row-Tow to the man for what is no favour.

Are not the Radicals in Scotland gay fellows to attack the military *sabre à la main?* Dear me! when a rebel-

x 2

lion not better organised, or very, very little better, made head against the reigning family in the year 1745, people laid down knife and fork, and began to pray, or to run, or to fight on one side or other. We are now so improved in philosophy that we do not even lay down our cards, or make the hanging up nineteen prisoners of war — within 300 miles of the Capital — any part of our conversation.

I am glad meanwhile that you intend to act as magistrate in these strange times. It were to be wished that the clergy might be exempted from that duty. They are enough hated as it is, and some one told me that the bishops were hooted and hissed going to a fine London dinner, I forget at whose house.

H. L. P.

To Sir James Fellowes.

No. 36, Royal Crescent, Clifton, near Bristol,
Tuesday, 27 June, 1820.

LORD, Sir! what heats are these? natural, civil, political : a conflagration of men's minds will make them tindery as your ship two hours before it took fire, and make all ready for a general burning. This place and weather are really very like Naples, and my face now is tanned like one of their biscuits. I recollect no such season since I spent mine at Exmouth. Dear Piozzi left me there a fortnight, while he went to London, and lived with Archdeacon Hamilton. My employment was to make up my "Journey Book" for the press ; my

amusements, to send him love-letters and verses, among
which these come most readily to my mind :—

I think I 've work'd exceeding hard
    To finish five score pages ;
I send you this upon a card
    In hopes you 'll pay my wages.
The servants all get drunk and mad,
    This heat their blood enrages ;
But your return will make us glad—
    That hope our care assuages.
To feel more fondness we defy
    All nations and all ages ;
And quite prefer your company
    To all the seven sages.
Then pr'ythee come, Oh, haste away
    And lengthen not your stages ;
We then will sing and dance and play
    And quit awhile our cages.

The plural number was used because Mrs. Mostyn,
then a child, was with me.

The heat was intense, I remember, and when he returned, we ran to see the lyons of the neighbourhood,
Plymouth, Powderham, Castle and Mount Edgecumbe.
I think 'tis exactly thirty years ago, when I was amused
by the ill-timed eulogium pronounced by a vulgar fellow
on Shenstone's Leasowes. We were going over the
Terrace with a heap of wonder-seers, just such a hot
day as this is at Lord Edgecumbe's : a man showing off
the prospect, &c. " Ay, Sir," says a rich looking in-

habitant of Highgate or Hampstead ; "it is very fine, sure, considering how far we are from London, but my wife likes a tower, and we always does go somewhere, seeing our pockets is pretty warm, ha, ha, ha! and so last year we goes to her relations at Hales Owen, and there I saw a sweet place — did not us, lovey? with an inland prospect, such as I can see with my eyes, not a good sight either—and river fish."

"Why," says dear Sir James Fellowes, "you are just like the man you laugh at, Mrs. Piozzi. To be telling old stories now, when every body is thinking, at least talking, of the Queen." Perhaps so, but I am ill-provided with argument *pour ou contre*, and feel towards a general topic, as a pretty woman feels towards a general mourning if black does not become her complexion. So here I sit crying—

> " All conquering heat, oh, intermit thy wrath,
> And on my throbbing temples, potent thus,
> Beam not so fierce."

But, at eighty-one years old, pride should be burned out, and shall be. I will set in the West, and find some sea-beaten shore to forget the fallacious world in. Three weeks more in this lovely spot will, I trust, suffice ; and then, as the Irish lady said, I may take lave of the company without an apology.

Wherever I am, you, dear Sir, will be sure to hear of yours and your family's

Faithful as obliged,
H. L. P.

To Sir James Fellowes.

No. 36, Royal Crescent, Clifton,
Sunday, 16 July, 1820.

"Nothing so dull as a consolatory letter," says some pert wit of the last age. True; but this need not be dull for that reason, as it will not try to obtrude insipid consolation. Lord Gwydir is dead, and I am very sorry; happiest that we were no better acquainted, for then I should have been more sorry at his loss.

I saw —— expected the stroke, though shrinking from it: and yet, without death, toils, virtues, hopes would make but one chimera. I will go wait for mine at the Land's End, a proper place enough, if bordering on the ocean of eternity. This place adds to the small but strong threads that fasten one to life; . . it is so beautiful. The situation so like Naples; the view so like that from Brynbella, but too expensive.

I will go feed on fish and chickens at Penzance, and if I ever should come back to the living world again, will hasten through dear Adbury to see if she who is now a queen regnant, despotic over the minds of multitudes, will have used her arbitrary power mildly, or set your metropolis o' fire, as she doubtless could to-morrow, if she chose it. "There is a tide, however, in the affairs of men," as Shakespear says, and if she misses it, must take the consequences. Thais carried a brand to Persepolis on less provocation, and Phryne delighted in building up the walls of Thebes, which Alexander destroyed. We must learn the lady's disposition before we pronounce on the future. The present is tremendous to be sure. Salusbury talked of visiting me in Cornewall, but will, I fancy, let that alone, as he will not find the derivation an exact one: Corno Wallia, horn of abundance to Wales. If I save any money, I will spend it on myself, doing my own way.

Mrs. Pennington lives here, and is most hospitably kind to me. What a proof of the mutability of taste does this little district exhibit! When she married from Streatham Park, where we passed much time together, Mr. Pennington was master of ceremonies at the Hot Wells, and considered his post as worth 400*l.* o' year. The place is now deserted, a spot for hospitals or national schools, and their house, with five elegant rooms on a floor, a perfect and positive incumbrance, such as they can neither let nor sell. Sidmouth, too, where I remember she ran with her mother one summer, afforded quite incomparable lodging and boarding for them and their maid: one guinea only o' week. A gentleman told me just now, he paid seven pounds o' week for a house there.

Let me find a letter directed to Post office, Penzance, and tell me dear Maria is never sick like Salusbury's children; which, however, do not die, thank God! but battle their way, as it appears, through dreadful illnesses — or they dream so. Oh, if we knew what babies coming into the world were born to see and suffer, with what different looks should we contemplate their growing beauties! but the distant hills always look soft and fair, not rough and rocky as on nearer approach. May your younglings be happy, and yourself, dear Sir, as happy as is wished you by her, who will ever retain a grateful sense of that partial good opinion which is the boast of poor

H. L. P.

To Sir James Fellowes.

Penzance, 12 August, 1820.

" How happy is the blameless vestal's lot,
The world forgetting, by the world forgot ! "

says old H. L. Piozzi at eighty-one, and dear Sir James Fellowes, as he well may, laughing at her; but any antiquated joke is better than too long and too seriously to lament, as I fear our dear-loved Doctor does, the common fate of humanity in poor Lord Gwydir. Whatever we lose in this world we cannot very long be sorrowing for. My life, and that of your excellent father, though drawn out to such uncommon length, are but as points imperceptible as this, in the folio-page of eternity, to which we are approaching like the second-hand upon a stop-watch, that moves round while we look off and on again.

" Yea, but all this did I know before," say you; " it would be better tell about Penzance."

The only place I know but little of. Why then Penzance, if I'm to live another fourscore years and rival old Harry Jenkins, will be to me what Minorca is to Dr. F——, a place of recollection for cheap living, and the best eating possible. Red mullets large and beautiful, 4*d.* o' piece; pipers and dories, herrings, almost for carrying home. Kid, as in the Tyrolese Alps, where we ate it, you know, stuck with rosemary; and mutton exactly like that in North Wales, small, fat, and tender. Now for the negative catalogue. No conversation, no circulating library, no rooms for purpose of assembling to dance, chat, or play at cards; no theatre, no music meeting, no pictures, and what is stranger far, no picturesque, the bay alone excepted. For the country—Churchill might have looked south as well as north when he exclaimed,—

> " Far as the eye can reach no tree was seen,
> Earth, clad in russet, scorn'd the living green."

Oh! 'tis a melancholy place for talking folks. Botanists, however, may justly delight in it. Every wretched habitation has a garden, perfumed by carnations and redolent of sweets from many a foreign shrub whose name I know not; for the whole place is in itself a sun-trap; and if they cultivated vines here, here they would grow. They are, however, occupied, and skilled too, I believe, in underground acquisitions. Mining is both the business and pleasure of people here; and while it does seem as if earth's surface at this time teemed with events capable of arresting attention, our Cornish neighbours set up a geological school, and spend what intellect they have on feltzspar and quartz; little heeding whether Paris is burned by incendiaries, or Spain torn in pieces by a civil war; whether condemnation or acquittal of a conspicuous princess endangers the safety of our own metropolis, or whether old Rome is to be destroyed at last by her own hands, avoiding threatened ills from foreign power, and expiring, as her scorpions do, by suicide.

Dear Mrs. Siddons, when I lived much with her and with the Kembles, used to say my principal characteristic was candour, giving the good and bad in every description of people and of things. I hope ill-fortune, ill-health, or ill-humour have not yet spoiled me for "an honest chronicler" like my countryman, Griffith, who in Shakespear's Henry VIII. gives an account of Cardinal Wolsey's death and conduct, balancing the good and evil.

'Tis really no bad thing now to possess my much-praised memory, for books here are none, and I left mine ("Thraliana" with them) in the good ship "Happy Return," bound for Penzance, in the Cumberland Bason, Bristol, with our cook, plate, linen, clothes, tea, wine, every earthly thing on board, three long weeks ago; nay, four, by the time my friends at Adbury receive this letter from a distant region.

Write to me, dear Sir James, oh pray write for pity on a poor creature starving for intellectual food, in danger of repletion from too much corporeal. Bessy has made herself sick with crab, a downright cholera, and Lord! how I was frighted; but we have a good physician, Dr. Forbes, and the danger is all over.

Adieu. Did we not once, in the little room, New King Street, agree that nothing but the consciousness of having done right could comfort solitary moments?

But alas! your honour's fine Bible, in three vols. folio, is even now tossing on the ocean. I would it were come to console yours and your father's, and your brothers', and dear, dear Fellie's everlastingly obliged

H. L. PIOZZI.

To Miss Willoughby.

Penzance, Fryday, 25 August, 1820.

FRANK or no frank, I rejoyce to see the handwriting of dear Miss Willoughby in this distant region to which I have condemned myself for a long portion of my short life. As I have lived, however, eighty-one years next January, I may exist on to April and May, if it should so please God; and then no fear but of my too great haste to join the living world again in a quiet way, for over-grown society is as great a burden — nay, greater to me — than solitude. At your age, however, it is not only pleasant but proper that somewhat of life should be learned, and you were fortunate in finding London gay and communicative. Doctor Johnson said that after the full flow of London conversation, every place was a blank; I wonder what he would have thought of dull Penzance? We had a Spenceiana in our hands at Streatham Park while he was writing the Poets' Lives; and when I borrowed the Anecdotes at Bath, there was little quite new, but it seemed to me that Spence was partial.

My paper, the "Morning Post," about three days

back mentions a case in point to the present upon tryal.* What can he mean? I have cudgelled my brains, and turned over Wraxall's " Memoirs " in vain, though the event was in 1780, the editor says, a year I remember but too well. Ask Mrs. Fox if she can guess what story he alludes to, and tell me what wonders Lord Byron is come home to do, for I see his arrival in the paper. His grandmother was my intimate friend, a Cornish lady, Sophia Trevanion, wife to the Admiral, *pour ses péchès*, and we called her Mrs. Biron always, after the French manner. The friends you live among are more likely to know facts concerning Atterbury's tryal than I am, and where to find the letter, for such a letter there is, sure enough. Pope's letter to the Bishop at parting is pretty, and tender, and *touchant;* but I have not a good edition of Swift here, and the reading people of this town study only what is under ground, neglectful of the superfices. We have a geological school here, and professors; better than Weston-super-Mare, you'll say, where two books only were to be found in the place, a Bible and a Paradise Lost. I bought them both.

To Sir James Fellowes.

Penzance, 23rd Sept. 1820.

My dear Sir James Fellowes should not have been followed up in this shameless manner, but that a letter

* The Queen's Trial.

from his brother Dorset, to whom I owe so much of
kindness and obedience, charged me to write immediately to Adbury, and say he was well and happy (as
it appears) at Paris. It made me so to understand how,
quiet all is there ; and but that I believe the calm pre-
cedes *bourrasque*, my heart might be easy as to poor
Louis Dix-huit, who I must love both as a king and individual. When he shall be removed, much misery
will befall that devoted nation, which having set fire to
all Europe, will herself perish first in the flame. You
know I cried *proximus ardet* long ago ; but no one listened.

Meanwhile, here am I at Penzance. " Ay," says the
fool, in Shakespear's " As You Like It," "here am I
in the Forest of Ardennes, thou fool I." But 'tis plain
my fancy was not guided by his, who admonishes mortal
man not to dwell either in a ditch, or on a terrace ;
you have always found me either in the one, or on the
other.   .   .   .   .   .   .

Meanwhile, Charles Shephard has written to me
from Santa Lucia, where he is Attorney-General, and
where, from the public newspapers, he heard of my
octogenary fête, and wished me joy with unabated good
humour.

Prosperity does make, or keep people good-humoured,
and if I can live to the 10th of July, 1821, I will be
good humoured too; unless the radicals break up our
funds entirely. For love of the Queen and the country,
Cobbett did say in some of his papers three years ago,
what a pleasure it would be to see 300,000 people starv-

ing; for then we should get rid of six individuals to him very obnoxious. A cheerful calculation! For my own part, however, I hope to come out next year with the swallows, if possible: they, and the sun, and your most humble servant, are all half torpid, or retired at least during winter; and they tell me there is no winter at Penzance. A lady said here the other day, that she went to Taunton last year, to see skaiting—a diversion she had often heard of, and that she was gratified during her absence from home with a heavy fall of snow. I rather fancy there is some truth in all this, because of the shrubs in every little garden plot: rhododendron now in beauty; myrtles covered with bloom, like Italy; and the arbutus high as an apple-tree, very handsome indeed, *sed non omnes arbusta juvant, humilesque myricæ;* and if I am doomed to six months' exile, the finding myself in Botany Bay, will afford small consolation. Old friends in leather jackets, the books, do not desert me, and new friends are civil, send me figs and peaches, and invite me to their little parties, where we play sixpenny whist comfortably enough. Apropos to whist, you see the Duke of Grafton's papers explained nothing concerning who wrote Junius.

To Sir James Fellowes.

Penzance, Wednesday, 4 Jan. 1821.

MIL Años y mas, viva V. M., my dear Sir James Fellowes, whom I hasten to make again my debtor, as dili-

gently as Tully*·would hasten to make me so. I owe
him but 10*l.* now, however, and dividend day is coming.
Apropos, my tenant, and your honour's not very
near neighbour—but neighbour compared to the distance I live at from all the world—is in arrears 91*l.*
he did squeeze out 109*l.* of the October money just
before Christmas, and promised the rest; but those
promises, like Tully's pie-crust, are made to be broken;
a *pâté vol au vent,* I suppose.

I, and Miss Willoughby, who followed me uninvited; came hither professedly to avoid winter; and
never in my sight did winter assume so terrific, so
formidable a form: the sea rising to a tremendous
height; fogs and snow thickening all around; and
when any one is able to stand the storm, and call at
the house, tales of shipwreck in every mouth. I will
come to Penzance no more.

Meanwhile, poor Bath has, as you say, been suffering by the other destructive element; what a mercy
that I was able to discharge Upham's long bill, before
he was burned out of the premises I have often felt
happy in. The fire-eaters would have been perhaps no
better, they could not have been more active or friendly
assistants than that charming Loder, the violin-player;
who volunteered his services, and resigned the ruining
those delicate fingers, by which alone he lives, to save
the property of a man whose prejudices all militate
against stage and orchestra. But virtue and genius
should go together, and they commonly do.

* The Bath confectioner.

The Bath newspaper tells of a clergyman at New-
bury, who has prayed for the Queen ever since George
4th's accession, but who is now forbidden to do so by
his Bishop.

Old Beadon, Bishop of Bath and Wells, is in *articulo
mortis*, I understand, and probably Dr. Hall, if he is
the bold man who stept forward with the prohibition,
will succeed him. Llandaff was treated very roughly
on less provocation by half.

Fine times! are they not. The retrospect may be
entertaining to the century; but this, young as it is,
will smart, I think, before the year 1850.

Pourriture avant maturité, as the great Frederick
of Prussia used to deprecate for his own government. I
have never had courage to look in "Thraliana" since
my arrival; so little does looking backward delight
me.

At eighty-one years old 'tis time to begin reconnoi-
tring, when we know that retreat is impossible. Twenty
years, *y mas*, have elapsed, since my two quartos were
sent out, like Hamblet's father, with all their imperfec-
tions on their head. Well! no matter.

Do you remember the Name Book? it ended with Zenobia, and I must tell a story of a Cornish gentlewoman
hard by here, Zenobia Stevens, who held a lease under
the Duke of Bolton by her own life only—ninety-nine
years — and going at the term's end ten miles to give
it up. She obtained kind permission to continue in the
house as long as she lived, and was asked, of course, to
drink a glass of wine. She did take one, but declined

the second, saying, she had to ride home in the twilight upon a young colt, and was afraid to make herself giddy headed.

Don't I hear you cry, bravo Zenobia?

——'s pretty wife is screaming, I believe: she has outlived two accoucheurs. No wonder: I do think a country practitioner (meaning a medical man of all work) should have an iron constitution.* Our agreeable Dr. Forbes seems so endowed: a Scotchman, a competent scholar, full of country anecdote, and he told me the true tale of Zenobia, whose daughter died the other day, aged ninety-eight only. Those who said no snow was ever seen at Penzance, dealt in fiction and fable: here is a heavy snow this moment, and but that the sea is open enough, God knows, I should call it a polar winter. Dr. Parry's son will go again, it seems, for another 5000*l.*; other inducement there can be none, and the most curious circumstance of the voyage is an account given by one of the officers, how his Irish setter, a tall smooth spaniel, attracted the attentions of a she wolf on Melville Island, who made love to the handsome dandy, and seduced him at length to end his days with her and her rough-haired family, refusing every invitation of return to the ship; a certain proof that dog, fox, jackall, &c. are only accidental varieties; while lupo is head of the house, penkennedil, as Welsh and Cornish people call it.

* In one of her marginal notes she quotes the saying of a distinguished lawyer, that a judge should have a face of brass, a constitution of iron, and a bottom of lead.

Adieu! I am going to eat a cod's-head, which you would be happy to give two guineas for, when Lord Carnarvon dines with you. My servants have the rest for their dinner to-day and to-morrow. The whole fish cost half-a-crown. But there is a mermaid coming to England I hear. That she ends in *piscem*, I partly believe, but *mulier formosa* I doubt. No room for more nonsense, scarce enough to say how many wishes for yours and your family's happiness are breathed in this distant region by, dear Sir, yours and their most obliged and grateful and faithful servant,

H. L. Piozzi.

To William Dorset Fellowes, Esq.

Penzance, 14 February, 1821.

Well, my dear Sir,—

> This day, whate'er the fates decree,
> Shall still be kept with joy by me.

Sir James had a long letter from me some weeks ago, but I believe his tooth ache was so bad he never minded it. There has been a new attack made on my property, of which I gave him an account; but it will end in smoke before I can have time to tell you the tale, which relates to dividends left standing, unclaimed, an immense while, in the names of Thrale and Gifford. Some Mr. K——, I know not who, flies at me to ask what I did with them? God knows I did nothing with them, nor ever heard a breath concerning the matter,

till his letter put me upon inquiry, and having written
to Mrs. Merick Hoare, she consoles me by bearing testi-
mony to my innocence of having ever touched this 600*l.*
which this gentleman believes himself heir to.

But this comes of too long life. My coadjutors and
brethren in the executorship were, it seems (but I knew
it not), every one dead, when this stock was sold; and
the name of poor H. L. Piozzi answers for all at the
distance of fifteen years. If Mr. K—— ever crosses
your way, do tell him I am an honest creature, incapable of wronging even a fly. My husband's illness, and
my attendance on him who took up my whole heart and
thought, did I suppose obliterate the transaction from
my mind; which certainly does retain no trace of it.

Your duty as Secretary to the Lord Great Chamber-
lain of England * will now become less irksome, I hope,
and friendship may have her share of your active bene-
ficence; your dear sister is silent, but I am willing to
believe pleasure helps detain her from her pen.

Conway is in high favour at Bath, the papers say; so
indeed do private letters. That young man's value will
be one day properly appreciated; and then you and I
will be found to have been quite right all along.

Tell me about Miss Wilson meanwhile, and whether
'tis somewhat in the Billington style, that she is excel-
ling all the world so. My heart tells me 'tis a long
continued warble like *hers* which ever fascinates both
skilful and unskilful critics; and which is more the gift
of nature than of art.

* Lord Gwydir.

But I hate reasoning down our own enjoyments; 'tis like burning down rubies in a concave glass : the French never do it, and you will soon visit *them*, I dare say. *En attendant je vous souhaite, Monsieur* — it was a bishop's wish you know — *Paris en ce monde, Paradis en l'autre.*

To Miss Willoughby.

No. 10, Sion Row, Clifton,
16 March, 1821.

SOMETHING tells me — vanity I suppose — that dear Miss Willoughby will be glad to hear I am where I wish to be, on the sweet Gloucestershire Downs, numberless old acquaintance, and some new, kindly expressing pleasure at my return. Poor Mrs. Yorke, 10,000*l.* richer than when we parted ; ten years older, and all in ten months' time ; Mrs. Lambart's death, Sir Philip Jennings' sister, caused the alteration. Our friend Conway is not younger ; he won't play Master Slender now ; his enquiries after you were very kind indeed, and he rejoyced for my sake that Penzance was your chosen retreat. Oh, how he regrets his Lesserillo ! But Mr. Green has secured 500*l.* per annum, with an agreeable woman, and must not, for shame, lament the profession, which will not soon cease to lament him. The benefits are thin I hear, but that for which we are interested gives good hope. Monday, 26th, will be the day, and Mirandola, with the Chevalier de Moranges, the night's entertainment. I have seen the future footman ; he will at worst be better than poor James, I suppose: who is gone to Bath now on a frolic: Bessy tearing her hair, and Mrs. Pennington exhausting all her eloquence in expressions of wrath and anger.

It is almost time to tell you what a providence watched over your old friend at Exeter, after my letter was written, at three o'clock, Sunday morning. The bed was very high, and getting into it, I set my foot on a light chair, which flew from the pressure, and revenged it on my leg in a terrible manner.

The wonder is, no bones were broken; only a cruel bruise and slight tear, and we trotted on hither, after cathedral service, at which I hardly could kneel to thank God for my escape. So Sir John may look to my demise now at his leisure, and my legacy [leg I see].

"Not a mouse stirring," the French translators of Hamlet rendered, "Je n'ai pas entendu un souris trotter." Our mouse could not trot without your assistance; with it, he performed his journey beautiffully; though I did feel a horrid pang about my own imprudence, running into a dirty cottage on the road, full of the small-pox. Long live vaccination, however, and Dr. Jenner who first devised it.

Sunday, 18.

Here is a storm worthy of Mount's Bay; your billows must roar finely this morning. Bessy would not trust me to church, I should have been blown down the hill, she says. So since Mr. Le Gris's blessing has helped bring me safe hither, I must not press it further, but sit pretty and put my leg upon a chair, instead of my foot. Was not it a horrid accident? and in the dead of the night so! Dr. Forbes will be very sorry, for poor H. L. P., always a blue, now a black and blue, lady, bruised, say you, from top to toe?—"My Lord, from head to foot."

The pet books, sent by waggon from Penzance (Pascoe's cart carried them), are not arrived yet. The ship things all came safe.

To Sir James Fellowes.

24 March, 1821, Sunday Morning.

Your letter only came last night.

My dear Sir James Fellowes, though a tardy correspondent is always a kind one. True it is, that your sister has seduced me to dine with her on Tuesday next; and rejoyce in our friend Conway's success, which I hope to witness on Monday evening.

True it is, that I arrived at Clifton on the 12th March, escaping the stormy equinox, which must have shaken poor Penzance to the foundation. It is built upon the sand, so no wonder. True it is, that I hope to shew myself to you unimpaired, as to appearance; but my value will be lessened because I have broken my shin. Is not that the case now and then with a quick goer? Sleeping in Russel Street, however, would not do. I have asked Miss Williams to dine with Mrs. Pennington and me at the Elephant and Castle, where I will set up my repose, and keep my l. e. g — my elegy — in good repair. Mrs. Pennington is quite poetical, always eloquent on that, and every subject. Since my arrival at Sion Hill, — for there I occupy a lodging till my house in the Crescent is ready, — two parcels directed by tying friends, have given me a mournful sensation: they are letters written by me to them in distant days, I know not how happy. You will have to look them over after my death, and I dare say they are better than those I write now. My intention, however, is not to be in haste: though Salusbury seemed to apprehend his journey would be long and expensive if I died at Penzance. So here is poor aunt at the embouchure of his favourite River Severn, and here he may come after (the 10th of July) to look after the demise and the legacy [leg I see]; but he must stay away till I have put my house in order.

* "On the day following the date of this letter, which was the last I received from Mrs. Piozzi, I called at the Castle and Elephant at Bath, and found her and Mrs. Pennington. She was in high spirits, joking about the *l. e. g.* She dined with my father and sister, at No. 7, Russell Street, and was throughout the evening the admiration of the company, amongst whom were Mrs. Pennington, the lady so often mentioned in Anna Seward's correspondence as the beautiful and agreeable Sophia Weston; Admiral Sir Henry Bayntun, G.C.B., a distinguished naval officer at the battle of Trafalgar; Mr. Lutwyche (Mr. Lutwyche's house in Marlborough-buildings was celebrated for its hospitality, and as the resort of all the most agreeable society at Bath. Mrs. L. was the daughter of Sir Noah Thomas, a baronet and distinguished physician); and Mr. Conway, the actor, who was held in high estimation for his excellent private character. He fell overboard and was drowned on his passage from New York." — *Sir J. Fellowes.*

MISCELLANEOUS EXTRACTS FROM "THRALIANA."*

Miss Streatfield.—I have since heard that Dr. Collier picked up a more useful friend, a Mrs. Streatfield, a widow, high in fortune and rather eminent both for the beauties of person and mind; her children, I find, he has been educating; and her eldest daughter is just now coming out into the world with a great character for elegance and literature. — 20 November, 1776.

19 May, 1778.—The person who wrote the title of this book at the top of the page, on the other side — left hand — in the black letter, was the identical Miss Sophia Streatfield, mentioned in " Thraliana, " as pupil to poor dear Doctor Collier, after he and I had parted. By the chance meeting of some of the currents which keep this ocean of human life from stagnating, this lady and myself were driven together nine months ago at Brighthelmstone; we soon grew intimate from having often heard of each other, and I have now the honour and happiness of calling her my friend. Her face is eminently pretty; her carriage

* These extracts reached me after the preceding sheets were printed off.

elegant; her heart affectionate, and her mind cultivated. There is above all this an attractive sweetness
in her manner, which claims and promises to repay
one's confidence, and which drew from me the secret of
my keeping a " Thraliana," &c. &c. &c.

Jan. 1779.—Mr. Thrale is fallen in love really and
seriously with Sophy Streatfield; but there is no wonder
in that : she is very pretty, very gentle, soft, and insinuating; hangs about him, dances round him, cries when
she parts from him, squeezes his hand slyly, and with her
sweet eyes full of tears looks so fondly in his face*— and
all for love of me as she pretends; that I can hardly,
sometimes, help laughing in her face. A man must
not be a *man* but an *it*, to resist such artillery. Mar-
riott said very well,

> "Man flatt'ring man, not always can prevail,
> But woman flatt'ring man, can never fail."

Murphy did not use, I think, to have a good opinion
of me, but he seems to have changed his mind this
Christmas, and to believe better of me. I am glad
on't to be sure : the suffrage of such a man is well worth
having : he sees Thrale's love of the fair S. S. I suppose : approves my silent and patient endurance of what
I could not prevent by more rough and sincere behaviour.

---

* "And Merlin look'd and half believed her true,
So tender was her voice, so fair her face,
So sweetly gleam'd her eyes behind her tears,
Like sunlight on the plain, behind a shower."
Idylls of The King.— Vivien.

20 January, 1780. — Sophy Streatfield is come to town, she is in the "Morning Post" too, I see (to be in the "Morning Post" is no good thing). She has won Wedderburne's heart from his wife, I believe, and few married women will bear *that* patiently if I do; they will some of them wound her reputation, so that I question whether it can recover. Lady Erskine made many odd enquiries about her to me yesterday, and winked and looked wise at her sister. The dear S. S. must be a little on her guard; nothing is so spiteful as a woman robbed of a heart she thinks she has a claim upon. She will not lose *that* with temper, which she has taken perhaps no pains at all to preserve: and I do not observe with any pleasure, I fear, that my husband prefers Miss Streatfield to me, though I must acknowledge her younger, handsomer, and a better scholar. Of her chastity, however, I never had a doubt: she was bred by Dr. Collier in the strictest principles of piety and virtue; she not only knows she will be always chaste, but she knows why she will be so. Mr. Thrale is now by dint of disease quite out of the question, so I am a disinterested spectator; but her coquetry is very dangerous indeed, and I wish she were married that there might be an end on't. Mr. Thrale loves her, however, sick or well, better by a thousand degrees than he does me or any one else, and even now desires nothing on earth half so much as the sight of his Sophia.

> "E'en from the tomb the voice of nature cries !
> E'en in our ashes live their wonted fires !"

The Saturday before Mr. Thrale was taken ill —
Saturday, 19th February — he was struck Monday,
21st February — we had a large party to tea, cards, and
supper; Miss Streatfield was one, and as Mr. Thrale
sate by her, he pressed her hand to his heart (as she
told me herself), and said "Sophy, we shall not enjoy
this long, and to-night I will not be cheated of my only
comfort." Poor soul! how shockingly tender! on the
first Fryday that he spoke after his stupor, she came to
see him, and as she sate by the bedside pitying him,
"Oh," says he, "who would not suffer even all that I
have endured to be pitied by you!" This I heard
myself.

Here is Sophy Streatfield again, handsomer than
ever, and flushed with new conquests: the Bishop of
Chester feels her power, I am sure; she showed me a
letter from him that was as tender and had all the
tokens upon it as strong as ever I remember to have
seen 'em; I repeated to her out of Pope's Homer —
"Very well, Sophy," says I : —

> "Range undisturb'd among the hostile crew,
> But touch not Hinchliffe *, Hinchliffe is my due."

Miss Streatfield (says my master) could have quoted
these lines in the Greek; his saying so piqued me, and
piqued me because it was true. I wish I understood
Greek! Mr. Thrale's preference of her to me never
vexed me so much as my consciousness — or fear at
least — that he has reason for his preference. She has

* For Hector.

ten times my beauty, and five times my scholarship —
wit and knowledge has she none.

May, 1781.—Sophy Streatfield is an incomprehensible
girl; here has she been telling me such tender passages
of what passed between her and Mr. Thrale, that she
half frights me somehow, at the same time declaring her
attachment to Vyse yet her willingness to marry Lord
Loughborough. Good God! what an uncommon girl!
and handsome almost to perfection, I think: delicate in
her manners, soft in her voice, and strict in her principles: I never saw such a character, she is wholly out
of my reach; and I can only say that the man who
runs mad for Sophy Streatfield has no reason to be
ashamed of his passion; few people, however, seem
disposed to take her for life — everybody's admiration,
as Mrs. Byron says, and nobody's choice.

Streatham, 1st January, 1782. — Sophy Streatfield
has begun the new year nicely with a new conquest.
Poor dear Doctor Burney! *he* is now the reigning
favourite, and she spares neither pains nor caresses to
turn that good man's head, much to the vexation of his
family; particularly my Fanny, who is naturally provoked to see sport made of her father in his last stage
of life by a young coquet, whose sole employment in
this world seems to have been winning men's hearts on
purpose to fling them away. How she contrives to
keep bishops, and brewers, and doctors, and directors of
the East India Company, all in chains so, and almost
all at the same time, would amaze a wiser person than
me; I can only say let us mark the end! Hester will

perhaps see her out and pronounce, like Solon, on her wisdom and conduct.

Miss Nicholson. — After stating that she went to London, early in June, 1784, to procure a suitable companion for her daughters, after her marriage with Piozzi should have taken place, and mentioning several disáppointments, Mrs. Piozzi goes on to say : —

" Providence, however, directed a Miss Nicholson to my door, and her peculiarly pleasing manners attracted me strongly. She referred me to Mr. Evans of Southwark for her character; and to every exterior accomplishment no objection could be made. Correct though sprightly, and steady though cheerful in her manner : the elegance of her form, the maturity of her age, and the soft expression of her countenance fixed my election, and I brought home to my daughters a woman of fashion fit for them to reside or converse or consult with. This sweet Miss Nicholson will make all still more smooth to me; she is a well-wisher to the cause, and will, when the girls are parted from me, keep them from hating or trampling on the memory of a mother who adores them; she professes to like me excessively, and if she does, oh, how happy may this connection, so accidental and so extraordinary, make my poor suffering heart! God bless her ! "

Baretti.—Baretti had a comical aversion to Mrs. Macaulay, and his aversions are numerous and strong. If I had not once written his character in verse, I would now write it in prose, for few people know him better: he was — *Dieu me pardonne,* as the French say — my inmate for very near three years; and though I really liked the man once for his talents, and at last was weary of him for the use he made of them, I never altered my sentiments concerning him; for his character is easily seen, and his soul above disguise, haughty and insolent, and breathing defiance against all mankind; while his powers of mind exceed most people's, and his powers of purse are so slight that they leave him dependent on all. Baretti is for ever in the state of a stream dammed up: if he could once get loose, he would bear down all before him.

Every soul that visited at our house while he was master of it, went away abhorring it; and Mrs. Montagu, grieved to see my meekness so imposed upon, had thoughts of writing me on the subject an anonymous letter, advising me to break with him. Seward, who tried at last to reconcile us, confessed his wonder that we had lived together so long. Johnson used to oppose and battle him, but never with his own consent: the moment he was cool, he would always condemn himself for exerting his superiority over a man who was his friend, a foreigner, and poor: yet I have been told by Mrs. Montagu that he attributed his loss of our family to Johnson: ungrateful and ridiculous! if it had not been for his mediation, I would not so long have borne trampling on, as I did for the last two years of our acquaintance.

Not a servant, not a child, did he leave me any authority over; if I would attempt to correct or dismiss them, there was instant appeal to Mr. Baretti, who was

sure always to be against me in every dispute. With
Mr. Thrale I was ever cautious of contending, conscious
that a misunderstanding there could never answer, as I
have no friend or relation in the world to protect me
from the rough treatment of a husband, should he
chuse to exert his prerogatives ; but when 1 saw Baretti
openly urging Mr. Thrale to cut down some little fruit
trees my mother had planted and I had begged might
stand, I confess I did take an aversion to the creature,
and secretly resolved his stay should not be prolonged
by my intreaties whenever his greatness chose to take
huff and be gone.   As to my eldest daughter, his behaviour was most ungenerous; he was perpetually spur-
ring her to independence, telling her she had more
sense and would have a better fortune than her mother,
whose admonitions she ought therefore to despise ; that
she ought to write and receive her own letters *now*,
and not submit to an authority I could not keep up if
she once had the spirit to challenge it; that, if I died
in a lying-in which happened while he lived here, he
hoped Mr. Thrale would marry Miss Whitbred, who
would be a pretty companion for Hester, and not tyran-
nical and overbearing like me.   Was I not fortunate to
see myself once quit of a man like this? who thought
his dignity was concerned to set me at defiance, and who
was incessantly telling lies to my prejudice in the ears
of my husband and children ?   When he walked out of
the house on the 6th day of July, 1776, I wrote down
what follows in my table book.

6 July, 1776. — This day is made remarkable by the

departure of Mr. Baretti, who has, since October, 1773, been our almost constant inmate, companion, and, I vainly hoped, our friend. On the 11th of November, 1773, Mr. Thrale let him have 50*l.*, and at our return from France 50*l.* more, besides his clothes and pocket money: in return to all this, he instructed our eldest daughter—or thought he did—and puffed her about the town for a wit, a genius, a linguist, &c. At the beginning of the year 1776, we purposed visiting Italy under his conduct, but were prevented by an unforeseen and heavy calamity: that Baretti, however, might not be disappointed of money as well as of pleasure, Mr. Thrale presented him with 100 guineas, which at first calmed his wrath a little, but did not, perhaps, make amends for his vexation; this I am the more willing to believe, as Dr. Johnson not being angry too, seemed to grieve him no little, after all our preparations made.

Now Johnson's virtue was engaged; and he, I doubt not, made it a point of conscience not to increase the distresses of a family already oppressed with affliction. Baretti, however, from this time grew sullen and captious; he went on as usual notwithstanding, making Streatham his home, carrying on business there, when he thought he had any to do, and teaching his pupil at by-times when he chose so to employ himself; for he always took his choice of hours, and would often spitefully fix on such as were particularly disagreeable to me, whom he has now not liked a long while, if ever he did. He, professed, however, a

violent attachment to our eldest daughter; said if *she*
had died instead of her poor brother, he should have
destroyed himself, with many as wild expressions of
fondness. Within these few days, when my back was
turned, he would often be telling her that he would
go away and stay a month, with other threats of
the same nature; and she, not being of a caressing or
obliging disposition, never, I suppose, soothed his anger
or requested his stay.

Of all this, however, I can know nothing but from
her, who is very reserved, and whose kindness I cannot
so confide in as to be sure she would tell me all that
passed between them; and her attachment is probably
greater to him than me, whom he has always endeavoured to lessen as much as possible, both in her
eyes and — what was worse — her father's, by telling
him how my parts had been over-praised by Johnson,
and over-rated by the world; that my daughter's skill
in languages, even at the age of fourteen, would vastly
exceed mine, and such other idle stuff; which Mr.
Thrale had very little care about, but which Hetty
doubtless thought of great importance. Be this as it
may, no angry words ever passed between him and me,
except perhaps now and then a little spar or so when
company was by, in the way of raillery merely.

Yesterday, when Sir Joshua and Fitzmaurice dined
here, I addressed myself to him with great particularity
of attention, begging his company for Saturday, as
I expected ladies, and said he must come and flirt
with them, &c. My daughter in the meantime kept

on telling me that Mr. Baretti was grown very old and very cross, would not look at her exercises, but said he would leave this house soon, for it was no better than Pandæmonium. Accordingly, the next day he packed up his cloke-bag, which he had not done for three years, and sent it to town; and while we were wondering what he would say about it at breakfast, he was walking to London himself, without taking leave of any one person, except it may be the girl, who owns they had much talk, in the course of which he expressed great aversion to me and even to her, who, he said, he once thought well of.

Now whether she had ever told the man things that I might have said of him in his absence, by way of provoking him to go, and so rid herself of his tuition; whether he was puffed up with the last 100 guineas and longed to be spending it all' Italiano; whether he thought Mr. Thrale would call him back, and he should be better established here than ever; or whether he really was idiot enough to be angry at my threatening to whip Susan and Sophy for going out of bounds, although he had given them leave, for Hetty said that was the first offence he took huff at, I never now shall know, for he never expressed himself as an offended man to me, except one day when he was not shaved at the proper hour forsooth, and then I would not quarrel with him, because nobody was by, and I knew him be so vile a lyar that I durst not trust his tongue with a dispute. He is gone, however, loaded with little presents from me, and with a large share too of my good opinion, though I most sincerely rejoice in his departure, and hope we shall never meet more but by chance.

Since our quarrel I had occasion to talk of him with Tom Davies, who spoke with horror of his ferocious temper; "and yet," says I, "there is great sensibility about Baretti: I have seen tears often stand in his eyes." "Indeed," replies Davies, "I should like to have seen that sight vastly, when — even butchers weep."

The Burneys. — August, 1779. — Fanny Burney has been a long time from me; I was glad to see her again; yet she makes me miserable too in many respects, so restlessly and apparently anxious, lest I should give myself airs of patronage or load her with the shackles of dependance. I live with her always in a degree of pain that precludes friendship — dare not ask her to buy me a ribbon — dare not desire her to touch the bell, lest she should think herself injured — lest she should forsooth appear in the character of Miss Neville, and I in that of the widow Bromley. See Murphy's "Know Your Own Mind."

Fanny Burney has kept her room here in my house seven days, with a fever or something that she called a fever; I gave her every medicine and every slop with my own hand; took away her dirty cups, spoons, &c.; moved her tables: in short, was doctor and nurse and maid—for I did not like the servants should have additional trouble lest they should hate her for it. And now, — with the true gratitude of a wit, she tells me, that the world thinks the better of me for my civilities to her. It does? does it?

Miss Burney was much admired at Bath (1780); the puppy-men said, "She had such a drooping air and such a timid intelligence;" or, "a timid air," I think it was, "and a drooping intelligence;" never sure was such a collection of pedantry and affection as filled Bath when we were on that spot. How everything else and everybody set off my gallant bishop. "Quantum Centa solent inter viburna Cupressi." Of all the people I ever heard read verse in my whole life, the best, the most perfect reader, is the Bishop of Peterboro'.

1st July, 1780.— Mrs. Byron, who really loves me, was disgusted at Miss Burney's carriage to me, who have been such a friend and benefactress to her: not an article of dress, not a ticket for public places, not a thing in the world that she could not command from me: yet always insolent, always pining for home, always preferring the mode of life in St. Martin's Street to all I could do for her. She is a saucy-spirited little puss to be sure, but I love her dearly for all that; and I fancy she has a real regard for me, if she did not think it beneath the dignity of a wit, or of what she values more—the dignity of Dr. Burney's daughter—to indulge it. Such dignity! the Lady Louisa of Leicester Square! In good time!

1781. — What a blockhead Dr. Burney is to be always sending for his daughter home so! what a monkey! is not she better and happier with me than she can be anywhere else? Johnson is enraged at the silliness of their family conduct, and Mrs. Byron disgusted; I confess myself provoked excessively, but

I love the girl so dearly — and the Doctor, too, for that matter, only that he has such odd notions of superiority in his own house, and will have his children under his feet forsooth, rather than let 'em live in peace, plenty, and comfort anywhere from home. If I did not provide Fanny with every weareable — every wishable, indeed, — it would not vex me to be served so; but to see the impossibility of compensating for the pleasures of St. Martin's Street makes one at once merry and mortified.

Dr. Burney did not like his daughter should learn Latin even of Johnson, who offered to teach her for friendship, because then she would have been as wise as himself forsooth, and Latin was too masculine for Misses. A narrow-souled goose-cap the man must be at last, agreeable and amiable all the while too, beyond almost any other human creature. Well, mortal man is but a paltry animal! the best of us have such drawbacks both upon virtue, wisdom, and knowledge.

September, 1781. — My five fair daughters too! I have so good a pretence to wish for long life to see them settled. Like the old fellow in " Lucian," one is never at a loss for an excuse. They are five lovely creatures to be sure, but they love not me. Is it my fault or theirs?

August 28th, 1782. — He (Piozzi) thinks still more than he says, that I shall give him up; and if Queeney made herself more amiable to me, and took the proper methods — I suppose I should.

1st October, 1782. — After analysing the state of her

heart and feelings towards Piozzi, and balancing the
pros and *cons*, she adds — These objections would
increase in strength too, if my present state was a happy
one: but it really is not. I live a quiet life but not a
pleasant one. My children govern without loving me.
My friends caress and censure me. My money wastes
in expenses I do not enjoy, and my time in trifles I do
not approve; every one is made insolent and no one
comfortable. My reputation unprotected, my heart un-
satisfied, my health unsettled. I will, however, resolve
on nothing. . .

April, 1783.— I will go to Bath: nor health, nor
strength, nor my children's affections, have I. My
daughter does not, I suppose, much delight in this
scheme [viz. retrenchment of expenses and removal to
Bath], but why should I lead a life of delighting her,
who would not lose a shilling of interest or an ounce of
pleasure to save my live from perishing?

Piozzi was ill. . . A sore throat, Pepys said it was,
with four ulcers in it: the people about me said it had
been lanced, and I mentioned it slightly before the girls.
" Has he cut his own throat ? " says Miss Thrale in her
quiet manner. This was less inexcusable because she
hated him, and the other was her sister: though, had
she exerted the good sense I thought her possessed of,
she would not have treated him so: had she adored,
and fondled, and respected him as he deserved from her
hands, from the heroic conduct he shewed in January
when he gave into her hands, that dismal day, all my
letters containing promises of marriage, protestations

of love, &c., who knows but she might have kept us separated? But never did she once caress or thank me, never treat him with common civility, except on the very day which gave her hopes of our final parting. Worth while to be sure it was, to break one's heart for her! The other two are, however, neither wiser nor kinder; all swear by her I believe, and follow her footsteps exactly. Mr. Thrale had not much heart, but his fair daughters have none at all.*

June, 1783.— Most sincerely do I regret the sacrifice I have made of health, happiness, and the society of a worthy and amiable companion, to the pride and prejudice of three insensible girls, who would see nature perish without concern . . . were their gratification the cause.

The two youngest have, for ought I see, hearts as impenetrable as their sister. They will all starve a favourite animal—all see with unconcern the afflictions of a friend; and when the anguish I suffered on their account last winter, in Argyll Street, nearly took away my life and reason, the younger ridiculed as a jest those agonies which the eldest despised as a philosopher. When all is said, they are exceeding valuable girls — beautiful in person, cultivated in understanding, and well-principled in religion: high in their notions, lofty in their carriage, and of intents equal to their expectations; wishing to raise their own family by connections with some more noble . . and superior to any feel-

---

* This is the very accusation they all brought against her.

ing of tenderness which might clog the wheels of ambition. What, however, is my state? who am condemned to live with girls of this disposition? to teach without authority; to be heard without esteem; to be considered by them as their superior in fortune, while I live by the money borrowed from them; and in good sense, when they have seen me submit my judgment to theirs at the hazard of my life and wits. Oh, 'tis a pleasant situation! and whoever would wish, as the Greek lady phrased it, to teize himself and repent of his sins, let him borrow his children's money, be in love against their interest and prejudice, forbear to marry by their advice, and then shut himself up and live with them.*

Character of Johnson.—One evening as I was giving my tongue liberty to praise Mr. Johnson to his face, a favour he would not often allow me, he said, in high good humour, " Come, you shall draw up my character your own way, and shew it me, that I may see what you will say of me when I am gone." At night I wrote as follows.—(Here followed the character which forms the conclusion of the *Anecdotes.*) At the end she writes:—" When I shewed him his Character next day, for he would see it, he said, ' It was a very fine piece of writing, and that I had improved upon *Young,*' who he saw was my model, he said, ' for my flattery was still

---

* After Buckingham had been some time married to Fairfax's daughter, he said it was like marrying the devil's daughter, and keeping house with your father-in-law.

stronger than his, and yet, somehow or other, less hyperbolical.'"

Baretti.—Will. Burke was tart upon Mr. Baretti for being too dogmatical in his talk about politics. "You have," says he, "no business to be investigating the characters of Lord Falkland or Mr. Hampden. . . . You cannot judge of their merits, they are no countrymen of yours." "True," replied Baretti, "and you should learn by the same rule to speak very cautiously about Brutus and Mark Antony; they are my countrymen, and I must have their characters tenderly treated by foreigners."

Baretti could not endure to be called, or scarcely thought, a foreigner, and indeed it did not often occur to his company that he was one: for his accent was wonderfully proper, and his language always copious, always nervous, always full of various allusions, flowing too, with a rapidity worthy of admiration, and far beyond the power of nineteen in twenty natives. He had also a knowledge of the solemn language and the gay, could be sublime with Johnson, or blackguard with the groom; could dispute, could rally, could quibble, in our language. Baretti has, besides, some skill in music, with a bass voice very agreeable, besides a falsetto which he can manage so as to mimic any singer he hears. I would also trust his knowledge of painting a long way. These accomplishments, with his extensive power over every modern language, make him a most pleasing companion while he is in good-humour; and his lofty consciousness of his own superiority, which made him tenacious of every position, and drew him into a thousand distresses, did not, I must own, ever disgust me, till he began to exercise it against myself, and resolve to reign in our house by fairly defying the mistress of it. Pride, however, though shocking enough, is never despicable, but vanity, which he possessed too, in an eminent degree, will sometimes make a man near sixty ridiculous.

France displayed all Mr. Baretti's useful powers — he bustled for us, he catered for us, he took care of the child, he secured an apartment for the maid, he provided for our safety, our amusement, our repose; without him the pleasure of that journey would never have balanced the pain. And great was his disgust, to be sure, when he caught us, as he often did, ridiculing French manners, French sentiments, &c. I think he half cryed to Mrs. Payne, the landlady at Dover, on our return, because we laughed at French cookery, and French accommodations. Oh how he would court the maids at the inns abroad, abuse the men perhaps! and that with a facility not to be exceeded, as they all confessed, by any of the natives. But so he could in Spain, I find, and so 'tis plain he could here. I will give one instance of his skill in our low street language. Walking in a field near Chelsea, he met a fellow, who, suspecting him from dress and manner to be a foreigner, said sneeringly, " Come, Sir, will you show me the way to France ? " " No, Sir," says Baretti, instantly, " but I will show you the way to Tyburn.' Such, however, was his ignorance in a certain line, that

he once asked Johnson for information who it was composed the Pater Noster, and I heard him tell Evans *
the story of Dives and Lazarus as the subject of a
poem he once had composed in the Milanese dialect,
expecting great credit for his powers of invention.
Evans owned to me that he thought the man drunk,
whereas poor Baretti was, both in eating and drinking,
a model of temperance. Had he guessed Evans's
thoughts, the parson's gown would scarcely have saved
him a knouting from the ferocious Italian.

When Johnson and Burke went to see Baretti in
Newgate, they had small comfort to give him, and bid
him not hope too strongly. " Why what can *he* fear,"
says Baretti, placing himself between 'em, " that holds
two such hands as I do ? "

An Italian came one day to Baretti, when he was
in Newgate for murder, to desire a letter of recommendation for the teaching his scholars, when he
(Baretti) should be hanged. " You rascal," replies
Baretti, in a rage, " if I were not *in my own apartment*,
I would kick you down stairs directly."

Piozzi.—Brighton, July, 1780.—I have picked up
Piozzi here, the great Italian singer. He is amazingly
like my father: he shall teach Hester.

13 August, 1780.—Piozzi is become a prodigious
favourite with me, he is so intelligent a creature, so
discerning, one can't help wishing for his good opinion ;
his singing surpasses everybody's for taste, tenderness,

---

* Evans was a clergyman and (I believe) rector of Southwark.

and true elegance; his hand on the forte piano too is so soft, so sweet, so delicate, every tone goes to the heart, I think, and fills the mind with emotions one would not be without, though inconvenient enough sometimes. He wants nothing from us: he comes for his health he says: I see nothing ail the man but pride. The newspapers yesterday told what all the musical folks gained, and set Piozzi down 1200*l.* o' year.

14 January, 1782, Harley Street.—I had a letter to-day desiring me to dine in Wimpole Street, to meet Mrs. Montagu, and a whole army of blues, to whom I trust my refusal will afford very pretty speculation, and they may settle my character and future conduct at their leisure. Pepys is a worthless fellow at last: he and his brother run about the town spying and enquiring what Mrs. Thrale is to do this winter, what friends she is to see, what men are in her confidence, how soon she will be married, &c.: the brother doctor, the medico as we call him, lays wagers about me, I find. God forgive me, but they'll make me hate them both, and they are no better than two fools for their pains, for I was willing to have taken them to my heart.

Harley Street, 13 April, 1782.—When I took off my mourning, the watchers watched me very exactly, "but they whose hands were mightiest have found nothing:" so I shall leave the town, I hope, in a good disposition towards me, though I am sullen enough with the town for fancying me such an amorous idiot that I am dying to take up with every filthy fellow. God knows how distant such dispositions are from the heart and constitution of H. L. T. Lord Loughboro', Sir Richard Jebb, Mr. Piozzi, Mr. Selwyn, Dr. Johnson, every man that comes to the house, is put in the papers for me to marry. In good time I wrote to day to beg the "Morning Herald" would say no more about me, good or bad.

Streatham, 17 April, 1782.—I am returned to Streatham, pretty well in health and very sound in heart, notwithstanding the watchers and the wager-layers, who think more of the charms of their sex by half than I who know them better. Love and friendship are distinct things, and I would go through fire to serve many a man whom nothing less than fire would force me to go to bed to. Somebody mentioned my going to be married t'other day, and Johnson was joking about it. I suppose, Sir, said I, they think they are doing me honour with these imaginary matches, when, perhaps the man does not exist who would do me honour by marrying me! This, indeed, was said in the wild and insolent spirit of Baretti, yet 'tis nearer the truth than one would think for. A woman of passable person, ancient family, respectable character, uncommon talents, and three thousand a year, has a right to think herself any man's equal, and has nothing to seek but return of affection from whatever partner she pitches on. To marry for love would therefore be rational in me, who want no advancement of birth or fortune, and till I am in love, I will not marry, nor perhaps then.

October, 1782.—There is no mercy for me in this island. I am more and more disposed to try the continent. One day the paper rings with my marriage to

Johnson, one day to Crutchley*, one day to Seward. I give no reason for such impertinence, but cannot deliver myself from it. Whitbred, the rich brewer, is in love with me too: oh, I would rather, as Ann Page says, be set breast deep in the earth and bowled to death with turnips.

Mr. Crutchley bid me make a curtsey to my daughters for keeping me out of a goal (*sic*), and the newspapers insolent as he! How shall I get through? How shall I get through? I have not deserved it of any of them, as God knows.

Philip Thicknesse put it about Bath that I was a poor girl, a mantua maker, when Mr. Thrale married me. It is an odd thing, but Miss Thrales like, I see, to have it believed.

3 November, 1784. — Yesterday I received a letter from Mr. Baretti, full of the most flagrant and bitter insults concerning my late marriage with Mr. Piozzi, against whom, however, he can bring no heavier charge than that he disputed on the road with an innkeeper concerning the bill in his last journey to Italy; while he accuses me of murder and fornication in the grossest terms, such as I believe have scarcely ever been used even to his old companions in Newgate, whence he was released to scourge the families which cherished, and bite the hands that have since relieved him. Could I recollect any provocation I ever gave the man, I should be less amazed, but he heard, perhaps, that Johnson

---

* She suspected Crutchley to be the natural son of Thrale.

had written me a rough letter, and thought he would write me a brutal one : like the Jewish king, who, trying to imitate Solomon without his understanding, said, " My father whipped you with whips, but I will whip you with scorpions."

January, 1785.—I see the English newspapers are full of gross insolence to me : all burst out, as I guessed it would, upon the death of Dr. Johnson. But Mr. Boswell (who I plainly see is the authour) should let the *dead* escape from his malice at least. I feel more shocked at the insults offered to Mr. Thrale's memory than at those cast on Mr. Piozzi's person. My present husband, thank God ! is well and happy, and able to defend himself : but dear Mr. Thrale, that had fostered these cursed wits so long ! to be stung by their malice even in the grave, is too cruel :—

" Nor church, nor church-yards, from such fops are free."—POPE.

1786.—It has always been my maxim never to influence the inclination of another : Mr. Thrale, in consequence, lived with me seventeen and a half years, during which time I tried but twice to persuade him to *do* anything, and but once, and that in vain, to let anything alone. Even my daughters, as soon as they could reason, were always allowed, and even encouraged, by me to reason their own way, and not suffer their respect or affection for me to mislead their judgment. Let us keep the mind clear if we can from prejudices, or truth will never be found at all.* The worst part of this disinterested

* " Clear your mind of *cant*."—JOHNSON.

scheme is, that other people are not of my mind, and if I resolve not to use my lawful influence to make my children love me, the lookers-on will soon use their unlawful influence to make them hate me: if I scrupulously avoid persuading my husband to become a Lutheran or be of the English church, the Romanists will be diligent to teach him all the narrowness and bitterness of their own unfeeling sect, and soon persuade him that it is not delicacy but weakness makes me desist from the combat. Well! let me do right, and leave the consequences in His hand who alone sees every action's motive and the true cause of every effect: let me endeavour to please God, and to have only my own faults and follies, not those of another, to answer for.

EXTRACTS FROM " BRITISH SYNONYMY."

AFFECTION, PASSION, TENDERNESS, FONDNESS, LOVE.

THE first four of these words, then, so commonly, so
constantly in . use, are, although similar, certainly not
synonymous ; and the last, which always ought and I
hope often does comprehend them all, is not seldom
substituted in place of its own component parts, for
such are all those that precede it. Foreigners, however, will recollect, that the first of these words is
usually adapted to that regard which is consequent on
ties of blood ; that the second naturally and necessarily
presupposes and implies difference of sex ; while the
rest, without impropriety, may be attributed to friendship, or bestowed on babes. I have before me the de-
finition of FONDNESS, given into my hands many years
ago by a most eminent logician, though Dr. Johnson
never did acquiesce in it.

" FONDNESS," says the definer, " is the hasty and injudicious determination of the will towards promoting
the present gratification of some particular object."

---

* *British Synonymy, or, An Attempt at Regulating the Choice
of Words in Familiar Conversation.* By *Hester Lynch Piozzi.*
In Two Volumes. London ᐧ 1794. This book has been long out
of print, and contains much curious matter. Sir James Fellowes
meditated a new edition of it.

" FONDNESS," said Dr. Johnson, " is rather the hasty and injudicious attribution of excellence, somewhat beyond the power of attainment, to the object of our affection."

Both these definitions may possibly be included in FONDNESS; my own idea of the whole may be found in the following example :

Amintor and Aspasia are models of true LOVE : 'tis now seven years since their mutual PASSION was sanctified by marriage; and so little is the lady's AFFECTION diminished, that she sate up nine nights successively last winter by her husband's bed-side, when he had on him a malignant fever that frighted relations, friends, servants, all away. Nor can any one allege that her TENDERNESS is ill repaid, while we see him gaze upon her features with that FONDNESS which is capable of creating charms for itself to admire, and listen to her talk with a fervour of admiration scarce due to the most brilliant genius.

For the rest, 'tis my opinion that men love for the most part with warmer PASSION than women do — at least than English women, and with more transitory FONDNESS mingled with that passion : while 'tis natural for females to feel a softer TENDERNESS; and when their AFFECTIONS are completely gained, they are found to be more durable.

AMIABLE, LOVELY, CHARMING, FASCINATING.

These elegant attributives — so the learned James Harris terms adjectives denoting properties of mind or body — appear at first more likely to turn out synonymes, than upon a closer inspection we shall be able to observe : while daily experience evinces that there is an almost regular appropriation of the words; as thus —an AMIABLE character, a LOVELY complexion, a CHARMING singer, a FASCINATING converser;—the first of these appearing to *deserve* our love, the next to *claim* it, the third to *steal* it from us as by magic; the last of all to *draw*, and to *detain* it, by a half invisible, yet wholly resistless power. Nor does the epithet ever come so properly into play, as when tacked to an *unseen* method of attracting : for positive beauty needs not fascination to assist her conquests; and positive wit seeks rather to dazzle and distress, than wind herself round the hearts of *her* admirers; while there is a mode of conversing that seduces attention, and enchains the faculties.

" When Foote told a story at dinner-time," said Dr. Johnson, " I resolved to disregard what I expected would be frivolous; yet as the plot thickened, my desire of hearing the catastrophe quickened at every word, and grew keener as we seemed approaching towards its conclusion. The fellow *fascinated* me, Sir; I listened and laughed, and laid down my knife and fork, and thought of nothing but Foote's conversation."

Some Italian lines set by Piccini, with expressive dexterity, represent this power beyond all I have read —as descriptive of *female fascination* * ; and every man

* Her own description of Miss Streatfield's fascinations (*antè*, p. 300) is a better example.

who has been in love with a woman, not confessedly beautiful, feels his heart beat responsive to the verses and the music, when sung with the good taste they deserve. Will the lines be much out of place here? I hope not.

In quel viso furbarello
V'è un incognita magia ;
Non si sa che diavol sia .
   Ma fa l'uomo delirar.

Quegli occhietti cosi vaghi
Ve lo giuro son due maghi,
E un sospiro languidetto,
Che fatica uscir dal petto
   Vi fa subito cascar.

Vengon per ultimo i cari accenti,
Le lagrimuccie, li svenimenti,
Ch'opprimer devono
   Perforza un cuor :

Innumerabile
Son l'incantesimi,
Son l'arti magichi
   Del dio d'amor.

The following imitation misses its effect, because the measure is unfavourable, yet may serve to convey the idea :

In that roguish face one sees
All her sex's witcheries ;

Playful sweetness, cold disdain,
Every thing to turn one's brain.

Sparkling from expressive eyes,
Heaving in affected sighs,
Sure destruction still we find,
Still we lose our peace of mind.

Touch'd by her half-trembling hand,
Can the coldest heart withstand?
While we dread the starting tear,
And the tender accents hear.

Numberless are sure the ways
That she *fascinates* our gaze;
Magic arts her pow'r improve,
Witcheries that wait on love.

ANTIPATHY, AVERSION, DISGUST.

The first of these disagreeable sensations we find chiefly excited I believe by inanimate things, or brutes. One man alleges his unconquerable ANTIPATHY to a cat; another encourages his AVERSION to a Cheshire cheese; and while English ladies think it delicate to faint at touch or even sight of a frog, or toad—Roman ladies, accustomed to noisome animals from the natural heat of their climate, fall into convulsions at a nosegay of flowers, or the scent of a little lavender water.* To

* So one hunting man complained that the violets spoilt the scent, and another that the singing birds prevented him from distinguishing the voices of his hounds.

such fastidious companions it would not be perhaps
wholly unreasonable to feel a certain degree of DISGUST ;
and Arnold of Leicestershire tells us from experience,
that increasing ANTIPATHIES should be particularly
dreaded, as an almost certain indication of incipient
madness.*

AWEFUL, REVERENTIAL, SOLEMN.

The last of these epithets begins the climax — A
Gothick cathedral (say we) is a SOLEMN place ; its
gloomy greatness disposes one to REVERENTIAL behaviour,
inspiring sentiments more sublime, and meditations
much more AWEFUL, than does a structure on the
Grecian model, though built for the same purposes of
piety.†

The word *aweful* should however be used with caution, and a due sense of its importance: I have heard
even well-bred ladies now and then attribute that term

* Shakespeare has put a plausible defence of antipathies into
the mouth of Shylock, *Merchant of Venice*, act iv. scene 1 ; and
Coleridge, in *Zapolya*, treats an instinctive dislike as a providential
warning:—

"Oh, surer than suspicion's hundred eyes,
Is that fine sense which to the pure in heart,
By mere oppugnancy of their own goodness,
Reveals th' approach of evil."

† See the description of the temple in *The Mourning Bride*, act
ii. scene 3. Johnson, to tease Garrick, used to say that it was finer
than any passage of equal length in Shakespeare. Mrs. Piozzi, in
a marginal note, questions its originality, but says she has forgotten from whence it was borrowed.

too lightly in their common conversation — connecting it with substances beneath its dignity — such *mésalliances* offend the sense of high birth natural to a Saxon.*

AY and YES.

The first of these affirmatives, derived from the Latin *aio*, is of the higher antiquity in our language, and still keeps some privileges of superiority, enforcing that which the other less decidedly asserts. It used to be represented in Shakespear's time by the single vowel *I;* see the long scene between the Nurse and Juliet, when told of Tybalt's death; but I recollect no later author who so corrupts it. We say in familiar talk, that Diana counsel'd her sister Flora against such a match; did she not, Sir? Yes, I believe she did.— *Counsel'd* her! exclaims a stander-by — Ay, and controuled her too, or she had been his wife now.†

BEAUTIFUL, HANDSOME, GRACEFUL, ELEGANT, PLEASING, PRETTY, FINE,

Are, however desirable epithets, by no means strictly synonymous; and though, upon a cursory view, the six

---

* The word "mighty" was common in the last century—as, "mighty tiresome."

† When Queen Caroline first came to England knowing not a word of English, a discussion arose what one word would be most useful or least dangerous for her to know. Lady Charlotte Lindsay suggested *No*, because it might be pronounced so as to mean *Yes*. A very pretty song of Lover's is called *Yes and No*.

last appear included in their principal, which takes the lead, conversation will soon inform us to the contrary, while, talking of a GRACEFUL dancer now upon the stage, we shall find in her person, if not put into motion, no claim at all upon our first attributive:—nor does that first necessarily comprehend the other excellencies—for though the situation of Mount Edgcumbe be confessedly more BEAUTIFUL than Shenstone's Leasowes, taste would lead many men to prefer the latter, as more PLEASING: and at the time when true perfection of female beauty appeared among us in the form of Maria Gunning, I well remember hearing men say that other women might justly be preferred to her as PLEASING, and perhaps GRACEFUL too, in a far more eminent degree; and so true was the observation, that her inferiors made it their amusement to steal away lovers from her, who commanded admiration they had no chance to attain.

The word ELEGANT can scarcely be used with more propriety than on such occasions, when people *elect* as PLEASING what produces a train of ideas most congenial to our own particular fancy. Pearls are, on this principle, accounted by many people to be more ELEGANT than diamonds; which we all allow to be FINER, HANDSOMER, and infinitely more BEAUTIFUL. And one says popularly, that Pope's Rape of the Lock is an ELEGANT poem, and Milton's Paradise Lost a FINE one. Greville's Stanzas to Indifference are however exquisitely PRETTY, and some parts of Mr. Whalley's Ode to Mont Blanc, uncommonly BEAUTIFUL. Burke—whose own

compositions include every species of excellence — says,
that BEAUTIFUL objects are comparatively small, but to
minute perfection I should give the adjective PRETTY.
Insects of various colours, and delicate formation, butterflies above all, are justly termed PRETTY.   Some
shells too, slight in their texture, and of tints as tender,
claim this epithet, and can claim no more; for, while
the apple and peach bloom have among vegetables the
same pretension—an orange-tree richly furnished, growing in the natural ground as I have seen them on the
Borromæan Islands to a considerable height, and rose-
trees in the Duke of Buccleugh's pleasure-grounds, or
those of Hopeton-House, are decidedly BEAUTIFUL.   One
large and wide-spreading beech-tree, or full-bodied oak,
single in a verdant meadow, I should select for a FINE
object* to repose the eye upon, in autumnal seasons
when the tint begins to shew more richness than mere
maturity produces, and excites a train of reflections full
of pensive dignity: while the old-fashioned avenue of
limetrees long-drawn and feathering down so as to hide
all stem, makes a HANDSOME appearance in July, when
filled with fragrance and redolent with bloom.

Were we speaking of architecture, I should direct
foreigners to call the Pantheon at Rome a FINE building,
Saint Peter's a BEAUTIFUL one, our own in London dedi-
cated to St. Paul a very HANDSOME edifice, the Redentore

---

* Fine (from *fin*) must have implied delicacy; but its original
sense has been reversed.   A fine face is one with a bold and
strongly marked outline; a fine child, a stout healthy one; a
fine woman, a well-formed one on a large scale.

at Venice, planned by Palladio — and our own sweet
Doric, done by Inigo Jones — I reckon ELEGANT fabrics;
while King's College, Cambridge, elaborately PRETTY,
gives delight to every beholder. The word HANDSOME
certainly annexes fewer ideas of pleasure than the rest,
because we have appropriated it now and then somewhat
meanly. We say a HANDSOME kitchen certainly in
English, and a HANDSOME piece of roast beef*; nor do
we give higher appellatives to a large woman painted
by Rubens with more strength of colour than dignity
or grace. When we speak of a HANDSOME house and
gardens, our hearers turn not, I believe, their imagina-
tions to recollect Villa Albani or even Castle Howard,
while a drive round London realizes the idea at less
expence of trouble nearer home. But, after all, the
words

BEAUTY, GRACE, EXPRESSION; CARRIAGE, ELEGANCE, AND
SYMMETRY;

Are substantives on which so many volumes have been
written, that one would think it impossible it should

---

* " Handsome elocution " occurs in Addison. Archbishop
Whately says that " Handsome implies not exactly an artificial
beauty, but the beauty of some person or thing which is *trained*
or *cultivated*." Thus he says we should not speak of a handsome
wild animal, or a handsome prospect, although the Irish and
Americans frequently do. The non-commissioned officer who gave
evidence on the prosecution of Frost, said that when the order
was given for returning the fire of the mob, the mayor (Sir
Thomas Phillips) " handsomely " threw open the shutters of the
room in which the soldiers were placed. In the performance of
this handsome and gallant action he received a severe wound.

be still agreeable to read about them; yet is every writer tempted to extend on such a subject — every student attracted to continue a page where those names begin the leaf. And it is perhaps not wholly tedious or uninteresting to observe, that more, much more, is required to describe BEAUTY, than is comprehended in the common acceptation of the adjective *beautiful* : for, while SYMMETRY suffices to constitute a perfect form in many works of nature, and some of art — as the mountain at the head of Loch Lomond in Scotland, and the Antonine column at Rome — far more is demanded by connoisseurs who deal in animated excellence. A horse, for example, is scarcely allowed to possess true BEAUTY, till his owner can boast for him a brilliancy of coat, whatever the colour may be — a decided ELEGANCE as well as SYMMETRICAL proportion in his shape—GRACE presiding in every motion, with eyes and ears expressive of a long-traced lineage, and even of apparent sensibility to his own praise and value. Haughty CARRIAGE is indispensable to brute perfection. The peacock is handsomer than the Chinese pheasant, because he is prouder; and the feline race take much from their own BEAUTY, by substituting the EXPRESSION of insidiousness instead of pride.

Indeed we are not correct when we require only EXPRESSION in a human face, for there are EXPRESSIONS which disgrace humanity. Among our own species we must meantime confess that we love a lofty consciousness of superiority, just stopping short of a vain-glorious ostentation. Os HOMINI SUBLIME DEDIT, &c. The late

Earl of Errol, dressed in his robes at the coronation of
King George the Third, and Mrs. Siddons in the character of Murphy's Euphrasia, were the noblest specimens of the human race I ever saw; — while he,
looking like Jove's own son Sarpedon, as described by
Homer,—and she, looking like radiant Truth led by
the withered hand of hoary Time — seemed alone fit to
be sent out into some distant planet, for the purpose
of shewing its inhabitants to what a race of exalted
creatures God had been pleased to give this earth as a
possession.

With regard to mere GRACE, I am not sure which
produces most pleasing sensations in the beholder—
which, in a word, gives most delight — well varied and
nicely studied ELEGANCE, carried to perfection, though
by an inferior form, as in the younger Vestris—or that
pure natural charm resulting from a SYMMETRIC figure
put into easy motion by pleasure or surprise, as I have
seen in the late Lady Coventry. To both attesting
spectators have often manifested their just admiration,
by repeated bursts of applause — particularly to the
countess, who, calling for her carriage one night at
the theatre—I saw her—stretched out her arm with
such peculiar, such inimitable manner, as forced a loud
and sudden clap from all the pit and galleries; which
she, conscious of her charms, delighted to increase and
prolong, by turning round with a familiar smile to
reward the enraptured company.

For she was fair beyond their brightest bloom,
   This Envy owns, since now her bloom is fled;

Fair as the forms which, wove in Fancy's loom,
   Float in light vision o'er the poet's head.
Whene'er with sweet serenity she smil'd,
   Or caught the orient blush of quick surprise,
How sweetly mutable! how brightly wild
   The living lustre darted from her eyes!
Each look, each motion wak'd a new-born grace,
   That o'er her form its transient glory cast;
Some lovelier wonder soon usurp'd the place,
   Chas'd by a charm still lovelier than the last.

In her description alone might then all our synonymy
be happily engaged; and truly might we say that her
unrivalled, her consummate BEAUTY was the effect of
perfect SYMMETRY, spontaneously producing GRACE in-
vincible, although her MIEN and CARRIAGE had less of
dignity and sweetness in it; and the EXPRESSION of her
countenance, illuminated by the brightest tints, although
lovelily mutable, as Mason says, in verses alone worthy
the original — was always the EXPRESSION of pleasure
felt or pleasure given. Her dress was seldom chosen
with ELEGANCE, as I remember; and I recollect no
splendour except of general BEAUTY about her.*

* The best portraits of Maria Gunning, Countess of Coventry,
confirm Mrs. Piozzi's theory of the enthusiastic admiration la-
vished on her. It must have been principally elicited by grace
and expression. Her sister, Elizabeth, afterwards Duchess of
Hamilton and (by a second marriage) of Argyll, was equally
beautiful, and her beauty has been inherited by her descendants in
three generations. The sisters set off each other, and their appearance together added to the charms of both. A corresponding

BROOD, CLUTCH, PROGENY OF FEATHERED ANIMALS.

It is distressing enough to foreigners when they find us arbitrarily calling the young domestic fowl which follow a turkey a fine BROOD, when we talked but two minutes before of a CLUTCH of chickens, and perhaps cry out in the next breath, Here's a *flock* of young geese on this water! The first of these words however must be their decided choice; as in saying *that* they cannot be wrong: the last word does not strictly allude to the goslings, but means the number all together; and the second word is only used from the trick a hen has to herself almost, of calling her little ones so *closely* round her in times of danger, that you may CLUTCH or make a handful of them, as we say. Mr. Addison, who was more an elegant author than good naturalist, teaches them in his Spectators to say a BROOD of ducks, when he expresses his admiration of the providence by which all the works of

effect may have been seen in our time, when three celebrated sisters were grouped together, or when the two Northumbrian beauties were the rage, or when more than one lovely mother, who shall be nameless, came forth attended by a fresher and lovelier self, *matre pulchrâ filia pulchrior.*

At a crowded London party, I was asked by a very distinguished Frenchman to point out the beauties in vogue. Those nearest to us happened to be no longer in the first flush of youth; they had not that *beauté du diable* which Frenchmen deem indispensable, and he exclaimed: " You English are as odd in this as in other matters: you cling to your established beauties as you stand by your old institutions." Among those he gazed upon was one who, after being for sylph-like loveliness the *beau idéal* of the poet's and artist's dream, had arrived at the perfection of ripened and developed beauty.

heaven are governed; and he is the best language master: though that very paper betrays the little skill with which he looked on such matters in a thousand instances.*

BROOK, RIVULET, STREAM, RIVER,

Are much in the same manner synonymous, so far as relates to poetical use, &c., but Mr. Locke shews us how to separate them in conversation, and how they really separate by nature, when he tells us that "SPRINGS make little RIVULETS, and these united form BROOKS; which coming forward in STREAMS, compose great RIVERS that run into the sea." Doctor Johnson, whose ideas of any thing not positively large were ever mingled with contempt, asked of one of our sharp currents in North Wales — " Has this BROOK e'er a name?" and received for answer—" Why, dear Sir, this is the RIVER Ustrad." " Let us," said he, turning to his friend, " jump over it directly, and shew them how an *Englishman* should treat a *Welsh* RIVER."

CLEVER, DEXTROUS, SKILFUL;

To which might be added another pretty word well taken into our language without alteration of spelling, and called *adroit.* This adjective should not have been

---

* The language of the sporting world is capricious and arbitrary; and to use *brace* or *couple* irregularly, is as fatal to a young man's reputation as a false quantity was once. The cant phrase now is, I *got* (not I killed or shot) so many brace, &c.

omitted on the list, as it will be very suitable to foreigners, and less approaching to vulgarity than CLEVER, which, if applied to things high or serious, frights one. We say, The minister managed ADROITLY in procuring men eminently SKILFUL in the art of engineering, and equally DEXTROUS in the manual use of such machines;—for let a fellow be as CLEVER as he can, without practice no person will arrive at being neat-handed and DEXTROUS about any thing, least of all in matters where complicated machinery is in question: I have therefore little opinion of those contrivances and modern inventions to prevent fire or thieves; particularly a piece of workmanship once shewn me of a ladder and fire engine combined, which alternately prevented the operation of each other.—Few things indeed are more offensive than those futile, and half impracticable devices to snuff a candle after some new method; by which tricks CLEVER fellows however are SKILFUL enough to get money from neighbours more rich than wise, who, like the lady in Young's Satires,

> "To eat their breakfasts will project a scheme,
> Nor take their tea without a stratagem;"

to the contriving of which we will leave them.*

---

* "Cleverness (from the verb to cleave) is correctly applied to a certain quickness and readiness in the operations of the mind, and especially in the art of acquiring knowledge. But the loose way in which ideas are expressed in ordinary conversation has led to a considerable abuse of this word, which is not seldom applied to every kind of talent."—*English Synonyms*, by the Archbishop of Dublin.

TO CRY, TO EXCLAIM,

Are pretty near synonymous in some senses certainly; but if a foreigner speaking of the London CRIES
called them the EXCLAMATIONS of the city, all would
laugh. 'Tis very strange meantime, and to me very
unaccountable, that the streets' cries should resemble
each other in all great towns—but sure I am that
Spaz-camin, with a canting drawl at the end, sounds at
Milan like our *Sweep sweep* exactly; and the *Garçon
Limonadier* at Paris makes a pert noise like our
orange-girls in the Pit of Covent Garden, that sounds
precisely similar. I was walking one day with my own
maid in an Italian capital, and turned short on hearing
sounds like those uttered by a London tinker—the man
who followed us cried *Cafferol, Cafferol* d'accommodar
—to the tune of his own brass kettle just as ours do:
and I believe that in a little time, many cities will be
more famous for the musick and frequency of their
cries than London; because shops there, increasing
daily, nay hourly, take all necessity of hawkers quite
away—excepting perhaps just about the suburbs and
new-built houses, where likewise shops are everlastingly
breaking forth, and afford people better appearance of
choice than can be easily carried about by those who
CRY them.

TO CRY, TO WEEP,

Are really and I think completely synonymous, only
that the last verb being always appropriated to serious

purposes, we never scarcely use it in colloquial and
familiar discourse, unless ironically—for 'tis as we say a
tragedy word—and Do not CRY so, is the phrase to
children or friends we are desirous of comforting. Tears
have a very powerful effect on young people, and indeed on all those who are new in the world :—but
veterans have seen them too often to be much affected;
and since the years 1779 and 80, when I lived a great
deal with a lady* who could call them up for *her own*
pleasure, and often *did* call them at *my request*, the
seeing one WEEP has been no proof to me that anything
sad or sorrowful had befallen : and perhaps some of the
sincerest tears are shed when reading Richardson's
Clarissa, or seeing Siddons in the character of Mrs.
Beverley. With regard to real anguish of the heart,
an old sufferer WEEPS but little.

> " Slow-pac'd and sourer as the storms increase,
>   He makes his bed beneath th' inclement drift ;
>   And scorning the complainings of distress,
>   Hardens his heart against assailing want—"

like Thomson's Bear, so beautifully described by a poet
equally skilled in the knowledge of life and of nature.
Such reflections however will lead my readers naturally
enough on to the next synonymes, which are

DEFORMED, UGLY, HIDEOUS, FRIGHTFUL.

Dyer derives the second of these unlucky adjectives
from *ough* or *ouph*, or goblin, not without reason, as it

* The charming S. S.

B B 2

was long written *ougly* in our language. FRIGHTFUL bears much the same bad sense, I think.—Goblins are still called *frightening* in the provinces of Lancaster and Westmorland; and the third word upon the list, from *hideux* French, is but little softer, if at all so. DEFORMED has a more positive signification than the rest; for we know not how easily delicate people may be FRIGHTED, nor how small a portion of UGLINESS will suffice to call forth from affectation the cry of HIDEOUS! while hyperbolical talkers have a way of giving these rough epithets to many hapless persons, who are in earnest neither more nor less than *plain;* by which I mean to express a form wholly divested of grace, a countenance of coarse colour and vacant look, with a mien possessing no comeliness; which quality would alone protect them from deserving even that title, because they would be then *ornamented.* Those however who most loudly profess being always scared when they are not allured, will in another humour be easily enough led to confess that many an UGLY man or woman are very agreeable, and display sometimes powers of pleasing unbestowed even on the beautiful; which could scarcely happen sure, were their unfortunate figures and faces *ouph* like, or terrifying:—it were well then if the English, who hate hyperbole in general, would forbear to use it so constantly just where 'tis most offensive, in magnifying their neighbours' defects.

Lord Bacon says the deformed people are good to employ in business, because they have a constant spur to great actions, that by some noble deed they may rescue their persons from contempt: and experience does in some sort prove his assertion; many men famous in history having been of this class—the great warriors, above all, as it should seem in very contradiction to nature—when Agesilaus, King William the Third, and Ladislaus surnamed *Cubitalis*, that pigmy King of Poland, reigned, and fought more victorious battles, as Alexander Gaguinus relates, than all his longer-legged predecessors had done.* CORPORE PARVUS ERAM, exclaims he—CUBITO VIX ALTIOR, SED TAMEN IN PARVO CORPORE MAGNUS ERAM. Nor is even Sanctity's self free from some obligations to deformity—while Ignatius Loyola losing a limb at the siege of Pampelona, and conceiving himself no longer fit for wars or attendance on the court, betook himself to a mode of living more profitable to his soul in the next world, and to his celebrity in this, than that would have been which, had his beauty remained, he might have been led to adopt.

That DEFORMED persons are usually revengeful all will grant †; and the Empress Sophia had cause to

---

* "It is probable that among the 120,000 soldiers who were marshalled round Neerwinden under all the standards of Western Europe, the two feeblest in body were the hunch-backed dwarf (Luxemburg) who urged forward the fiery onset of France, and the asthmatic skeleton (William) who covered the slow retreat of England." (*Macaulay's Hist.* vol. iv. p. 410.) All readers of Shakespeare will remember the Countess of Auvergne's speech to Talbot:

> " It cannot be this weak and writled shrimp
> Should strike such terror to his enemies."

† Shakespeare puts their justification into the mouth of Richard the Third.

repent her insulting letter to old Narses, when she
advising him to return and spin with her maids — he
replied, "that he would spin such a thread as her
Majesty and all her allies would never be able to un-
twist."—Nor did he in the least fail of fulfilling the
menace; which reminds one of Henry the Fifth's answer,
when the Dauphin of France, despising his youth and
spirit of frolicking, sent over tennis balls as a fit present
for a prince addicted more to play than war.—Our young
hero's reply being much in the spirit of that sent by
Narses to the Empress, one might have thought it borrowed, had not eight centuries elapsed between the two
events. These matters may for aught I know be all
mentioned in a pretty book I once read when newly
published, and have never seen since: it came out three
or four and thirty years ago, and gained to its author
the appellation of DEFORMITY *Hay*. He likewise translated some epigrams of Martial, but for his Essay on
Deformity I have enquired in vain; and if I am guilty
of plagiarism it is *à mon insçu*, as the French express
it. Meantime UGLINESS in common conversation relates
merely to the face, whilst DEFORMITY implies a faulty
shape or figure. FRIGHTFUL and HIDEOUS may be well
appropriated to delirious dreams; to the sight of
mangled bodies, or human heads streaming with blood,
such as France has lately exhibited for the savage
amusement of a worse than brutal populace: but the
words *plain* or *homely* are sufficient to express that
total deficiency of beauty too often termed UGLINESS in
our friends and neighbours. That such is not the pro-

per expression is proved by that power of pleasing, universally allowed to the late Lord Chesterfield, who had nothing in his person which at first sight could raise expectation of any delight in his society: and perhaps to overcome prejudice in private life, and make an accomplished companion out of an ill-cut figure and homely countenance, may be more difficult than by warlike prowess and acts of heroic valour to gain and keep celebrity in the field of battle.

Where there is a talent to please however, pleasure will reside; and one of the best and most applauded minuets I ever saw, was danced at Bath many years ago by a lady of quality, pale, thin, crooked, and of low stature:—my not wishing to name her is notwithstanding a kind of proof that her elegance would not (in her absence) compensate for her DEFORMITY: so surely do readers in general take up and willingly cherish a disadvantageous idea, rather than a kind one. Pope, who was DEFORMED enough to have felt the truth of this position, and ingenious enough to have found it out had he *not* felt it, disobliged his patron Mr. Allen so much by these lines,

" See low-born Allen, with an *awkward* shame,
Do good by stealth, and blush to find it fame ;"

that he was forced to learn by experience how one of the best and humblest of mankind suffered more pain by having his awkwardness and mean birth perpetuated, than he enjoyed pleasure in having his virtue celebrated

by a poet, whose works certainly would not fail of con-
signing it to immortality.

TO DEFY, TO CHALLENGE.

These words are synonymous when applied to a single
combat between particular people ; but the first verb is
vastly more comprehensive than the second. Antony
CHALLENGED Augustus to commit the fate of universal
empire to his single arm, conscious that in such a contest (as his opponent easily discovered) the advantages
lay all against Octavius, who for that reason laughed at
his proposal, and with due dignity DEFIED such empty
menaces.* A man whose situation is wholly desperate,
may indeed CHALLENGE the seven champions if he
chooses, without fear of losing the victory, because no
loss can set him any lower: but who is he that would
be mad enough to enter the lists?

Our two words were not ill-exemplified in a very
different line of life, when a flashy fellow known about
London by the name of Captain Jasper some twenty
years ago, burst suddenly into the Bedford Coffee-
house, and snatching up a hat belonging to some one
in the room, cried out—"Whoever owns this hat is a
rascal, and I CHALLENGE him to come out and fight."
A grave gentleman sitting near the fire replied, in a
firm but smooth tone of voice, "Whoever does own the

---

* Napoleon, when challenged by Sir Sidney Smith in Egypt,
replied that he would think of it when his proposed antagonist
was a Marlborough.

hat is a blockhead, and I hope we may defy you, Sir, to find any such fool here." Captain Jasper walked to the street-door, and discharged a brace of bullets into his own head immediately.*

TO DROP, TO FALL, TO TUMBLE, TO SINK SUDDENLY.

These neuter verbs are not synonymous; because, although whatever DROPS must in some measure FALL, yet everything that FALLS does not necessarily DROP. A man climbed a tree in my orchard yesterday, for example, where he was gathering apples; having missed his footing, I saw him, after many attempts to save himself by catching at boughs, &c. FALL at length to the ground—the apples DROPPED out of his hand on the first moment of his slipping. To SINK SUDDENLY, half implies that he FELL in water, unless we speak of such an earthquake as once destroyed the beautiful town of Port Royal in Jamaica, when the ground cleaving into many fissures, people SUNK IN on the sudden; some breast-high, others entirely out of sight. To TUMBLE is an act of odd precipitancy, and often means voluntary FALLS endured, or eluded by fearlessness and adroit agility: 'tis then a verb active, a trick played to get

* A stock story at the *Grecian* was, that a bully, who insisted on a particular seat, came and found it occupied by a templar; " Who is that in my seat ? " " I don't know, sir," said the waiter. "Where is the hat I left on it?" " He put it into the fire." " Did he! d—n—n!—but a fellow who would do *that* would not mind flinging *me* after it ; " and so saying he disappeared.

money, and shew the powers of humanity at an escape, as in feats of harlequinery; or the strange thing done many years ago by Grimaldi, a famous grotesque dancer, eminent for powers of this kind, at the Meuse Gate in London; where having made a mock quarrel, and stripped himself as if intending to fight, previously collecting a small circle to see the battle, he suddenly sprung over his antagonist's and spectators' heads, and TUMBLING round in the air, lighted on his legs and ran away, leaving the people to gape. When the well-known Buffo di Spagna, or Spanish buffoon, who delighted to frequent such exhibitions, was asked what person he thought to be the first TUMBLER in the world, he archly replied: "Marry, Sirs, I am of opinion that 'twas *Lucifer*; for he TUMBLED first, and TUMBLED furthest too, and yet hurt himself so little with the FALL, that he is too nimble for many of us to escape him yet."

DULL, STUPID, HEAVY.

Of the first upon this flat and insipid list Mr. Pope has greatly enlarged the signification, and taught us to call everything DULL that was not immediately and positively witty. This is too much, surely; and indeed one finds it received so only in the Dunciad or Essay upon Criticism. Information may be HEAVY sometimes without being STUPID or DULL, I think; its own weight of matter may render it so; and he who conveys useful knowledge should neither be mocked nor slighted because he happens to be unskilled in the art of levigating his learning to hit the strength or rather feebleness of moderns to endure it. There is, however, a kind of talk that is merely HEAVY, and in no sense important. Such conversation has been lately called a *bore**, from the idea it gave some old sportsman originally I believe of a horse that hangs upon his rider's hand with a weight of STUPID impulse, as if he would *bore* the very ground through with his nose; tiring the man upon his back most cruelly. The cant phrase used at those public schools, where they call a boy who is not quick-witted, and cannot be made a scholar, a *blunt* †, is so good, that I sigh for its removal into social life, where blunts are exceedingly frequent, and we have no word for them. Dullard is out of use; we find it now only in Shakespeare.

MARRIAGE, WEDDING, NUPTIALS.

Although these are all common conversation words, they can scarcely be used synonymously. There is a treaty of MARRIAGE going forward in such a family, say we, and I expect an invitation to the WEDDING dinner, as 'tis reported the parents are disposed to celebrate

---

* The word *bore* is even more abused than *clever*, and frequently creates the very feeling it affects to describe. Young ladies and gentlemen who are suffering from mere vacancy of mind, make a merit of their emptiness by exclaiming, in a tone of conscious superiority, that they are *bored*. The mechanical operation of *boreing* may have suggested the word.

† The *ne plus ultra* of insults at a German University is *Dummkopf*.

these NUPTIALS with great festivity, and very few friends
of the family will be left out.

Meantime our great triumph over foreigners, who
visit us from warmer climates, is in the superior felicity of our married couples; nor do I praise those
superficial writers who so lament the infidelities committed among *us*—in papers which carried to the Continent tend to make them believe there is no more
conjugal attachment in Britain, than at Genoa or
Venice.—Truth is, we find in all great capitals an ill
example set by a dozen women of distinction who give
the *ton* as 'tis called; and with regard to such, London
confesses her share: — yet is the mass of middling
people left untainted; and even among our nobility,
those of the first fortune and dignity in England live
with an Arcadian constancy and true affection, such as
can very rarely happen in nations where a contrary
conduct is neither punished by the Legislature, nor
censured by Society; for there is no need to resolve
virtue and vice into effect of *climate*, unless we are
supposed to improve or degenerate like animals which
whiten as they approach the Pole — human nature will
go wrong if religion forbears to restrain, and government neglects to punish.

MELODY, HARMONY, MUSICK.

These terms are used as synonymes only by people who
revert not to their derivation; when the last is soon discovered to contain the other two, while the first means
merely the air—or, as Italians better express it, *la can-*

tilena—because our very word MELODY implies *honey-sweet singing, mellifluous* succession of simple sounds, so as to produce agreeable and sometimes almost enchanting effect. Meanwhile both co-operation and combination are understood to meet in the term HARMONY, which, like every other science, is the result of knowledge operating upon genius, and adds in the audience a degree of astonishment to approbation, enriching all our sensations of delight, and clustering them into a maturity of perfection.

MELODY is to HARMONY what innocence is to virtue; the last could not exist without the former, on which they are founded; but we esteem him who enlarges simplicity into excellence, and prize the opening chorus of Acis and Galatea beyond the Voi Amanti of Giardini, although this last-named composition is elegant, and the other vulgar.

Where the original thought, however, like Corregio's Magdalen in the Dresden Gallery set round with jewels, is lost in the blaze of accompaniment, our loss is the less if *that* thought should be somewhat coarse or indelicate; but MUSICK of this kind pleases an Italian ear far less than do Sacchini's sweetly soothing MELODIES, never overlaid by that fulness of HARMONY with which German composers sometimes perplex instead of informing their hearers. *His* chorusses in Erifile, though nothing deficient either in richness or radiance, are ever transparent; while the charming subject (not an instant lost to view) reminds one of some fine shell coloured by Nature's hand, but seen to most advantage through the clear waves that wash the coast of Coromandel when mild monsoons are blowing. With regard to MUSICK, Plato said long ago, that if any considerable alteration took place in the MUSICK of a country, he should, from that single circumstance, predict innovation in the laws, a change of customs, and subversion of the government. Rousseau, in imitation of this sentiment, which he had probably read *translated* as well as myself, actually foretold it of the French, without acknowledging whence his idea sprung; and truly did he foretell it. "The French," says he, " have no MUSICK now—nor can have, because their language is not capable of musical expression; but if ever they *do* get into a better style—(which they certainly soon did, changing Lulli and Rameau for Gluck and for Piccini)—*tant pis pour eux.*"   .

Rousseau had indeed the fate of Cassandra, little less mad than himself; and Burney justly observed, that it was strange a nation so frequently accused of volatility and caprice, should have invariably manifested a steady perseverance and constancy to one particular taste in this art, which the strongest ridicule and contempt of other countries could never vanquish or turn out of its course. He has however lived to see them change their mode of receiving pleasure from this very science; has seen them accomplish the predictions of Rousseau, and confirm the opinions of Plato; seen them murder their own monarch, set fire to their own cities, and blaze themselves away — a wonder to fools, a beacon to wise men. This example has at least served to show the use of those three words which occasioned so long a specu-

lation. MELODY is chiefly used speaking of vocal MU-
SICK, and HARMONY means many parts combining to
form composition. Shall I digress in saying that this
latter seems the genuine taste of the English, who love
plenty and opulence in all things? Our MELODIES are
commonly vulgar, but we like to see them richly drest;
and the late silly humour of listening to tunes made
upon three notes only, is a mere whim of the moment,
as it was to dote upon old ballads about twenty or thirty
years ago; it will die away in a twelvemonth—for simplicity cannot please without elegance: nor does it
really please a British ear, even when exquisitely sweet
and delicate.

We buy Blair's works, but would rather study War-
burton's; we talk of tender Venetian airs, but our
hearts acknowledge Handel. Meantime 'tis unjust to
say that German MUSICK is not expressive; when the
Italians say so, they mean it is not *amorous*: but
other affections inhabit other souls; and surely the last-
named immortal composer has no rival in the power
of expressing and exciting sublime devotion and rap-
turous sentiment. See his grand chorus, *Unto us a
Son is born*, &c. Pleyel's Quartettos too, which have
all somewhat of a drum and fife in them, express what
Germans ever have excelled in—regularity, order, dis-
cipline, arms, in a word, war. When such MUSICK is
playing, it reminds one of Rowe's verses which say so
very truly, that

> " The sound of arms shall wake our martial ardour,
> And cure the amorous sickness of a soul

Begun by sloth and nursed with too much ease.
The idle god of love supinely dreams
Amidst inglorious shades and purling streams;
In rosy fetters and fantastic chains
He binds deluded maids and simple swains;
With soft enjoyment wooes them to forget
The hardy toils and labours of the great:
But if the warlike trumpet's loud alarms
To virtuous acts excite, and manly arms,
The coward boy avows his abject fear,
Sublime on silken wings he cuts the air,
Scar'd at the noble noise and thunder of the war."

What then do those critics look for, who lament that
German MUSICK is not *expressive?* They look for
plaintive sounds meant to raise tender emotions in the
breast; and this is the peculiar province of MELODY—
which, like Anacreon's lyre, vibrates to amorous touches
only, and resounds with nothing but love. Of this
sovereign power,

" To take the 'prison'd soul, and lap it in Elysium,"

Italy has long remained in full possession: the Syrens'
coast is still the residence of melting softness and of
sweet seduction. The MUSICK of a nation naturally re-
presents that nation's favourite energies, pervading
every thought and every action; while even the devotion of that warm soil is tenderness, not sublimity;
—and either the natives impress their gentle souls with
the contemplation of a Saviour newly laid, in innocence
and infant sweetness, upon the spotless bosom of more
than female beauty — or else rack their soft hearts with
the afflicting passions; and with eyes fixed upon a

bleeding crucifix, weep their Redeemer's human sufferings, as though he were never to re-assume divinity. Meantime the piety of Lutherans soars a sublimer flight; and when they set before the eyes of their glowing imagination Messiah ever blessed, they kindle into rapture, and break out with pious transport,

"Hallelujah! for the Lord God Omnipotent reigneth, &c."

They think of Him that sitteth high above the heavens, begotten before all worlds!

"Effulgence of the Father! Son beloved!"

With such impressions, such energies, such inspiration — Milton wrote poetry, and Handel composed MUSICK.

MISTAKE, ERROR, MISCONCEPTION.

Whoever thinks these words strictly synonymous will find himself in an ERROR; while he who says he wandered out of his way between London and Bath, from mere MISCONCEPTION, makes a comical MISTAKE—for he only committed an ERROR in neglecting to punish those who turned him out of the right road *for a joke*. These are the niceties of language that books never teach, and conversation alone can establish. Let foreigners however settle it in their minds, that the word first used in this catalogue of false apprehension, is used when one man or one thing is taken for another: the second applies much wider, and we say it of all who deviate from the right path, whether that deviation is or is not

caused by a mere MISTAKE: the latter seems less an act
of the will than either of the other two; 'tis more a
perversion of the head than any thing else, and its
resistance against conviction carries with it somewhat
laughable.   A nobleman, for instance, employing his
architect to show him the elevation of a house he intended to build, the artist produces a drawing made
with Indian ink.   This is no bad form of a house, says
my lord, but I don't like the colour — my house shall
be *white*.   By all means, replied the builder, this is a
white house.   No, this is black and white, methinks —
evidently so, indeed — and striped about somehow in a
way that does not please me.*   Oh dear! no such
thing, my lord — the house will be white enough.
That I don't know, Sir; if you contradict my senses
now, you may do the same *then*: but my house shall
not be patched about with black as this paper is — it
shall be all clean Portland stone.   Doubtless, my lord;
what you see here is perfectly *white*, I assure you.
You are an impudent fellow (answers the proprietor),
and endeavour to impose upon me, because I am not
conversant in these matters, by persuading me that I do
not know black from white; but I do know an honest
man from a rogue — so get about your business directly,
no such shall be my architect.

This was MISCONCEPTION.   When the faux Martin

* This recalls the reply of a distinguished lawyer (now a peer)
to the late Mr. Justice Gaselee, who remarked that Canning was
not so tall as the bronze statue of him near Westminster Hall:
" No, nor so green either."

Guerre came to France from India, and took possession
of the house, lands, wife, &c. of a man whom he
strongly resembled, and who, by four or five years' absence from his family, was so forgotten by them that
neither brother nor sisters found out the imposture —
their caresses and obedience, their rents and profits,
were all intended to the person of another man, and
were only paid to him by a fatal but innocent MISTAKE.
But when the jury condemned a man wholly uncon-
cerned in the business to suffer for a crime one of themselves had committed, nor ever found out that good
evidence was wanting to prove his guilt, till the real
perpetrator of the murder owned it himself in private
to the judge — they acted with too little caution and
delicacy, and have been always justly censured for the
ERROR. The facts are all acknowledged ones.

NARRATION, ACCOUNT, RECITAL.

In order to give a good ACCOUNT of the fact (say we),
'tis necessary to hear a clear RECITAL of the circumstances,
but if we mean to make a pleasing NARRATION, those circumstances should not be dwelt on too minutely, but
rather one selected from the rest, to set in a full light.
Whoever means to please in conversation, seeing no person more attended to than he who tells an agreeable
story, concludes too hastily that his own fame will be
firmly established by a like means; and so gives his
time up to the collection and RECITAL of anecdotes.
Here, however, is our adventurer likely enough to fail;

for either his fact is too notorious, and he sees his audience turn even involuntarily away from a tale told
them yesterday perhaps by a more pleasing narrator;
or it is too obscure, and incapable of interesting his
hearers. Were we to investigate the reason why narra-
tives please better in a mixed company, than sentiment;
we might discover that he who draws from his own
mind to entertain his circle will soon be tempted to
dogmatize, and assume the air, with the powers, of a
teacher; while the man, who is ever ready to tell one
somewhat unknown before, adds an idea to the listener's
stock, without forcing on us that of our own inferiority.
—He is in possession of a fact more than we are—that's
all; and he communicates that fact for our amusement.

NATION, COUNTRY, KINGDOM,

Are all of them collective terms, well understood,
and at first sight only synonymous. A moment's reflection shews us many COUNTRIES which are not kingdoms,
and some KINGDOMS which include not the whole NATION
to which they apparently belong. The first of these
words is used in some universities for the distinction of
the scholars, and professors of colleges. The faculty of
Paris consists of four, and when the procureur of that
which is called the French NATION speaks in public, his
style is *Honoranda Gallorum Natio.* I hope they
have changed their phrase now, when all KINGDOMS,
COUNTRIES, NATIONS, and LANGUAGES, unite in abhorrence
of their late disgraceful conduct towards the good house
of Bourbon, so named from Archibald Borbonius in the

year 1127, whose impress was a globe, and round it this anagram of the earl's name, *Orbi bonus.* The times how changed in this fatal year to Frenchmen, 1793 !

Strokes of national character, national humour, however, still exist: with regard to the latter, we see *their* bons mots still untranslatable beyond those of other kingdoms; and our authors plunder French comedies in vain; the humour loses and evaporates: witness Farquhar's endeavour to force into his Inconstant, the gay reply made by Le prince de Guemené, when Louis Quatorze's queen, a grave Spaniard, seriously proposed putting the famous Ninon de l'Enclos among *les filles repenties.*—" Madam," answered the courtier, " *elle n'est ni fille, ni repentie.*"* This was NATIONAL pleasantry, and will not translate for that reason.—No more will that proof of John Bull's NATIONAL character, told of a fellow, who, when King Charles the First of England lay before Rochelle, was employed by that Prince as a diver, to carry papers, &c. which having done most dexterously, the good-natured sovereign bid him name his own reward.—" Something to drink your majesty's health, that's all," quoth the man. " Blockhead!" exclaimed the duke of Buckingham, who stood in presence and was provoked at his stupidity for asking nothing better, " why didst not *drink* when thou wert under water?"—" Why so I did, master!" replied the

---

* When an English lady appeared in a *tableau vivant* as a Magdalen, it was observed that she looked like a Magdalen who had *not* repented.

man; " but the water was salt you know, so it made
me the more a-dry."

NOW, AT PRESENT, THIS INSTANT.

While metaphysicians expand their subtleties into im-
perceptibility upon this fatal monosyllable, one would
hope that conversation might go on without dispute
concerning what flies away like the witches in Macbeth,
who, while we contend about the nature of their existence, *make themselves air, into which they vanish.* So,
alas! does NOW; the present moment passing away even
before the word is written that explains it. We may
tell foreigners, however, that 'tis usual in our language
when calling in a hurry, to cry NOW, NOW, as the quick-
est expression, I suppose, for urging another to immediate haste. "AT PRESENT we cannot come to you"—is
a common phrase—He was here THIS INSTANT, means,
'tis not an instant scarcely since he was here : but it
does certainly mean time *past;* for one says to a person
who, looking round, misses the individual sought for—
"Why, she is here, NOW, cannot you see her?"

"I thought we were to begin upon the subject NOW,"
says a man impatient of decision. "We *will* begin THIS
INSTANT," replies his cooler friend (meaning a *future*
time, though near); "AT PRESENT it would not be so
proper." These things are difficult to foreigners; nor
can I guess why both time past, and time to come, should
be hourly and commonly exprest by THIS INSTANT, which
at first view appears improper enough.

TO NULLIFY, TO ANNULL, TO DISANNULL, TO MAKE NULL AND VOID.

These verbs stand in conversation chiefly in the place of the verb to annihilate, or rather between that and the softer phrase of, to render ineffectual. Horatio's arguments, say we, were rendered NULL and VOID, at least in my opinion, by what our friend Cleomenes urged against them : but no man better knows than he how to NULLIFY the discourse of his competitor without annihilating the speaker either in his own eyes, or those of the auditors; as a good legislator will see the way to ANNULL a statute no longer useful or necessary, without taking away by direct annihilation all trace or remembrance of its former utility. The third verb is a favourite among the vulgar here in England, who mis-apply it comically enough. I asked the late Lord Halifax's gardener for a walk and summer-house I used to see at Horton : " There was such a walk once," re-plies the man, " but my Lord DISANNULLED it."

In 1815, Mrs. Piozzi sent a copy of "British Syno-nymy" to Sir James Fellowes with the following note and verses, which will appropriately conclude this com-pilation :

5 Nov., 1815.

Accept, dear Sir, this second-hand copy of your poor little friend's favourite work, now completely out of

print.   That it should bear the name of Samuel Johnson on the title page, is so curious, that I would not
erase it.

Ten years at fewest must have elapsed since the
author of the " Rambler" had breathed his last, when
this book saw the light; and he to whom I have now
the honour of presenting it, was struggling between
the perils of fire and water in the midst of the At-
lantic Ocean.   Awful Retrospect!   Yet a lightly volant
pen traces the following lines, only to say that

> In this Synonymy you'll find
> Portraits from poor Floretta's mind ;
> With many a tale and many a jest,
> By which her fancy was imprest.
> Oh! had that fancy been acquainted
>   With characters too late display'd,
> Far happier pictures had been painted,
>   Far stronger light and softer shade.
> Beneath the life-preserving hand,
> How had we seen the soldier stand!
> Or kneel, instructed to adore
> Him who bestow'd the healing pow'r.
> But merit, dazzling men to blindness,
> Was still reserv'd for Piozzi's *Finis*.

INDEX.

THE END OF THE SECOND VOLUME.

www.ingramcontent.com/pod-product-compliance
Lightning Source LLC
Chambersburg PA
CBHW030816110726
47900CB00006B/1638